THE DAWNING OF THE DAY

BOOKS BY ELISABETH OGILVIE

*Available from Down East Books

Bennett's Island Novels
The Tide Trilogy
  High Tide at Noon*
  Storm Tide*
  The Ebbing Tide*

The Lovers Trilogy
  The Dawning of the Day*
  The Seasons Hereafter*
  Strawberries in the Sea*

  An Answer in the Tide*
  The Summer of the Osprey
  The Day Before Winter*

Children's Books
The Pigeon Pair
Masquerade at Sea House
Ceiling of Amber
Turn Around Twice
Becky's Island
How Wide the Heart
Blueberry Summer
Whistle for a Wind
The Fabulous Year
The Young Islanders
Come Aboard and Bring
  Your Dory!

Other Titles
My World is an Island*
The Dreaming Swimmer
Where the Lost Aprils Are
Image of a Lover
Weep and Know Why
A Theme for Reason
The Face of Innocence
Bellwood
Waters on a Starry Night
There May be Heaven
Call Home the Heart
The Witch Door
Rowan Head
No Evil Angel
A Dancer in Yellow
The Devil in Tartan
The Silent Ones
The Road to Nowhere
When the Music Stopped

The Jennie Trilogy
  Jennie About to Be*
  The World of Jennie G.*
  Jennie Glenroy*

THE DAWNING

OF THE DAY

by Elisabeth Ogilvie

Down East Books / Camden, Maine

The Dawning of the Day

Jacket illustration © 1999 by R.B. Dance
ISBN 0-89272-464-1
Printed and bound at Capital City Press, Burlington, Vermont

5   4   3   2   1

Down East Books
P.O. Box 679
Camden, ME 04843
BOOK ORDERS: 1-800-685-7962

Library of Congress Cataloging-in-Publication Data

Ogilvie, Elisabeth, 1917–
        The dawning of the day / by Elisabeth Ogilvie.
            p.   cm. — (Bennett's Island saga ; 4)
        ISBN 0-89272-464-1 (pbk.)
            1. Islands—Maine—Fiction. 2. Women—Maine—Fiction. I. Title.
        II. Series: Ogilvie, Elisabeth, 1917–   Bennett's Island saga ; 4.
        PS3529.G39D34   1999
        813'.52—dc21
                                                                99-17860
                                                                CIP

Principal Characters

Philippa Marshall
Eric, her son

Stephen Bennett, brother of Joanna and Mark

Young Charles Bennett, nephew of Stephen,
  Mark, and Joanna

Nils and Joanna (Bennett) Sorensen
Their son, Jamie
Their daughter, Linnea

Mark and Helmi Bennett
Rob and Kathie Salminen
  (nephew and niece of Helmi)

Jude and Lucy Webster
Their children, Rue, Edwin, Faith, and Daniel

Syd and Viola (Campion) Goward
  (sister of Asanath and Foss)
Their daughter, Ellie

Asanath and Suze Campion
Their son, Terence

Foss and Helen Campion
Their children, Perley (son of Helen by
  her first marriage), Peggy, and Schuyler

Randall and Ella Percy
Their children, Fort, Ralph, Clare, and Francis

Gregg, who belongs to no one

Sou'west
Ledges

Sou'west
Point

Cranberries
and
Wild Strawberries

Spruce
Woods

cemetery

Bull Cove

Goose Cove

"To The Rock"

High
Ledge

Goose
Cove
Ledge

⊱ BENNETT'S ∙ ISLAND ⊰

2½ miles from Sou'west Point to Eastern End Cove

Harbor Ledges

Western Harbor Point

To Brigport

Barque
Cove

Big
Wharf

Eastern
Harbor
Point

① Clubhouse
② The Well

Paths -------

① Nils
and
Joanna ②

Harbor Beach

The Homestead

Long Cove

Schoolhouse

School-
house
Cove

Ice pond

Barn

Woods

Windward
Point

Pudding
Island

Eastern
End Cove

To Tenpound Island

W

N

S

E

Shag Ledge

What isn't woods is ledge (all around shores) and field.

Map by A.B. Venti

THE DAWNING OF THE DAY

Prelude

The island lay alone on the sea. Though it was less than two miles, as the gulls and cormorants flew, from the larger island to the north of it, its solitude was genuine and complete, a thing of the spirit as well as a physical reality. There were some fifty islanders, including the smallest child, and on this morning in early September, each went about his separate business as he had done for the past year and expected to do for some time to come. Each was the center of a world that revolved around him with the comforting regularity of the tides and the sun.

Though among them there were twisting frustrations, silent agonies, and secret terrors, as a group they were self-sufficient; they wanted nothing from Brigport or from the mainland twenty-five miles to the north, whose mountains made a lovely but uninviting line along the sky. Their work, their homes, and their futures were here, on the long strip of meadowland and spruce woods that rose from the Maine sea, steeply buttressed with rocks and forever salted with flying spray. Here the lobsters crawled in plenty on the clean bottom, in the dark deep waters that were guarded even from Brigport men by an invisible but powerful line. The lobstermen were rich when inshore lobstermen could barely pay for a day's gasoline. If they wanted the mainland, they went to it in their big competent boats, and when they walked the streets, everyone knew them for islanders. When they went home, they looked with complacent possessiveness on the moat between them and the rest of the world.

For them this was like any fine late-summer day. It would end as all such days ended; there was no reason to believe otherwise. When the last boat was on the mooring, the last skiff hauled up to high-water mark, when the stars appeared in the pure cold blue of the

3

evening sky, when the lamps were lit and the men kicked off their boots and settled down to an evening of radio and knitting trap heads, when the derelict who lived in the Binnacle began to play his clarinet, the self-sufficiency of the islanders would be a thick and warming cloak against the rest of the universe. They would have no reason to believe that on this day their lives would have begun to change.

The men went out to haul their lobster traps in the early morning of this day. Most took to their boats eagerly enough. The air was fine, the horizon set in crystal. The boats bounded across the dark blue water; the wet buoys, red, yellow, white, flashed in the sun. The women got the week's washing out where the wind could blow it.

In midmorning a lobsterman's boat went out of the harbor to meet the mail boat at Brigport. She plunged proudly into the tide rip, and the wake reached the moorings and set the skiffs and the dories to bouncing on the dark glittering water. But in a little while the wake died out, and the sound of the engine was lost behind the eastern harbor point. The island settled back into the cradle of familiar things that would go on forever: the rote on the far shores, the wind blowing, the gulls over the water, and the crickets and sparrows on the land. It was a day that began as thousands of other days had begun.

Chapter 1

The mail boat for Brigport and Bennett's Island had been rolling ever since she'd poked her stubby nose out past Owl's Head Light two hours earlier. The wind was northwest, and the *Ella Vye* took the boisterous seas on her quarter. She was eminently seaworthy and had been making the twenty-five-mile run across Penobscot Bay in all kinds of weather. A northwest blow in early September was nothing to her. But she shuddered with each comber that came smashing aboard, recovered herself, rushed boldly forward on a carrying sea only to pitch abruptly as if the waters had suddenly departed altogether.

Philippa had felt a mild regret when she boarded the boat that morning because she was the only passenger. Now she was glad. She could not have endured the shame of seasickness in front of anyone. It was true she had not been sick yet, but the terror of it had been with her constantly. At first she had stayed out on deck, up before the pilothouse, her arm around the mast. She had been exhilarated by the expanse of water that was a surge of dull silver in the wake and a cold pure blue-green everywhere else; she had felt excitement as the foaming crests rushed toward the boat and as the gulls had followed them out of the harbor, soaring overhead. At first, too, there had been the islands all around them, clear blue shapes that robbed the horizon of its wilderness look.

The boat's wake bubbled behind them in a constantly widening path, back to the mainland whose roofs were melting into obscurity, whose hills were purpling with distance. She looked back with the fascination of one who has entered into a strange dream and knows there is no waking. *There* was the reality, the yellowing elms rooted in the unshaking earth, the square houses that could not be changed

5

to wilderness even by the sea gulls that came to perch on their ridge-poles. *There* was her son, tangible flesh that was hers.

Here—here was the narrow wet deck tilting and shuddering under her feet. The mast to which she held went up and up to pitch crazily against the blowing clouds. The bow rose and fell against a bare horizon. Her destination lay beyond that horizon, but try as she might, she could make out no faintest cloud of land against the hard clean curve of the sky.

She tightened her arm around the mast and looked behind her and up. In the window of the pilothouse the captain's face was blank mahogany. His gaze went over her head and beyond the bow as if she were not there. When she'd come aboard the boat that morning, he had been supervising the loading of the freight, rope and laths, paint, kegs of nails, crates of food, bags of grain. He had been civil to her, taking his cigar out of his mouth when he spoke and looking at her squarely.

Now the captain was part of the dream. He was secure, this boat was all the world he needed; for him and the lanky, expressionless deck hand she was not a person, she was only freight.

A sudden need for her child cried out sharply in her. She pressed the palm of her hand against the sun-warmed curve of the mast's side, remembering how, early this morning before she left Eric at her sister's home, she had dampened his fine mouse-brown hair and tried to comb his cowlick flat. She remembered the shape of his head under her hand and the smell of him as he hugged her good-by. It could have been a month ago.

The boat seemed to be rising up and up without stopping, up and forward, and Philippa's head spun. Holding tightly to everything and moving in cautious steps like someone very old, she went aft then and down into the passengers' cabin. The fear of seasickness began.

From that time on, the trip lasted for an eternity, yet curiously there was no time to think. She must hold herself on the narrow locker, pick up her typewriter case when it was hurled across the cabin, rearrange her luggage, and try to keep her balance at the same time; when the nausea came, she went up the steep ladder and slid back the hatch cover, and stood there breathing the cold salty air and trying not to watch the ceaseless forward rush of seas now at

6

eye level. If she looked at them, their motion was duplicated in her stomach. When a shower of icy spray broke over her, she went below again. She found herself thinking in time to the chugging of the Diesel engine. She had found out at the first that it was a Diesel; Eric had told her to ask. She must know the length of the boat and the captain's name, all this for Eric. He would be in school now but thinking of her and envying her this fabulous adventure; he had hoped, for her sake, that it would be rough. She laughed and shuddered at the same time.

Once, when a brutal jolt caught her off guard and she cracked her head sharply, she almost burst into tears, and she was amazed to discover how thin the veneer of adult self-assurance really was. Her sense of loneliness was perilously close to the surface. She held her throat rigid until it ached, and by then the danger was past. She put her sister's steamer rug on the floor and sat on it, bracing her feet against one locker and her back against the other, and shut her eyes.

I know now, she thought, what the other teacher meant when she said that teaching on Bennett's Island had put ten extra years on her. They're on me already.

She felt an unwilling sad-edged humor, and suddenly she could visualize her husband appearing at the top of the companionway and gazing down at her as she sat on the floor of the cabin, her hair on end, her long legs jackknifed under her chin.

"Why, Philippa." She could hear his gentle amazement. "Whatever are you doing? You look drunk." There would have been a glimmer of mirth behind his glasses. His strong mouth would have twitched in a mild smile.

"The teacher should personify poise and dignity at all times. You'd better mend your ways before your new employers get a look at you and think they've been had."

She burst into laughter, and the sound of it was bold in her ears and drove off her megrims as the cold wind had blown away her nausea. At the same instant the whistle shrieked over her head, and she lurched to her feet and looked through the salt-misted portholes. To the left a high craggy island bare of trees rose from a ring of white surf. A row of unfamiliar dark birds perched along its ridge, their wings outspread.

She looked out the other side and saw a long natural bastion of tawny rock, with pale glistening seas breaking continually against it and sending sparkling showers of spray into the air. There was a high clamor of gulls, and she saw a lobster boat rolling in the tide rip like a clam shell, heading past the end of the tawny ledge with the gulls following. The boat disappeared beyond the ledge, and the *Ella Vye,* whistle shrieking, veered in the same direction.

Philippa sat down on the locker and opened her handbag, her fingers stiff and chilled, her whole body trembling. If only Brigport were the end of the journey; then, in a few moments, she would be on land, with the firm ground under her feet, the warm ripe smell of autumn in her nostrils, and the sun striking through her aching flesh. But Bennett's Island was three miles beyond. Still, three miles would be nothing to her after this nightmarish twenty, and perhaps it wouldn't be rough between the islands. Of course not, she thought with assurance. It will be sheltered, and I can stay out on deck and really enjoy it.

She would have a great deal to write to Eric. Planning her first letter to him, she worked methodically to remedy her appearance. She was thirty and quite tall, with long strong bones; when Eric was a baby and Justin was living, she had had an appearance of firm and luminous health. But in the last few years she had become very slender, as if the flesh had been chiseled away from the bones, leaving her rib cage hard as armor under her breasts and accentuating her cheekbones and jaw line in a way she would have thought elegant when she was seventeen and had pined for a romantic willowiness.

She combed her hair back hard from her forehead; it was brown hair, neither chestnut nor richly dark but merely brown. It shone after brushing and had a faint wave so that when she pushed it back from her broad forehead, it gave her a softening for which she was grateful. There was one other feature for which she was also grateful. Her eyes, wide set under the gentle curve of her brows, were a clear and penetrating gray-green.

Once again her son's face came sharply to mind. Eric, she thought, we are thankful for this job, I should be thanking God at this moment, I have no right to miss you so.

She took her lipstick angrily from her bag. This was no time for self-pity.

She realized that the boat had been running with a blessed steadiness for the last few minutes, and she put on her beret and her topcoat and went up on deck. They were in the harbor of Brigport, and the rough weather outside the long natural breakwater might have been a cruel joke on her senses. For here inside, the scent of warm spruce blew mildly on her face, the water was the tame blue of cornflowers. The boats lay above their own pure reflections. Children played in dories and skiffs around the wharves built out from the rocky shores. The houses gleamed among the spruces, the fields were golden with approaching autumn, the whole scene spoke peace.

Chapter 2

The captain went up the wharf with the mailbags, assisted by two barefooted small boys in khaki shorts, and the others on the wharf trailed after them. Philippa was relieved. Some had gazed down at her with curiosity and some with indifference; she had felt exposed and vulnerable, the sole passenger on the mailboat, an outsider and a schoolteacher at that. She had understood their interest, it was a natural thing. But how does one respond? she thought. Do I smile up at them winningly or look haughtily into space?

Now she was alone, even the deck hand had disappeared. She sat quiescent in the hot silence. A little boy rowed out in a big dory from a nearby wharf, and a man who was painting a boat beached in the shade of the wharf spoke after him in a deep patient voice, "Take care, now."

"Ayeh," the child piped back.

She thought with pleasurable anticipation of the children whom she was to teach. They would be island children, far different from any others she had known in the cities and suburbs. There would be a wildness in them. She longed to call to the little boy in the dory, to have him come alongside and look up at her so she could talk with him; he could not have been much older than Eric, about eight. His hair is fair where Eric's is mouse-brown, she thought, but he has the same tremendous energy in that thin straight back and those skinny shoulders. She watched him send the big gray dory across the harbor, standing up to row with one knee on the seat, pushing on the long oars. He would not be able to talk as glibly as Eric about turbojets and Roy Rogers and the television he had seen in friends' houses when they lived in Boston. But how wise he must be in the rhythm of the tides, the recognition of sea birds, the ways of seals, in foretelling the wind, in the feel of a boat under him, in the intricate construction of a lobster trap.

She hoped there would be an eight-year-old boy in her school on Bennett's Island. There must be, out of twelve children ranging from five to fourteen. She hadn't asked the island people who had come to her sister's house to interview her; she had wanted the job with such intensity her poise had been alarmingly uncertain, and for almost the first time in her adult life she had been at a loss, afraid of saying too much or too little.

The islanders had come to see her on the recommendation of the former teacher. There had been two brothers, Foss and Asanath Campion, and Mrs. Asanath. Even in their good blue suits and white shirts, the men were marked by their livelihood. Their pale blue eyes were narrowed by folds of flesh finely wrinkled; they were bright and far-seeing eyes, deep-set above hard cheekbones and big high-bridged noses. Their skin was burned to a color darker than their sandy hair, except at the back and temples where it had been newly clipped. They held their hats in knotted brown fingers and their clothes seemed to fit them stiffly. Mrs. Campion was a slight graying woman with small features that appeared indistinct; she didn't speak after the introductions were over but sat without moving during the interview, her gloved hands folded on her bag, her feet close together in neat shoes. Her eyes were a misty hazel behind her glasses, and when she shook hands with Philippa, her hand had been either timid or reluctant. She seemed as without substance as a shadow. Philippa had had no time to wonder. She had been too nervous, amused and angered by her ridiculous trepidation and then fiercely justifying it all in one moment. She had to have this job, to keep Eric in Maine and out of the city life that had been stifling them both.

She knew the men were not confused. They were as rugged and

immovable as their island, unimpressed by her manner and accent that said she was "from away," though she had been born in Maine. They spoke in the leisurely fashion of men who liked to talk and who took time to choose their words. They were much alike, but Foss Campion was the younger; she guessed he was in his forties. Whenever she glanced toward Mrs. Campion, there was no change in the vague eyes or the prim pale mouth. But Foss Campion always smiled, as if to reassure her, with a slow quizzical narrowing of his eyes in their net of distance wrinkles.

He rarely spoke, however. It was Asanath, the older, who was clearly in command. "Bennett's Island always had its own school, Mis' Marshall," he explained in a deep deliberate voice. "When the war come along and folks began scattering, why, there warn't enough young ones for a school, so we shut up shop. Now there's more'n enough kids again. We could have the state help us out, which would mean having our books and schoolma'ams chosen for us. But we're islanders, a stiff-necked bunch. We figger we can live without having the state wipe our noses for us." His mouth twitched in sudden humor, and then the smile grew upward over the craggy face.

"We don't want anything, Mis' Marshall, but to take care of ourselves without outside help or interference for the rest of our days." He sat back in his chair.

Foss Campion smiled at her. "We choose two to pick a teacher when we need one." His voice was smoother than his brother's; it had an undertone that was almost a caress.

"Joanna and Helmi Bennett chose Mrs. Gerrish," Mrs. Campion said unexpectedly. "They come back talking of her college degree like it was Holy Writ—"

Under Asanath's calm gaze she ebbed into silence, her gloved fingers fidgety.

"Now, Suze," Foss said agreeably, "let's give the devil his due. May Gerrish was all they could get at the time, and after awhile they didn't like her no better than we did." He nodded at Philippa. "We thought, might be we could do better."

She felt that he liked her, but she knew he was not the one to consider. Two might be picked for the delegation, but she sensed that Asanath would be the one to make the decision. Fright made her resent him. How quietly arrogant he was, watching her with those bright and calculating eyes.

"Do you have a school committee?" she asked, relieved that her words came out so clearly. "Besides yourselves? Or are you the committee?"

He shook his head. "Not liking interference," he said, "we figger the teacher feels the same way. School's her business, so long as she knows what her business is." He placed the tip of his fingers together and over the tent looked at her squarely. "We teach our young ones to be honest and hard-working and God-fearing, Mis' Marshall. We expect the teacher to keep a firm hand over 'em and set 'em a good example. . . . Wages is forty dollars a week and found. You'll board at my house."

She was lightheaded with surprise, hardly able to believe it was over. Through the short silence she heard Eric calling out from the yard, "Johnny, can I ride your bike?" I can get him his own bicycle, she thought as if in a dream. Aloud she said gently, "I'm looking forward to this more than I can say. I wanted this job very much." She couldn't keep from smiling, and she turned impulsively toward Mrs. Campion. "It means something splendid to my little boy and myself."

Mrs. Campion said in a vague way, "If Asanath thinks you'll do—" The words trailed off. Foss Campion, getting up, seemed amused by something.

"I think it'll be mighty pleasant for all of us," he said. "A real good change."

"May Gerrish was a mite wearing toward the last of it," his brother said dryly. He looked down at her from under hawklike lids. "When can we expect you to arrive, young woman? Boat goes three times a week."

"How about a week from today?" she said.

"*Good.* Suze'll be glad of a young female in the house." He looked at his wife and chuckled. "Sometimes she kind of feels she needs moral support."

It was a strange thing, how Mrs. Campion seemed to take on body only when he turned toward her; it was like the moon soaking up the sun's light.

"Yes, it'll be real nice having you, Mis' Marshall." Her voice was less vague. "Helmi Bennett wanted you, but Asa told her, 'twould be better for you with us." She gathered depth and momentum. "It's real close to the school and you'd have an ungodly long walk from over there in the winter, besides her being under Joanna's thumb—"

Asanath's voice calmly overrode her. "We figgered 'twas better for the teacher to board where there was no school-age young ones, Mis' Marshall. Well now, you've got things to do. And so have we."

Suze started faintly. "Ayeh." She turned toward the door, and Philippa took a long step to reach it and open it for her. She looked down at Suze, smiling.

"My grandmother always used to say she hated lady boarders, Mrs. Campion. They were always fussing around in her kitchen, wanting to wash out a pair of stockings or make a cup of tea. I can promise you I shan't get in your way."

"Ayeh." Mrs. Campion's eyes were blank again behind her glasses. Asanath made an odd, courtly, little duck of his head.

"It's an honor for us to board the schoolma'am, Mis' Marshall. She's kind of important to us."

"Thank you," said Philippa. "Thank you very much." She was dismayed by the strange sensation in her throat. She had never been a sentimentalist.

Foss Campion was the last to go. "My kids'll be relieved to know you aren't eighty and deaf. They gave us orders to find somebody pretty."

The sensation in her throat blossomed into laughter. She laughed with Foss Campion as if they were old friends.

When they had gone, she felt wanted and cherished; these were island people, sensitive and shrewd, demanding much, and they had chosen her for something beyond her city clothes and the timbre of her voice with its alien accent. For the first time in years she felt the solemn rapture of dedication which she had brought to her first school. She met it with a deep thrill of recognition; she had believed it dead. Perhaps on this unknown island, so far out that it was not even a dim blue cloud on the horizon, she would find a renascence in more ways than one.

She watched them go down the street, the woman and the two lean, angular figures in dark blue who walked like the proud fishermen they were. Justin would have been impressed, she thought. He would have called them the men of Thoreau and Emerson.

On the grassy rise beyond the wharf at Brigport, the people milled in and out of the store like bees around a honeysuckle bush. The captain of the *Ella Vye* returned to the boat and went down into the cabin. Philippa was surprised to see him put her luggage out on deck.

"Wind's not lessening," he said around his cigar. "It's too rough for me to try to work in and out of that small harbor down there. It's all right for a small boat. And there's one coming to fetch ye." He looked over her head down the length of the harbor. "Here she comes now."

Philippa turned and looked. The boat came up through a narrow passage between walls of rock that flung the echoes back and forth. The tranquillity of the harbor was gone; as the water curled back from either side of the high white bow, small waves rushed at the wharves, the moored boats rolled and danced, the gulls flew up from the rockweed and circled, crying. The little boy in the dory pulled at the long oars until he had turned the dory's bow into the wake.

The powerboat slid swiftly toward the wharf, its engine cut down to a throaty murmur. The sides had a wet gleam and the two men in the cockpit wore oil clothes and sou'westers. If it was too rough for the mail boat, Philippa thought with dread, why should the mail and herself be entrusted to this *smaller* boat.

The man at the wheel shut off the engine. "Got the mail for you, commodore!" he sang out. "What you scared of, Link? That little old tide rip out there?"

He had a soft merry voice. When he took off his sou'wester, she saw he was hardly a man after all, but a boy with a thick short curly crop of black hair and skin as dark as that of the gypsies who had come recently to her sister's door on the mainland with their baskets and fortunes. "Throw those mailbags at Link, Fort," he said to the other boy, "and see if you can wrap 'em around his neck."

Fort was a red-headed and stocky boy with a clownish grin. He laid hold of the *Ella's* rail with a gaff and pulled the powerboat in close. The captain shifted his cigar and received the mailbags. "I guess you got more than a little tide rip down there," he said without expression. "With all that wind blowing off the island, it's too bad the government couldn't use it for something."

"I ain't said a word, Link," said the red-headed boy. His grin danced continually all over his broad face, like sunlight on the water.

The dark boy's gaze moved to Philippa's face and settled there, with a child's steady, opaque curiosity. The mail-boat captain flung another set of mailbags down into the smaller boat's cockpit and handed Philippa's luggage down after it. She felt a sudden constriction of anxiety in her stomach; the roar of surf outside the harbor and along the far shores of the island seemed deafeningly loud. What a letter this will make for Eric, she thought. He mustn't ever know what a jelly his mother was at this historic moment. She walked to the side of the boat, and the captain unhooked a short length of chain that formed part of the railing around the deck.

"Here's your passenger," he said to the boys. The red-headed Fort came quickly up onto the wide washboards and took her arm in a strong grip. "Step aboard," he said. "She's steady as a rock." His face with its wide cheekbones and freckles shining through the tan was all honest, earthy good humor. "And if your legs go out from under ye on account of the way Link's cement mixer tossed ye around, Charles'll ketch ye, he's awful good at that."

She looked down at the other boy as he put a box in place for a step. "I'm sure he is," she said. Charles glanced up at her and smiled; his eyes had a soft beguiling twinkle.

"Link, you've gone and forgot to bring us our schoolma'am." He spoke past her. "Sure you didn't see her standing all forlorn on the wharf? Stiff in one leg and sprung in the other?"

"Sure, I saw her," said Link without expression. "But she warn't what I'd call enticing, so I brought this one. You better put for home with the mail. Try not to go aground on Tenpound just because you got an interesting passenger."

Philippa waved her hand to him. "Good-by, and thank you," she said. The boat was backing away from the *Ella Vye,* and Philippa went to sit down on the clean crate placed for her in the lee of the cabin. She watched the two boys in yellow oilskins by the wheel, her first Bennett's Islanders, except for the Campion brothers.

The boat made a slow circle and slipped forward, the water rippling and chuckling along her sides. I hope I don't get frightened out there, Philippa thought. Or if I do, I hope I can hide it. It will be a good thing for me if they tell the rest that I didn't turn green with terror or seasickness no matter how bad it was.

And with a desire to armor herself in all ways possible against what was coming, she got up from the crate, turned, and folded her arms on the shoulder-high roof of the cuddy. Suddenly the engine moved into a higher speed; the boat made a long smooth lunge forward that reminded her of a deer leaping over a fallen tree, and seemed to rush headlong toward the open water and the wind.

Chapter 3

She did not have to pretend. The boat reassured her with the even rhythm of the engine beating through the sturdy planking; at the same time it might have been composed of feathers and air, like the medricks that skimmed over the water just outside Brigport Harbor. In spite of the tired ache in her bones, Philippa felt a springing of exhilaration as she watched the shape of Bennett's Island grow large and sharply defined upon the horizon.

The magic of islands, Justin said, was as old as life. They had been talking of other islands, then, the ones they planned to visit and explore, the isles of the Aegean, the Hebrides, Skye. But they'd had no time to find out about them.

Halfway between Brigport and Bennett's they passed a hump of islet, all sun-washed rock crowned with green turf. Gulls flew up from it, balancing on the wind and crying; a black ram stood on a high place and looked down at the boat as it rolled in the backwash from the shore.

"Tenpound Island." the red-haired boy shouted to her. "Lots of good grass there for sheep!" She looked back for a long time at the ram braced arrogantly against the pale turquoise sky. She wanted to get the picture complete for Eric.

When she turned toward the bow again, Bennett's Island had changed from a low blue mass to a definite shape composed of thick green spruce woods, steep rocky beaches wet in the shade and shimmering in the sun, and a sudden wide field of yellow grasses that seemed to stretch across the island to open sea.

They came abreast of a ledge rearing out of the surf; a spruce-covered point loomed above them. Suddenly the boat lunged and bucked as if in panic. Philippa was thrown off balance and gripped at the cuddy door for support. As the boat seemed to sink away from her feet, she had a moment of instinctive terror. An arm went firmly around her waist and held her hard.

"Just coming into the harbor," Charles Bennett said. His face was so close to hers she could feel on her cheek the warmth emanating from his flesh. He was staring straight ahead, but there was a rush of color under his brown skin.

"Do you always come into the harbor so violently?" she asked, and moved casually away from him. "Thanks for catching me. I haven't got my sea legs yet."

"Tide rip right here," he answered, still without looking at her, and went back to take the wheel from Fort. She was amused by his embarrassment.

The boat went along the inner side of the high, wooded point and headed toward the first wharf beyond the descent of the point. A man stood on the wharf watching them, and suddenly she knew it was Asanath Campion. In duck-billed cap, blue shirt and work pants, and rubber boots, he looked far taller than he had been in her sister's living room. There was a stack of new traps behind him as high as his head.

The engine was shut off, and in a sort of entranced silence the boat slid close to the green-slimed spilings. Asanath sat on his heels at the top of the ladder, smiling in the shade of the duck-bill. "Been a miserable long trip, hasn't it?"

"The last part was the best." She looked around at the two boys. Charles was taking off his oil clothes, his head studiously bent, but Fort grinned.

"We ain't lettin' her land till you get the red carpet down, Asa."

"Why son, it's been down for seven days hand-running, with me holding one end and Suze at the other. So start handing her up!"

Asanath's hard brown hands reached down to help her over the top of the ladder. She looked down at the boys in the boat. Charles was getting her luggage out of the cuddy.

"Thank you both," she said. "I meant it, you know. The last part of the trip was the best."

"Ma'am," said Fort, sweeping off his cap and holding it over his stomach. Charles looked up and smiled. *How that face must excite the island girls,* she thought wryly.

"Any time," he said. "It was a pleasure. But you'd better thank my uncle, she's his boat."

"You thank him for me. Tell him she's a beautiful boat."

"See, you're learnin' the lingo already," said Fort. "You made a real good choice, Asa."

"Of course I did," Campion said benignly. He shook hands with Philippa. "Good to see you, Mis' Marshall. I'll hand you over to Suze while these hellions get your gear ashore."

They went up the wharf between the walls of new traps, each with a clean blue and white buoy lying on a coiled warp inside. The planks seemed to lift under her feet, and she put her hand out to the weathered shingles of the fishhouse. Campion said, "Place'll be heaving under you for the rest of the day."

Then the wharf gave way to the land, and the ground felt warm and firm through the soles of her shoes. She stopped and looked back at the harbor, beginning at the breakwater and the big wharf on the other side, and following the shore all around to the place where she stood. She knew she would soon become accustomed to the wharves rising out of the water and the houses that were so close to the shore they must shudder in their foundations whenever there was any great surf. But now everything had the high savor of strangeness. Here were the great winds and light and space. She thought of Justin; he used to say there were places that could exalt a man or beat him down to nothing. She knew in this moment that Bennett's Island was one of them.

The solitude of noon hung over the island. There was no one in sight but Asanath Campion, lighting his pipe as if he had all day to wait while she stood and stared, and the two boys in the boat heading out across the harbor toward the moorings. She had been expected, yet no one was out to see her arrive. It seemed like an instinctive delicacy on the part of the islanders, to go on with the regular details of their existence as if she were not a curiosity.

Then she saw someone after all, a young man coming along the shore path between clumps of bay and wild rose. His dungarees rode low on his lean hips, and the inevitable duck-billed cap shaded his face. He walked slowly, with his thumbs in his belt, as if his whole inner self were far from the spot and there was no force to move him but the wind.

There were two houses besides Asanath's on this side of the harbor, the further one white-painted and with zinnias and dahlias a glitter of color in the dooryard, flowers that must have often felt spray from the rocks on the other side of the path. But the house between this one and the Campions' was boarded up and needed paint. The young man stopped and looked at it. He pushed back his cap, and Philippa saw the craggy profile of a Campion.

"My boy," said Asanath briefly. "Terence." The curtness of his remark seemed to imply criticism.

Terence came toward them aimlessly as a feather. Asanath introduced him, and Philippa shook hands. He had the Campion eyes, pale and bright as aquamarine, and a thin straight mouth. He was in his mid-twenties, Philippa guessed, and wondered what preoccupied him.

"Git Mis' Marshall's stuff up off the wharf, son," Asanath said, and Terence nodded and left them. A faint sound of whistling spun out like a thread behind him. His father said in his leisurely voice, "Terence is some absent-minded. Always thinking something he ain't telling."

They went up toward the house, and she saw Suze Campion behind the screen door. But in that instant she was not so real for Philippa as the sweet whistlings of the goldfinches in the thistles at the edge of the woods, the sheets snapping like sails on the clothesline in the side yard, and behind them a yellowing field that stretched to the sea. Beyond she saw again the island called Tenpound; in the clear air the black sheep were visible against the sky.

Chapter 4

At midnight she was no nearer to sleep than she'd been two hours before when the last of the callers had gone home and she'd come to her room to write to Eric and then go to bed. She lay on her back with the high headboard rearing above her and watched ripples of moonlit water move endlessly toward the shore below her windows. The wind had died out at sunset, but the room was filled with a sort of murmurous hush, like the big conch shell that was her door stop.

Foss Campion and his wife had come to supper. Foss was the same as she had remembered him, except for the change from the blue suit to cotton slacks and moccasins. His wife, Helen, was a big woman with short wavy dark hair, only slightly gray, a fine color, and a brilliant hazel gaze. She appeared to overshadow Foss, who had little to say but whose eyes glinted in an amused and friendly smile whenever they met Philippa's.

"I understand you're a widow, Mrs. Marshall," Helen said. She didn't drop her voice, as if widowhood were a faintly disgraceful condition, but said it heartily. "I'm a widow myself, or was, till I married Foss. I have a boy by my first marriage, too, so it gives us something in common."

"So it does," said Philippa. "How old is your boy?"

"Seventeen. Perley's real smart. I wanted him to go to high school, but he was so set on being a fisherman he just wouldn't work for his pass. Stayed in the eighth grade for three years!" She laughed heartily.

"Have a roll, Helen." Asanath held the plate out to her. "You look about starved. I can see your ribs."

She enjoyed the joke thoroughly, flinging herself back in her chair till it creaked, her laughter pealing around the kitchen, her solid bosom heaving. When the last of the spasm had died away in a diminishing series of breathless gurgles, she wiped her eyes and said faintly, "Oh dear, Asa, you'll kill me yet!" She took two rolls. "If you can see my ribs, you're a lot better off than Foss; he says he hasn't *felt* 'em for ten years!" She began to shake again but subdued the paroxysm and buttered her rolls. "I was telling you," she said to Philippa, "Foss gave Perley a peapod last year and he's been in it ever since. Loves lobstering, he does, and his father was a farmer! So I guess the smell of manure don't get into the blood after all."

Suze, a vaguely disapproving look on her face, got up from the table and went over to the dresser. Helen's laughter burst forth again; the men looked at her with bemused smiles, except for Terence, who continued to gaze past Philippa's shoulder at the woods outside and seemed unaware of anything that happened in the big kitchen. Helen stopped laughing to bite a roll, swallow hastily, and go on.

"Foss and I have two more. Peggy, she's thirteen, and Schuyler, he's eleven. May Gerrish, she and Peggy never hitched horses at all, but I always say an old maid's got no business handling high-strung sensitive children. Now Peg—"

Foss stirred himself lazily. "No sense bragging on 'em to the teacher, old woman. Leave her something to find out for herself. Your victuals are getting cold, and here's Suze got a lamp lit and the pie ready."

Helen threw up her head. "I guess you can hold forth when you get going on that fancy new engine of yours!"

"That takes care of you, boy," Asanath drawled. Suze came and set the tall nickel lamp in the center of the table and turned up the wick so that the yellow light spread over them all.

After supper Terence went out. Suze and Helen talked, the current of their voices running fast and light over the deeper, slower stream of men's conversation. Philippa knitted on a sweater for Eric and listened first to one set of words and then to the other. The men talked of lobstering, of seining, of winter gales to come, and of the best places to set traps; the phrases had an alien, half-poetic flavor for her. The women talked of personalities, touching the pattern of daily events and giving the island the substance and dimensions of a world in microcosm.

Later in the evening Viola Goward came in. She was sister to Asanath and Foss, a tall lean woman in whom the Campion features had a curious distinction. Her hair was straight and sandy, and pulled harshly back from her angular face into an untidy knot at the back. There was a penetrating intelligence in the pale eyes.

"How do you do, young woman," she said brusquely. "I've come over to offer my sympathies. I was a teacher myself."

"But I like teaching," Philippa protested, laughing.

"That's because you've never taught on Bennett's Island. I never did either, for that matter, but I've watched the battles from afar. Matter of fact they offered me the school more than once, but I told them I was no fool, thank you very much."

"Are you trying to scare me off?" Philippa asked in amusement. "Because you can't."

"She's real brave," said Foss. "Never turned a hair when we showed up on her doorstep that day. That's courage."

"Besides, it's the most beautiful place I've ever seen," Philippa added.

Mrs. Goward shrugged. "It's no Eden. Wait till they start a lobster war, and then you'll wish yourself a thousand miles away."

"Lobster war!" Helen Campion shrieked it. "How you talk! This is modern times, Vi!"

"Is that *so*?" Mrs. Goward pounced triumphantly on the words like a lean rusty-red fox on a mouse. "Then why did the wardens close off the waters around Shag Island last year? Just for something to do? I suppose none of *you* would come right out and call it a lobster war when the Brigporters and the Rockhaveners were slashing traps off right and left, and heaving ballast rocks at each other, and carrying rifles with 'em when they went to haul!"

Foss grinned at her mockingly. Asanath leaned back in his chair. "You'd ought to be on the stage, Vi. You're real good at making an entrance. Ain't life exciting enough for you without them horror stories? We're neither Brigporters nor Rockhaveners on this island. We're halfway civilized."

Vi's long jaw grew longer. "Well, it'll be a real horror story, as you call it, if the rest of the Bennett brothers get tired of going dragging and decide to come back here. They're liable to figure the island's not big enough for Campions and Bennetts both. *Then* what, Asa Campion?"

"Now that you've spoke your piece, you can set, Viola," said Asanath.

Mrs. Goward shrugged and sat down. "Well, big night on Bennett's Island. Steve Bennett took a crowd to the dance over to Brigport. Gregg's drunk and playing that devilish clarinet of his." Her eyes flickered around the room. "Where's Terence tonight? I thought he'd be right here honeying around the schoolma'am."

Suze's cheeks blotched with red. She didn't look up from the heavy sock she was knitting. "Well, he isn't."

"Speaking of the absent," said Asanath, "where's Syd?"

There was a moment's uneasy silence. His sister gazed back at him steadily. "He's got his migraine again."

"Thought it was coming on him." Asanath leaned forward to knock his pipe empty into the stove. "I was over in his fishhouse this afternoon, and he warn't in much of a condition to nail laths." He sat back, getting out his tobacco pouch.

Viola sat erectly in her chair. "He's just about blind with it," she said in a dry, expressionless voice. She put her long freckled hands up to stab a loose hairpin in her pug. "So I got clear out of the house. It's about the only thing anybody can do for him. I sent Ellie up to play with the Percy kids, and I took the long way around here, through the orchard. It's been stripped, green ones and all. If the day should ever come when one of those apples was left on the tree past Labor Day, I should think it was the end of the world and prepare to meet my Maker!"

"Websters?" said Helen eagerly.

"Well, 'twasn't chipmunks or porcupines. They're one thing the island hasn't got, though I don't know as I wouldn't rather have them than some of the things we do have."

"Now, Vi," Foss said, "you're not being one bit charitable. Those Webster kids can't help it because they're a mite slow."

"Who are they?" asked Philippa.

"Just some oddities," said Asanath. Whenever he spoke, mild as he was, all other voices stopped and everyone turned toward him. "You'll see 'em the first day of school. Hope it don't depress you too much. Jude Webster's a good enough carpenter. But his wife's sickly —in her head as much as in her body, I should say—and the kids are a queer lot. Maybe if you put 'em all together you'd get one average set of brains."

"I think the state ought to do something about them," said Helen vehemently. "They shouldn't be mixing with normal children."

Asanath squinted at her through his pipe smoke. "Well, what they got ain't catching."

Philippa thought of Eric, with the finely balanced intelligence in his eyes, the straight back and perfect coordination, and was thankful enough to make a little silent prayer of gratitude. Suze was saying in her wispy voice, "I'd like to see those Finns go. That girl's as brazen as a brass monkey."

"I saw her this morning," said Helen, her eyes alight, "out there in that dory of Mark Bennett's, standing up in it and leaning over the side of Terence's boat while he worked on his engine. Maybe she's only fourteen, but she's a big fourteen. My Peggy now, she's still a nice modest little girl."

"Probably Kathie thinks Terence is a real good catch," suggested Viola. "Those Finns marry young. You want to be ready for Terence to come bringing home a bride any day now, Suze, all set to move into the house next door. You know what the men say about girls—when they're big enough they're old enough." She chuckled without sound.

Asanath cleared his throat gently. "One thing Terence don't have," he murmured, "and that's migraine."

Viola stood up abruptly. "I'll be getting back to Syd," she said. "Good night." She went without waiting; the goodnights of the others trailed after her. Suze hurried behind her to the door. "Goodnight, Viola!" she called faintly into the crisp still night.

But no one else seemed discomforted by Viola's sudden departure. In a little while Foss and Helen left. Asanath went out with them, and Suze and Philippa stood in the doorway while the men looked out at the moonlit harbor and the boats gleaming on the slate-blue water. The wind had died out and there was only a faint whispering along the shore. "Hear the rote," Suze said, and Philippa listened and heard the dim, far-off roar that was the surf on the outer shores of the island. Yet at first she would have said there was silence everywhere, except for the crickets and an occasional swish and surge around the rocks.

"Be a fair day tomorrow," Asanath said.

"Ayeh," Foss answered.

Their voices were low, the voices of people with all time to spare. The air was cool and aromatic with an indefinable blend of sea and land scents. Philippa was very tired, and she thought how strange it would be to go to bed without first looking in on Eric; but she was faced with the enchantment of an island night in early September, and Eric was safe and happy, looking forward to his new bicycle. And so she was at peace.

Now she lay in bed, with all the faces and voices circling in her brain and no suspicion of sleep in her bones. The kitchen clock struck one. She got up and put on her robe and knelt by the window that looked out on the harbor. In the white light the shore curved away from her, the water flashing suddenly in shadowy spots around the rocks as a ripple caught the moon. The island was like a creature lying asleep on the dark sea. She must add that to Eric's letter, she thought.

Kneeling there with her arms folded on the sill and her chin down on them, her eyes wide with gazing, she tried to remember when she had last dreamed that Justin was alive and had simply gone away from her. She realized she hadn't dreamed it for a long time, which meant she had accepted the fact of his death. Yet in moments like this she was as conscious of him as if he were an articulate presence in the moonlit room.

She stayed by the window a long time, thinking of Eric and Justin and staring at the harbor, the moonlight like snow on the village roofs, the spruces on the opposite point saw-toothed and black against the pale sky. Then she went back to her bed, to burrow into the clean-scented sheets, pull the Lone Star quilt up around her head, and fall asleep.

Chapter 5

It seemed a shameful thing to begin school when the year was moving into its full glory. Philippa finished classes early for the first few days, knowing how the scents and sounds of the island's late summer flowing in at the windows must have tortured girls fresh from long hours in their playhouses in the woods, and boys who had spent the summer in their father's dories. When the winter came they would be glad of school, and, if Philippa could keep to her ideal, the one room would become for them a world of many horizons. She had no reason to anticipate a failure; she knew what she possessed to give to children and was certain of her ability to reach them. At the same time she realized that every teacher since the first one must have begun each year with the same ardent hope that he would be something more to his pupils than the wind blowing or the tides changing.

Her acquaintance with Eric—in analytical moments she looked upon it as an acquaintance because there was so much she did not and could not know about her son—had deepened her perception of children; she always approached them with respect, an open mind, and a certain wariness.

She had no illusions about country schools, where she had learned just how frustrating, and how rewarding, a teaching career could be. She thought she knew what to expect in the schoolhouse on Bennett's Island.

There were nine pupils instead of twelve who came the first day. They ranged from the third to the eighth grade. She was grateful for the single third-grade pupil, for he was just the age of Eric. Jamie Sorensen was a fair and serious eight-year-old who returned her gaze with grave attention. It was all she could do not to smooth down the cowlick at the crown of his yellow head whenever she leaned over to look at his work.

It was toward the two eighth-graders that she looked for the first signs of unrest. Yet in the beginning days she met nothing in Peggy Campion and Kathie Salminen but what she brought to them, a guarded willingness to take her at face value. Peggy, the daughter of Foss and Helen Campion, was tall like her mother and had the same fine carriage. Her sweater and skirt outfits were well chosen, her fawn-brown hair was brushed to a sheen. She considered Philippa with bland blue eyes that neither promised nor threatened.

Kathie was the girl whom Philippa had heard discussed—in a somewhat unfriendly manner, she remembered—in Asanath Campion's kitchen, the one who rowed out across the harbor to hang over the edge of Terence Campion's boat while he worked on his engine. It was hardly credible that they should be friends, for Kathie had so much gusto, and the young man seemed nothing more than a vague shadow, withdrawn and preoccupied. And he was at least ten years older than the girl.

She wasn't an islander, but she and her younger brother, Rob, were living with their aunt, Mrs. Mark Bennett of the store and post office. Kathie was sturdy and square shouldered, with bright blue-green eyes set at a faintly Oriental angle above broad cheekbones powdered with freckles, a snub nose, and a wide mouth. Often she gazed at Philippa over the heads of the others with a certain air of comprehension, as if they shared a common sophistication. Yet with the others she had a good-humored straightforwardness, and the first time Philippa heard her robust laughter ring out in the schoolyard, she laughed too, from sheer pleasure in the sound. Kathie will be my friend or my enemy, she thought. And whichever it is, she'll be superb at it.

The others were less distinct at first, but she had them sorted out in a few days. Of the three red-headed Percy children, Ralph showed the strongest resemblance to their older brother Fort. He had the same comic good nature in his broad freckled face. He and Schuyler Campion shared the seventh grade. His two younger sisters were plain, fidgety youngsters with shrewd little faces and sharp elbows.

Schuyler, called Sky, resembled neither his father, Foss, nor his sister, Peggy. He was a short, black-haired, plump boy with a round intelligent face, his eyes dark and unwinkingly intense behind his glasses. His constant companion was Rob Salminen, Kathie's brother, a lank faunish towhead who made it clear to her at the first that the reason he wasn't in the seventh grade with Sky and Ralph was the stupidity of previous teachers who had never been able to teach him fractions.

The fifth grade consisted of a prim little girl whose tight sandy curls appeared to have been formed on a pencil; she was Ellie Goward, Viola Goward's daughter, and therefore niece to Asanath and Foss. Ellie had the Campion eyes but none of the Campion assurance, and Philippa wondered if she would ever be able to get by that small, locked face.

These were her pupils sitting before her, nine of them, looking at her from hour to hour with varying degrees of expectancy or suspicion. But there should have been several more children, she realized—the disputed Websters. She had heard of them for the first time, as she had heard of Kathie, in Asanath's kitchen. But when on the first day of school she asked about the Websters, not one of the nine raised a hand. After a long moment of silence, she thought that Kathie Salminen shrugged slightly.

"Do you have some information, Kathie?" Philippa asked.

"Nobody's seen them around the harbor all summer. They don't play with the other kids."

Their absence was easily explained, then. If they kept to themselves and the home was an unsettled one with an ailing mother, it was possible they didn't know or care about the opening of school. At the close of school the first day she asked Kathie where the Websters lived, intending to walk around there directly and look for them.

"I'll go with you," Kathie volunteered helpfully.

"Oh, I think I can find it," Philippa said. Kathie looked disappointed for a moment. Then her grin came, broad and debonair.

"Wish you luck!" She sang out over her shoulder, and left.

Alone in the room, Philippa heard the ticking of the old wall clock become wheezily loud in the silence; it was a great silence to follow a day filled with the multiple stirrings of children. It was a familiar silence, unaltered in texture by the fact that this was a one-room schoolhouse on an island whereas last year she had experienced it in a modern classroom in a city school. This building had no indirect lighting, no solar heating, no colors planned to rest young eyes. It was a square white schoolhouse with a belfry; under the belfry at the end of the dark entry the firewood was stacked. There were outdoor toilets. It didn't matter. She was pleased with it all and looked forward to a precious sense of freedom in her work that she had never felt before. This school was *hers*.

The desks and seats were a concession to progress, but around the walls were the narrow and supremely inhospitable benches of the past. She was sure that the New England poets over the west windows, and the British poets over the east windows, had been the benign ghosts of the place for generations. There were books in the corner bookshelves upon which Philippa's mother had been raised. There were later ones, too, but Philippa was relieved to see that no one had invaded this schoolroom with progressive nonsense about the unfitness of *Black Beauty, What Katy Did,* and *The Five Little Peppers. Robinson Crusoe* and *Moby Dick* in Victorian editions had been much handled. A cottage organ stood in the opposite corner.

There was a certain charm in the stove's bulky ugliness and long stovepipe, a promise of aid and comfort in the months to come. The lighting might not have been scientifically the best, but in those

28

early September days the big windows held a sweep of stunning color. The west windows looked across the russet marsh to the harbor and the activity of the beach where the men rowed ashore from the moorings or hauled up their powerboats to be painted. From Philippa's desk, through these same windows, she looked in an opposite direction, up the long easy slope of mown grass to the Bennett Homestead and the solid mass of spruce woods over beyond. The children at the back end of the room on one side could see the mail boat come out around Tenpound Island and go past Long Cove on her way to the harbor.

At recess they played "steal eggs" or "giant steps" in a yard edged with thickets of goldenrod, great puffs of asters, and wild rosebushes turned wine-red. The smell of the marsh was pungent here, and the great wild brightness of the sun on the sea cast a peculiar clarity all around. Sometimes the children went down over the old sea wall onto the shore of Schoolhouse Cove. Black duck and sheldrakes flew up at their approach, but if there was a seal he would ride in the swell, looking like a swimming dog, fascinated by the children's noise.

A lovely place to play, Philippa thought, remembering the paved or graveled schoolyards she had known.

She went around the harbor that first day and found the Webster place as Kathie had described, set back against the woods and hidden by big spruces in front. It was like an empty house. No one answered her knock, no cat came crying, though the Percy children were playing around their house a little distance away. She waited for a little while, hoping to hear a stir inside, but there was nothing. She went home, not deeply concerned. There was no need to rush anyone. She would wait a day or two; then if they hadn't come, she would go to the house again, in the evening, when the father would be home.

Almost immediately there were events in school that required extra attention and took her mind off the Websters. Schuyler Campion and Rob Salminen were neither insolent nor mischievous. But they began to stay away from school. In the mornings they came and behaved well. In the afternoons they did not appear.

Chapter 6

The first time Philippa asked their older sisters where they were, she expected some casual story about upset stomachs and too many green apples. Peggy Campion looked at her as blankly as her cousin Terence did. "I don't know anything about Sky," she murmured.

Kathie said, "I started back to school before Rob did." She was frankly entertained by the mystery. No one else had seen the boys, a rather astonishing fact in view of the size of the community. The next morning they were there with the rest. They had no written excuses.

"Forgot to bring it," Sky Campion said.

Rob grinned at Philippa without shame. "Forgot mine, too. I'm numb, I guess."

"Bring your excuses this afternoon," Philippa told them pleasantly. They went back to their seats and worked hard all morning. At noon she reminded them again of their excuses.

"Sure," said Rob.

"Yes, Mrs. Marshall," Sky answered.

They did not come that afternoon. This time Philippa did not ask if anyone had seen them. In the morning the boys were there. When she called them to her desk and asked for the notes from home, there was a familiar atmosphere in the room.

The first time she had encountered it, in her first school, her stomach had been cramped with panic, and all her sentimental fancies about children had fled in the same instant. She might have been facing a roomful of monsters. There was a terrible ten minutes of hating them and being terrified by them simultaneously, until by some groping, sweating method that was nothing she had been taught but a product of pure, desperate pride, she had gained control of the situation. Now, as she felt the collective tensing of the class, their anticipation as tangible as smoke, she understood. This business of Rob and Sky, and the way she handled it, would tell the rest whether she was to be respected or fair game. With a certain wry amusement behind a serene face, she leaned back in her chair and folded her hands. The boys were as serene.

"No notes?" she asked.

Sky snapped his fingers. "Forgot it again!"

"I told you we're regular numbheads," Rob reminded her.

"This afternoon," she said gently, "will be the last chance. You may go back to your seats." They went, docilely. Only the smaller children watched; all other heads were bowed in concentration. Philippa studied the variety of partings, cowlicks, ribbons, and barrettes. The atmosphere was thick with suspense. This afternoon was the last chance. They could hardly wait. Philippa knew exactly how they felt. She called the fourth grade up to her desk, and while they read aloud she thought, Last chance for what? It was a matter of importance that she handle the situation herself, if it was humanly possible. It was inexcusable to go to the parents at the first sign of trouble.

The afternoon took care of itself; the boys didn't come. Whenever her back was turned, Philippa felt the eyes upon her and wondered what sort of precedent May Gerrish had set. Did they expect that in the face of this candid defiance she would show trembling hands, a nervous flush, outright anger? She would prove to them that the world of school could revolve tranquilly without Sky and Rob. For the last half-hour she read *Moonfleet* aloud and was amused to see them trapped into exchanging one sort of suspense for another.

In the morning Sky and Rob were in their seats again. "Do you have your notes?" she asked, as if she had never asked it before. Sky gave her a luminous and steadfast hazel glance and then looked out the window as if the question bored him. Rob said cheerfully, "Nope!"

"Then you'd better go home," she said. "Both of you. Don't come back until you have your excuses." She nodded at the door. "Run along. We'll be right here when you get back."

Ralph Percy laughed aloud, as if she had said something very witty; he had a broad, comic face like Fort's. Everybody watched Sky and Rob go down the aisle to the door. Sky walked straight out with a purposeful air, but Rob, as token that he wasn't greatly disturbed, tweaked Kathie's ear when he passed her. She grabbed her ruler and gave him a violent swipe across the seat of his corduroys.

Rob burst out laughing, and ran after Sky. While Philippa read Psalm 101, she watched to see them go past the windows on their way home, but they didn't appear. They could have taken a round-about way, she thought, crawled under the windows on their hands and knees, and thus saved face with the others by keeping them in suspense as to whether or not they had decided to obey her. She knew. Once she had been eleven years old and had lived by her own incredibly complex code.

The morning routine swept them all in its wake, and the boys did not come back. Philippa was not surprised when they didn't come in the afternoon. Neither were the children. There was a certain bustle about them, a flattering alertness to her every gesture, a sub-dued air of carnival. They were not sure who was to be thrown to the lions, but they expected a worthy climax to three days of anticipa-tion. Then they would know whether they were to respect or despise Philippa for the rest of the year. Oh, they would be impartial enough, she knew. They would go over to the winner, no matter who, and woe betide the loser.

Before the first class of the afternoon started, Kathie Salminen came and sat jauntily on the corner of Philippa's desk, swinging her long, scratched brown legs, her pale fine hair flaring out from her face like a dandelion blossom. "Rob never came home this noon," she said. "He's run away. So has Sky. You can ask Peg."

Philippa glanced past her at Peggy and met a long and speculative gaze. After a moment the girl bent her head deliberately over her English grammar.

"Did you tell your aunt what's going on?" Philippa asked Kathie, knowing nobody had told anything at home that could possibly curtail the full development of the drama.

Kathie shrugged her square shoulders. "Why should I? It's not my funeral. . . . What'll you do to them? Put the strap to them?" She was far more casual asking the question than Philippa was hear-ing it.

"Is that what everyone's waiting for?" she asked coldly.

Kathie was not embarrassed. "Miss Gerrish used her pa's razor strop all the time. Brought it with her. It made everybody mad, but she didn't care. I guess toward the end she just didn't give a darn."

"You may go back to your seat, Kathie," Philippa said.

32

"O.K." She slid off the desk, stretching lazily; she was well developed for a fourteen-year-old under the boy's white shirt. She tucked her thumbs into her cowboy belt and looked down at Philippa. She wasn't offended; her eyes twinkled with humor and a sort of primitive wisdom. "I just wondered, that's all. Maybe you don't think much of pounding them up, but you'll come to it. You can't beat up the fathers and mothers, so you'll take it out on the kids." She tipped her hand to Philippa in a cocky salute and went back to her seat.

So that was the story of May Gerrish. Philippa remembered the nervous fingers traveling over the badly made-up mouth, the eyes darting behind the glasses, the voice that was calm enough at the start but soon trembled and grew shrill. "Your sister says you're a good teacher. You're young and look strong and got a stubborn jaw. That's enough for you. I'll recommend you, if you think you can stand it."

"I'm not afraid of bad weather or of isolation," Philippa had said innocently, and the other had laughed. It was a high, bleating sound.

"There are other things," she had said.

Philippa wondered then, as she wondered now. But one thing she knew; Kathie must be kept in her place as a fourteen-year-old who was neither hay nor grass. In her candor and her complete self-assurance, she was a rich personality. But she must never be allowed to forget, razor strop or not, who ruled the schoolroom.

Chapter 7

The way led home through a little lane behind the schoolhouse that came out between Foss Campion's white house, with its dahlias and zinnias, and the empty house with its boarded-up windows. Philippa always experienced a sharp pleasure in the sudden transition from the lush shadows of the lane to the full afternoon sunlight flooding the harbor and shore. Today the wind was east with a salty rockweed smell. The air had a peculiar soft luminosity, the water was a warm quiet blue.

The tide was not yet high, and an adult gull paddled around in the pools among the rocks, where the seaweed streamed bronze across the water. The gull's child, brownish gray and black billed, paddled hard behind her, bobbing its head and crying in a persistent, penny-whistle voice. Across the harbor, children were fishing for pollack off Mark Bennett's lobster car. When someone sang out triumphantly, "I got another one!" the words were as loud and pure as a bell in the still afternoon.

Nothing moved around Foss Campion's house, except the money cat washing herself on the front doorstep. But as she came abreast of Asanath Campion's house, Asanath called to her from the fishhouse doorway. "Got a bone to pick with you, girl."

She walked down toward him, and he went back into the shop and began painting buoys again. Philippa sat down on a nail keg and looked at him expectantly. She had already learned it was no use to hurry Asanath. He talked in deliberate pauses and phrases. The sun came in through the long low window over his workbench, and the reflection of the water shimmered on the ceiling over his head. He drew a blue stripe around a buoy and said, "I was hauling down the west side today and saw two people who warn't s'posed to be there. S'posed to be somewhere else. I know for a fact nobody's graduated 'em from school yet." He glanced around at her then, his eyes narrowed and smiling in the fine tissue of sun wrinkles. "You missing any of your scholars? Couple of 'em come to me a little while ago—careful as the devil to wait till *after* school was out— with some of my buoys they'd picked up on the back shore. I didn't let on I'd already seen 'em."

Philippa said honestly, "Today isn't the only day. It's been three days hand-running. I thought I could handle it without involving the parents."

"You figger to threaten the kids or bribe 'em?" He put the brush and the buoy down, and leaned against the bench. "Lord, girl, what are parents for? Nobody expects you to deal with these hellions singlehanded. I can't speak for Mark Bennett and his wife, of course, but I guess I can speak for my brother." He said Mark Bennett's name with a peculiar emphasis of distaste.

"I don't want them whipped." She wondered if Asanath Campion thought her a stubborn and sentimental fool. "In a way I don't blame the boys. They're choosing what they think is the better part. But the rules have been made."

"Foss ain't much of a hand with a switch," Asanath said. "He never gets too haired-up about anything. He's easy, is Foss. Helen's got the temper in that family." He laughed softly. "Times when Foss walks Spanish, I can tell ye."

He looked over his shoulder at the harbor. "He's out there now. I'll give him a hail." He went out onto the wharf and shouted at Foss, who was on the bow of his boat taking up the mooring.

"Be right there," Foss called back. Asanath began to fill his pipe. "No sense dragging this thing out," he said. Philippa was not sure whether she was amused or annoyed to have the question taken so smoothly out of her hands.

They waited on the wharf, watching Foss row toward them. Suze Campion appeared around the fishhouse, her small face pale in the bright sunlight, her glasses turned toward Asanath as if Philippa were not there. "What's all that noise about, Asa?" she asked plaintively.

"Thought you was cranberrying, Suze."

"You *know* they're not near ripe enough yet. I've been washing the windows on the back of the house. Seems as if I can't keep the spray off 'em five minutes."

Foss's skiff nudged the spilings, and he came up the ladder.

"What's this, a special meeting of the Bennett's Island vigilantes?" He pushed his cap back and winked at Philippa. "Haven't had a chance yet to inquire how my two are behavin' themselves in school."

"Suze," Asanath said gently, "why don't you put the kettle on, in case Mis' Marshall'd like a cup of coffee to hold her till suppertime?"

"Coffee's all made, Asa," said Suze with a ghost of triumph in her eyes.

"Well, let's go inside," said Asanath and didn't look at his wife again. He went into the fishhouse and the others followed.

"Acts real portentous, don't he?" Foss winked at Philippa. "He'd be good in politics. Specially in giving them fireside chats."

"Mis' Marshall's giving the fireside chats today, Foss," said Asanath mildly. "She's got something to say to *you.*"

"It's nothing much," said Philippa. "I told your brother I was going to handle it myself, although I don't know just how. Sky and

Rob have me cornered." She laughed. "I admire them, really. They're so calm about it. They've skipped school for three days in a row, but why worry? They've almost convinced me that being out of school in this weather is far more important than anything I could teach them."

Suze caught her breath excitedly.

"Well, I'll be—!" Foss exclaimed. "Excuse me, Mis' Marshall. But Sky, up to tricks! Peg never said a word to home about it."

"Children stick together," Philippa said. "Don't whip him, Mr. Campion. Just tell him to come to school. He's an awfully nice little boy and a bright one. He'll settle down."

Suze said vehemently, "He wouldn't have thought of running off if that Rob Salminen hadn't put it in his head. Mark Bennett's responsible for Rob! He's condoning this, most likely to plague you. Just because the Campions chose you—"

"Hold your tongue, Suze," Asanath said.

"Now, Suze." Foss shook his head at her. "Sky don't need anybody to do his thinking for him, any more than Terence did when he was that age. Sure, Terence looked like a proper little minister, the way you dressed him, but warn't he the tyke? Many's the time I've sent him up over the beach holdin' onto his bottom where I warmed it. He could put the curses to me too. The air'd be blue." He squinted out at the path. "Here he comes now, walking in a dream. Wonder what could have happened? Must have lost his voice when it changed."

Asanath cleared his throat. They all looked out at Terence on the sunny doorstep. Terence, oblivious, leaned down to rub the yellow tom's arched back. Then he went into the house. Suze left the shop quickly, hurrying up the path without a backward glance.

Foss lit a cigarette and blew out smoke. "I'll talk to Sky," he said to Philippa. "He'll be there Monday, and every day afterward."

"With a written note," said Philippa smiling. "We've been having a silent duel about it."

"He'll have his note. Next time anything comes up, you hike straight to me. If the people on this island can't work with the teacher, there's plenty wrong with them."

"Or the teacher," said Philippa. She did not feel like smiling now; she was inexplicably touched by the forthright goodness and common sense of these people. She stood in the doorway and looked at the two brothers, her eyes shadowy and grave, her mouth relaxed from its firmness into an unexpectedly young curve. The incident of the truants was a small one, but there was nothing small about the sincerity of the Campions. One feels, she heard herself explaining to Justin, that if something big happened—though I don't know what it could be, these children don't have a chance to be delinquents —it would be considered frankly and honestly by all concerned.

"Thank you," she said to them both. "It's something off my mind. Or it will be, as soon as I see Rob's people."

"Good luck," Asanath said. Foss, leaning against the bench and smoking his cigarette, smiled and said nothing.

She went up to the house thinking of coffee and a square of Suze's gingerbread. Justin used to laugh at her conviction that it was necessary to have something in her stomach before she plunged into a new element. As she came into the sun porch that reached across the front of the house, she heard voices in the kitchen and hesitated. Suze Campion's words rose and fell, faint and dreary, like the little wind that sometimes blew all night past the eaves.

"When your father was twenty-five, he had a home and a family and money in his strongbox—he wasn't letting brazen little girls hang on his coattails till all the tongues was wagging—"

"Whose tongue is wagging besides yours and Vi's and Helen's? Sure, the old man's got plenty to say, but then he never did have much use for me."

Philippa was astonished. She hadn't thought Terence was capable of such vigorous bitterness. Up in her room she could still hear Suze; not the words, but the monotonous, woeful tone. Again Terence slashed across it.

"Your father says, your father says. Why doesn't he tell *me* what he says, the oary-eyed old hypocrite? No, he can't, he's too busy being 'good old Asa.' Everybody loves him, everybody harks when he opens his mouth, even the schoolma'am listens like he was God—"

"Terence, *hush!*" his mother cried.

There was a short silence. Then suddenly he began again, his voice soft but venomously clear. "And I'm not getting Kathie Salminen in trouble, if that's what you're all so green about the gills for. Maybe I'm a disgrace to the Campions, but I haven't got around to misusing fourteen-year-old kids yet. You're all fit to be tied because she's a Bennett, or just the same as one. Listen. If you've got any more gurry to throw, you keep it off her, or I'll give you something to howl about for the rest of your life."

The screen door slammed. Philippa looked out and saw him going along the path. There was a rather alarming stillness from the kitchen, and she wondered if Suze were all right. *If Eric ever turned on me like that,* she thought, *I would die inside.*

Then she heard the teakettle move on the stove and let her breath go normally again. It was time now to think of the Mark Bennetts. Rob Salminen's truancy also had to be stopped. She went down the front stairs and out the front door without meeting Suze at all.

Chapter 8

After the brilliance of the day outside, the low-roofed store on the wharf was dim. It had its own peculiar atmosphere, a blend of oranges, oil clothes, and trap-head twine. Kathie was alone, sitting on a nail keg, her feet braced against the potbellied stove. She was reading a Western story magazine. When she saw Philippa, she got up quickly, lean as a boy in her dungarees.

"Gosh, hello, Mrs. Marshall. Can I get you something?"

"I don't want to buy a thing," said Philippa. "Just tell me where to find your aunt and you can go back to the rootin' tootin' West."

"She's up at the house. Follow the path around the corner. Is it about Rob?"

"I'm afraid so."

Kathie laughed happily. "Don't worry about it. Rob won't. He doesn't care a hoot. That's the way I am, too." Footsteps sounded on the wharf outside the door, and Fort Percy and Charles Bennett came in. "Look what a gull dropped," Kathie said, and went behind the counter. She crossed her arms on her chest and leaned against the shelves, looking inscrutable. Fort grinned.

"What's eating you, Kit-kat? Hello, Mis' Marshall. How you standing this rarefied air we got out here?"

"You brought a lot of it in with you," Kathie said. "Right out of the bait butt. I need a gas mask."

"Nothing the matter with the smell of good bait." Fort sniffed vigorously. "How are you, Mis' Marshall? You doing any better than Lady La-de-dah, here?"

"I haven't needed oxygen since I came," said Philippa. "Not even when I pass your bait shed."

Fort exploded into laughter, and Kathie snickered. Young Charles, standing with his back against the door so that his features were in shadow, made no motion or sound. Kathie said abruptly, "What's the matter with *him?*"

"Oh, he's in one of them brown studies," Fort explained. "It's an awful dark kind of brown."

As Philippa went toward the door, the boy moved to one side. "Hello, Charles," she said.

"Hi." He swung away from her and turned his back. Philippa said good-by to the others and went out. Behind her Kathie said with forceful clarity, "Anybody doesn't have to be so ugly! What'd she ever do to you, old frosty face?"

No answer from Charles, but Fort was bland and conciliatory. "Now, Kathie, he's setting out to be a woman hater, and it takes a lot of studying."

Mark Bennett's house at the crest of the point was built low to the ground. When no one answered her knock at the front door, Philippa waited on the wide porch long enough to look over the island. It lay below her in a bath of yellowing sunlight that made it look like a painting by Innes.

Beyond the gulls walking pontifically on the store roof, the fringe of wharves around the harbor, and the gilded village, the school-house sat by itself like a toy building that could be picked up by its belfry. On the far side of the island the sea reached endlessly toward the east. Northward, Isle au Haut was a mystic blue bubble that seemed to float above the horizon.

She left the porch with reluctance to search for the back door. A small shaggy brown dog came trotting around the corner of the house, saw her, and threw back his head in a hysterical outburst. She stopped and let him come up to her. The man who came behind him snapped his fingers and said without haste, "Hey, Max. Let the lady by." The dog gave him a perfunctory look and returned to Philippa's ankles, his nose cold against them but not hostile.

"It's all right," Philippa said. "I don't think he's going to bite."

"He puts on kind of an impressive front, considering he hasn't got a tooth in his mouth to back it up with." His voice was both deep and slow, what she had come to think of as an island voice that had learned never to hurry. The dog trotted back to him, and the man leaned down to touch the rough head.

He was a spare, tall man with the deep coppery tan that comes to dark skin, his hair black as a crow's wing when he pushed back his cap. He had none of Young Charles's handsome arrogance, but the cheekbones and the lean squared lines of his jaw made him undeniably a Bennett.

"Are you Mark Bennett?" she asked with an inexplicable air of hope. "I'm Mrs. Marshall, the teacher."

"I'm Steve. Mark's around at the back." His dark eyes were gentle and incurious. "Is this a duty call or trouble?"

"A very minor trouble." They smiled at each other. Philippa walked beside him to the back of the house as he said, "Then let's get it over with." The dog bounded before them, barking with irrational enthusiasm.

"I've ridden in your boat," Philippa said. "She's lovely."

He looked at her gravely from under thick black brows. "That wasn't too good a day for a newcomer. But the boys said you didn't turn a hair."

"I didn't know I could be so convincing," she said, but at the same time she felt a twinge of pride that the boys should have given her a good report. He walked beside her, moving with a slow ease. A scent of washed and ironed cloth came from his shirt, and suddenly this scent carried a sense of overpowering masculinity with it; she remembered breathing the same aroma, made particularly intimate by the hard warm flesh below it, when she was in Justin's arms. The sensation was so keen now that she was shocked.

She glanced sideways at Steve Bennett and felt a loosening like relief in her chest muscles. He appeared lost in a pleasant reverie, watching the dog's wild noisy circles. And Justin's skin, there where the open collar of this man's shirt lay back from his neck, had never been so brown. There was not the slightest similarity except that all freshly ironed shirts smelled the same.

They came into a small grassy yard bordered with bright flowers and sheltered from the wind by spruces. A tall blond woman in a green skirt and sweater rose from a deck chair and stood looking at them in watchful yet expressionless silence. Across the yard a man was painting the storm sashes leaning in a row against a shed wall.

"Here's company, Helmi," Steve Bennett said. "Mrs. Marshall, Mrs. Mark Bennett." He gestured with his head toward the painter. "That's Mark. Turn around, boy."

The other glanced around at them. He was like Steve and at the same time curiously unlike him. He was angry. He nodded abruptly at Philippa and turned back to his work, painting fast; the set of his big shoulders under blue chambray was rigid.

If she had come into a family scene, it was too late for embarrassment. Philippa said, "How do you do, Mrs. Bennett?" and put out her hand. Mrs. Mark Bennett murmured an answer and took Philippa's hand in a cool brief grip. Her face was wide at the cheekbones and vigorously cut, her skin darker than the pale hair that sprang away from her high temples. Her eyes were like Kathie's, the lucid color of the eastern sea in this day's light; but they had none of Kathie's friendliness, and Philippa thought that the farthest reach of the ocean could not be more distant.

Steve Bennett was moving another deck chair close to his sister-in-law's. She said in a low voice, "Sit down, Mrs. Marshall."

"Thank you," Philippa said. They sat down. Mrs. Bennett took a package of cigarettes from the knitting bag hung over the arm of her chair and held it out to Philippa, who shook her head. She lit one for herself, without flourishes. Steve Bennett took one of his own and sat on his heels against the wall of the shed. He scratched Max behind the ears. Both man and dog seemed peacefully absorbed.

"It's not just about Rob that I've come," Philippa began in the tone of smooth, cheerful confidence that she had learned over the years, to dispel antagonism and tension in parents. Sometimes it worked. She wondered if she would be automatically on the defensive if someone came to her about Eric.

Mark Bennett stopped painting. He took a few steps toward her, the brush in his hand. His dark face was hostile. "What's Kathie done?"

"Nothing," said Philippa in surprise. "Kathie's a wonder. She's a great addition to the schoolroom."

The hostility turned doubtful. His black brows drew down. His wife was smiling faintly.

"Does Kathie strike you as a sensible girl, Mrs. Marshall?" she asked in her low voice.

"Shrewd beyond her years, I should say." That's not to say she isn't vulnerable, Philippa added silently, but she felt that what she had spoken aloud was the right thing for the moment. Steve Bennett, his back against the warm shingles, smiled at her.

"That's what we've been trying to tell Mark. Maybe he'll believe you. He's getting all worn out with the cares of parenthood."

"Other people's children are a tremendous responsibility," she said tactfully. She felt as if she were walking in the dark; each remark must be essayed with caution, like a tentative footstep that might plunge her into conversational disaster.

"*Responsibility!*" Mark repeated violently. He wiped his hands on a rag and took out his cigarettes. The hostility had given way to angry bewilderment. He shook his head at the crumpled package. "Good Lord, I wish she had buck teeth and bowlegs. But even that wouldn't keep some of these ginks to home."

She recognized, then, the source of his anger; it was fear more than anger, the same fear that motivated Suze Campion when she whined at Terence . . . "brazen little girl hangin' on your coattails."

"Well," said Steve softly, "you can always send her back to the main."

"I've suggested it," said Helmi with pleasant calm, studying the tip of her cigarette. Mark got up and looked at the rest of them morosely.

"She won't go back to run the streets if I've got anything to do with it." He turned to Philippa. "Give her plenty of homework, make her help you after school, all that stuff. How about it?"

She said, "I'm sure Kathie would run the school for me, if I'd only give her a chance."

"She would, at that! She's already running the store!" He broke out into relieved laughter, a strong hearty sound, and Steve joined him. His wife looked at them both, smiling. The atmosphere had become subtly warmed, as if a crisis had been passed.

"But you said it wasn't Kathie you came to see us about," Helmi reminded Philippa. "Is it Rob? Or just a social parent-teacher call?"

"Both."

"What's he done?" asked Steve. "Smoked a stogie out behind the schoolhouse?"

"I guess I've still got that to look forward to. Rob hasn't done anything very terrible. He and Sky Campion have been playing hooky for the last three days."

"I told you to go easy on those tales of your misspent youth," Steve said to his brother. "Putting ideas in the kid's head."

"He doesn't need any help," said Mark. "Neither him nor Sky." His voice roughened. "What does Foss Campion say?"

"He says that Sky will be in school Monday with a note from home, and he won't run away from school again."

Helmi said quietly, "Rob will be in school Monday, too. With a note, and all the rest of it."

"There's one more thing," said Philippa. "Sky isn't going to be whipped. So it wouldn't be fair to take a switch to Rob, would it?"

"He needs his bottom warmed, I should say," Mark growled. He picked up the can of paint and went into the shed.

"Better break out your bull whip," Steve called after him. Helmi arose.

"Will you have some coffee, Mrs. Marshall?"

"I'd love it, but I'll pass it up today. I'd planned on a walk before supper to see what I could of the island." She hadn't planned anything of the sort, but for some time she had been aware of a great uneasiness in her that had nothing to do with the Mark Bennetts, Kathie, or Rob. It was at once frightening and ludicrous. She stood up quickly as if to shake herself free of something.

"Well, there'll be plenty of days for coffee when the snow flies," Mrs. Bennett said. They smiled at each other conventionally. Philippa looked out past the line of spruces and down over the sloping ground to the first of the coves that notched the west side.

"How do I get down there?" she asked.

"I'll show you," Steve said. She felt a start of surprise; he had got up and come close to her while she wasn't looking, and his easy voice so near to her seemed inescapably personal.

"If you'll just point out the path to me—" she began.

"I'll start you on it." He dropped his cigarette and ground it out with his heel. His brown face was grave and kind as he looked down, lids and black lashes hiding the darkness of his eyes. She said good-by to Helmi and followed in the direction he indicated. He

43

walked before her down the slope, light-footed in moccasins. His shoulders were not as broad as his brother's, he was leaner altogether. The fresh white shirt dazzled; she thought she could smell it again and wished passionately that he had not come with her. She could be silent no longer. She said, more crisply than she intended, "What is the position of the Salminen children in your brother's home? Why are they there?"

He stood against the glitter of the western water and waited for her to come up to him. He held a deep lavender aster between his fingers. "You don't often see them as dark as that," he said thoughtfully. Then he looked directly at her.

"The kids came a year ago. Their mother is Helmi's sister. She had to divorce the father, and then she had to get out and go to work. He's an alcoholic, spends more time in the lockup than out of it. That's their story."

"I was wondering—" she began hesitatingly, forgetting what it was that she had wondered.

"They get along all right, if that's what you're wondering. Mark and Helmi don't have any kids of their own, and these fill the gap. Helmi's a cool critter on the surface, but she's not cold. Mark growls at them as if he ate kids for Sunday dinner, but he dotes on them and they know it." He twirled the aster. "Be better for them if he made good some of his threats, I suppose. But they're sound kids, and Kathie's got a lot more sense than most people credit to her."

"I could see he was proud of her."

"He is. But he worries about her, and it makes him bad-tempered. We've got a sister—we're five brothers, by the way, two of us living here on the island, and the sister—and she tells Mark he's got a guilty conscience remembering what a heller he was in his youth." He laughed, and then held the aster out to her. "Here you are. Don't ever say we didn't greet the new schoolma'am with flowers."

"I shan't." The stem was warm and moist from his fingers. Smiling steadily, she tucked it through a buttonhole in her blouse. "Now which way do I go?"

"The path is clear right down to Sou'west Point." He gestured to the distant point beyond the scalloping coves, and the long ledges showing black in the blue water, with the surf creaming slowly over them. "No need for you to get lost."

44

"I always go by the moss on the tree trunks, anyway."

"I can see that you're the practical kind." They both laughed. The action was a relief to her; all at once she felt natural again. She said good-by and went off down the path without looking back.

Chapter 9

The slope was rank with goldenrod and asters, dense tangles of blackberry vines where some fruit still hung shiny as lacquered ornaments, clumps of raspberry canes with a few late berries. Where the land reached the rocks, the wild rosebushes burned against the granite, wine-red leaves and scarlet haws. In the midst of all this hot color, the clumps of bay were cool oases of green.

She descended into steep coves and examined driftwood stumps worn to a silver moiré finish. She followed narrow trails over dry and aromatic turf that was sometimes strewn with dry rockweed from past storms. There was a springlike trilling and fluting of song sparrows from the woods, an occasional twittering flurry of young birds around an alder patch, and grasshoppers everywhere. Philippa walked until the last angle of the Bennetts' roof was out of sight, and she was alone between the sea and the thick dark belt of spruce woods that crested the island like an Indian's roach.

Then she found a place where she could sit on a warm red rock and put her back against another one. From her feet, the rocks shelved in a flight of giant steps to the water that rippled in quietly over the swaying, shadowy rockweed. A little way out, two gulls appeared to be standing in contemplative silence on the water, their ledge barely submerged.

Philippa sat with her chin in her hands, letting herself go into the stream of the day as if she had an animal's consciousness of the warmth of light, of the smooth cold of shadows, of space and scents and the hundreds of tiny pin points of sound that made up the island's peculiar silence. Boats were coming home. A thick-shouldered boy in yellow oil pants and a duck-billed cap rowed by in a peapod, so close to the rockweed he would have seen her if he'd looked up.

It was Perley Fraser. He rowed standing up and pushing on the oars, and the shallow boat slid as swiftly over the water as its canoe ancestors must have done in the days when the Indians fished these shores.

Perley was Helen Campion's son by her first marriage, a stocky, swarthy boy of seventeen. He had barely answered the few times Philippa had spoken to him, and his stolid face with the narrow opaque black eyes never changed. Unless he was working around the fishhouse with Foss, he was always alone. He did not seem serene or self-contained in his loneliness; he appeared only to endure existence. She wondered if he were a little subnormal. Certainly he was very unattractive, and for this she found him pathetic and his mother's references to him pathetic also.

"Perley just wouldn't study," his mother had explained to her emphatically. "Crazy to be on the water—part gull, that one. 'Course we were set on him having an education, he's smart enough, but he broke us down! Just kept on in the eighth grade, wouldn't work for his pass into high school!" Her face and neck had turned dusky red in remembered anger, her tone sharp. "May Gerrish told me to my face he was stupid, but I told *her* that he was smarter than all the rest of us put together. He knew what he wanted, and he knew how to get it, too!"

Philippa watched him now and wondered if the warm lustrous day, the silver eddies behind his oars, the motion of his boat, had any power to move him.

Others came after him. The calm was broken into continuously changing patterns of wake crossing wake, of water splashing against the rocks, of gulls that flew up with a strong beating of wings and then settled into the swells again. Whenever Philippa recognized a boat, she had a warming sense of achievement. She liked to fill Eric's letters with details about the *Kestrel,* the *White Lady II, Joanna S., Susan C.,* the *Sea Pigeon.* She wished now for a notebook to record all that she had seen and smelled and heard this afternoon.

But writing wouldn't be enough; she could feel the words crowding painfully into her throat, the need to see the fast blaze of understanding in Eric's eyes. Her consciousness of Sky and Rob only increased her longing. Why should she be dealing with other little boys and not her own? She thought, I must do something about getting him out here. . . . If I could have a couple of rooms somewhere . . . perhaps in that boarded-up house.

She saw him in shorts and jersey, standing at the edge of the water where the *Kestrel's* wake still rushed against the rocks, a slender and yet not fragile silhouette with an indomitable resilience to it. Justin's boy and hers; brown hair that grew back from his forehead as hers did, with the widow's peak; Justin's eyes, as purely gray as rain; a way of standing that was Justin's, too; but he had her own swift excitement in a new experience and her way of secretly hoarding it afterward.

Where there had been two who loved, there became three. They had created him between them, Justin and Philippa. And as she saw Eric on the rocks, she saw Justin beside her, in his old slacks, smoking and watching the goldfinches. Why had they never known a place or a time like this? They had been cheated of too much. It gave her no comfort to tell herself, as she had been telling herself for eight years, that she was only one of millions of women to whom the war had become as intimate as a disease working fatally within them. There was no comfort anywhere, ever again. The knowledge had not grown less in eight years. She still felt that the injury which had been done her was irreparable.

When she smelled tobacco smoke sharp across the redolence of spruce and grass, she wondered for a panicky moment if her grief were turning to madness. She turned her head carefully and saw Young Charles standing at the edge of the trees. He looked back at her without speaking, then blew smoke from his nostrils, dug a hole in the earth with his heel, ground out the cigarette carefully and buried it. Then he walked down the slope toward her. He had a slim, compact build and wore his dungarees and rubber boots with an air that surely would have impressed Eric much more than any television cowboy.

"Did I scare you?" he asked in his soft voice, and smiled.

"Yes," she said. The past receded and she was grateful to him. He sat down on the rock beside her, pushing back his cap and narrowing his eyes against the sun until they were a dark glittering line behind the thick lashes. Philippa looked across the blue miles to the dark lilac waves of the mainland hills, and Charles looked at her. Why? she asked him silently. I'm thirty years old and tired from fighting battles with myself. Thirty is young enough when

47

you count it in years, but I'm not young. The years don't matter when you count it my way.

She wanted so much to say it aloud that she spoke hastily. "I've been watching the boats come home. Little boats, big boats, all kinds of boats."

"Guess you wonder why I haul from a peapod instead of a power-boat." He sounded stiff. She glanced around at him and surprised a rush of red in his face.

"No, I wasn't wondering. I don't know enough about it to wonder. Perley Fraser has a peapod, too, hasn't he?"

"That fumble-foot!" Charles jerked his cigarettes out of his shirt pocket. "He'll always be a pod fisherman, if he don't fall over his own fat—if he don't get in his own way and drown himself one of these days." He raked his thumbnail over the match head and lit his cigarette. His voice went stiff again. "I had me a good boat. Twenty-four feet. She wasn't much size to her, as they go around here, but she was all boat."

"Did you lose her in a storm?" Philippa asked.

"No. You can see her any time in Brigport Harbor. I lost her on account of gambling."

"Oh," she said without inflection, wondering if he had expected her to be shocked. He shrugged, and pushed out his lower lip.

"Family raised pure hell about it. They had to get together and chew just so much. But I didn't care. Just kept on playing poker. Lost my shotgun up at the choppers', and the Squire—that's what I call Cap'n Charles, my old man, when I want to gowel him—he thought I'd lose my peapod next and then I'd go out on my ear because he paid for it." He laughed softly. "They figgered when Bob Pierce came and took my boat that'd cure me of gambling. It didn't. So they think I'm the numbest thing ever feet hung on and was called a man."

He looked at her with a wide dark stare that was incredibly young, like a colt's. "I guess they'll be relieved when they find out I'm cured now."

"When did that happen?"

"Last week." He kept his eyes on hers, but the color was in his face again, and she had to struggle to hide her sudden dismay. "One day last week. I guess I was gambling because I didn't have anything

48

else to think about. I always wondered how my uncle Owen could stop raising hell so quick after he met Laurie."

"I'm glad you've stopped," she said pleasantly. "Perhaps you'll get your boat back now." She stood up, hoping it seemed casual. He got up too.

"I'll have her back. Man can't do much from a peapod. I've been playing at lobstering, that's all. No sense of responsibility, the Squire says." They walked along the path toward the next cove. "Most people call me the black sheep of the family," he went on, "ever since Owen stopped drinking and got married."

"You don't look terribly black to me," said Philippa. "I'm sure they don't think too badly of you. I know when I was nineteen or so I thought everybody disapproved of me. It's something we all go through."

"I'm twenty-one," he said tensely. "And they think I'm a black sinner. Maybe they're right. I broke into a store once and almost went to jail. And I've been out with a married woman." He strode off ahead of her without looking back. She walked slowly behind him, amused, touched, and appalled all at once. It had come to her suddenly that he had not been bragging to show her that he was a man, but confessing.

This was what her sister and her brother-in-law had warned her against, laughing across the dinner table. . . . *You'll be courted, Phil. It's more than recreation, it's one of the purest traditions. You should come out of this experience either a broken woman or an accomplished diplomat.*

Perhaps it could be a joke, if she were callous enough. But at the moment she was very unhappy about it.

Charles was waiting for her, lying back against the trunk of a small twisted spruce and gazing up through its sparse boughs at the sky. He looked like some youthful deity caught unawares on the shore of a Grecian island. He turned his head and smiled at her as if the past moments had not existed.

"Careful there," he said. "The grass is some slippery."

They went down into the next cove. A warmth arose from the rounded beach rocks driven into a ridge by violent tides. The great ribs of a ship were silvery under the matted beach peas. On the other side of the cove the ground rose up into a rounding green shape against the sky, like a Viking barrow, and she had sense of the land's end. Suddenly she could not wait but hurried on alone across the shifting stones and began to climb the steep slope.

"Are you part goat?" Charles called after her. She laughed, and scrambled upward. When she reached the top, she felt as if she had attained the peak of the world. The ground fell away; the rocks that were a volcanic black jumble in one place and shelves white as marble in another went down into the sea and seemed to emerge again as long ledges, over which the swells broke. She heard the small cracking sound as a sea urchin hit the rocks and the gull that had dropped it came down with a great fanning of his wings.

But beyond the broken shore and the leisurely pattern of the surf, past the barriers of the ledges, was the sea itself—not the twenty miles or so that lay between here and the mainland, but the thousands that reached beyond the tower of Matinicus Rock to Europe. The wind of distance blew against her.

Charles didn't come. She looked back and saw him sitting on the bleached timbers down in the cove, smoking. She wandered around for a little while. She found the fine white skeleton of a sea urchin gleaming in the short coarse grass, and wrapped it in her handkerchief and put it in her pocket. The sun was dipping toward the sea and her shadow was long behind her. The energy generated in her by the meeting with the Mark Bennetts had taken her a great distance today, and she had worked off most of her sense of frustration.

She went down into the cove again. "Do you know a short cut home?" she asked him.

He gave her a sideways look under his lashes. "Now you've seen what's at Sou'west Point, is it worth it?"

"You're a cynic, Charles."

"Oh, I know it's something to see." He got up, stretching. "I used to come down here in all weathers when my father kept sheep on here. Tell you when it's real handsome. Dawn on a winter morning when you're trying to get you a sea bird. One of those calm pretty mornings when the land's all black but the east turns the color of a ripe peach." He spun his cigarette at the water. "Come on, there's an old cow path through the woods."

He went up from the shore by an easier way, toward the long

dark crest of forest, and she followed him, bemused by the number of facets he had shown in an afternoon. A little more than a week ago she had seen him a simple creature, vividly handsome as a young horse, all gloss and fire and pure animal instinct. Now he was something more.

She considered the other Bennetts. Mark was older, more heavily set in his ways. But Charles and his uncle Steve had the same quality of ease about them. That is, Charles had it at intervals; with his uncle it was probably more lasting. He seemed a tranquil personality; there was no tension in even his most preoccupied gestures.

In the woods the warm red-brown light under the trees was flecked and striped with dusty gold.

"Nice thing about these woods," Charles remarked across the silence, "you don't have to think you'll meet a bear or a moose. There's not even a squirrel."

"But they feel haunted," said Philippa. "Hear my hushed tones? I don't dare speak up for fear of scaring someone—or something." She laughed.

"Nils Sorensen says that when his grandfather was alive he had all the kids on the island, and some of the grownups too, scared foolish of the Little People. He swore he'd seen 'em, and he was an awful religious old fella, so the kids believed him. Even Nils."

"I believed in fairies for years," said Philippa. "I felt cheated when I finally realized I didn't believe any more." Whichever way she looked through the dark columns of the trees, there was the warm mysterious gloom spangled with sun. "There should be *something* here," she insisted. "A deer or a fox or even a rabbit—" Her voice broke off abruptly, but the memory of it hung in the stillness. Something had moved at the edge of her vision. She stopped walking and turned around, searching down the long corridors of spruces for another flicker of light and action, but there was only the deepening shadow.

"There is something here," she said softly. "I saw it."

"Ghosts," suggested Charles.

"All right. Ghosts. They've scurried off into the underbrush, over the way, I think." She pointed. "By that fallen tree."

Charles did not look where she pointed. He was staring at her with an air of wild discovery; the words seemed to tear themselves out of him against his will. "Your eyes are—are green. Like the water, in the shade of the woods—" He stopped abruptly.

She felt a twist of pain. Without knowing it, conscious only of his own angry, embarrassed longing, he had spoken to her in pure poetry. "Charles," she said, putting out her hand to touch his shoulder as if he were Eric. But he was not Eric, and she drew her hand back. "Charles, it was a lovely thing to say to me. It makes me proud, for once, of my green eyes. It wipes out all the nasty, teasing things that were ever said about them. And now will you believe me when I say I saw something over there among the trees?"

The intensity ebbed away like the red leaving his brown cheeks. "It was one of the Webster kids, most likely." He took out his knife and began chipping at a blob of spruce gum on the nearest tree. "They've got a camp down here somewhere."

"Webster?"

"Don't you know 'em?" He worked carefully at the spruce gum. "Looks like more than Rob and Sky played hooky if Jude's kids haven't showed up at school yet."

"Maybe they don't know school's started yet. Aren't they supposed to be mentally deficient?"

Charles shrugged. "If you mean a little slow, mebbe Edwin is. He's a crazy-acting kid, but they're not foolish enough to *look* foolish. They're more like a bunch of scairt rabbits."

Philippa gazed off toward the woods; the darkness was flowing in like a tide under the trees. "Could you find their brush camp?"

"No more than I could find a bird's nest. Look here, we've got to be high-tailing it for home, or they'll have a posse out looking for us, and it'll be a real fancy scandal."

She walked along reluctantly. "I'd like to see these children. I'm curious about them."

"Well, you'll see 'em, don't worry about that. Jude's set on his kids learning—he's always holding forth down to the shore about education. . . . We turn here. Careful of that swampy place." He took her hand, his fingers hard and impersonal, and let her go quickly when they reached firm ground again.

They walked rapidly, without conversation. Why can't I be a realist, she asked Justin in her mind, and think placidly that every boy falls in love with an older woman, that it's just growing pains and he'll get over it? Why can't I accept it with amusement and a little vanity because he could have his choice among the girls ten years younger, and fresher, than I? He is making poems for me, Justin, and I can only feel pain for him because I am so tired from eight years of trying to keep on an even keel without you.

Suddenly they came out of the woods above Goose Cove. The cove lay like a dark mirror below the high wall of trees, but the chimneys of the Homestead, on the high land opposite, caught the last red light of the sun. The westward windows seemed to hold fire.

"That's a lovely house," Philippa said, wanting to break the silence. "Why doesn't someone live there?"

"If my old man ever goes back to lobstering, we'll live there. He and my brother Owen have a dragger now. They go out of Port George."

"You don't like dragging?"

He shrugged. "I'm an islander. If my aunt Jo wouldn't have me, I'd rent me a shack to live in or move into the Binnacle with Gregg." Standing there looking across the cove at the Homestead, he seemed as securely rooted in his environment as the trees behind him, and suddenly he acquired, without knowing it, new stature in Philippa's eyes.

They went down toward the shore, skirting the beach, and climbed over the stile into the meadow. A marshy coolness rose up around Philippa's legs. The crickets and sparrows were already quiet for the night; the gulls were flying homeward to their ledges by two's and three's. She felt anxiety stirring in her, as if Eric were lost in the woods. The Webster children had better go home soon before it was really dark. They couldn't be very big children.

She and Charles had reached the place where the path down to the Sorensen place joined the one that crossed the meadow toward the marsh and the schoolhouse.

"We've had a good walk," she said. "Thanks for coming along and showing me the way home."

"I'm taking you to the door," he protested.

"There's no need of it. . . . I may stop at Foss Campion's," she lied.

"O.K." He shrugged. "I liked the walk, too. So long." He swung toward his path without looking back.

"So long, Charles." What shall I do with him? she thought, going down the road. But the Websters, formless and elusive, came like the fog, blotting him out.

Chapter 10

In the morning the fog was thick and wet. Philippa walked through the lane to the schoolhouse after breakfast. Sitting at the desk in her raincoat, she studied the attendance records for the last year, and Mrs. Gerrish's rank book. She found what she had missed in her first quick survey of them; she had not noticed, that other time, that the Webster children's names did not appear after a date in early April, last spring. Before that they came with scarcely an absence, Rue, Edwin, and Faith. There was no explanation of their sudden departure, no note in Mrs. Gerrish's handwriting.

As she read the marks for the past year, she became first puzzled and then angry. She could not say at first against whom her anger was directed, but it was there, forceful and inescapable. *Not foolish enough to look foolish,* Young Charles had said. There was nothing about Rue's marks to show a retarded child. She had been in the sixth grade. Faith, a third-grader, had done adequate work. It was only Edwin whose ranks were consistently bad. It was quite possible that Edwin, who wasn't even honored by a grade number, was mentally deficient; but surely the girls were not.

She sat there looking at the records for a long time, her anger growing at what she termed a senseless, unnecessary mystery. Mrs. Gerrish should have given her some explanation of these children. Perhaps her dark hints and forebodings had meant the Websters. It was strange, too, that apparently none of the adults on the island knew that the Websters had left in April. Only the other children knew; but none of the other children had told.

Afterward she locked the schoolhouse and went out to stand on the old sea wall. The Bennett meadow was invisible in the fog. Unseen waves crashed on the shingle beach a few feet away from her,

54

and there was the rhythmic moan of the foghorn at Matinicus Rock Light. She smelled the clean salty scent of deep sea water and fresh rockweed. The dampness curled her hair round her face and made her skin feel cold and smooth. She should have been enjoying it, she knew, but she kept thinking of the Webster children in the woods, hiding from her and Charles like small wild animals. She had dreamed of them last night; the trees had seemed alive and tortured, and she had seen one of the children with a clarity that had awakened her; it had Eric's face.

Not foolish enough to look foolish, Charles had said, dropping the crystalline lump of spruce gum in his pocket.

She would not be satisfied until she had seen them for herself. She walked home slowly, meeting no one in the fog. The life of the harbor was at a standstill, but a whiff of wood smoke blowing down on the thick wet wind meant that work went on in the fishhouses. She passed Foss's shop on the way home, and he called to her cheerfully from the doorway. Perley, ripping broken laths off a trap outside the door, didn't look up. Asanath and Terence were working in their fishhouse with the door shut. She wondered what they talked about when they were alone, or if Asanath talked and Terence painted buoys or patched pots in silence.

Viola Goward, Asanath's sister, was in the kitchen with Suze, sitting down but still wearing her coat as a token that it wasn't a visit, she'd just run in. Ellie Goward, nine years old, sat at the table eating gingerbread. She was a shy, plain child who had none of her mother's tart assurance. When she saw Philippa, she smiled uncertainly.

"Hello, Ellie," Philippa said. Ellie blushed, and stared hard at the rope-company calendar over the table. Vi gave Philippa a fast, shrewd survey. *"Somebody's* got nice red cheeks from the fog. Unless maybe she met somebody over in Schoolhouse Cove."

"Now that you've driven me to confessing," said Philippa, "there was a perfectly fascinating seal. Such acrobatics in the surf."

"Same seal who took you walking around Sou'west Point yesterday?" asked Mrs. Goward. Suze, rolling out cookies on the dresser, glanced around with an apprehensive and yet eager motion, fixing her glasses on Philippa. Vi's lips curled back, smiling, from her strong, faintly yellow teeth. "Nobody can keep anything secret on Bennett's Island," she said. "Not from me."

"I didn't think there was anything secret about my walk," Philippa said mildly.

"It's a good thing you feel that way. Then you won't ever be surprised at what folks know about you."

"Or what they guess." Philippa smiled back at her. "No, I shan't be surprised. I've lived in small places before." And I know all about the local Gestapo, she finished silently. There had been a time when she would have said it aloud. She looked at the little girl. "All set to lick that spelling test Monday, Ellie?"

"I guess so," Ellie said in a hoarse whisper and continued to stare at the square-rigged ship on the calendar. Philippa touched lightly one of the sandy curls. "Ellie's the best speller in the fourth grade," she said.

"I was always the best," Mrs. Goward snapped. "Nobody's ever spelled me down yet."

As Philippa went into the hall and up the stairs, Mrs. Goward's dry resonant voice began again.

"Syd was coming in from hauling yesterday, and he saw her and Young Charles Bennett fooling around on the shore, and then start up in the woods. You know how all those Bennetts are about women."

That was meant for me to hear, Philippa thought. She had a moment of anger, but she kept climbing steadily toward her room. You're fair game, my dear, Justin would have said. You knew what it would be.

In her room she turned on her portable radio softly to a record program and began to prepare her next week's work.

Chapter 11

On Sunday afternoon Philippa sat under an apple tree in the orchard, a book open in her lap. The little plantation of fruit trees was ringed around with big spruces, but when it had been first laid out, some seventy years ago, it had been part of the Bennett meadow. Now the woods had come down in silent possession, making of the orchard on this windy day a hidden lake of heat and light. Here there was the somnolent richness that belonged particularly to the beginning of autumn, a warm perfume of rotting apples from the windfalls in the tall grass, the silent hovering of the big black and orange butterflies over the asters that banked the path.

Philippa put her head back against the tree trunk and shut her eyes. From far off, soft but insistent beyond the crickets and the birds, there came the rote. It was always there. She could never forget the sea; it was as if the island were like one great shell held to the ear.

Sundays were difficult for Philippa because she and Eric had always done something together on Sunday afternoon. These days in the early fall had been among the best, when it was not too hot to go by subway to the zoo or aquarium or museum. She did not want the city now, but she wanted Eric. What a splendid thing they could make of a long Sunday on the island! She wondered if he missed her and decided that he didn't. Jenny and Roger would be driving out in the countryside today, and as one of the carful of children, eating apples bought at a roadside stand, Eric would be too busy to want or remember anything else.

She was satisfied with this and would not have had it otherwise. A boy of eight should live in the moment or in his heroic plans for a future as a surgeon or a space pilot. Eric was all right; it only remained for Philippa to conquer the sensation of emptiness with which she awoke on Sunday morning. It was not a sentimental feeling. She had no desire to cry a little, imagining Eric dressed for Sunday school with someone else tying his necktie. It seemed to be a purely physical manifestation, as if on Sunday she became conscious of a missing limb.

Sometimes chunks of the past came to her with a startling lucidity that was more than memory. It had to be when she was as relaxed as this, lulled by the buzzing and humming warmth around her, eyes closed against the sun. Then she was set free of her body and all that had happened to her; all experience became as constant as the rote; whatever had happened to her once kept on happening again and again.

Now she could be fifteen years old, sitting immobile under the grape arbor at home, with the sun falling hotly on her face through the flickering leaves, and the perfume of the Concord grapes in her nostrils. If she opened her eyes, she would see her tanned bony hands, large and boyish, clasped over her knees that were scraped from a recent fall on the tennis court. Her book lay open beside her on the grass. She could remember the words she had just read; she had tilted back her face toward the trembling green roof of the arbor and shut her eyes to say them over to herself:

> *O, clasp we to our hearts for deathless dower*
> *This close-companioned inarticulate hour,*
> *When two-fold silence was the song of love.*

Had Rossetti written those words to his Elizabeth? she wondered. It didn't matter, she had found them, Philippa Hathaway; now they were hers.

The girls' voices were a chattering blur out under the apple trees, sometimes sweet and sometimes as harsh as the squawk of blue jays. Then Jenny's voice stood out alone, with the alluring huskiness that Philippa so bitterly envied.

"Poor Phil, it's good that she's bright because she'll never be pretty. She'll never be a man's woman. . . . She's all legs and jaw. It's father's jaw, of course, but on him it's distinguished."

"The only thing for a girl with Phil's bones," Mary Taylor said judiciously, "is to be terribly sophisticated."

There was a peal of laughter. "Can you imagine Philippa being *sophisticated*? A setter pup like *her*?"

"And she's such a horrible little Puritan!"

I should go out there now, the fifteen-year-old thought, trembling. They'll be sick when they realize I was here all the time. I should smile at them a little, as if they amused me beyond words, and walk by them into the house without speaking.

But she could not do it. She was terrified of what might happen. Her smile would be sick and pitiful; they would look at her as if they'd wronged a baby. If she walked with her head in the air, she'd fall over something. So she stayed where she was, her throat aching with the sobs of self-pity she fought to hold back, her hands clawing into her knees. She knew how badly she was stricken because she was not angry; she did not want to fight them, but to stay out of their sight forever.

But Jenny and Mary Taylor and the rest had been only seventeen or so, she thought now with a rush of tenderness. They'd been as stupid and innocent in their judgments as she had been to believe them. But they had felt so sure in their opinions, and it had gone on for so long. She wondered how many years it had taken her to forgive them for driving her to such frantic efforts to be sophisticated, to stop being a little Puritan.

There was Jenny coming into her room at two in the morning, her delicately cut face so stern she looked like an avenging angel. "I just wanted to tell you, Philippa," she began in a low intense voice, "that the way you acted at the dance tonight was a disgrace to the entire Hathaway family. When it gets to Mother and Father, it will break their hearts. And *then* maybe you'll be satisfied."

Philippa, flat under the covers, felt her stomach begin to quiver with sickness. Cousin Robert, the battered plush rabbit of her babyhood, who usually sat enthroned on her pillow when the bed was made, had fallen to the rug when she pulled back the covers a little while before. Now, instinctively, her arm swung down and her hand groped for Cousin Robert's ears. She smiled at Jenny.

"What did I do that was so awful?"

"The way you danced with that George Masters, for one thing. So close it was absolutely disgusting, and then you went out into his car, and don't you deny it. He gave you something to drink, didn't he?"

But it had made her sick. It had been horrible. She yawned, patting her mouth insolently with her fingers. "Well, there's more than one way of being popular. Maybe I'm turning out to be a man's woman."

Let her ask where I got that idea, and I'll tell her, all right. I'll tell her once and for all that she's to blame if I'm a disgrace to the Hathaway family. I'll tell her—

"If I'd ever *dreamed*," Jenny hissed at her, "that a sister of *mine* would get to be a byword! And with just *anybody*!"

"Not with anybody," said Philippa. "Just with boys." She giggled at Jenny's face. But when Jenny went out, Philippa tightened her grip on Cousin Robert's ears and hurled him with all her strength at the door. He fell to the rug, and she saw with horror that his stuffing had begun to come out. She burst into tears, scrambling blindly out of bed, and went to gather him up in her arms. Holding him against her breast, she tried to push back the cotton.

"I'm sorry," she whispered to him, choking. "I'm sorry." But it was a long time before she could stop crying. She knew it was too much weeping and storm over a little old rabbit whose seams had burst. After all, he could be mended. But still she cried, burrowed under the covers with her mouth pushed against Cousin Robert's back, until she was exhausted enough to fall asleep. . . .

I suppose everybody goes through it in one form or another, Philippa thought sitting in the orchard on Bennett's Island. The fortunate ones, like Jenny, aren't so plentiful. And even Jenny had her bad moments. The important thing is that she and I have grown up to be friends. But can I deny that there is a certain elemental satisfaction in leaving my child with Jenny? He must remind her at every turn that the setter pup wasn't so hopeless, after all.

Philippa smiled, and opened her eyes on the orchard. The excursion into the past had refreshed her so that she saw everything with a heightened sensitivity. Whatever has happened to me in the past eight years, she thought, I have had more, felt more, and seen more than I ever dreamed possible for me. I have no right to feel resentment, except for Justin's sake. He is the one who has been bitterly served.

It's just that I've been left, she finished wryly, without any. Cousin Robert.

At that moment she thought she saw something moving in the shadows on the slope. She shaded her eyes against the sunlight and stared into the dimness. Then she saw the children, running down the slope. The first to pass through the slot of light was a little girl in a short skimpy dress, with pale hair flying. She ran on into the duskiness among the tree trunks like a gauzy apparition. An older girl followed her through the long ray, leading a small child by the hand and giving an impression of desperate haste. She had the same pale, flying hair, and for an instant her face shone clearly out at Philippa, strained and unseeing; then she, too, was out of the light. The last was a boy who seemed no bigger than Eric. He came down the steep path in a series of leaps, swinging a heavy stick and looking back over his shoulder.

60

It was a fantastic little procession, a frieze of figures running from light to darkness. They disappeared completely, but a young growth of spruce at the fringe of the orchard must have hidden them, for suddenly they broke out among the apple trees and stood in a cluster in the tall grass, their heads turned toward the woods in strained alertness.

Philippa didn't move. A bank of goldenrod half concealed her, and her dress was a muted grey-green. The children stood tightly together. The tallest girl kept her arms around the smaller two. The boy in thin and shrunken overalls gripped his stick and kept staring into the woods.

"He's gone, I guess," the girl said hoarsely.

The boy cried out something; the words were unintelligible, but the intent was clear as he swung the stick back.

"No, he's gone," the girl repeated. She turned her head toward the wood in a listening attitude. Her profile showed white against the dark trees, the features pointed and delicate. Her neck was too thin, her shoulders sloping. The younger children pressed against her in an unnatural stillness.

There was another movement at the outer rim of Philippa's field of vision. She looked back to where she had first seen the children and saw Perley Fraser coming down the steep path. He plunged heavily over the slippery needles. The long ray of light caught him like a spotlight, and his thick features were transfigured with an intense alertness. He had no cap on, and a cluster of black curls fell over his forehead. Then he disappeared the way the strange children had done, but the image of his face stayed in Philippa's mind, coarse and eager and wild.

She realized that the children hadn't seen him yet, but presently he would appear behind them. He had been tormenting them, she supposed. They'd be fair game for teasing, such white nervous creatures, as high-strung as deer though not beautiful like deer in any way that she could see.

She stood up and walked around the bank of goldenrod; just as Perley came into her view behind the children, she appeared before them. They gazed at her in an appalled stillness, but she looked over their heads at Perley. The intentness was gone from him, his face was as blankly sullen as it had always been.

"Going for a walk, Perley?" she asked pleasantly.

Her voice released the children from their spell. They began to sidle away; then one of them saw Perley, and all four of them broke into a frantic run toward the end of the orchard. It seemed kinder not to watch them.

"Those are the Webster children, aren't they?" she asked.

Perley grunted. He looked around her and beyond her, and then squinted at the dim trail behind him. "Got to go back and get my gun."

"What were they afraid of, do you know?"

He pulled at his lower lip, rolling it out so that the moist inner part showed. "I d'no. I was tryin' to find out. I was amblin' along mindin' my business when they come stuggerin' out of the pucker brushes and took off like a lot of fool pa'tridges. So I come after them to see what scared 'em."

You're lying, Philippa thought. It was you who frightened them, somehow. He disappeared behind the bright green young growth and reappeared on the slope, moving fast in spite of his lumpishness. Then she walked down through the orchard. When she reached the alley of trees, there was no sign of the children. One way the path led to a gate, beyond which she caught a glimpse of the gables of the Fennell house. The other way led out to the Bennett meadow. She went this way.

The vision of the running children stayed with her. If they had been attractive, she would not have been moved so deeply. But they had been as fragile and as unwholesome as the Indian pipes that grew in the darkest part of the woods, pushing blindly out of the sterile carpet of needles. Because of this, there had been something in their fear to infuriate her.

She remembered the time when Eric wanted a kitten and she had finally decided they might keep one in the apartment. Someone promised her a chunky yellow male as soon as it could be weaned. But in the meantime Eric came home from the park one day bearing tenderly in his sweater a weak, lanky, thoroughly ugly, and pregnant female. Eric called her Strange. She never grew to trust Philippa and was only grudgingly civil with Eric, but once she had thrust herself upon them there was no forgetting her. Eric and Philippa tended her, Eric with patient love and Philippa with a grim sense of duty, until the night she had died having her one kitten. The kitten died too. Philippa had been unwillingly moved by their deaths, but when she suggested the promised kitten, Eric refused. He would have no other cat. Strange had been his cat, he had found her, or she had found him. She had never liked him very well, but it didn't matter. In her weakness and wildness she had claimed him completely.

The cat had rearranged their lives around hers, and they had allowed it because the duty of the strong toward the weak was an inescapable thing. After she died, the change was still there. In Eric it was irrevocable because it was his first experience of the sort. For a long time afterward Philippa had wished, with a surprising passion, that Eric had taken a different route home from the park that day. Now, walking out into the Bennett meadow, she wondered if the time would ever come when she would wish with the same passion that the Webster children had never run down into the orchard this afternoon.

She repudiated the idea. Premonitions, she could hear Justin enunciate clearly, are a fine stock in trade for a medium, but not for a schoolteacher. He trained me so thoroughly, she thought, that I wouldn't even let myself imagine that he might be killed.

She was out of the shelter of the trees now, and the wind blustered coldly across the meadow. At the same time a dog came racing toward her through the tall grass, barking—a large dark dog of the indeterminate shepherd type seen in old engravings of farm scenes. His bark was tremendous, as if he were trying to outdo the wind, but the plumed tail was waving.

"*Dick*!" a woman's voice called, clear and imperious as a bell. "It's all right, he doesn't bite!"

"I know." Philippa answered. As the woman came nearer, she recognized Joanna Sorensen, Mark and Steve Bennett's sister. She was as tall as Philippa, with a strong supple build. Her coloring was warm and dark.

"Hello! I've been wanting to meet you. We wanted to plan a sort of party for you at the clubhouse, but with the men out after herring every night it's had to be put off." She put out her hand. "Jamie's very much impressed with you. But when I said I'd visit school one day, he was horrified."

"They hate it," Philippa said. "My son's always been thankful

I've had something to keep me busy in school hours, so I can't embarrass him."

"How old is he?"

"Eight. Just the age of Jamie." They stood there in the wind, smiling at each other. Birch leaves blew past them in a dry gilt shower, and the meadow grass billowed like a pale sea.

"I've been out for a walk. Looking for cranberries, incidentally." Mrs. Sorensen pulled open the pocket of her old leather jacket, and Philippa looked in at the berries.

"They're so pretty. They must be fun to pick."

"Come with me some time. You can get enough to supply all your relatives with genuine, rare, sea- and sun-kissed, Bennett's Island cranberries." She had a way of throwing back her head when she laughed, and her strong throat was as smooth and round as a girl's. She might have been forty; there was gray glinting in the black hair that ruffled out from under her beret.

Philippa felt a quick reaction from her introspective mood. "They look a lot healthier than the children I just saw. Nothing sea- and sun-kissed about them, but I must say they were rare." Mrs. Sorensen's black eyebrows lifted. "The Websters," Philippa explained. "That name was beginning to sound like a species of elf or gnome long before I laid eyes on them, and now I know why. I saw them for the first time about ten minutes ago."

"Haven't they been in school?" Mrs. Sorensen demanded. "Wait a minute. I remember, now. Young Charles said something one night, but I was making biscuits and the children were at each other's throats, so all I heard was the name and something about school."

"Tell me about them," said Philippa.

"I'll tell you all I know to tell," Mrs. Sorensen answered. "But not out in this wind. Come home with me and have a cup of coffee."

They walked toward the grove of big birches and ancient alders that bounded the meadow on the side toward the harbor. The dog loped ahead of them with an air of good-natured importance. For him there would be no nonsense about barking at a sparrow flushed out of the grass or chasing off on the trail of a cat.

"There's nothing much to say about the Websters," Mrs. Sorensen said as they came into the sheltered path through the alders. "Jude's an intelligent man, but he doesn't have much 'git up and git'. He's had a lot of bad luck, and maybe it's broken his spirit. I don't know. But he's ambitious for his children. If it was left to Lucy, they'd be as wild as squirrels." Her laughter was faintly cynical. "I don't know but what they are, anyway. They've had all summer to go woods-queer in. But if they haven't been to school, I know why. They've got nothing to wear. Lucy's taken to her bed and hasn't fixed up anything for them, poor young ones."

"I've been to the house, but nobody answered."

"She's having one of her spells, I suppose. Well, I'll get up to see her tomorrow and stir her up." Joanna Sorensen frowned thought-fully. "The men have been seining every night, getting in way late, and I've been so busy I've been right out straight, or else I'd have seen her earlier. I like to go up there every so often and blow in like a nor'easter, to see if I can't shake her up." She gave Philippa a dark amused glance over her shoulder. "That sounds as if I was just plain mean, but I honestly believe Lucy likes it. Jude fairly lives on tiptoe for fear of snapping her nerves like violin strings."

"There's nothing more maddening than watching someone trying to handle you with gloves."

"You know, that's exactly what I think. Nils lets me get just so far with my vaporings, and then he starts hauling me back to earth again." She led the way across the plank bridge that spanned the little brook between the alder swamp and barnyard. "Here we are. It's getting late—can't you make it supper instead of just coffee?"

Dick, who had been to the house and back several times, leaned against her legs, and she bent to scratch his ears, looking up earnestly at Philippa. "I'll send Jamie around the harbor with a message."

"All right," said Philippa. They smiled at each other with a mutual sense of pleasant discovery. "But there's one more thing, be-fore we go into the house. I'm still thinking about the Webster children. I'd like to see them and talk to them, if it's possible, before I see their parents. What do you suggest?"

"I can send Jamie up now to tell them to come down for some eggs. They'll all come. They never get tired of the hens and the pig and Jamie's banties."

"They won't scatter when they see me?"

"I don't know, but it's worth a try, isn't it?"

There was something exciting about the instant sparking of

Philippa's mind to this woman's. Philippa felt a stirring of expectancy, and then her training and experience assumed firm control over instinct. In a small community it was not wise for a teacher to have a particular friend among the mothers. Besides, a person who appeared as vital and candid as Joanna Sorensen was sometimes a cruel disappointment. Their charm wore thin, their directness had other less pleasant manifestations.

Am I telling this as a consolation, Philippa wondered ironically, so I won't be tempted to give in and choose her as a friend?

It was a thing to consider later. Meanwhile Mrs. Sorensen was halfway across the yard to the back door. From somewhere out of sight a pig that had heard her voice was lifting up its own. The Rhode Island Reds in their big enclosure crowded conversationally to the fence, and the privileged bantams scurried like blowing leaves around her feet and Dick's big paws.

How Eric would love this, Philippa thought. Mrs. Sorensen was waiting for her at the end of the walk between the tall lilac bushes. None of the barnyard citizens followed them. "Dick keeps them in their place," she said. "Kind but firm. Just like Nils." She laughed, and opened the door into the warm house.

Chapter 12

Steve Bennett walked home with Philippa later that evening. Charles, who had been excited and gay all through supper, didn't speak to them when they left. Philippa felt sorry for him, and oddly guilty, as if she had hurt a child's feelings. But as she walked beside Steve, the faint discomfort was lost in the night's splendor. The wind had dropped at sunset and the air was still. The northern lights moved over Brigport, sweeping across the sky, shooting toward the zenith and withdrawing, slipping sideways like the sticks of a fan.

"It'll be warmer tomorrow," Steve said. "The wind will be southerly."

"Weather is as important out here as food, isn't it?" Philippa asked. "Even the children talk about it. The boys come into school saying, 'It's airing up,' or 'It's a weather breeder, be an easterly to-morrow.' And while we're on the subject, what's a hand-bill? And fog crumbs?"

"Hand-bills are little clouds, sort of round, that race before the wind. And fog crumbs are the thin wisps without much shape."

"Thank you," said Philippa. "I'll write it all to my child, so he can have something to impress his friends with."

"That's important. I could never impress anybody at home, being the youngest, but I could make my chum's eyes pop. He was Nils's kid brother, by the way. I went down one day chewing raw prunes and spitting through the gap in my teeth. Told Dave it was tobacco. He believed me till he got close enough to smell." His laughter was low and reminiscent, going past Philippa to a far-off place that excluded her. "I was eight then."

"When I was eight," Philippa said, "I impressed people by telling whoppers. The stories varied with everything I read. I impressed people, but not the way I'd hoped."

"Who thinks a kid's life is simple?" He held a package of cigarettes toward her.

"No, thanks." While he got one out and lit it, she looked around her. They were on the path that led to the shore and had stopped by the house called the Binnacle. It was a lofty old place set close to the harbor. On the side toward the path only one window, a lower one, was lighted. Philippa could see the smoky hand lamp on the table close to the pane. In this room someone played the clarinet. The key was a minor one and the melody woeful, but the tone was poignantly true.

"That's Gregg, isn't it?" she whispered. "Who is he?"

"A derelict," he said. "We've always had one in the Binnacle. Sometimes two or three at a time. No one knows where they come from or where they go when they leave here. One of them comes chugging into the harbor some day in a little one-cylinder putt-putt and wants to rent a place. We put 'em in the Binnacle—it belongs to our family—and if they make enough, hand-lining or lobstering, to pay rent, all right. If they don't—" He laughed. "Well, they stay just the same. My father never hounded them for the rent, and I guess his reputation still goes on—they expect to get a roof over their heads on Bennett's Island."

"Your father's reputation seems to be upheld by his sons," said Philippa. "It's a rather nice thing to discover in this day and age— a true haven for derelicts."

"Don't flatter us." He sounded amused, though she couldn't see his face distinctly. "Maybe we're not good, just lazy. We used to think my father was soft, and we had plenty to say about it then. But I don't think any one of us is half the man he was." He went on before she had a chance to comment. "Gregg's no addition to the place, none of them are, but he does no harm. He drinks himself into the D.T.'s now and then, but he can play that clarinet in a way to break your heart. He told me once he played it in the Navy Band. That's about all anyone knows about him."

The tune followed them from the Binnacle, pure and unearthly clear in the quiet night. Philippa had seen Gregg sunning himself on his doorstep or wheezing around the shore to the wharf on boat days, a balding untidy little man with watery eyes, and pants that always sagged under the round of his belly. As she listened now, she tried to see him young and slender in his uniform, his hair thick and his eyes unfaded. And she saw him playing the music she heard, the young man, not the grimy old stray the island knew as Gregg.

For a moment, as she walked beside Steve along the shore, she felt as if the situation were completely unreal; the great unseen presence of the sea whose nearness was proved by the quiet breathing on the beach, the ghostly light fanning the sky, and now the melancholy clarinet. And through her awareness of the strange night moved the memory of the Webster children, who a few hours before had come shyly into the Sorensen house out of the dusk, like small white deer coaxed from the woods. They had been torn between the trust of their friends and their extreme consciousness of the stranger, even though Philippa made no move toward them. She had sat on the woodbox, holding four-year-old Linnea Sorensen in her lap; and while she was appalled by their suspicion of her, she was not surprised that Joanna Sorensen could draw them to her.

Nils Sorensen was a squarely built man in his forties with fair hair and unequivocal dark blue eyes; he didn't speak to them or move from his chair. He took out his knife and began to hone it on a small oilstone. The smallest child, a thin waxen boy who could have been four or an undersized six, went to him without hesitation to watch the process. Jamie slung his arm around his father's neck in a proprietary manner, but at the same time he smiled at the other child with a sweetness that touched Philippa.

The younger girl kept close to the older one, who made what answers were required of her in the hoarse breathless voice Philippa had heard in the orchard. Her pale straggling hair was tied at the nape of her neck with a bit of bait-bag twine. She stood stiffly quiet in the kitchen. Sometimes her eyes darted toward Philippa and then quickly away. They were an odd light color Philippa couldn't distinguish and shallow set above the sharp, narrow cheekbones.

The boy who had carried the stick said nothing at all and never advanced farther into the kitchen than just inside the door. He stood warily, and Philippa, by means of casual glances, saw that he was older than eight. He looked much like the girl, Rue. What a strange and sad name that was: Rue.

When the children began to fidget, Steve took down a lantern and lit it, and led them out to the hen house.

"Steve is a genius at getting eggs out from under hens," Joanna said. "They all hate me. And it's not because I'm another female. Gromyko hates me too. That's the rooster."

The spell was broken and Philippa was glad. She found herself stiff with strain. A cat appeared and Linnea hurried out of Philippa's lap to greet her. Jamie went back to his airport spread out on the sitting-room floor and made loud engine noises. Nils turned on the radio for news and weather.

"What do you think?" asked Mrs. Sorensen, taking dishes out of the cupboard.

"I don't know," said Philippa frankly. "I never saw such frightened children. The embarrassing thing is that they seem as afraid of me as they are of—anybody." She had almost said *Perley*.

"Naturally!" Mrs. Sorensen laughed. "You're the teacher, you're going to drag them away from this heavenly existence, building brush camps and all the rest. And what's more you'll be telling their father what they've been up to."

"That's what I don't want to do. When you go to see Mrs. Webster —" She paused as Charles came in by the front way.

Joanna Sorensen nodded. "I won't mention it," she murmured. "If you can get them back by yourself, that'll be best."

Philippa became aware suddenly that Steve had finished lighting his cigarette and was watching her. "I'm sorry," she said. "I was looking around."

"There's a good deal to see, even at night. And to hear." He sounded as if he had seen nothing odd in her abstraction. "Gregg's probably in bad shape, but he stays in tune."

They began to walk again, not hurrying. The night was too still for hurry. It was good to be leisurely and have a companion. In some remote way she was reminded of the long walks with Justin through empty city streets at midnight. They had moved slowly, savoring the quietness, feeling the place to be particularly their own because they were almost alone in it. It was an alien thing for her to be so much at ease with a stranger. Perhaps, she thought, it was because his own affairs left no room for interest in hers.

There were no lights on the far side of the harbor, and very few behind them. They went by the long fishhouse, divided into small sections where some of the men kept their hogsheads of bait. An indescribable blend of freshly salted herring and herring long dead hung about this place, as if not only the damp boards of the floor but the beach rocks outside were saturated with it. On the opposite side of the path was the long pebbly beach where the boats were hauled up to be painted and where the men came ashore in their skiffs. Tonight the tide was high, almost to the road, and the water flooded the beach in a black, uneasy stillness. Two dories that had floated were mysterious pale shapes, moving gently; when one nudged the other, the sound seemed incredibly loud.

When they reached the big anchor that had been sunk deep into the soil where the marsh reached the beach, Steve stopped. "Let's walk over past the schoolhouse," he suggested. "It's too pretty a night to shut off so soon." A cricket sounded almost under their feet. "He thinks so too. And somebody else."

There were footsteps somewhere behind them, faint and unhurried on the pebbles.

"If I was about ten, now," Steve murmured, "I'd be lying in wait in the tall grass to see if that was a smuggler. . . . Jamie's talking smugglers. It's that book you're reading to the kids."

The idling footsteps came closer; the man was a vague figure approaching them. "Evening," Terence Campion said.

They answered him and he went on. They waited until the sound of his feet died away on the boardwalk.

"How about that walk?" Steve asked.

"I'd like it." She wondered how long it would be before Asanath's sister, Viola Goward, would ask her about this. They took the path across the marsh toward the schoolhouse. The ground was spongy underfoot, and the night scent of the marsh grass was pungent.

"I wonder what Terence thinks about," she said. "He seems fairly well insulated from the world around him."

"You should hear him firing buoys at the wall of his fishhouse sometimes," Steve said dryly. "You'd know then the insulation's worn pretty thin in spots. It'd be more to the point if he chucked the buoys at Asanath."

"Why? Because his father doesn't trust him not to get into a mess? That's about the size of it. They're worried sick over him."

"They should have been worried sick about him a long time ago, and not because of Kathie. She's got more sense, that kid, than most of the grown women I know." It was the first time she had heard him so definite. "When Terence was born, they already had Elmo, and from what Suze said when they first came here, Terence was a surprise to them and not a fancy one. They hadn't planned on having any more besides Elmo. Suze talked a lot about it when the women got together to do Red Cross work during the war. But I guess she hardly mentions it now. Maybe Elmo hadn't been dead very long."

"I didn't know about Elmo. They haven't mentioned him. There's not even a photograph."

"He was killed in the war. Battle of the Bulge." He said it without expression. They passed the schoolhouse and went out of the school-yard into the rough road leading past Schoolhouse Cove. A long sword of light, far more brilliant than the display over Brigport, swept the southern sky.

"Matinicus Rock Light," Steve said. He took her arm gently and turned her to face open sea. The light came again. "It shone into my room when I was a kid. There used to be twin towers then. Two eyes, watching us and watching over us. Nothing could get us, I used to think, but we couldn't get away with anything, either."

He took his hand from her arm, and she was faintly regretful. This was a moment that demanded contact with someone or something. Without it she felt a vast and devouring loneliness all around. The ghost fires in the north and this finger of light probing in the south only served to emphasize it. She thought of Terence walking through it like the ghost of his older brother. Elmo, the wanted brother. She remembered the Webster children with a sure and despairing knowledge that she was predestined to fail with them.

I must be tired, she thought. I've been up and down all day, exalted one moment, nostalgic the next, angry, touched, excited about first one thing and then another. After a night's sleep everything will come all right. I'll be myself, the efficient Mrs. Marshall to whom all things are possible. . . . It was as if someone was mocking her, and she shivered.

"Cold?" Steve said.

"I hate to admit it. It's so lovely out here." It wasn't lovely. She wanted to get back to her room and secrete herself in it as if it were her shell.

"There'll be other nights," he said. They began to walk back. "Wait until it's winter and we have those windy nights with a full moon, and the surf crashing in all along the wind'ard side of the island, and the spray flying. Then there's the way it is before a storm, when the stars blaze so close and there's not enough wind for a sigh. The water lies so quiet around the ledges you could land on any of them from a skiff."

She listened, trying to fight against depression. "Did you ever do that?"

"Enough times so my father would've tanned my bottom if he'd known. I still like to take a dory and go rowing late at night after everybody's climbed under the kelp."

The short cut behind the schoolhouse lay in a heavy, cold shadow, like a grotto. Philippa imagined Steve rowing in the starlight with long unhurried strokes, lifting the oars sometimes and letting the dory glide of its own momentum over the dark water, past coves that had become mysterious with the advent of night. She could not conceive of anything more peaceful.

"Take me some time," she said. The sound of her voice startled her, and her face grew heated. But he was already answering her, without surprise.

"All right. Some night when the water's firing."

72

"I won't talk and spoil the stillness."

"No. You're not a gabbler."

Justin used to say it a little differently: *You weren't afraid of a short silence and you literally bask in the long ones.* "Thank you," she said to Steve. They came out by Foss Campion's house and went onto the boardwalk, moving quietly.

Chapter **13**

Rob Salminen was the janitor of the school, which meant, principally, bringing in wood from the supply stacked in the entry and building a fire when it was necessary. He was responsible also for a fresh pail of water every day and for ringing the bell. The work was neither arduous nor exacting, but Rob found it impossible to carry on without assistance, usually in the figure of Ralph Percy. Sky Campion was Rob's closest friend, but Ralph, by design, managed to arrive at school early enough to help. This meant simply that he and Rob could stay inside the schoolhouse and keep the others out until the teacher arrived. It gave them a fine sense of superiority.

When Philippa reached the school on Monday morning, Rob and Ralph were inside, and the younger Percys were storming a locked door. Ellie Goward stood by, clutching her new pencil box against her chest and staring at them with awe. No one else had come yet. The Percy girls were kicking the door and shrieking at the tops of their voices when Ellie saw Philippa, gasped, and clapped a hand over her mouth.

"It's Ralph's fault!" Clare Percy shouted defiantly. She was the older. "If he'd a let us in, we wouldn't a kicked the old door!"

"But it's too early for you to go in," said Philippa reasonably. "And it's warmer out here in the sun than it is in there."

"Well, what's *he* in there for?" asked Clare. Frances, whose upper lip refused to close over her big cramped teeth, added, *"He's* not the janitor!"

"No, he isn't," Philippa agreed. "But kicking the door won't make any difference either way. Please don't kick it any more. Why don't

you girls"—her casual glance took in Ellie, who was still rigid—
"pick a nice big bouquet of asters for the bookshelves?"

"Well—" Clare managed to get two syllables into the word. "Are
you going to make that old Ralph come out?"

"I have something for Ralph to do. Frances, Ellie, there are some
really deep purple asters in the path."

Ellie went, as smoothly as a small seal diving, and Frances ran the
length of the doorstep and jumped off, her skirt flying. Clare looked
after them uneasily and then went down the steps, walking with
dignity.

Philippa had been conscious of the organ for some time and of
Ralph's voice rendering "When the Roll Is Called up Yonder" with
the gusto of a drinking song. It seemed a pity to interrupt. She
knocked, and no one came. Ralph went on singing, striking vi-
brant though haphazard chords. Rob shouted over and around him.

"Git away from that door, you little brats!"

Philippa knocked with what she hoped was an unmistakable ring
of authority, and there was a stricken silence inside. The gentle wash
of surf in Schoolhouse Cove and the racket of crows in the woods
beyond became audible. After a moment someone unlocked the door
and opened it. It was Rob. He stared at her, stroking his jaw with his
hand as if to keep from bursting into dismayed laughter.

"Good morning, Rob," said Philippa, and walked by him through
the entry and into the schoolroom. Ralph sat on the organ stool,
solid in his tight dungarees and plaid shirt, his hands on his knees,
innocence on his round face.

"Good morning, Ralph," said Philippa. Ralph ducked his red
head.

"Good morning, Mis' Marshall."

"The music was very nice," said Philippa, "and I don't mind your
helping Rob to build the fire. But once it's started, I think you'd
better go outside until it's time to ring the bell."

"I'll warm their backsides for kicking that door," said Ralph virtuously.

"I've spoken to them about the door. But they're right about it,
you know. You're not the janitor." She gave him a sideways smile on
her way to hang up her coat, and he grinned and stood up. "You
don't have to go out this moment," she said over her shoulder. "I
want to talk to you. You too, Rob."

74

She sat down at her desk. Ralph stayed on the organ stool, and Rob lighted on a first-grader's desk with an air of impermanence, like a grackle lighting on a treetop.

"Why did the Webster children stop coming to school?" she asked.

The good-natured expectancy in Ralph's face was smoothed to nothing. Rob gazed at the New England poets. Philippa waited, listening to the crackle of the fire. She looked out and saw Sky Campion sauntering through the lane, studying something in his hand. She returned to Ralph and Rob.

"What was the matter, couldn't they keep up with the work? Did Mrs. Gerrish ask them to leave?"

"Gorry, no," said Ralph. "She didn't say anything, not that I know of. But she didn't say anything when they stopped coming, either. She didn't act very surprised, come to think of it."

"Maybe she was relieved," said Philippa. "It's not easy, trying to teach children who aren't very bright."

Ralph stopped swinging on the stool. "Who ain't very bright?" he demanded. "I know I'm a numbhead when it comes to those foolish problems, but—"

She laughed. "Present company always excepted, Ralph. I mean the Webster children."

Rob's fair eyebrows lifted in a movement like Kathie's. "They aren't foolish. Unless maybe Edwin. He doesn't talk so good, and the other kids used to plague him."

"Rue's the smart one," Ralph said. "She's as queer as a two-dollar bill. They all are. But she's smart. I live right next door," he explained importantly. "She gets the work done, fixes Jude's dinner box for him, cleans up the other kids, and they go out about the time we're starting for school and stay all day."

"I wonder why she left school," Philippa said. "I wish someone could tell me." She began to straighten things on her desk. It seemed to her that she could feel the glances darting back and forth beyond her. "I wonder," she murmured, "why Mrs. Gerrish didn't try to get them back. Rue, anyway."

Rob's voice was jerky. "I guess they made her nervous. She acted —well, kind of afraid of them, because they were different from us. It was like she didn't know how to handle 'em."

"She didn't like Rob and Kathie either," Ralph said, "but she could fight with them. Kathie used to throw the—" He blushed. "Throw it right back at her."

"But why did the Websters really go?" She appealed to them as if they were two reasonable adults. "Because she was stiff with them? Did she ignore them?"

"I guess they got tired of being tormented," said Ralph.

Philippa sat back in her chair. Her lack of surprise was in itself a surprise to her. "How were they tormented?"

"You know how kids plague other kids that are kind of queer." His freckled face was stolid. "They prod at 'em, stand in their way and won't let 'em by, call names like—well—" he flushed. "Ask 'em if they lived under rocks and ate cutworms, and if their mother was so crazy they had to keep her locked in the cupboard under the sink. . . . They took an awful lot of it, when they were standing around before school and when they were passing back and forth on the road. But they didn't leave until it got warm enough for them to stay in their brush camp. I guess they didn't have anywhere to go before that. Jude wouldn't stand for them to stay out of school."

"But if he'd known what was going on—"

"They knew better than to tell. It would've been worse for them if he'd made a chew about it."

"Who did it?"

Ralph shrugged. "Different ones, different times. Perley Fraser was in school then." He glanced up at Philippa uneasily. "Guess we all thought it was fun to plague Edwin, he makes such crazy noises. But my brother Fort came out from behind a boat on the beach one day and caught me at it, and like to knocked my head off." He rubbed his ear reminiscently.

"I sort of outgrew it," Rob mumbled. "Almost everybody did. Edwin, he'd get so riled up he'd go down on the beach and heave rocks at everybody. Mad enough to go out of his head. It scared me. And Rue never did anything but stare back at you with those funny eyes of hers." He looked at Philippa defiantly. "But I never did anything *bad*. Just to tease."

"But somebody must have done something really bad." Suddenly Philippa saw the Webster children running silently through the woods, and Perley Fraser behind them. She said the name into the quiet schoolroom.

"Perley?"

Ralph nodded. "He's dirty," he said with violence. "He was bigger than all of us. And what he did was worse than anything we ever did." The flush ran into his face again, and he stared stiffly past Philippa. "He could think of things like bending back your little finger till you was down on your knees crying and begging. . . . He's had me down, and Rob too. We know all about it. And taking you by the back of your neck and digging his fingers into those soft places under your ears—" He winced, and tenderly felt his neck. "And knocking your books out of your arms into mud-puddles, and stepping on your hand when you grabbed for them. And punching you in the belly when you wasn't expecting it. He could make us all holler," he confessed defiantly, "all of us but Rue. But when he'd make Edwin croak out in that funny voice, Rue'd get feather-white."

"And we couldn't do anything!" Rob burst out. "He'd just as soon knock you dead. Kathie flew at him once, and he like to broke her arm, twisting it behind her."

Philippa folded her hands on the desk and looked at her thumbs. "Why didn't any of the parents do anything?"

Ralph gazed at her with wonder for her ignorance. "Nobody told. The little kids was off by themselves. They most always had a different recess-time, anyway. And the older ones—like us—well, they never tell at home. You get the grownups mixed in, and it's an awful mess. It could even lead to a lobster war, or something."

"It seems to me it was a dirty mess anyway," said Philippa dryly. But it was too late now to lecture. Besides, she had come up against this before, this obstinate code of silence that amounted to a conspiracy against the entire adult world. Even the victims joined it, seeking their own way of escape. "And Mrs. Gerrish didn't know anything that was going on?"

"She never looked out the windows that I know of," said Rob.

"Couldn't some of you have ganged up on Perley?"

"There was just Ralph and me to do it," said Rob. "Maybe Kathie. She's a good fighter. But even if we could lick him, we didn't want it to get to Foss. You know—Perley's stepfather." He glanced anxiously at Ralph. "O.K. to say why?"

Ralph shrugged and looked at the floor. "Go ahead."

"Ralph's father owes Foss a pile of money. If Foss ever decided to collect, Ralph's father would be in awful trouble. He'd lose his house, boat, gear, everything. So Ralph couldn't do anything or say anything about Perley, see? Even if Perley wasn't so big, we still couldn't do anything."

His eyes were bright on hers, begging her to diminish the guilt he felt. Philippa nodded.

"I see why you had to stick with Ralph," she said. "But why shouldn't Foss Campion have known what was going on? He could have stopped it."

"Some people," said Rob witheringly, "think everything that goes on in the schoolyard and in the bushes out back is just *pranks*." He stood up, a slim gangling boy whose expression at the moment was curiously mature. "I guess it's time to ring the bell."

Philippa looked at her watch and simultaneously became conscious of voices and activity outside. "All right, Rob." She smiled at them. "Thank you both. You've been a great help to me."

Ralph got off the organ stool. "Are you figgering on telling this to anybody?" He wet his lips nervously.

She shook her head. "Not unless I have to use it in some big emergency, which I hope will never arise. I wanted to know why the Websters left school, because I'm going to get them back. Perley's out of school now, and busy lobstering. And I like to know what goes on in the yard at recess. So we'll start from scratch and leave the past behind us. . . . In any case, Ralph, nothing that I ever say will make trouble for your father."

His smile came back. "And we'll be good to those kids—you wait and see." He climbed over desks as if his spirit had suddenly been restored to him, and there was a scuffle in the dark entry just before the bell began to ring.

Chapter 14

Afterward, when Philippa looked back, she remembered it as a quiet week. The weather was unbroken in its mildness. One day melted into another as the sea melted into the sky in a lilac haze. There were sweet, mournful scents in the air, a heat like summer in the sun at midday and a frost-flavored chill at morning and night.

It was a week of waiting. The island waited, in its farewell to summer, for the winter to begin. Philippa waited for the chance to find the Webster children. There was nothing she could do until the end of the week. There was no chance of finding them in the woods in the late afternoon after school was out. Perhaps she wouldn't be able to find them on Saturday, even if she began in the morning and searched all day. But she had to try. And when she found them, how could she talk to them and tell them she knew what had frightened them and that it was safer for them in the schoolyard than in the woods? Against her will she retained the picture of Perley crashing down the steep dark path under the spruces, bursting out into the sunlight. The frightening thing about it was not so much Perley himself, but the power of the instinct that drove him to commit his acts of cruelty. And when she thought of Rue, as fragile as a stalk of silverrod, it was impossible to be dispassionate, not when one senseless explosion on Perley's part could destroy the child utterly.

Indeed, the whole business of the persecution that began in the schoolyard, the scenes conjured up for her by the boys' admissions, carried a nightmare atmosphere with them, as if deep within the shell of experience that had made her adult, there still existed the lanky, vulnerable child who had been everybody's game.

She tried to talk to herself like Justin. Don't become too passionate over these children. Don't let them turn your life inside out, as Eric's cat did. Get them into school, see that they're protected, but don't identify yourself with them. You aren't really Phil, you know. She's dead, actually. Consider her a sort of ancestor of yours, and forget her.

It was easy enough to say. But she spent most of Saturday tramping around the Western End and saw nothing, not even the flicker of a pale head or a dress; and she was too oppressed with foreboding to enjoy the sheldrakes and coots feeding in quiet coves or the unexpected sight of a dozen seals taking the sun on a long ledge. She remembered them dutifully, to describe to Eric, but where was her own gusto? She felt resentful to be thus cheated, but it was inevitable. She could quote Justin or use her own hard-earned logic, but the Websters were too strong for her in the end. She went to bed early, and wrote to Eric while the Campion brothers and their wives played Sixty-three in the sitting room downstairs. Whenever she heard Helen's peculiar exuberant laugh, she thought, How much does she know about her son? How much does she guess or suspect? Or does she see Perley simply as a projection of the baby she fed at her breast?

She looked down at her letter. . . . "The sheldrakes have cowlicks like yours," she had written. "Except they look more uncombed than you, if possible. . . . Two of the seals kept slapping at each other with their flippers. The men around here say a baby seal is easy to tame. . . ." She saw Eric reading the letter, the expressions constantly changing across his narrow face, the thin wiry hand going up unconsciously to smooth his cowlick, his mouth quirking in amusement as he caught the gesture. What if, she thought, there is something wrong with Eric that I don't know? What if I am as ignorant as Helen Campion, who laughs at the men's jokes, and preens herself on her children, and loves her food and relishes her gossip as if she were the wealthiest, most fortunate woman in the world?

She felt chilled, and too tired to write, but she read her sister's last note and felt her world—the world of herself and Eric, and no one else, no Websters—take on its normal climate again. "Eric is such a sensible child," Jenny had written. "Not too good to be true, but both Roger and I agree he has a sturdy core of common sense." Common sense, Philippa thought gratefully. Such a splendid pair of words.

She went to sleep prepared to think no more of the Websters or of Perley until tomorrow. But when she awoke on Sunday morning, her heart was beating in a hard heavy rhythm as if she had just experienced some sort of terror. She lay there trying to recollect the dream, but it belonged in darkness and could not be called up into the bright room with the ripples of light flowing endlessly across the ceiling, the windows full of blue light in which the gulls flew, crying, with sunlight on their wings.

When she went downstairs, Asanath was alone in the kitchen, sitting on the woodbin smoking, and looking out across the field to Long Cove. His nose with its thin, high-humped bridge and the sharp rake of his jaw had a curious distinction. The yellow tom was stretched along his leg.

"Hello," Philippa said. "You look like Sunday, the two of you."

"We always observe the Sabbath, real faithful. No mice, no lobsters. Always glad when Monday comes, ain't we, boy . . .? Note for you on the table. Young Jamie just left it."

As she turned to pick it up, Suze came in, a blue bowl of eggs in the round of her arm. "Terence has gone off in Perley's double-ender," she said fretfully. "Going to look for what cultch he can find along the shore, he says. I don't like it. A peapod's like an eggshell, and there's a swell around them ledges."

"Lord," Asanath said. "Perley goes out in that peapod every day, and he's a dull young one and clumsy as a hog on ice at that. Terence ain't altogether in a dream, old woman. He won't be runnin' aground on any sharp rocks."

Philippa smiled at Suze. "Good morning. What's prettier than warm brown eggs in a blue bowl, I wonder?" She read her note, written in a dashing and resolute black script and signed Joanna S. Her pleasure was comforting after the formless fright in her sleep. "I'm invited to a picnic," she said. "And to pick cranberries." Asanath nodded, looking benign. Suze said distantly, "They're always strammin' around in the boat on Sundays."

Asanath pointed his pipe stem at the blue bowl. "Suppose you boil up a couple of those new-laid eggs for Philippa and let her get off on her picnic." He turned to Philippa. "It's too bad you can't have your boy here today. We'll have to figger something."

Chapter 15

Nils Sorensen's boat swung gently at anchor outside the cove where Philippa had once come with Charles. She realized that the scene had changed since she had been there. The dark green tangle of the beach peas was the same, but rough seas had shifted the ovoid shimmering rocks around the wreck.

She felt a faint regret, and said to Nils Sorensen, "Will the wreck disappear completely, do you think?"

He shook his head. "It's been there almost as long as I can remember." He watched Jamie and Linnea jumping from one great silvery rib to another, and said, "Every kid on the island has played on that wreck, for twenty years or more."

"I'd like Eric to see it and know the story."

"It's nothing very spectacular," said Joanna. "She was a coaster, loaded with lumber. Nobody was drowned, but the entire population of the island nearly killed itself off salvaging the lumber."

She held out a shiny two-quart lard pail to Jamie and a tin cup to Linnea. "No, keep your shoes on, honeybunch, for the thistles and thorns." The children went off toward the woods, and she looked at Philippa and laughed. "I understand most of the island feuds started when the *Martha Ames* went ashore."

"My grandfather made more enemies at that time than at any time in his career," said Nils. "He was able to enlarge his barn right afterward. A few small-minded people thought he was a little careless when he was passing by their lumber after dark." He went over and laid his hand on a silky-grained rib. "But nobody drowned in the wreck. Only the ship, and that was hurt enough for the master."

They scattered, looking for the sheltered places on the slopes where the first-ripened cranberries grew pink and red in their beds of vines and mossy turf. Philippa climbed up the hillock she called a Viking barrow and looked off, again experiencing the sensation of greatness and insignificance all in one. How tall she stood, how far she could see; below her in the calm water she could see the pale luminous green of sun-flooded shallows and the purple-brown shapes of submerged ledges like sleeping undersea animals. Where other ledges broke the twinkling surface in long dark reefs, there were the gulls and the shags, immobile in the sun. A cock old squaw and his hens paddled in a sort of lagoon, leaving long glittering V's behind them. Their voices rose to Philippa in a sweet, faint bugling.

The horns of elfland, she thought, and looked beyond them to the distant lighthouse on its rocky islet, riding the horizon like a tall, turreted ship.

Here, then, was where the insignificance began. She saw herself standing small and solitary in space, a doll trying to think great cosmic thoughts when it would be better occupied to be filling the empty lard pail. She laughed aloud suddenly, and began looking for the cranberries. When she found a patch, dark red with a purple bloom, she felt a ridiculous excitement. Warm and cool at once in her hands, they made a satisfactory drumming on the bottom of the pail when she dropped them in. If only I could gather in the Webster children as easily, she thought.

Jamie and Linnea were on the slope toward the woods, their heads gleaming gold against the damp shadowy trees. Eric had never picked cranberries, or any kind of berries that she could remember. This business that Jamie conducted with such grave pleasure had no similar thread in the texture of Eric's short past. Eric would be bored, perhaps, but at eight even a city child wouldn't have grown too far away from the earth. There was an affinity between young animals and the soil.

Joanna and Nils were in the slight depression between the two slopes, and suddenly Jamie stood up and called to them. "I've got a coo! You can pick in it if you want to!"

"Thanks, but we've got a coo of our own," Joanna called back. "Pick it clean, now."

"Ayeh!" Jamie went down on his knees again. Linnea was wandering down toward her parents, singing a formless little song.

Philippa looked guiltily at her own patch to see if she'd picked it clean, then took her pail and moved within conversational distance of the Sorensens. Joanna was busy, but Nils sat with his back against a boulder, smoking his pipe. "What's a coo?" she said.

"I don't know where it comes from," said Joanna, "but when a man finds a place where the lobsters come good, he has a coo. What does it mean, Nils?"

He lifted a blond eyebrow at her, and shrugged.

"A man of few words," said Joanna. "After ten years with me Nils is just as quiet and I'm just as noisy. Is that good or bad?"

"It sounds like an ideal arrangement," said Philippa. "You've each preserved the integrity of your personality, it says in the book."

"All wrong," Joanna said darkly. "I'm supposed to spring alive only when I hear my master's voice, and let him pick out my shoes for me in the catalogue. 'Asa, these are the ones I kind of like—'" It was Suze's voice, tentative and without hope. "'Waal, I'll tell ye, old woman, seems like you're gittin' a dite giddy, choosin' a heel like that.'" Joanna narrowed her eyes. "Giddy! He doesn't care what she wears, he hardly ever looks at her, but if he doesn't keep her in line, maybe she'll forget for one second that he's the Big Man. And if he had that Joanna Bennett for a wife, the way *she* rampses over the island, he'd put the wood to her, all right!"

"Did you ever hear him say anything like that?" asked Nils.

"I only have to look at him, darling. And he only has to look at me." She drew her finger fast across her brown throat, and laughed. "Now Foss likes women with spirit. He figures he's great shakes as a lion tamer. It's in his voice. It's supposed to gentle you into a state of coma."

Nils pointed between them with his pipe, out at the mouth of the cove. "Tell us about Terence," he said. "You're doing fine."

They looked and saw the double-ender going by, moving like something entranced on the summery sea. The rounded side of the boat was patterned with glimmering reflections. It shone between water and sky like a pearl. Terence was not alone. Kathie sat opposite him, on the stern seat. Her head was bright against the water. They were too far away for the others to see their faces, but there was a peacefulness about them. Terence rowed with long effortless strokes, and Kathie sat with one elbow on a bare knee, her chin in her hand.

Philippa's reaction was first pleasure and then dismay. She glanced warily at the others. Nils's eyes, a cool withdrawn blue, were almost shut. He seemed intent on the action of his pipe. Joanna watched the peapod pass out of sight beyond a point of red rock, her lips parted. There was a faint crease between her black eyebrows.

"Steve says there's nothing to it," she said. "He doesn't know much about Terence, but he says Kathie is sound. Charles says Terence isn't—well, I'll say virile, but that's not his word."

"The rest of the place maintains an open mind," said Nils dryly. "Just waiting for Kathie to get in trouble." He nodded at Philippa. "You have Kathie in school. What do you think? Mark would appreciate some backing. He and Helmi don't jibe on it."

"Helmi's like Steve," said Joanna. "She thinks Kathie has common sense."

Philippa said reluctantly, "I couldn't make any guesses about what's going on. Terence never says two words to me. Well, he says

84

'Good morning' or 'Good evening,' sometimes. I like Kathie. We get along well, and I'm sure she'd give me a lot of helpful advice, if I'd just *ask* her."

The Sorensens laughed, and Linnea, coming to them with her empty tin cup, laughed too. "That's Kathie," said Nils. "Efficient as all get-out."

"She feels sophisticated," Philippa went on. "She was very airy when she told me her parents were divorced. It makes her different. At that age you can either suffer the torments of the damned if you think you're different, or you can be pretty well set up over it. Kathie is. She despises Peggy Campion for a smug brat who's barely beyond the Bobbsey Twins. I think Kathie feels she is equal to mastering any situation in the world. She's as brash as a fox terrier, and so likable that I don't know what I'd do without her." She smiled from one to the other and lifted her hands in a gesture of defeat. "And I can't say she shouldn't be associating with Terence Campion because there's no magic way of telling what sort of relationship it is. It might be a beautiful friendship, and it might be something not beautiful at all."

"When I was fourteen," Joanna began, and Nils said lazily, "When you were fourteen, you were on your brothers' coattails, and they couldn't raise hell and neither could you. And you were mad all the time because girls couldn't go lobstering for a living."

She looked at him with a charming air of surprise, as if there were something new about him. "Why, Nils. I didn't know you remembered so much."

"I remember everything about you." He sat up and knocked his pipe empty against the rock. "Pick your berries, woman. You've been talking about this all summer. Now you're here, and you'll pick."

They smiled at each other. Philippa felt lonely all at once and would have moved away from them if it could have been accomplished gracefully. But after the instant of withdrawal into their own world, they came back to her, so casually she knew they had not even been conscious of the withdrawal.

"I suppose Kathie and Terence don't amount to a hill of beans," said Joanna, "when you think about what's going on in the world." She brought up a handful of berries and looked at them somberly.

"Times when I wake up before dawn and lie there sick with the most awful sense of responsibility, as if I had a big share in the blame and ought to be doing something—but I don't know what. Then when everybody's stirring, and there's breakfast to get, and the men's dinner boxes to fix, and the boats go out of the harbor, then everything falls back into place and I think, Why, nothing can happen to the island."

Yes, I know, thought Philippa. I know about waking before dawn. Waking alone, without Justin. She said, "Things are always worse when you're lying still."

"Nils never worries," said Joanna. "Neither does Stevie. They've been through the fighting. I suppose that teaches anyone to be so grateful to be alive that you can't waste precious moments worrying." Suddenly she flushed deeply and stared at Philippa with anger and remorse. "Listen to me running on! Nils, why didn't you slap me?"

Linnea, who had been lying on her stomach helping a cricket through the grass, crinkled her small nose with excited interest. "No slaps. Use an alder switch."

The uncomfortable moment passed in their laughter. Joanna said, "I suppose you think a few licks with the switch would be good for me, punkin. Well, I guess you're right."

Nils reached for one of the short blond pigtails, and tucked an aster under the rubber band. "I'll go and see how Jamie's doing," he said. He walked up the slope and toward the woods, not a tall man, but tidily built. The close-clipped hair on the back of his neck was lighter than his skin. The aroma of his pipe smoke floated behind him in the motionless air.

"He's very nice," said Philippa.

"I wish he'd shut me up before I made a fool of myself."

"Why do you feel like that?" Philippa asked in a casual way. "Do you feel guilty because your husband lived through the fighting and mine didn't?"

"I don't know. No, I don't think I feel guilty. But when Nils was away, and I wasn't hearing from him, and I was having the most hellish nightmares, there was a cousin of his who used to come in and prattle on and on, saying nasty, thoughtless things. . . . I felt like murdering her. And a few minutes ago I heard myself, and all I could think of was Thea."

Philippa laughed. "I had an aunt once who was a widow. That sounds as if it was her occupation, and it was. Nobody ever mentioned her without using the word 'noble,' and I'd swear that's how she thought of herself. Then one day a few years ago I heard someone refer to me as 'noble' and my blood ran cold."

Joanna let out a long breath and began energetically to pick cranberries. "I feel better. What a lovely day it is, after all!" They picked for a while without speaking, and the varied sounds of the place sang about them: a distant murmurous undertone, like the wind blowing through a pine forest, that was the sea on the shore; Linnea's singing as she toiled up over the Viking barrow; the cricket; all the nameless rustlings and stirrings in the grass.

Philippa looked up at the yellow-green curve of the barrow against the sky, expecting to see Linnea there. Instead, there were the Webster children, motionless and staring.

"Visitors from another world," she said in a low voice.

"What?" Joanna, on her knees, straightened up and looked around. "Oh. Hello, up`there! Come down and see us!" They came uncertainly on bare feet that looked too large for the thin knobby ankles. Rue led, holding the waxy little boy by the hand. She kept her yellowish eyes fixed on Joanna, as if by ignoring Philippa she could keep her outside an invisible wall. Her light hair was strained back from her rounded, childish forehead and tied as usual at the back with a bit of twine. The faded, skimpy dress was very clean. All the children looked bleached and parboiled with cleanliness. Edwin was scowling bitterly and carrying his stick, and the little girl with flyaway hair came sliding down over the short turf hand in hand with Linnea. She laughed; it was a gay, entirely natural sound of childhood. Then, as if she felt Philippa's glance, she let go of Linnea's hand and looked down at her feet.

Joanna sat back on her heels. "Isn't this nice? Come over here, Dan'l, and let me see if you're putting on weight." The smallest child looked at her, his upper lip lengthening as if he was trying not to smile, and Rue let go of his hand and gave him a little nudge. Joanna held out her arms, and he went to them at a trot and was cradled against her breast. How small he is, Philippa thought, like a shadow beside Linnea, who is so solid.

Joanna's tanned hand, patting gently, covered the thin little bottom. "He must be drinking his milk, Rue," Joanna said. "There's more meat on his sit-down and his ribs." She held him back to look into his face, and now he couldn't hide his smile, the one-sided quirk to his mouth. "You're a scamp, Dan'l," she said. "There's two tiny devils in your eyes, I can see them. Yes, I can." Daniel wriggled with pleasure in her hands, bumped his forehead gently against hers, then tore loose and rushed back to Rue.

"Hello, Edwin," Joanna said. Edwin dug savagely at the ground with his stick. Joanna smiled and put out her hand to the little girl, who looked at Philippa sideways through her pale lashes and went stiffly to Joanna.

"You're at least two inches taller," Joanna said with awe, "since the last time I saw you." She touched with a finger the sun-bleached hair at the girl's temples. "Rue, this child is going to have a natural wave, I'm sure of it."

There was a tinge of color in Faith's cheeks. Rue said hoarsely, "How could she get it? It's a lie to say carrots will do it."

"I never believed in that myself," said Joanna, "but Faith's got a tendency to wave, and if you keep her hair clean and brushed, you can help it along."

The child touched her head with delicate sticks of fingers. Her pale hazel eyes were luminous.

"*Well*," said Joanna briskly, "have you been looking for cranberries? Had any luck?"

"We've got some." Rue's glance slid toward Philippa, and her uneasiness hung strong between them.

"We want to pick for money!" Faith burst out, as if her exhilaration about her hair were too big for her spindly body to contain. "We want to earn—"

"You shut your mouth, Faith Webster!" Rue cried.

Philippa stood up. "If you want to talk to Mrs. Sorensen alone," she said to Rue, "I'll go down on the beach or over where Jamie is."

Rue looked at her steadily. "I guess it's all right," she said after a moment. "It ain't so important as all that. Everybody'd know it soon enough." She turned back to Joanna. "We want to pick to sell, like Faith said. I heard Mark say once in the store he was figgering to sell cranberries over to the main this year if he could get enough picked, and so I thought he'd hire us."

"And you want me to ask him, is that it?"

Rue nodded. Joanna said, "I'll ask him, then. I can't promise you anything except that. Mark whiffles around. Maybe he's changed his mind. In the meantime, though, you go on picking because I've got to send Bennett's Island cranberries to everybody and his brother, and I'll hire you for that."

"We don't need any favors."

"Land of love, it's no favor, except to me!" Joanna's heartiness blew around them like a salt wind. "I can't get down here the way I'd like to, and you'll be saving me some steps and some worry."

Rue reached for Daniel with one thin tense hand and for Faith with the other. "Thank you," she said.

"Thank *you*. And I'll talk to Mark right away."

"We're goin' to save up," Faith chanted, irrepressible, "and buy a blackboard! So we can have a school in our brush camp!"

"You hush up your noise, Faith Webster!" Rue's head swung irresistibly toward Philippa. There was a perceptible stiffening of the girl's pale delicate lips, as if to hide a tremble. Then she turned and started up the slope, jerking Faith with her. The younger child whimpered and dragged back. Edwin sprang toward the top, driving his stick before him like a lance.

Philippa said in a low voice to Joanna. "I must speak to them." But she was reluctant, knowing she would be defeated. The irony was that the presence of Joanna Sorensen, which had drawn them here, was to keep Philippa from saying the one thing that might reach through Rue's defenses. She took a few steps after them.

"Rue," she said. "Listen to me." The girl looked back, but the sight of that face, a blank mask, dismayed her. "Won't you come to school? I want you all, very much. Bring Daniel too. We can keep him busy."

There was no answer. Holding the younger children tightly, Rue ran to the top of the hillock and down the other side.

"That's that," said Philippa. She sat down tiredly on a rock.

Joanna said, "They've gone wild as hawks. I wonder if it's because of Edwin? Maybe it's that more than the clothing question. Last time I was up to the house Rue had just done a big ironing, and there was more than enough to dress them all decently. You may have to go to Jude after all."

"I want them to come of their own free will. If I have to go to the father in the end, so be it. But I'll give them, and myself, another week."

"I wish you luck," said Joanna. She smiled and reached for Linnea's hand. "I'm one of those people who think a nice cup of tea is a great help. So let's have lunch. I'll give Nils a hail."

She went off toward the woods with her long purposeful stride, Linnea trotting beside her. They stopped by one of the thick widespread clumps of bay that gave a Mediterranean aspect to the land rising harshly from the brilliant blue sea. Joanna herself, with her lustrous darkness, her warm uninhibited gestures, might have been Latin. She broke off some bay leaves, crushing them in her fingers and holding them for Linnea to smell.

Philippa watched them until they disappeared behind the feathery green screen of some young spruces. She wished she could have told Joanna about Perley. But the only action at this point must come from the children themselves. Philippa, sitting on her rock in the strong sunshine, saw again the spirit in Rue's face; the rigid and terrible pride.

Chapter 16

After lunch Linnea slept, sprawled on a blanket in the shade of the woods. Jamie went off on his own affairs. The adults made low, desultory conversation. From the cool tent of the woods they looked out on the sunny landscape of a dream. Words became scarce, voices trailed off. Philippa found herself sinking into a warm lethargy. She resisted it; for her, these interludes often slid imperceptibly into depression, as if the degree of her body's quiescence had some bearing on the defenses of her mind. Nils Sorensen lay on his back, his fair head close to his daughter's; he gazed with half-closed eyes at the shifting green canopy overhead. Joanna might have been asleep, lying curled on her side. One hand touched her husband's.

Philippa got up and walked down over the rough terraces of turf and granite ledge that descended to the sea on the other side of the point. She found a trail winding along between the fringes of second-growth spruce and the sprawling jumble of volcanic rock, and followed it around bay and wild rose thickets. The trees grew closer to the shore now, so that she sometimes walked in shade stippled with sunlight. She came to a little cove, where the beach was no more than a slanting wall of pebbles between two spits of black and rufous rock. The resinous scents around her were spiced with smoke; she saw it rising in a mauve streamer from the rocks at the far side of the cove, and then she saw Kathie and Rue tending a small fire, with the curiously votive air that comes with kneeling before a flame. Daniel and Faith came into view from some further beach, their arms full of driftwood which they dumped beside the fire. Kathie said something and they all laughed, even Rue. She did not look like anyone Philippa had ever seen before. Certainly not like the creature who had turned on her the shallow inscrutable mask.

On a flat rock beyond the fire, at the edge of the sea, Terence was cleaning fish while Edwin watched. Edwin, without his stick, with his thin body hunched in repose and his bleached head canted forward, was also a stranger. Terence, too, had a new aspect. As he rinsed the fillets in the water, the white meat flashed in the sun. Then he washed his hands and his knife, and handed the knife to Edwin. The boy held it reverently. Philippa knew from the movements of his hands that he was opening and closing all the blades. He followed Terence back to the fire, not running or leaping nervously, but carrying the knife with care.

Kathie, talking cheerfully, arranged the fish in a frying pan. The children squatted on the rocks to watch the cooking. Their faces, defenseless in the full flooding of the sun, were soft with their childhood.

Terence stretched out on a level place and propped himself up on one elbow. He pushed back his duck-bill and took out his cigarettes. As he put one in his mouth, he seemed to look directly toward Philippa. She blushed and grew tense; suddenly she felt like the worst sort of Peeping Tom. She waited stiffly for him to make a sign that he had seen her among the tree trunks, but now he was fishing out a match and scratching it with his thumbnail. Edwin came and sat down near him, and Terence glanced over his shoulder and smiled; she saw the flash of his teeth.

She moved backward, cautiously, until she was out of sight. Because she knew Terence was on the defensive about his relationship with Kathie, innocent or not, she felt guilty at coming upon them like this. If Terence had seen her, he would have suspected her of spying. He would have classed her at once with the rest of the island.

She walked back along the path to the Sorensens much faster than she had walked before.

Chapter 17

Steve Bennett was on Nils's wharf to catch the dory painter when they rowed ashore in the late afternoon. The children went up the ladder first. As Steve swung Linnea over the top, he said, "Six new freckles."

"They're sun kisses!" Linnea shouted furiously.

"Freckles," said Jamie, propping himself against a hogshead as if he were blasé instead of sleepy. Linnea screamed, "Sun kisses!" and burst into loud weeping. Steve held out his arms to her, but she beat him off. Joanna stood up, balancing herself expertly in the dory. "It's airing up," she said. "Small craft warnings. Very small craft." She went up the ladder with an ease that Philippa admired, smiling affectionately at her brother. "Never mind, Steve, you can make up with her later. She's so tired she doesn't know whether she's afoot or on horseback. See you later, Philippa," she called down. "You can leave your berries with ours till you want to send some to your friends. We'll keep them in the cellar where it's cool. Hasn't it been a wonderful day?"

She went home, leading Linnea by the hand. Gregg sat on his doorstep, taking the mellow heat of the sun, and she gave him a serene greeting as if Linnea's wails were not drowning her out.

Steve took Philippa's arm as she reached the top of the ladder. "Will you scream if I tell you how many new freckles you've got?" he asked soberly.

"No, I'm old enough to face up to the bitter realities. There comes a time in a woman's life when she has to admit that freckles are freckles, and if she has them she'll just have to be gallant about it." He laughed and sat on his heels to reach for the water pails of cranberries that Nils handed up. There were also four pot buoys and a collection of strangely gnarled, curved, and antlered driftwood.

Steve touched one of the buoys with his foot. "That's mine, isn't it?" he said.

Jamie, in the middle of a yawn, sprang to attention. "I found it. It was hung up in the rocks near the Devil's Den, and I lugged it clear around the point to the dory." His blue eyes, glistening, watched his uncle's face.

Steve brought out a handful of change, picked out a quarter, and gave it to him. Jamie put it in a pocket of his faded dungarees and carried the other buoys to the fishhouse. Nils put the dory on the haul-off and sent her out away from the wharf. "Better get that driftwood under cover too, son," he said. "Know which is yours?" he asked Philippa.

"This one that looks almost like a gull in flight." She picked it up, stroking the thin satiny curve of the wings.

"Never knew it to fail," said Steve. "Let a woman get near a beach, and she's always lugging home driftwood. May I carry your driftwood around the beach for you, ma'am?"

"Oh, *thank* you!" she exclaimed effusively. "But I'm stronger than I look, really!"

Nils's eyes flickered behind his thick light lashes. "Try again, boy. Maybe she'll let you carry along some berries for Suze and Helen." He handed up a lard pail full of cranberries.

Steve pulled at an imaginary forelock, saying gravely, "Bless your kind heart, Cap'n Sorensen. You was always a good friend to the young folks." Jamie looked on in mild astonishment as the adults laughed.

"Thank you for a wonderful day," Philippa said to Nils.

"I'm glad you could come with us," he answered. "Be neighborly."

Coming onto the path, with Steve beside her, she felt a ludicrous embarrassment at Gregg's hail from the doorstep. Then, between the long fishhouse and the beach, they met Rob, Sky, and Ralph, who chorused a little too loudly, "Hello, Mrs. Marshall! Hi, Steve!"

I'm tired, she thought irritably. And the man bothers me. She looked at him sideways; his dark profile was imperturbable except for the agreeable lift of his mouth. She looked away again, and saw Young Charles and Fort far down the beach at the edge of the tide, bailing out a skiff. Young Charles didn't glance up. There was something obdurate about his shoulders as he knelt on the middle seat of the skiff. But Fort grinned and waved his bailing scoop.

"Hey, teacher, can I come to school tomorrow, huh?" he shouted.

"I'll be looking for you," she called back, but still Young Charles didn't look up.

At the beginning of the boardwalk she stopped and reached for her cranberries. "Thank you very much for carrying them."

"You're welcome," he said equably. "I'd like to carry them all the way, but you seem to have your mind made up. . . . It'll be a fine night. No moon, but plenty of fire in the water. Let's go rowing."

She was unprepared for her own reaction. It was as if two entirely separate entities had shouted their answers simultaneously at her, the *yes* of one and the *no* of the other resulting in chaos. For an instant the chaos held, and then she said in a voice of suave reluctance, "I'd love it, but I wouldn't enjoy it the way I want to. I'm almost asleep on my feet now, and I still have a little work to do for tomorrow." She looked past him, across the green and russet of the marsh to Schoolhouse Cove, and groped for the rest of the words; she came back to his face and said with the right anxiety, "But you *will* ask me again, won't you?"

"You're half drunk with air and sun. You won't need to be rocked tonight." He added, without emphasis, "I'll ask you again. Don't doubt that." He turned back.

Chapter 18

In the morning her alarm clock awakened her to a raw gray chill in the room, and a booming of surf on the harbor points. Her windows rattled in a long, sustained gust. She slid from under the covers, wincing at the icy sea of linoleum beyond the island of braided rug, and shut the windows. Eric had let her know he considered the weather to be disappointingly fair, but here was his storm. She was excited enough on her own account.

It was a northeasterly; the wind came down between the islands with a wailing rush. Foam-smeared seas ran high past the harbor mouth and crashed on the end of the breakwater. The high point out beyond the Campion house helped to shelter the harbor. Cat's-paws struck downward over the trees and hurried continually across the gray water, but there was very little action of the boats, and the usual gulls walked on the wet black roofs of the fishhouses or stood, breasts to the wind, on the half-submerged ledges outside Nils Sorensen's wharf.

The house strained in the wind. The buildings on this side of the harbor had no real protection from a northeaster, with the open meadow behind them. The wind baffled capriciously around corners, unlatching doors and then slamming them, shaking windows that should have been in the lee, sending strong drafts down stairways, whining in the chimneys.

When Philippa went into the hall, she looked out at Long Cove and the meadow. The rain was beginning to patter like hail on the glass. Through the blurred panes she saw the dead yellow grass, blown toward her in a smoothly rippling sea. Beyond Long Cove there was the tumbling race of whitecaps and fountains of spray shooting high off the end of Tenpound.

Where would the Webster children stay today? Perhaps they would come to school. She didn't really believe it. A brush camp, Nils Sorensen had told her, could be as tight and snug as a house, if it were built well and deep enough in the woods.

But I will get to them soon, she thought, too excited by the storm to be depressed. Down in the yard the yellow tom chased a whirling leaf with fierce abandon. She laughed, and started downstairs.

"I'm going by the way things look," Asanath was saying. "I'm going by the human element."

"The human element!" Terence shouted derisively. "You know everything, don't ye? You're the bully boy with the glass eye!"

"You spent the whole day with the girl down on the Western End," his father went on as if he had not paused, or even recognized Terence's violence. "You picked her up over behind the point somewhere. You took her down there and you stayed. I want to know the truth here and now; what went on down there?"

Terence made a strangled sound, but his father's voice ignored the interruption. Philippa looked at her watch. She must eat and get to school; it was a damnable situation. She walked back toward the stairs, wondering how to make a noise they'd hear above their own. "Your mother and I have a right to know if you've been up to some deviltry with this girl. We want to know so we'll be prepared for Mark Bennett to walk in here some day and say, 'The girl's in trouble and your son's the one who did it.' The Bennetts would be mighty glad to have something to yammer about, make no mistake. They don't like us any more than we like them. So I want to know if they've got a right to have you arrested."

Was this the Asanath she knew? Philippa wondered in shocked surprise. The Asanath who seemed to preach moderation and tolerance in every word he spoke? It was not so much his questioning Terence that startled her; sometimes plain language was necessary between father and son. It was his comments about the Bennetts.

Terence was shouting no longer. He was saying in his singularly quiet voice, "I'll tell you nothing. For the same reason I never did tell you anything. Because you're so *very* sure of yourselves. Everything I ever thought of, you knew beforehand it wouldn't work. You could knock it down with a grin. Supposed to be fatherly love. To keep me from thinking too proud of myself."

Suze was weeping. The sound was swallowed sometimes by the wind.

"You've been living under a sorry misapprehension, son," Asanath said slowly.

"A misapprehension that I shouldn't have been born?" Terence answered. "Unless maybe I'd got set to be a girl. You already had your boy."

Suze made a pathetic bleating cry, and Asanath cleared his throat. "That'll be enough, son. You've had your say."

"But you still haven't found out anything, have ye? And you won't find out anything. You've got your mind in the gutter, and you can keep it there. You can just stew in your own juice."

It was out of the question for Philippa to go into the kitchen now. She took her coat from the closet and went out the front way. As she stopped in the lee of the sunporch to knot her kerchief, the back door slammed, and Terence came out and around the corner of the house. He passed her, saw her, and came back. He looked at her without speaking, his long jaw thrust forward like a weapon, his eyes glittering under the lids.

She guessed at his thoughts, and spoke to him calmly. "I didn't tell them, Terence. I'm not a tattle-tale."

He turned abruptly toward the fishhouse and she fell into step with him. At least he was no longer a shadow; in his anger he had become violently alive. She followed him into the building and shut the door. He began to kindle a fire in the rusty stove, while she spoke to him above the splashing and chortling of water around the spilings.

"I think I know who might have told," she said. He was pouring kerosene on the kindling, and didn't look around. "It might have been Perley," she said, and waited.

He dropped a match into the stove and stepped back; the leaping flame threw an orange light on his face. "Did you see him?" He was alert now, still without looking straight at her.

"No, but there was a good chance that he was around where the Webster children were."

"What in the devil do you mean by *that*?" He came toward her, pushing back his cap and reaching automatically for a cigarette.

She told him what she meant, keeping her words sparse and to the point. "The boys weren't lying," she said. "They were too nervous and uncomfortable to be lying. I'd seen Perley following the children, but I didn't know then what it meant. Now I know. Perley's quite a specialist at torture, I understand, and the Webster children are fair game. Nobody cares about them, and besides, they're so puny they can't put up much of a fight. They're like sickly kittens."

"Ayeh, like kittens," Terence repeated softly. "Kittens never stood much of a chance with Perley. Helen always figgered it was funny their kittens met up with so many accidents—if she ever caught on it was Perley, she didn't say anything, for fear somebody might think her baby was a mite cruel." The cigarette in his fingers broke suddenly, he dropped it and ground it with his boot. "That cat they got now belongs to Peg. That's the only reason it lived to grow up. Peg can find a way to get even with anybody that crosses her, and I guess that's got through Perley's thick skull."

He went back to the fire, and Philippa spoke to the back of his head. "The reason I've told you all this," she said, "is to see if you'd get a message to those children, the next time you see them. Will you tell them that nobody will dare to tease them any more, and they'll be safe from Perley, if they come to school?"

He stood looking out at the harbor, giving her no sign that he had heard. She waited, her stomach queasy with hunger and tightening nerves. It was getting on toward schooltime. The echo of her voice seemed to hang in the smoky air, above the crackling in the stove. She tried to recall just what she had said. If it was simply an affair of wasted breath, at least she needn't fear that Terence would carry the story. She wasn't even sure that he had heard her.

But after a time he said idly, "Why don't you let Kathie do it?"

"Because it's nothing to concern any of the other pupils. Besides, Rue saw Kathie try to fight for her in the schoolyard, and lose. Perley is a great one for twisting arms, I hear." Terence moved. He went to the stove and looked in, but she felt now that he was listening.

"She wouldn't believe Kathie half as fast as she'd believe you, because you're an adult. If you tell her, it'll be all right—there's a chance that it's the truth. Rue hasn't gone to anyone with this thing, but I have a feeling that if she thought some grown person—not her father —*knew*, in spite of her secrecy, she'd be relieved. It's a terrible strain for a child." She remembered Terence's accusation flung so viciously at his father, and added, "A youngster can feel awfully alone sometimes."

Terence said, "Well—" He looked at his cigarette. Apparently he was capable of standing immobile for moments at a time, and Philippa had a compulsive desire to shake him or at least to shout, "Will you or won't you?"

"I'd better get my breakfast," she said curtly, and left him.

Chapter 19

The lane that led off behind Foss Campion's place to the school was somewhat sheltered, by a growth of young spruce, from the wind and rain beating down across the field. Coming back after the noon hour, Philippa didn't hurry. Dinner had been a silent and yet ominous meal, as if at any moment some wild outburst might take place.

Though the trouble in the house was no concern of hers, the portentous atmosphere was inescapable. Philippa walked slowly in the sodden lane, finding a peculiar relaxation in the tumult around her. The dark cloud masses scudded overhead; with each long, high gust the branches were whipped about in a frenzy, the small tender tips were torn loose and lay bright green against the drowned dead grass in the path. The rain beat through the trees in icy showers. The sound of surf lay over and beneath all other sounds. The cold wet air reeked of the fresh rockweed ripped loose and thrown up on the beaches. It grew stronger as she reached the end of the lane.

She rounded the huge boulder that was a beleaguered fortress or pirate island during recess, and came into the lee of the schoolhouse. A man in oilskins was leaning against the wall, smoking. The oilskins gave him a broad, bulky look, and he wore a sou'wester. He looked up. It was Steve Bennett. Above the yellow oil clothes and against the white clapboards, he was very dark.

At the sight of him she felt an extraordinary degree of surprise, keen enough to be unpleasant. She was aware of its strangeness and of her impulse to retreat as she walked toward him, smiling conventionally.

"Are you just out for a stroll in the fine weather?"

He tipped back his sou'wester. "I had an errand."

"Oh?" She took her handkerchief from her raincoat pocket and wiped the wet hair around her temples, where the rain had beat past her hood. He watched her, and his smile began around his eyes, a faint narrowing at the corners.

"A nor'easter looks good on you," he said. "You must like it."

"I do. I love rough weather, but not in people. I suppose a psychiatrist would say I was fundamentally violent, but civilized about it, or inhibited."

"I'm not much of a stormy petrel, myself." He looked off peacefully across the drenched and wind-flattened marsh. There was no hurry in him. The incongruity of the situation struck her, and she laughed aloud.

"Here we stand, looking at the view as if it's midsummer, and the wind's shrieking through the belfry like a banshee. I've got to see to the fire." She went around to the door.

She felt comfortably normal again; the shock of astonishment, as if he had no right to be leaning against the schoolhouse when she came along, had gone all in an instant.

Following her, Steve said, "When I took my turn at janitor I almost burned the schoolhouse down."

"I'd have thought you were the efficient type." They went up the steps; there was a little lull in the wind, and for a moment there was only the low thunder of the surf behind their voices.

"I was. I stuffed the stove with good dry spruce, opened up everything, let her go Gallagher, and went out to ring the bell." He opened the door. "I was a real fancy bell ringer, as fancy as you can be with one bell. Thought I was ringing Dick Whittington's Bowbells that day—we'd been reading about him." The wind struck the schoolhouse with a shuddering impact; the door was slammed violently shut. They were shut in the narrow dark space of the entry.

"All but took my hand off," said Steve in mild astonishment. His voice was suddenly too close, and the stiff crackle of oilskins became deafening. They had a queer, pungent scent she had never noticed before. Half stifled, she groped for the knob of the inner door. Always her hand had gone straight to it; this wasn't the first time the door had blown shut and left her in the dark. Nerves prickled in the small of her back as she searched, using the flat of both hands. It was as if the close black area of the entry had some unique symbolism which she feared. Idiot! she cried contemptuously within herself.

"Lost the knob?" Steve said. "Wait, I've got a match." His oil clothes rustled loudly. A new gust struck, forcing a faint clang like a cry from the bell. She found the knob just as the match flared up behind her.

"I've got it!" she said eagerly. She laughed, out of breath; she might have just been running. The gray light of the schoolroom was inexpressibly dear to her, the torrents of rain streaming down the windows on the windward side, the familiar scents of the birch fire, chalk dust, the recent occupancy of children. She was safe now in her own frame of reference.

"Anyway," he said, "I set the chimney afire, and they wouldn't let me be janitor any more."

She turned toward him, smiling. He sat on a desk in his bright oil clothes, looking ruefully at the stove. She said, "You sound as if you were still unhappy about it."

"I was remembering how I used to wish I'd burned the place to the ground. Everybody disapproved of me for so long afterward, and then when they got over the scare, it got to be a good joke, even on Brigport. . . . 'Here's the tyke who set the chimney afire, hey? You think you was Steamboat Bill, chummy?' I wished I'd burned the schoolhouse down so they'd look at me as if I was a famous criminal instead of a joke."

Philippa laughed. "Funny how we go through the stage when we ache to be wicked and have everybody look at us with horror. There's a certain respect with that; it gives you some kind of stature. But ridicule turns you into nothing."

"You sound as if you'd been through it too."

"I have." She went to her desk. "Was your errand to do with me?" she asked.

He looked at her as if he was thinking of something else. She waited, and then he came back from his remoteness, smiled and rubbed the side of his jaw. "The boys are getting up a dance at the clubhouse Wednesday night. I'd like to take you. You can see I'm getting my bid in early, while the others are working out their strategy."

"Does it take strategy to invite the schoolma'am to a dance?"

"On this island," said Steve, "it takes strategy for everything. Saves us from monotony."

"Well, yours worked today. I'm so flattered by the way you beat through a storm that I couldn't think of refusing. Will there be square dances?"

"Square dances and waltzes are all you get around here. If any reckless feller comes up with something later than 1900, he learns right off that nobody approves of those flighty modern ideas."

"I can see that this is my spiritual home," said Philippa solemnly. "At school dances I was always stuck with some bright boy who had a lot of original steps to try out. It'll be nice to know exactly what to expect."

"Our dances aren't that cut and dried. The boys got Gregg to say he'd play his clarinet, and now they're trying to think of a way to keep him sober till Wednesday night. Then they'll give him a bottle of wine because he plays the best when he's had just enough. The problem is to keep him from going past the margin of safety."

"I can see it's going to be a very interesting affair," said Philippa.

The outside door opened and crashed shut, and there was a series of thuds and gasps in the entry. "My janitor is arriving," she said. "In two parts."

"Well, I'll get back to the harbor." He picked up his sou'wester. "I'll call for you about eight Wednesday night."

When he opened the door, Ralph and Rob fell in through it, locked in an extremely original wrestling hold. "Break it up!" one of them exploded. They got up, Ralph rubbing his ear and blushing. Rob looked quickly from Philippa to Steve.

"Hey, what are *you* doing here, Uncle Steve?" he asked. Ralph snickered, and Rob whirled on him, punching. Their laughter went rapidly from hysteria to idiocy. Philippa said, "No roughhouse in the schoolroom, boys."

They fell apart, wet-eyed and panting. Steve said, "When I was that age my father said I should be kept in a barrel and fed through the bunghole."

"That's a good idea," said Philippa. "Or the sort of zoo with no fences but nice deep moats they couldn't possibly cross."

The boys, trailing odd wheezes and gurgles and clumping unnecessarily in their rubber boots, hung up their damp jackets. Ralph sat down at his desk and became deeply involved with his English grammar. Rob squeezed by his uncle without looking at him and went out into the entry to ring the bell.

"I'll get out of here before anyone else has the high fantod at sight of me," said Steve. Over Ralph's head they exchanged faint smiles that couldn't escape a tinge of intimacy. Steve went out and Philippa walked back to her desk. In the brief hiatus before the others came, she tried to think objectively of the sensation she had experienced when she came from the lane and saw Steve standing by the schoolhouse, and of her more frightening reaction to the dark entry. She had been like someone blindfolded and spun around three times and then told to find the doorknob. For a matter of seconds her world had gone off its axis.

If it had happened to someone else who told her about it afterward, she would have said with some amusement, "You didn't want to find your way out of the dark entry. You knew where the knob was, but you wouldn't let yourself find it."

She felt a wash of heat rising over her body. You deserve to be uncomfortable, she told herself ruthlessly. You have read too much sensational drivel and taken it seriously.

She saw herself sitting at the desk in her russet dress, gracefully erect, her hands folded before her, her face serene, the events of the past until this moment wiped from it as if they had never taken place. This was the way to begin the afternoon, to begin a lifetime. Never carry into the next hour what should be left in the last.

Rob Salminen's view of fractions was hazy in the extreme. But his candor about his limitations as a scholar charmed Philippa while she deplored it. He was not ashamed of being in the third-grade arithmetic class while Schuyler Campion did knotty problems with the eighth grade. While the rest of the school worked, Rob dreamed, his round face with its tilted Tartar eyes and snub nose rapt with the visions that passed gloriously across his mind. Whenever he became conscious of Philippa's glance, he grinned, scratched his head, and shrugged, as if the whole question of study were a quaint fable which neither he nor Philippa believed. It was a pity to recall him to base reality. But there was the matter of his pass from the sixth grade to the seventh. She had until June to get him through three years of arithmetic. Studying his papers, which showed great ingenuity in getting nine-eighths or five-fourths out of a whole, she wondered what Mrs. Gerrish had done with her time.

Rob had agreed with Philippa from the first that something must be done about his work, if only to please her. Kathie had agreed to supervise his homework. "Helmi was going to help him once," she said, "but Mark nearly blew his top listening. He said he didn't believe Rob could be so stupid. So he took it over. And then he said to keep Rob out of his reach after that because he couldn't be responsible for his own actions. But I won't have any trouble. I'm younger so I can stand more of him." She went back to her seat, too sure of herself to swagger.

On this afternoon of the northeaster, Philippa kept Rob in. Clare Percy stayed to wash blackboards. She switched importantly about the room, doing her chores with elegant flourishes of elbows and wrists. The swing of her red bob and the firm clatter of her shoes expressed her efficiency. Sometimes she allowed herself a cynical smile at Rob's struggle. Philippa sat beside him, unveiling the arcanum of fractions by the most elemental means. The rain still rattled at the windows, but the fire mulled comfortably and the clock ticked with a sleepy beat. A sort of coziness settled over the room.

They were startled when the outer door slammed and the inner one flew open. Clare exclaimed dramatically and flapped her hand against her flat gingham chest. Rob and Philippa looked around. Young Charles stood there in his oil clothes, his skin moist and ruddy from the cold rain. He dropped his sou'wester on the floor, and grinned at Clare.

"Hello, Gingertop. You been up to deviltry and got kept in?"

Clare's freckles were orange against her blush. "I'm helping the teacher," she said with dignity.

"Clare's a real help to me, too," said Philippa.

"What about this one then?" He moved forward and lifted Rob's head by one long tow-colored lock. Rob said amiably, "I'm stupid."

Clare stood watching, an eraser in each hand. Charles winked at her and she blushed again.

"I'm not entertaining today," Philippa said. "Have you come on business?"

"Sure I've got business," he said. "Real important business. We're going to have a time at the clubhouse Wednesday night. Fort and I got it up. I'll take you."

Rob whistled. Clare turned her entranced gaze on Philippa, her lips parting over her big front teeth. Philippa stood quickly, gathering up her book and pencil.

"Wait a minute, Charles. . . . You can go now, Rob. Work on the things I've marked. You've done beautifully, Clare. Thank you very much." She went up the center aisle to her desk. Charles had come in with such a happy assurance. At least she could clear the children out before she answered him.

Rob prepared noisily to leave, giggling when Charles told him he was a proper gorm. But Clare looked about her in a distracted way and then back at Charles as if he were the sun.

"I think you've done everything, Clare," Philippa said. "I'm leaving in just a few minutes." To reassure her that she was not being sent out just because Young Charles had come in, Philippa closed up the stove for the night. Clare went sulkily to get her boots and raincoat. It was an existence without a future, to be eleven and so cruelly plain, and to be called Gingertop by anyone as beautiful as Young Charles.

Philippa began to set her desk in order for the night. In a few moments she saw Clare running across the marsh. Rob was already out of sight.

"Now, Charles," she said briskly. A change from good humor to resentment had come while her back was turned. He walked down the aisle and stood in front of the desk, his thumbs hooked in the bib of his oil pants, looking at her from under the black bar of eyebrows.

"I'm not one of the school kids. So don't talk as if I was."

"I didn't mean to," she said, trying to sound remorseful. "I'm sorry. It's just that I've been using that tone all day. Occupational disease, I guess." She began to straighten the books between the leather-covered book ends that had been Justin's. Now I am being a coward, she thought. And why? He can't have everything he wants in this world; he can't walk in here and tell a woman of thirty what is to be done, and expect to be humored simply because he wants it so much. Her fingers rested on the rough binding of *Leaves of Grass*. If she opened the book, Justin's writing would be inside, but that would be no help to her now.

Charles's hand shot over the books and caught her wrist. For a moment she was too astonished to speak. She gazed quietly at his hand, as if she were making a study of the broad back with the bronze-tipped hairs, the sheen of the tight knuckles, the arrogant thumb. Then she sat back in her chair and looked at him.

"You're stopping the circulation, Charles."

"Will you listen to me, then?" He dropped her hand and came around the desk. His full lower lip moved out sulkily.

"Do you think I should listen, after that?"

"Then I'll be gettin' out of here!" He turned angrily with a crackle of oilskins.

"Wait," she said in a low voice. "You came to ask me to go to the dance, and I didn't want to answer in front of the children. You know how they'd love to carry it. I'm sorry, Charles, but I've already accepted another invitation."

"Fort?" he demanded.

She had to smile. "Not Fort. Your uncle Steve."

He stared at her in incredulous outrage. "How in Tophet's name did he know about it?" he demanded hoarsely. "We only got it up this morning!" His eyes half shut. "Ayeh. I remember now. We were having a mug-up at Jo's. He was knitting trap heads in by the radio. I thought he was listening to news and weather. Well, I made a horse's—a fool out of myself, didn't I?"

"There'll be other dances, won't there? But if you feel you've been had, I won't go at all."

He shrugged savagely. "All right, all right. I'll be a good loser. But right here and now I'll put my oar in for the next dance." He glared at her.

"That's a date then."

"Sorry I mohaggled you," he muttered.

"I know you won't do it again."

He said something else she didn't understand and went back to the door. He bent down and picked up his sou'wester; when he straightened up, he smiled at her. The hostility might never have been there at all.

"Always a tomorrow, anyway. Huh?"

"Always a tomorrow," she repeated, and smiled too. If there was a tenderness about her, it was because at the moment when he left he seemed hardly older than Eric.

Chapter 20

The weather turned fair and seasonably cool after the storm. Fresh breezes blew across the island, not enough to keep the men from hauling but sufficient to keep the water in a continual diamond sparkle. At recess the children kept warm by practicing square dances in the schoolyard. Everyone who knew the figures would be sure of partners on Wednesday night.

Sky Campion brought his harmonica to school. He sat on the steps, tapping his foot and playing "The Irish Washerwoman" over and over while the others clapped, swung, and promenaded through the dances. Sometimes Rob played so that Sky could take his turn at practicing. He danced with the preoccupied expression of a young scientist, even while he was swinging one of the Percys so fast she whitened under her freckles. Nobody was too self-conscious to take part; even the smallest ones were lined up and shunted through the figures. Entirely engrossed, the most gangling of the boys moved with the innocent grace of all young creatures. Kathie responded fluidly to the rhythm, even when she wasn't dancing. Peggy Campion moved through "Hull's Victory" with the proud, somber detachment of an Infanta performing a court pavane.

Everybody talked about the dance in one way or another. Helen Campion had come in after supper the night before. "My Lord, if they had a dance twice a week, 'twould suit me fine! We haven't had a thing in that clubhouse since Labor Day. Herring! That's all I've heard for weeks. I told Foss that if any man on this island comes in tomorrow night and says there's herring in the harbor, I'll shoot him myself, *personally!*"

She stamped her foot and flung herself back in the chair, shaking with laughter. Philippa laughed too, it was impossible to resist. She imagined Helen as a girl, strapping and handsome, going to dances and flinging herself headlong into the music and noise as a swimmer dives into the sea. She wondered if Helen were ever intimidated by the poise of her blasé daughter, Peggy.

Suze twisted her forehead and blinked at her knitting as if their laughter interfered with the counting of stitches. Asanath said, "I b'lieve you *would* shoot him, Helen. I b'lieve you would. I never saw anybody so set on dancing as you."

"And light on my feet, Asa! Light as goosedown, for all my size!" Her eyes flashed. She rocked back again, triumphant.

Viola Goward had come in quietly, and now she stood in the kitchen doorway. "You'll be all worn out before you get there," she said dryly. "Shouting like you'd been in a rumshop." Smiling mysteriously, she came into the room. She dropped her coat and adjusted a loose pin in her knot of sandy hair. Her gaze flashed around the kitchen, probing even the shadows outside the lamplight, and came back to Philippa.

"Got you a beau for tomorrow night?"

"Of course," said Philippa, laughing.

Asanath pulled on his pipe. "Shouldn't think you'd ask such personal questions, Vi. Why don't you wait and see?"

"Oh, I'll know who it is before the time comes! Likely I know now." Her air of omniscience was cheerfully arrogant. "But I'll keep my mouth shut about it."

"For once," Asanath murmured. Vi pretended not to hear. Helen said gayly, as if she were trying to regain her mood of anticipation, "If it's a clear night, there'll be a crowd over from Brigport. I like plenty of couples on the floor for 'Lady of the Lake.'"

"Be plenty of cuddling going on outside too," said Vi. "At the last dance you couldn't go out back without seeing nature in the raw under every spruce tree."

Helen said, "Oh, Vi, it wasn't *that* bad! What'll Philippa think of us?"

"What indeed?" Viola's eyes challenged Philippa with a spirited cynicism. "She's human, isn't she? She's young. She knows what happens at dances, whether it's our kind or the fancy ones she's used to. Liquor is liquor, and people are people."

"That's an incontestable point, Mrs. Goward," Philippa said, smiling. "People are people, all right. But I can't tell you much about dances these days because I haven't been to one for years."

Viola adjusted a hairpin with a sudden stabbing motion. She seemed peculiarly exhilarated, high color on her shiny cheekbones. "There were three schoolteachers rented a cottage on Brigport last summer. I guess they were out for their last fling, by the looks of some of their actions! One of 'em made a perfect fool of herself over Young Charles. A woman *her* age taking up with that boy!"

"How did they behave at the dances?" Philippa asked politely.

"I wasn't talking about that. They knew better than to act up in public. That's the best I can say of them."

"Well, that's quite a lot," said Philippa lightly. "Now as for me —why, I haven't been to a dance for so long I can't be sure how I'll react to all the excitement. It's like liquor, you know. Some people take just one drink and disgrace themselves." Vi stared at her suspiciously. Philippa added, "You just can't tell, what with my being a schoolteacher and all."

There was an instant of silence before Helen flung herself back in her chair, shrieking with laughter. Asanath chuckled; even Suze, looking at Viola's bleak face, smiled. When Helen's tumult had died down, Vi folded her hands tidily in her lap.

108

"Well, you're quite a joker, Mrs. Marshall. A real wit. I'm sure there's plenty on Bennett's Island who'll appreciate that in the teacher." She turned squarely in her chair. "Have you tried that new heel yet, Suze? It wears like iron in Syd's socks, but maybe it's me more than the heel. I was never one to let him wear a pair of socks more than two days in those stinking old rubber boots."

The light flashed on Suze's glasses. "Well, *I'm* not one to let Asa wear dirty socks either," she answered with unusual determination.

Chapter 21

On the night of the dance Steve came for Philippa. The afterglow had deepened to blue dusk, which became night with the clear starry stillness that precedes frost. Two boats came from Brigport; their engines were audible on Bennett's Island from the time they came around Tenpound.

Steve and Philippa were walking around the harbor when the boats came up Long Cove, and they could hear singing over the hum of the engines. It was the final touch; she felt deep within herself, like a young bird held carefully in the hand, a tremulous and youthful anticipation of the night ahead. The irony of it amused her. When she was fifteen or so and should have felt like this, she had approached such occasions with an aggressive blend of valor and antagonism. It was nice to have grown beyond all that. When you were young and yearned for the privileges of maturity, you could not guess what the best of the privileges would be.

"Security," she said.

"What?" asked Steve. "Did I miss something?"

"No, I was thinking aloud. I was thinking about the security of being thirty, and all the things you can enjoy in a calm, unqualified way without trembling on the verge of ecstasy or woe."

"Does that end when you're thirty?"

"It should, if a person is sufficiently mature."

He didn't answer, and his silence piqued her.

"What's the matter?" she asked. "Don't you think it's possible to reach a state of calm after storm? Oh, I know I have a boy to raise, but I don't anticipate any more than the usual amount of confusion that goes with an ordinary child. And I hope I can take that as an adult should. Apart from him, I expect to do my work and live my life with no great heights and no great depths. I've had them all."

Suddenly she felt as if she were talking too much. She hadn't planned on sounding so smug. My noble aunt, she thought, blushing. They were safely in the dark again, walking along the path by the well toward the lane that led to the clubhouse. She thought angrily, Why did I have to start this? It's quite possible that I've spoiled my evening.

"I wasn't sniping," Steve said after a moment. "I was admiring you."

"What about you?" she said quickly. "You've been to war and come back, you go quietly from one day to the next. You must have achieved some sort of compromise with life."

"I have. But the trouble is, I don't know how long it will last."

They turned into the lane. Ahead of them, light fell from the open door of the clubhouse; there were the sounds of scuffling and laughter from the porch, children shrieking as they ran around the building in a game made mysterious and terrifying by the dark. Above it all, the music floated in random, disembodied fragments—a liquid run on the clarinet, the thin unworldly merriment of a violin playing a phrase of a reel for the accordion to follow. There were people coming behind Philippa and Steve in the lane. The little Percys pounded by like foals. A flashlight bobbed across the field from Nils Sorensen's house. Philippa looked up at the black lances of the spruces reaching for Orion; she breathed the quiet cold of frost, sweet with the sad fragrance of dead leaves in the lane. She heard the voices ringing out like bells in the island night, and the scraps of music coming together suddenly into a tune.

"Sometimes we've had dances up here that have been wicked disappointments," Joanna said to Philippa. "Sometimes there's a feeling—it's hard to describe—that everybody's been flung out to a different point of the compass, and even if we all gather up here, we might as well be perfect strangers because we can't get together in our minds. But when there's a *good* dance, it's like this. Everyone wants it to be good, and they've got it in them to make it a fine thing. It's another sort of feeling, an outgiving. For a little while, all the grievances are stowed out of sight."

"I shouldn't think there were too many grievances on a place like this," said Philippa.

Joanna gave her a dark, subtly mocking glance. "It's not Utopia."

They were sitting out a dance not from lack of partners but from choice. With thirty couples or more to take part in "Lady of the Lake," there was so much swinging that Philippa had been grateful to be on her feet at the end of the last one. The clubhouse had kept on whirling, and she clutched at her partner's arm. It was Nils Sorensen. He had laughed and led her back to her seat with his arm snugly around her waist.

"You've got no head," he told her. "You'll have to do better than this. We had a schoolma'am once who could swing all the men off their feet."

Philippa had been guided through the first of the dances by Steve, Young Charles, and Nils. After that her partners had been varied; Foss Campion, young Ralph Percy, Mark Bennett, Sky Campion and a Brigport fisherman in lusty middle age. When she counted up the changes of partners in "Liberty Waltz," she realized she had danced with almost everyone and had not found a poor dancer yet. Young boys and girls learned how to dance in the most natural manner possible. There was no artificial segregation of age groups; neither the young nor the old were embarrassed in one another's company.

Steve went out on the porch for a cigarette. Joanna went off down the hall to speak to a Brigport woman, and Philippa sat peacefully alone for a few minutes. She followed first one person and then another through the play of light and shadow under the hanging lamps. Now and then someone stood out against the involved pattern as if spotlighted. Once Kathie came toward her, her hair like an aureole under the lamps, and then was swung away. She saw Young Charles, bending in a courtly way to swing Clare Percy, whose small face was frozen with happiness. Helen Campion danced with Asanath; she was as light on her feet for her great size as she had claimed. Nils's partner was Suze. She still looked confused and indefinite, but she knew her way perfectly and didn't lag.

Fort stood propped against the cold stove and went from one tune to the other without a change of pace. She knew some of the more common ones: "Turkey in the Straw"; "Old Zip Coon"; "Golden Slippers"; "Little Brown Jug." Joanna had given her more names: "The White Cockade"; "Stack of Barley"; "The Rakes of Mallow"; "My Love Is But a Lassie Yet"; "The Dawning of the Day." She loved them; she would write them all to Eric, but how was she to tell about Fort with his fiddle snugged under his round chin, his red brush coppery in the lamplight, his eyes shut to slits, his thick fingers marvelously agile on the strings, and the bow dancing with its own wild, unearthly music?

Fort played alone at the moment. The accordionist, a Brigport boy, had gone out for a smoke and some of the beer his friends had hidden in the tall wet grass across the lane. Gregg had gone out too.

The whole island, except for the Websters, seemed to be represented, either in the hall or out on the porch. She had seen Perley standing in the doorway once, in the group that didn't take part but loitered outside, looking on. Terence had come in briefly, he had waltzed once with Kathie, and then he had gone out again.

Philippa wondered if the Webster children heard the music. Their house was the nearest to the clubhouse. They must have heard it jigging and ringing in the windless night. All this warmth and joy, and they were shut away from it by their fear; they were afraid even to come and peek in at the windows because someone might touch them in the dark. She knew their father by sight, a man who looked frail and awkward in the guise of a fisherman, as if it were an ill-fitting costume. She tried to picture the mother; what sort of fey creature was she?

She became aware suddenly that the music had stopped and the hall was emptying; it was a sort of breathing spell, with the men going out to the porch and the women moving around to visit with one another. Fort put his fiddle in the case and went out.

Young Charles leaned over her suddenly. "What are you dreaming about?" he murmured.

"Island life," she said. "I like it."

"Let's talk about it some. Let's go for a walk, down to Mark's wharf and back." His eyes glistened. "It's some-handsome out. Know anything about the stars? Andromeda, the Great Square of Pegasus?" He gave off an aura of ardent vitality, the way a spruce forest under a hot sun gives off an exciting resinous breath. If I were seventeen, thought Philippa, I should be thoroughly intoxicated by now.

She let him talk on and watched Viola Goward with Mrs. Percy; they sat directly opposite. Mrs. Percy was a small, sere woman with a wry face, as if her teeth were forever being set on edge. They were talking fiercely against the buzz of other voices and the noise of the children who kept lashing themselves awake by sliding on the dance floor. They were also watching Philippa. The shrewd glances flicked toward her and Charles at rhythmic intervals.

"Did you ever go rowing when the water was firing?" asked Charles. "Come on, Philippa."

She said with amiable firmness, "No, Charles."

His face tightened. He got up quickly and walked toward the open door. Philippa was sorry for him and at the same time annoyed. His self-assurance would have been crass in someone with less charm. She had liked him better when he had walked through the woods with her; then he had been a little shy, a little stricken with the newness of what he felt.

He passed Steve in the doorway without speaking to him. Steve turned his head and looked after him briefly. Then he came inside, and his gaze moved without apparent direction around the hall. He was thin and straight, with a way of holding his narrow, neat dark head that expressed an inherent self-command.

When he reached Philippa, his face changed. He came and sat down beside her. "Got your breath back? You'll need it."

"Why? It isn't possible that there's another faster, more complicated dance, is it?"

"Gregg's got at the beer. They've been trying to steer him away from it, but he could smell it at forty fathoms." His eyes puckered at the corners. "It was quite a thing. Everybody falling over everybody else in the dark, looking for him, and he was farming off down the lane with his arms full of beer cans. When the beer meets up with that sherry, there'll be some mighty interesting results."

"And the boys worked so hard to keep him in shape," Philippa said. Poor Charles, she thought. Something else to frustrate him.

"It's nothing unexpected. We could get along without him if he'd go home and stay. But he's had his beer and he's back again. They asked him to play for a dance, by crikey, and he'll play for a dance."

A roar of laughter went up from the porch. Fort came in, moving rather rapidly, and picked up his fiddle. He winked at Philippa. Then Gregg appeared, flanked by Nils Sorensen and a lanky Brigport man. They were laughing still, but Gregg was solemn. He pulled himself free of them and tried to straighten his tie, which had got worked around under one ear. His faded eyes were wet with concentration, and his mouth was prim. He walked the length of the hall with short, precise steps. In spite of his pudginess and the tendency of his rumpled blue serge trousers to drop below his belly, he achieved a queer sort of dignity, perhaps because he was so intent.

The accordionist took his place, sank his chin moodily on his instrument, and waited with indifference for orders.

"Choose your partners for a waltz!" Charles shouted angrily from the doorway, and went out again. Fort began "Let Me Call You Sweetheart," and the accordion joined in. Steve and Philippa went out onto the floor with the rest.

"Optimists," said Steve.

"Perhaps he won't play," said Philippa. "He looks sleepy." But over Steve's shoulder she saw Gregg lift his clarinet.

There was a wild and intricate soaring of notes like the flight of a singing bird. For a few minutes the others plunged doggedly on, but Gregg was too close to them; they could hardly hear their own music. Fort gave up first, undone by his sense of humor. The accordionist played like a mechanical toy wound up until he saw that no one was dancing. Gregg played on, his eyes shut; he was lost in a world of his own making, starred with a glittering swarm of notes. He swam among them as effortlessly as a fish. It was, for Gregg, his moment of truth.

The Brigport people who had never heard Gregg drunk gaped at him; the children roused from their sleepiness. Someone said loudly, "Well, I never! It's a disgrace, allowing that man inside the clubhouse! He's tight as a coot!"

Steve and Philippa were near the door. "Let's go out," he said. "The dance is over. Gregg is all set for hours."

"My coat —" she began.

"I'll get it." When he came back, they went out through the knot of men listening at the door. When they were away from the chuckles and the crude jokes, the music sounded fiercely sweet in the night. Halfway down the lane, Philippa stopped to listen.

"He's good, Steve. No wonder he was so dignified. He knew."

"Yes, he's good. He played in the Navy Band once. Funny what the spontaneous combustion of beer and sherry brings out, isn't it?"

"I wish they wouldn't laugh at him," she said angrily. "Don't they realize what they're hearing? How many of them could get even one decent sound out of that clarinet?"

"That's why they laugh, to keep Gregg in his place as an old derelict. But he doesn't hear them. There's your security for you. All he hears is his music."

"Poor Fort and Charles," she said. "It's spoiled their dance."

"It was almost over. They're lucky Gregg didn't smell the beer earlier." His fingers tightened on her arm. "Where shall we go?"

"It's time for me to go home." Her voice sounded shallow in her ears. To stand like this in the dark put her at a disadvantage. The place seemed completely unfamiliar to her; she might as well have been dropped from space onto a mountain peak.

Steve was a presence in the dark, disembodied except for fragments—a slow voice, fingers on her arm, the scent of a tweed jacket worn by a clean and orderly male who smoked. What was her own sum total as a presence? she wondered.

"It's a beautiful night on the water," he said. "I have a little dory that goes like a gull feather before the wind." He didn't release her arm. His voice brushed her in the shadow like the first warm airs of spring. "Now do you want to go home?"

It was a warm air, but she felt somehow cold. "No, I suppose not," she said slowly. She wanted to keep talking, to ask bright vivacious questions about the dory, but she couldn't think of anything. When he moved, she wasn't surprised. He took her by the shoulders and kissed her. It was as gentle, and as positive, as all his movements were. Her mind tried frantically to right itself; her heartbeat seemed to shake the frail cage of her bones. She saw the pale powdering of the Milky Way going down toward the woods, and they were the same as they had been a minute before, but she had changed. Something had been liberated which she had barely known to exist. If only I had gone home! she kept thinking. The thought tolled like a bell. If only I had gone home.

He put his arms around her and kissed her temple and cheekbone. She felt a sadness, but at the same time her hands, moving independently, pressed against his hard lean sides under the tweed jacket, and she turned her mouth toward his. The dismay and rejoicing whirled together until she could not tell one from the other.

In a few moments they moved apart as naturally as they had come together. The sound of his breathing had a peculiar intimacy for her.

"Look," she said. "They're coming." She saw the flashlights on the far side of the field and heard the voices in the lane. Gregg was still playing, but the lamps in the clubhouse were being blown out one by one. She was looking across the black frosty space into another world which held no significance for her whatever. One flashlight bobbed toward them. They heard Joanna's strong, gay voice. "Good night, Ella! Good night, Vi!"

Steve took Philippa's hand. "Come on," he whispered. "Through the windbreak." They ran over the uneven ground, passing through a gap in the long row of Sorensen spruces, cutting across by the village well and down by the Binnacle to the shore.

They went into Nils's fishhouse and stood there hand in hand in the close darkness smelling pungently of marlin, spruce laths, and paint. The Foss Campions were going by. Helen broke into uninhibited laughter, and Philippa began to tremble. She felt as unpredictable as a cat before a storm. Steve put his arm around her shoulders.

"What's the matter?" he said close to her ear.

"I want to laugh," she said helplessly, and turned her face against his jacket. He caressed the nape of her neck, rumpled her hair, and then smoothed it. Suddenly her eyes filled with tears.

"Come on," Steve said at last. "They've gone. We'll go rowing now."

Chapter 22

Philippa had always been amazed at the way the human personality could make itself accept the irrevocable. She had come to realize that the power of acceptance was a partner of the will to survive. If you refused to agree, with your whole spirit, that certain catastrophic events had already occurred, you battered yourself to pieces eventually against the brutal wall of your dissent.

The thing happened; in a matter of minutes your life was altering its flow around and over the incident. In fifteen minutes or less Philippa had accepted this new circumstance. But with an instinct for self-defense, she was trying not to think about it until she felt calm enough to sort motives and emotions into their proper places.

She sat in the stern of the dory while Steve rowed down along the western side of the island. The land rose on her left, a long, massive black shape, saw-toothed against the gun-metal color of the sky and the pale glitter of stars. Tonight there were no coves or uneven projections of rocks. The shadow of the island lay on the water, and there was no telling where the water left off and the rocks began. It bore no relation to the sunny slopes where cranberries ripened, and ground sparrows flew up from tussocks, and the young spruces were brightly verdant at the edge of the woods. This was dream country, another planet.

She could see Steve clearly now in the starlight. He didn't talk to her but seemed to have gone into another mood entirely. The little dory slid over the water as fast as he had promised, the white water bubbling and hissing at her bow. The oars dipped up cold white fire; the blades were outlined with light and left luminous eddies behind. Once Steve said, "Look over the side. Don't move fast."

The dory felt as airily unsubstantial as a mussel shell. She looked carefully over the side and saw a crowding, darting mass of silver arrows in the water all around and under the boat, "What is it?" she whispered.

"Herring."

"Is that what you see when you go seining, then? Is that how you find them?" She hunted eagerly for questions. Herring made a safe subject.

"That's the way. You should see them in the seine. Then you'd know what molten silver means."

"It's too bad to catch anything that can go as fast and look so beautiful."

He didn't answer that, and she wasn't surprised. There was really no answer. He shipped the oars and got out his cigarettes. There was a swell, as quiet as the breath of a sleeper, and the dory was carried on it without a sound. From the end of the island came the low whisper of the rote. Steve's match flared; his skin showed ruddy. He was glancing downward, intently, at his cigarette. But just before he threw the match overboard, he looked at her. She felt as if he had touched her.

When the match had gone overboard, he didn't pick up the oars again. The dory moved quietly with the tide.

"What are you thinking about?" he asked. "Don't say herring. I know better."

"I was thinking about you and me," she said in a low voice. "I was wondering why it happened."

"Do you have to wonder? Can't you just let it be?"

"I'm sorry," she said humbly, "but I have to understand my part of it, at least. Didn't you ever do something that seemed so strange and unpredictable—for you—that you were bewildered?"

He looked up at the black mass of the island drifting by. After a moment he said, "Yes, I guess I have. There was one thing I couldn't figure out for a long time. It bothered me for about ten years, and then one day I let it go."

"Just like that?"

"Just like that."

"Why was it so easy to let go? Had it worn itself out in ten years, lost its importance? Or were you just tired of wondering?"

"I don't know. After ten years I was still having dreams about it that brought me awake all standing." He turned his head toward her; she could see in the starlight that he was smiling. "But maybe the sting of it had gone. It was easy to let go, finally, because something had come along that there was no question about."

She loosened her fingers consciously from the side of the seat. "What was it?"

"You."

"When you say there was no question about it, what do you mean?"

"I mean I love you," he said.

"But you *can't!*" she said, desperately. "Love—what I call love—isn't like that. It's not sudden, it's slow. It doesn't hit you like a bolt from the blue. And even if it did—well, I have no illusions, Steve. There's nothing about me to fascinate a man all in an instant—"

118

She stopped, and Steve said mildly, "Go on."

"I'm independent, I'm opinionated, I talk like a schoolma'am even out of hours." Fleetingly she saw Young Charles glowering at her across the desk.

"You're a lot of other things," he said. "You think they don't show, but they do. Mrs. Marshall's one person, but Philippa's another. She looks out sometimes, past the mother and the widow and the teacher."

She didn't know what to say. His words enchanted her; she could not help a fierce and secret rejoicing that this was no dream, that this was actually happening to her.

"You can't doubt me, Philippa," Steve said. "I'm thirty-eight. I'm not Young Charles. You know in your heart that I'm telling you the truth. It's yourself you're doubting."

"Why shouldn't I?" He gave her no quarter; he was using honesty as a weapon against her. "My husband has been dead eight years. He was the sum and substance of everything I'd ever wanted. When I knew he was dead, I expected I would never be stirred by another man, that I'd never feel even the faintest sort of physical attraction. I thought that phase of my existence had died with Justin. I was wrong, I know that. I must have thought I was superhuman. But now—tonight—and it started before tonight, if you want to know—" she flung at him defiantly—"I've been shaken out of my common sense, and I don't know what I feel. I can't tell whether it's *you* who has done this to me or the smell of your clean shirt!"

Her laughter sounded a little wild to her. Steve said, "I wish this darn dory wasn't so tittle-ish, so I could move without drowning us both. What's that about the clean smell of my shirt?"

"I noticed it the first time I met you, outside your brother Mark's house. For a moment—well, it didn't exactly remind me of Justin, but of *something,* a mood or an atmosphere. It's deceptive, can't you see?"

His voice was tenderly amused. "What happens when other men wear clean shirts just scrubbed and ironed by their loving womenfolk?"

"Nothing," she said unwillingly. She wished she could see him more clearly. The starlight was an aggravation.

"Listen, my darling," Steve said, leaning toward her. "The world isn't going to end tonight. You've got plenty of time to find the facts.

119

I'm not going to come down on you like Young What's-his-name out of the west and carry you off on my horse." He took up the oars. The blades dipped with a whisper and stirred up fire. "We'll go back to the harbor. I've kept away from you too long."

The village was quick at putting itself to bed after the dance. There were no lights anywhere when they came into the harbor; there was nothing to suggest that Gregg's music had once soared out over the island like a bird.

Philippa stood on the narrow strip of sand that appeared between Nils's and Sigurd's wharves when the tide was out, waiting while Steve put the dory on the haul-off. He came back to her then and put his hands lightly on either side of her waist inside her coat. She tensed instinctively, but without antagonism. "My clean shirt," he murmured. "So that was it. I thought it was tweed and tobacco that was supposed to do it."

"I was always different," she whispered back. "Awfully home-spun."

"You don't feel homespun." He put his arms around her all the way, under her coat, and held her close to him. As her arms went round his neck, she knew she must have wanted to do it the other time. He kissed her without violence but with a steadily deepening ardor, and her response came in a pure, free current.

He lifted his head and said, "That was Philippa." The words were a little unsteady. She stared at him in the dimness without speaking, knowing the new, soft unsteadiness of her mouth, the whole new defenselessness that would be part of her now.

He turned her toward the little rocky path that led up between the fishhouses. They walked around the harbor in silence. Steve took her hand and laced his fingers through hers. There was something irrevocable about the entwining grip of bone and sinew, the warm contact of palms. *And palm to palm is holy palmers' kiss,* she thought; she knew that even if there should be no more, this night could be enough to break her heart.

At Asanath's back door they stood for a moment facing each other. An interrogative chirrup sounded in the darkness, and the firm, furry body of the yellow cat leaned against Philippa's legs. She said gratefully, "Here's Tom."

"Good night, Philippa," Steve said.

"Good night, Steve."

He didn't offer to touch her, but said softly, "Don't go to bed and think. Dream. Maybe you'll dream what you want to know." He walked away quickly. The cat went into the house with her.

Chapter 23

As the lamp flame grew in her room, she looked around at the familiar things, the tidiness that was at once chaste and fussy. She half believed that in the morning she would discover the interlude with Steve had become detached from her existence, that the atmosphere of intimacy and longing had been a form of self-deception brought on by the night.

But sleep would have to come in between, and it looked as if there would be no sleep. Resolutely she relaxed each muscle and breathed deeply. She tried poetry, the sedative rhythms of "Evangeline" and "Hiawatha." But fragments of verse she thought she had safely outgrown with her adolescence came winging into her consciousness like goldfinches across the fields. Ernest Dowson, Rossetti, Swinburne. Swinburne! She laughed softly. How greedily she had devoured the pages out in the arbor or in bed at night by the beam of her scout flashlight. The words had scorched and intoxicated her. She had memorized things she barely understood, reciting the rich cadences as she walked to and from school, feeling that she lived an ecstatic life apart. But at twenty she had laughed at herself for the Swinburne episode. Why Swinburne now? He was a ridiculous and unnecessary adjunct to a difficult situation. She sat up in bed, looking at the streaks of star reflections trembling on the black water, and repeated wryly the words that kept plaguing her.

> Have we not lips to love with, eyes for tears,
> And summer, and flower of women and of years,
> Stars for the foot of morning, and for noon
> Sunlight, and the exaltation of the moon:
> Waters that answer waters. . . .

She hadn't known, at sixteen, what the poem really meant, but it didn't matter now; the words were still lovely after all. *Stars for the foot of morning, waters that answer waters.* She heard the long-drawn rote, and a slight wash of water on the shore outside as the tide turned and the wind freshened.

> *. . . And like me*
> *The landstream and the tidestream in the sea.*
> *I am sick with time as these with ebb and flow,*
> *And by the yearning in my veins I know*
> *The yearning sound of waters. . . .*

You're still sixteen, Philippa. Sitting up in bed and reciting Swinburne. What about tomorrow? Will Swinburne carry you through a day with a roomful of tired children?

She lay down meekly and fixed her eyes on the brightest star she could see. Perhaps it would hypnotize her. Sleep would turn everything back to its normal level.

She awoke at daylight, and Steve was in her mind before she was fully conscious. Nothing was detached. No perspective had shifted. She awoke remembering his fingers smoothing her hair and stroking the nape of her neck.

She wanted to finish a letter to Eric, now that she was awake and had time to spare. But she felt ill at ease when she began to write, and eventually she put the letter aside.

Routine had its uses besides efficiency. By the time school was under way, she felt almost natural again. There were no chances for reverie. Most of the children were tired from the night before, and a variety of small annoyances went on continually. Someone was forever being tripped by a foot thrust into the aisle; pencils prodded the sensitive spot between the shoulder blades; almost everyone sent to the board had the questionable gift of making the chalk squeal.

With no need to practice square dances, the older boys at recess began a campaign against the girls. Kathie and Ralph were after each other tooth and claw when Philippa discovered it. Though these two showed the greatest potentiality for damaging each other, the whole schoolyard was embroiled. Philippa dismissed the younger grades until the afternoon session and sent the older ones to the blackboard to work out some complicated problems.

She was watching Rob's heroic battle with his work when she

heard the hiss of Peggy Campion's indrawn breath and a choked spasm of snickers. When she looked along the board, everyone but Peggy was working hard, scowling intensely to indicate concentration, and with only a contorted stiffness of feature to suggest repressed emotion. Peggy stood back, chalk in hand. Her face was immobile. She stared at Ralph without blinking.

Philippa walked to where Peggy stood, and looked at the board. Peggy's numerals were always gracefully formed—they never soared up or staggered down; they were the same height, and their conclusions were invariably correct. The word scrawled across them was as blatant as if it had been shouted aloud.

Philippa looked at Ralph. The back of his neck became a rich red, contrasting unpleasantly with the bright color of his hair. The sound of his chalk took on a frenzied rhythm. Numbers appeared at a dizzy speed and with no meaning whatever. Then he erased furiously and filled the space with new figures. The rest of the class slid into a state of suspended animation; heads turned as slowly but irrevocably as sunflower heads followed the progress of the sun.

"Ralph," said Philippa at last. Ralph's shoulders jerked violently. He dropped his chalk on the floor, went down to find it, and came up with an incredible return of composure.

"Ma'am?" he enquired, looking like an eager spaniel.

"Are you responsible for that?" She moved her head toward the word.

"Ayeh," Ralph said. "Guess I am." He looked at the word with no visible shame but rather as if he were appraising a paint job. "Yep, I did it."

"Any explanation?" she asked coldly. Ralph scratched his head, looked at the floor, and then smiled at her.

"Dunno as there is. It just come over me, sudden. Like one of them big waves comes up out of nowhere." He snapped his fingers, and the rest gazed at his outflung hand. "I s'pose I hadn't ought to've yielded to temptation, like the feller says," said Ralph, "but I did. That's the way I am."

"What did Mrs. Gerrish do when anything like this happened?"

"Strap," said Ralph cheerfully, looking at his hard-calloused palms. Philippa took a large sheet of paper from her desk and handed it to him.

"Go to your seat, please, Ralph," she said, "and write your word five hundred times. After you've yielded to that temptation five hundred times, perhaps you won't find it so irresistible."

Ralph gaped at her as if he hadn't heard correctly. He took the paper gingerly, as if he expected it to burst into flame, and went to his desk. "You'd better sharpen your pencil," Philippa said after him. Moving like a sleepwalker, he went to the sharpener. When he had finally sat down, Philippa glanced at the class, and they returned to their own work.

"Erase Ralph's place," Philippa said to Peggy, "and copy your work there. Then you can erase the other." She walked over to the windows that looked out on the marsh and stood there watching the yellow grass rippling in the wind.

There was a notable change in the atmosphere of the schoolroom. Some gazed at her in somber awe, others in confusion. In their experience, anyone who spoke or wrote such a word in the presence of an adult was strapped—usually by both teacher and parents—and sent off to mull over his offense in solitary confinement. This new punishment had an Olympian tinge to it. There was no pain with it, but neither was there the excited admiration of friends who watched you stand up to the teacher and take your strapping with insouciance. It carried only the most stultifying of emotions, boredom.

Ralph began his chore with a certain dash, but it was plain that his bravado was false. By the hundredth time and the third sharpening, he looked as if he were being forced to cross the Sahara Desert on foot, and there was still an hour of school to go.

He regretted, too, the death of the word. It was like saying goodby to an old friend, not quite reputable but exciting and often very helpful. Never again would he scribble it or shout it with such an exhilarating knowledge of his own wickedness. After being written five hundred times, it would not even be a mildly bad word, just a dull one. The others knew it too, and so they looked at Ralph with a sort of compassion, and at Philippa with the admiration that otherwise would have gone to Ralph.

Philippa looked toward the harbor and saw the gulls. Their wings twinkled as they caught the sun. Perley came across the marsh with his shotgun in the crook of his arm and went up into the Bennett meadow. It was too rough for him to go to haul in his peapod today, or else he had his traps in to dry out and repair. In the fall the men set their traps in deeper waters. The boys who fished in fine weather from a peapod would go out with their fathers in the winter weather.

Perley walked clumsily in his rubber boots, his free hand in his pocket, his head pushed forward; he stared morosely at the path ahead of him. He was a lonely figure in the high-colored gusty day. Philippa could have been sorry for him if it were not for the Websters.

She came back early to school after dinner and worked on her letter to Eric. She described the dance, the music, and then told him how the island looked from the water after dark, and how the water blazed when the oars stirred it, and about the herring. Again she was disturbed by a peculiar self-consciousness. But she took a resolute stand. The thing to do, she thought, as if she were setting someone else in order, is to remember that Eric and I are two separate persons; if I want him to live his own life, I mustn't be afraid to live my own. . . . But in this case, it's idiotic to think in terms of the future. In twenty-four hours this may have all died down to nothing.

At that thought, meant to be encouraging, she felt a qualm like illness at the pit of her stomach.

She put Eric's letter away, finally, and considered the afternoon session. They might begin work on Halloween decorations; they needed some sort of occupational therapy today.

She heard the outer door open and shut with stealthy ease. Ralph and Rob must have been sobered by the morning's experience. She smiled, and leaned down to open the bottom drawer of her desk and find the patterns for the Halloween cutouts. When she straightened up, the inner door was open, and Rue Webster stood on the sill. She had young Daniel by the hand and the others were behind her, their pale pointed faces peering round her like background figures in a medieval tapestry. Rue looked at Philippa from exhausted eyes.

"Come in," Philippa said pleasantly. They came forward. Daniel looked around him and Faith had a spasmodic little smile like a grimace, but Edwin and Rue moved warily. They had thin sweaters over their clothes; the little boy was fitted into a pair of dungarees made crudely over into his size. The legs were wide and clumsy, but at least his tender skin was not exposed to the weather.

When they had reached the desk, they stood there in a silent knot. Rue's eyes were ringed in muddy shadows. She lifted her hand to brush a lank strand of hair back from her forehead, and when her sweater sleeve pulled up, Philippa saw that her skinny wrist was braceleted with bluish-red welts. Philippa looked away quickly, but the girl pulled her sleeve down to her knuckles.

"Where do you want us to sit?" she asked hoarsely.

"Where did you sit before?"

Rue jabbed her sharp forefinger. "I sat there, 'n' Edwin over there, and Faith—"

"*I* sat here." Beaming at Philippa, Faith slid into the seat. She wriggled around a little, as if to fit herself into a nest, folded her hands on the desk, and looked happily at the others. The seat belonged to the youngest Percy.

"But that was your seat last year," said Philippa, "and now you're a grade ahead, so I think you can move back one row."

"I don't know if Mis' Gerrish gave us our passes," Rue said suspiciously.

"We'll settle the grades later. Meanwhile we'll arrange the seats. No one happens to be using yours, Rue. Edwin—" He was staring past her at the board. There was not the slightest flinch of perception when she spoke.

"Can't he sit by me?" Rue broke in rapidly. "Mis' Gerrish wouldn't let him, because he was in a different grade and all, and she thought he'd act up worse, anyway. But he'd be a lot better if he could sit by me."

Color streamed into her meager face. Her tired eyes took on a sheen of intensity. Philippa said, "Sit down, Rue. Anywhere. Make Edwin sit down too. And then tell me about him. You know what he can do and what he can't do."

Rue touched Edwin, and he shook his head and went over to the windows. Rue sat down stiffly.

"Edwin's deaf," she said.

It was that simple.

Daniel wandered around the desk, sucking a parboiled thumb. Philippa lifted him into her lap. "Doesn't anyone else know?" she asked.

"Just us in my house. I never told anybody before now because I promised my mother I'd never tell. Faith promised too." Her color-less young mouth trembled slightly. "But I've got to tell now, if we're coming to school. Edwin's been beat enough. I promised him nobody'd strap him any more."

"That's right, Rue," Philippa said. "Nobody will."

"He acts so bad people think he's either a devil or foolish. He started school all right, back on the mainland, and learned to read, and then after he had diphtheria he began to get deaf. We didn't know he was deaf for a long time. We just knew he got to be so aw-ful acting nobody could do anything with him. First we thought he was born to be bad, and maybe took after Mamma's brother that had to be put in Thomaston prison. But when we found out he was deaf, it was worse."

The words came out flat and fast; they had been shut up in her for too long. "Papa's a good carpenter and he could pay a doctor. He wanted to take Edwin to Waterville or Portland, but every time he talked about it Mamma got so sick it scared him." There was a fierce defiance in her; she was shamed by the thing she hardly understood. "Papa tried to tell her there wasn't anything to hide, but she wouldn't believe him. She thinks because Edwin's deaf, he's tainted some-how."

Philippa wished she could hold Rue as she held Daniel. The girl must have ached with her rigidity. Edwin stood by the windows looking out.

"Wasn't there anyone else who took an interest?" she asked. "What about school?"

"They put him out, finally, because he acted so, and then when a woman came to talk to Mamma about him, and maybe find out what ailed him, Mamma got scared and carried on till Papa decided to move out of town right off, the next day. He didn't want to go, he had to leave his job, but Mamma wanted it." Rue spoke relentlessly, neither lifting nor lowering her voice. Red blotched her face. "Edwin never went to school again on the mainland. Mamma told people in the new place he wasn't bright enough to go. She said he fell out of his high chair when he was a baby and hurt his head. . . . I helped him all I could at home. Then Cap'n Charles hired Pa to come out here and work, and Mamma said it would be a good place to hide Edwin." Her light eyes shifted toward her brother's back.

"I took him to school here, but Mrs. Gerrish didn't like him much. The kids plagued him in the yard about the way he tries to talk, but he could keep 'em off by plugging rocks at 'em."

Her mouth curled in a humorless smile. "Couldn't throw rocks at Mrs. Gerrish, and she liked to work out her strap on him. Now I can feel kind of sorry for her. She was awful tired of this place by Christmas, and she thought Edwin was possessed to torment her."

Philippa stroked Daniel's back with a steady hand, but inwardly she was shaken with rage. There was no need to ask if Mrs. Gerrish had ever called on the Webster parents. "I don't hold with letting parents get involved in school affairs," she had told Philippa. "As soon as you call on a mother, she starts telling you how Johnny is different from the rest, and then she'll be dropping in every other day to make sure you're treating him with the proper respect."

Philippa had laughed at the time. Now she wondered if Mrs. Gerrish would have shown more forbearance with Edwin if she had known he was handicapped. It was not likely. She would still have found him unmanageable. Perhaps he would be a problem to Philippa; she could only try. Now he stood by the window, set free from his tension by something he saw outside, a fish hawk beating its wings in space high over Long Cove. Thus relaxed, he was simply an undersized boy with a pinched, bony face and big eyes that moved with an animal's preternatural swiftness.

"How old is Edwin?" she asked.

"Eleven."

"And you're sure you can take care of him in school?"

Rue's smile was faint but proud. "Last year he'd have been all right if she'd let him sit by me. The way it is in a school like this one, after the teacher gets through with your class, you've got plenty of time to get your own lessons and still help somebody else. We'd have made out fine if—" Her eyes shifted to a point past Philippa's head. "If they'd let us."

"Well, I think you'll have a chance to show me how well you can manage, Rue. We'll put Edwin by you and move Peggy back a seat. And Daniel can be the whole preprimary." She sat the little boy down at the table in the corner beyond her desk.

"Look, it's just your size!" she exclaimed in creditable surprise.

Daniel was amazed at the coincidence. He wriggled around to look at the back of his chair and bent over to look under the table. He came up giggling. Philippa found a box of wooden beads in the cupboard and started a string for him.

"Don't forget me!" Faith burst out of the silence she had kept long enough. "I'm in the fourth grade now!"

"That's no way to speak to the teacher," Rue said sharply. "Her name's Mrs. Marshall, and don't you forget it." She went to Edwin and touched him. He followed her to his seat.

"You'd better hang up your sweaters," Philippa suggested. But Rue, without looking directly at Philippa, pulled her sweater sleeves down hard over her wrists.

Chapter 24

The return of the Websters was accepted with equanimity by the rest of the students. The Websters had left; now they had come back. It was not an earth-shaking event. It would cause not the faintest tremor in the island alone.

Ralph Percy gave Philippa an oblique glance that was oddly adult. Peggy Campion, at finding her desk moved, showed no emotion. She ignored the Websters as if their scrubbed poverty were repellent to her. Meanwhile Edwin and Rue, alike in their immobility, turned the pages of their new books. Daniel strung beads, gloating over the varied shapes and bright colors. Faith switched about in her seat in an excess of happiness. The younger children stared at her, and most of them returned her eager smile. She reminded Philippa of one of those homely white kittens with pale eyes and unbecoming splotches of fawn, who make up for their plainness by exuding a humble, ingratiating friendliness toward all the world.

Kathie was the last to come in. She was always the last unless she felt in a sociable mood and wanted to chat with Philippa before the others arrived. Now she tossed her jacket at its hook and went to her seat, her thumbs tucked in her cowboy belt. She wore a bright blue-green silk kerchief knotted under the collar of her white shirt, and the wind had blown her yellow hair into its usual wild halo. She grinned across the schoolroom at Philippa, as one friend to another.

Suddenly she saw the Websters at the other side of the room. She lifted an eyebrow at Philippa and called out, "Hi, Rue!" Rue turned and smiled, and for an instant there was something shyly humorous and wise in her.

Steve did not come that evening. He had promised to give her time to think. He had no doubts about himself. In another man it might have been complacence, but complacence didn't go with Steve any more than it had with Justin. She thought of Justin with affectionate detachment; she had often wondered, in the calm fashion of one who is certain such a thing will never happen, how she would consider Justin if she should ever become interested in another man. But her theories had not gone very far. Now it had happened, and the matter was taking care of itself, which should prove the absurdity of theories, she thought.

She went around the harbor in the early evening to drop Eric's letter through the post-office slot. The store was open until nine o'clock, a place for the men to gather and talk; the women often made a little ceremony of walking to the store in the evenings for ice cream or candy. An island was no place to take such things casually. Philippa had fallen into the mood and looked forward to her after-supper strolls around the harbor.

Tonight some men were torching herring from a dory in the harbor, and as they put more fuel on the dying torch, it flared up in a burst of glory. Wharves and fishhouses and the black squares of un-lit windows were turned red and fiery gold by the great shaking, streaming, glare. The dory raced across water illumined to a bright, translucent green. The men in oilskins, two at the oars and one standing in the bow with a dip net, were like anonymous figures in a painting, and thus were touched with a sort of primitive radiance. Philippa stood outside the store watching until the cold breeze across the harbor drove her indoors.

Mark Bennett sat on the counter, smoking his pipe. Randall Percy, a stocky red-headed man with a weak good-natured face, was playing checkers with Syd Goward. Syd was slight and graying, his hands tremulous from his last bout, called by courtesy migraine. Nils Sorensen sat beyond the stove, his chair tilted back against the shelves and his hands behind his head. They all spoke to her pleasantly.

130

"Quite a sight out there, isn't it?" Nils said.

"It's spectacular," she answered. "It should be in a painting. I want to write to my son about it, but it just can't be told in ordinary words."

"You'd ought to be a poet," said Syd Goward, shyly ducking his brindled head. He had a small, meek face. "Then you could write it up like old Shakespoke."

Nils smiled. "Wonder if the old boy could've written something elegant about the fragrance of those herring six months from now?"

"The only poetry that sinks real deep into his heart," Mark said to Philippa, "is the number of lobsters that good corned herring tolls into his traps."

"I don't notice you getting low in your mind when the lobsters are crawling," said Nils. "You can stand on the wharf and earn your money while the rest of us are out pounding around."

"Who the devil looks out for the lobster car nights when it's blowing a gale through this harbor and you're snoring under the kelp? I've been down on this wharf sometimes and seen sights that'd make you suck wind, son!"

"Oh, sure," said Nils mildly. "You slave to make your millions. We know you do."

"Why, Mark." Randall Percy tilted his glasses downward and looked over them. "I didn't know you was the family Croweesus."

"What's that word?" demanded Syd. "Sounds like somethin' nasty."

Randall's king took three jumps. His fat, freckled face was sad. "Just because it rhymes with Jesus is no sign it's swearin'."

Philippa dropped her letter hastily into the slot. Mark caught the quirk of her mouth and said, "Songs and patter. Hear 'em free almost any day in the week." He went to peer through the low window at the harbor.

"Looks like Steve's struck it rich out there," he said. "Well, he's a good man with a dip net. Those bean poles always are. Randall, here, he'd have a stroke if he had to move that fast."

"I never see you out there strainin' your gizzard," said Randall.

Philippa said good night to them and went out. She moved to the corner of the store where the path began up the hill to the house, and stood there watching the harbor. No one could see her from the

131

store. Steve's name had been cut out from the other words to stand before her in a burnished solitude; she had been unprepared for its effect, the sudden violent wish to see him, to be near enough to touch him, to reaffirm their intimacy. She had wished urgently for him to come into the store, in rustling oilskins spangled with herring scales. They would glitter on his dark face, too, and among the fine black hairs on the backs of his hands. He would talk with his brother and brother-in-law about the torching, and she would study the candy counter indifferently. But their knowledge of each other, unsuspected by the men, would lie strongly between them.

The wind was beginning to stir through the spruces on the hill and the torchlight danced wildly. The sound of water splashing under the wharf was louder. She didn't know anyone was near until Kathie spoke behind her.

"What are you doing, out alone in the dark?"

"Looking and listening," said Philippa. Her poise, lost for a moment, flooded back. "I'd never seen torching, or even heard of it, before I came to the island. There's something tremendously exciting about it."

"Oh, sure," Kathie agreed with more politeness than conviction. "But there's more to see and hear, if you know where to look and how to keep quiet." She chuckled. "Not as much as there used to be. I wish I'd been here in the old days! My lord, the things that happened when they were hanging May baskets!"

"How do you know what went on then?"

"Mark tells me about it. Then they all get talking over coffee up to Joanna's."

"I suppose you live a pretty tame existence," said Philippa, "compared to the good old days."

"Jeeley Criley, yes! Thirty years ago there were all sorts of actions going on. There was a woman used to live in the Binnacle—" She sighed. "Well, all they do now is talk. But some of 'em can do the simplest fact upon in red ribbons and holly berries so you'd hardly recognize it."

"That's the way in all small places."

"There's going to be a heck of a lot of packages going around with your name on," said Kathie with what seemed unnecessary relish. "You tolled the Webster kids into school, and so you've stepped

132

on a lot of toes. Squashed 'em flat as those woolly caterpillars."

Philippa said pleasantly, "The Webster children have a right to come to school. Their father pays taxes and contributes toward my salary. Everybody knows that. . . . Are you walking my way?"

"I'll walk anywhere," said Kathie. They started along the path. "Sure, the kids have a right to come. But rights don't matter to some people, some who think the Websters shouldn't breathe the same air their kids breathe. They might taint it."

Kathie was waiting, Philippa knew, to be asked who these people were. She made one of the veiled ambiguous answers she herself hated. "I'm sure everything will work out all right, Kathie."

"Ayeh," said Kathie with cheerful insincerity. They stopped by Nils's fishhouse and looked out at the harbor. The torch was out except for a falling shower of red sparks hissing into the black water, but they could hear men's voices over the soft wash on the shore.

"They're through," said Kathie. "They must have loaded the dory. She looked to be riding pretty low in the water. Well, I'm going home. I was only supposed to go as far as the store." She giggled as if at her thoughts. "I hope you've got a good suit of chain mail to wear under your clothes, like Joan of Arc."

Philippa laughed. "Well, *thank* you, Kathie! Good night." She walked home quickly, wanting to pass the long beach before the men came ashore. Her desire to see Steve had gone out like the torch; an instant of meeting could only disturb and get in the way of her thinking. When she had first known Justin, she had let herself go gladly, as if on a broad, delightful tidal stream. But Justin had been like the rock around which the stream was diverted, and now she was different.

Chapter 25

Friday night Steve sent her a message by Jamie, inviting her to go to haul with him the next morning. She told the Campions about it. Asanath nodded benevolently. "That's something you ought to see, and now, else you'll have to wait till spring. Good days are few and far between this time of year."

"Everybody comes here wants to go out to haul," said Suze fretfully. "Like it was an excursion. What they can see in it, I don't know."

"It's local color, Mrs. Campion," Philippa said.

"Local fiddlesticks! Going around in circles, rolling and lolloping, and the bait sinking. I can't hardly eat a lobster when I think of the stuff *they* eat!"

"Don't you grieve about your weakness, Suze," said Asanath. "You're real brave when I bring in a mess. You always manage to choke down a few."

Suze looked at him uncertainly, flushing. For an instant Philippa guessed at the girl whom Asanath had married; a creature with a fragile, tremulous prettiness like Sweet Alice. The quality had not ripened with the years but had become dried, insubstantial, and faintly acid.

The morning was cold and sunny, with a little breeze to riffle the water and make a lively frill of white on the shores. She was supposed to be at Mark Bennett's wharf at half-past eight. Most of the other boats had gone, leaving their skiffs bobbing at the moorings. Sometimes a gull stood nonchalantly on a punt seat, facing into the wind. Steve's boat was still at her mooring, and he was busy in the cockpit.

When she reached the wharf, Viola Goward and Mrs. Percy stood talking in the little sunny spot in front of the store. It was boat day, and they had come early to get their money orders and put in their bids for a share of the meat, fresh fruit, and vegetables that would come on the boat. They didn't see Philippa at once; they were looking out at the harbor as they talked. Philippa glanced in at the post-office window and saw Helmi working at her desk, her fair hair making a silvery glint in the dim little room.

"Good morning," Philippa called to the others. They turned hastily. Mrs. Percy's dry, taut skin reddened, and her gaze seemed to hold guilt and then defiance. Viola laughed.

"Good morning! You're just the lady I want to see!"

"I'm flattered," said Philippa cheerfully. Mrs. Percy sat down on the bench and took her cigarettes from a pocket of her leather jacket. She kept tapping one on the back of her hand.

"I don't know whether you'll be flattered or not when you hear what I've got to say," said Viola heartily. "But somebody's got to do it, and it might as well be me. I was never one to shirk my duty, and if there's one thing I *have* got, if I do say so myself, it's a civic conscience. There's some folks, on account of being islanders all their lives, who don't know what it is to think of the *community*." She showed her strong teeth in a smile. "With them, it's every man for himself and the devil take the hindmost."

Mrs. Percy jabbed her cigarette at her mouth and brought out a lighter. "Dog eat dog," she said in a shrill voice.

Philippa pushed her hands a little deeper into her raincoat pockets, and set her back against a nearby hogshead. "This is going to be interesting, I can tell."

"There's no need of me going all around Creation and half of Brighton," said Viola. "If you've been given the wrong advice, and been taken advantage of in your innocence, what's happened is no fault of yours."

"Ignorance is bliss," Mrs. Percy contributed, blowing smoke through her nostrils.

"It seems to me I'm being damned with faint praise," said Philippa, "or praised with faint damns. And why?"

Viola pounced. "Do you know *what* you've got in your school, being allowed to associate with normal, healthy children?"

"I suppose you're referring to the Webster children?"

"I am." Mrs. Goward's pale blue eyes glittered.

I think she hates me, Philippa thought. She's going to slash away at me and my airs and graces, my insolence and stupidity. Aloud, she said, "But there's nothing wrong with the Webster children, Mrs. Goward. I know they're nervous, and probably undernourished. But they're intelligent, and so far very well behaved. They belong in the school, and I'm glad they've come."

"But there's things we know about that mess that you *couldn't* know," Viola went on with a show of patient generosity. "You've had bad advice, like I said, or you'd have waited to find out how *all* the parents felt. Some of us are fussy about our young ones, Mrs. Marshall, even if you think of us as just ignorant fishermen's wives."

"I don't think of you like that at all," said Philippa.

"It's too bad you were encouraged to go stirring things up that are better left alone."

"Let sleeping dogs lie," said Mrs. Percy.

"Fools rush in, Mrs. Percy," Philippa said. "That's another good one." With Viola Goward she was still gentle, with the softness of controlled anger.

"No one gave me bad advice, Mrs. Goward. I'm quite capable of making my own decisions and drawing my own conclusions. I did everything in my power to get those children back into school. It's true, there are a few people on the island who were as horrified as I was to find them wandering in the woods like refugees, but they didn't know the situation until I mentioned it." Out in the harbor Steve's engine started. The sound was sweet, but she didn't look toward it. "Their father pays his share. They have a right to come."

Viola reached up to adjust a hairpin in the familiar violent gesture. "Rue is *unwholesome*. You'll find out what I mean. You'll find out, all right. And Edwin is dangerous. I don't want my Ellie in the same room with him."

"I think I can control Edwin," said Philippa. "Without a strap."

"Daniel's under age," said Mrs. Percy suddenly. "He's not even pre-primary age. You're not supposed to be having a nursery school."

Surprised that Mrs. Percy could speak in anything but clichés, Philippa said, "I understood from Mr. Campion that the little children could come if the teacher wanted to bother with them."

The boat cut toward the wharf. Gulls flew up from the ledges in a strong beating of wings. Steve stood at the wheel, his thin dark face peaceful under the duck-bill. Philippa felt a sudden lift, as if inwardly she had gone up with the gulls. The day throbs with color and life, she thought. These women don't matter, they or the things they say with their cruel tongues and their nervous ringing voices. Viola is like a sandy-colored wolf and Mrs. Percy is a little jackal, but when I turn my back on them and face Steve, they will cease to exist.

She smiled at them with a generous friendliness. "I'm going out to haul. I've never been. It'll be a lovely day on the water, don't you think?" She waved to them as airily as Kathie might have done, and went down through the long damp shed to the open part of the wharf.

When they were going out of the harbor, Steve told Philippa to take the wheel while he put on his oil clothes. "Run out past the breakwater toward that spar buoy out there," he said. "That's Harbor Ledge buoy."

The answer of the boat to the wheel ran into her hands. She took a long breath. All her soul searchings about Steve were gone for the moment; she was caught up and enmeshed in a purely sensuous response to the cold stream of air against her face, the shimmer of sunlight on the sea, the bow's peak rising and falling against the distant hills of the mainland. Every new detail evoked more pleasure, whether it was the gull poised on the tilted spar buoy, or the sun shining on the buff-painted washboards and the green water boiling past.

Steve reached past her finally and took the wheel, heading the boat down the side of the island. "You look happy," he said.

"I am."

"What was all that backing and filling for, in front of the store? I saw Viola jabbing hairpins as if she was sticking a pig."

Philippa laughed. "Woman talk, Steve. Nothing more."

"I wouldn't have been surprised if Madam Goward told you she'd stowed away under the forward thwart of the dory the other night."

"She didn't even drop a hint," said Philippa. "So I guess she didn't think there was anything to find out. I have an idea that's how she gets most of her information. She does it very delicately, like a trout fisherman casting with a special sort of fly—she uses a different kind of fly for each victim—and they snap at it, and end up by giving their all."

"That's Vi." He put on a pair of white cotton work gloves and picked up the gaff. "The island's had 'em before. They come and they go, and the island's still here with never a dent to show where they've been." He steered for a yellow and white buoy, leaned out and gaffed it, and started the dripping warp around the wear-polished brass cylinder of the hauling gear. The warp spun tightly, flinging moisture in a bright shower, while the slack spiraled into a loose coil on the platform. The big trap appeared dimly in the depths, and then rose up to the side of the boat. Steve lifted it onto the washboards and brushed off the sea urchins. He reached over and gave the wheel a turn that sent the boat out away from the rocks, and then opened the door of the trap.

As he began to take out the lobsters from the dark green, spiny tangle, he gave Philippa a sideways smile. "You're no Jonah."

She felt ridiculously pleased, and said inanely, "That's a help."

"Four counters." He dropped the big ones in a barrel. Two were doubtful, and he measured them and found them legal. Three more went flying overboard, and the crabs with them. He took out the empty bait bag and put in a fresh one, bulging with herring. Another turn of the wheel, and the big boat, rolling a little in the brisk chop, circled to drop the trap approximately where it had been. Then as if with a leap of eagerness personal to herself, the boat headed for the next buoy.

When they hauled around the western end of the island, they anchored in a little cove where the trees came down to the rocks in a thick growth. There was a family of old squaws paddling peacefully in the shallows where the rockweed lay gold and bronze, breathing with the tide. They flew up when the boat came into the cove, but after the engine had stopped and silence flowed back over the dying ripples, the old squaws settled down again. It was out of the wind here and so warm in the noon sun that Philippa took off her kerchief and her raincoat. Far away, among the ledges that dotted the sea at half tide, other boats moved from trap to trap. She watched them idly, not wondering who was in them; she sat quiescent in the sun and silence.

Steve got out of his oilskins, washed his hands, and opened his dinner box. "Look, a tablecloth." His dark eyes narrowed in amusement, and he spread the big napkin on the engine box. "Jo fixed me up for a lady guest, all right. Would you care to dine at the captain's table, Madam?"

He set out lobster sandwiches and poured hot coffee into the thermos cups. There were filled cookies and two dark red winesaps polished like garnets.

"It's the most beautiful meal I've ever seen," Philippa said. "I'd like to take a picture of it."

"The background helps," said Steve. "And the company." He came around the engine box and sat down on the washboard beside Philippa. He took her hand and said soberly, "This is our first meal together. Supper at Joanna's that time doesn't count. Nothing had happened then."

"Our first meal," she repeated. The laughter had gone. She looked at him without defenses.

"What do you know, Philippa?" He almost whispered it. "Tell me what you know."

"Only that this is one of the happiest days of my life."

138

"I think you love me, Philippa." He put his arm around her. "I think you do." He took her jaw in his fingers and turned her face up toward his. She wondered for an instant if the woods were as empty and innocent as they appeared, if the flurry of chickadee voices and the squawk of crows meant anything more than a hawk. But Steve kissed her before the wonder could complete itself.

She looked into his eyes and saw the reflection of her own, lid and lash, against his dark chestnut-brown iris and black pupil. In this ghost of her, fragmentary and lost in him, there was an inescapable symbolism. For her who was shy and aloof to the marrow, it should have been intolerable. She tried for a moment to think that it was. Why, the man is a stranger! she rebuked herself. But the shock and the withdrawal didn't come. She returned his kiss instead. Steve was no stranger. She knew now that he had never been a stranger.

They separated with an outer casualness, only the flicker of a small, tender smile between them, and began to eat.

Chapter 26

The week began with fog and cold southeast winds. The earth oozed moisture, filling every footstep, and the black soil that showed in the marsh, where the tough grass had worn thin, was sticky and spongy. The children tracked it into school, as well as the fine damp gravel from Schoolhouse Cove. On Monday the wind was strong enough and the sea fierce enough to have given most of the exposed traps a serious beating. Foss, Asanath, and Terence were discussing it in the kitchen before Philippa went downstairs that morning. She heard them through the register. They sounded neither depressed nor optimistic. With cynical humor they laid bets on how many traps they'd have left of the strings set to the southeast of the island.

The children went beachcombing before school and at recess. The seas rolled into Schoolhouse Cove out of the fog; each rose in its towering greenish curve the length of the beach, and crashed with uneven thunder; then there was the hissing and foaming on the shore, the churning of pebbles, the sound of gravel sucked out hard and fast as the sea withdrew to form again.

There were treasures to be grabbed from the uneven white scallops spreading up the beach and sliding back. The children ran at the edge of the water like sandpipers, their voices small and tattered on the wind. When they came in to school, they were hoarse from shouting, their feet were wet where water had sloshed in over their boots, their hands were red, cold, and puckered. But their eyes were wild and shining. They were the wind's children today, greedy, drunken, possessed.

The back of the schoolroom was stacked with their loot. A broken toy boat and a buoy only a little damaged by someone's propeller—that was Jamie's; a pot warp, green-slimed but sound, that Sky Campion had cut from a smashed trap. He'd also taken off what laths were left whole. Rue had found a short pine plank in the surf. It was soaked and heavy, and she and Edwin made slow progress up the beach with it, but they looked suspicious when Rob offered to help them, and struggled on alone. One of the Percys found a teakettle. "For my playhouse!" she screamed, and the other little girls looked at her enviously and then looked away, as if they coveted the teakettle too much to bear.

Philippa heard Ralph telling Rob, rather too succinctly, not to lay a finger on the piece of manila hawser he'd found. When he turned and saw Philippa he blushed, but explained: "Some people'd steal the boots off your feet when you were sittin' down, and then say to your face, 'Well, you wasn't standin' in 'em.' " In spite of the ethics of beachcombing, it seemed that there were times when you couldn't expect others to be incorruptible.

After the first half-hour in school, when the warmth from the fire could exercise its gently persuasive spell over them, they settled down well to work. The Websters seemed to have fitted themselves into their own particular niche.

Rue worked grimly. Sometimes she had an old, anxious expression, as if she thought she would never get caught up. Edwin read; he watched Rue, the blackboard, and Philippa. He sat too tensely. Sometimes the cords of his neck stood out with the strain, and it was obvious that his teeth were clenched. Philippa's own jaw and neck ached for him. He needed a hearing aid and lip reading; he should have training to shape his crude, ugly sounds into words that would make him understood. But she could not even begin to conjecture how it could be accomplished.

It was only when he read to himself that he relaxed. She decided to put off reading aloud until she could get a duplicate of the book for Edwin.

His first penmanship papers were as neat as Rue's. He could control his pen, and the ink did not jet mysteriously out of the inkwell onto him and his paper. Rob Salminen was hopeless; Sky was average; Ralph viewed his pen with aggressive suspicion, and at the end of a penmanship session his paper was speckled and fingerprinted, and Ralph was hissing all the bad words at his command in stage whispers.

For the middle of the week she assigned compositions to all but the younger children. She wrote the usual list of suggestions on the board: The Season I Like Best, My Secret Ambition, My Favorite Place on Bennett's Island, Pets. They could write the first draft of their papers at home, and copy them in ink at school.

The fog continued into the next day. Violent wet winds blew in strong gusts into the schoolroom whenever a door was opened. The floor was damp with muddy footprints. The excitement of the storm had worn thin, the children were tired of it, and besides, there was nothing on the beach this morning. When the school settled down to work there was an undercurrent in the room. It was a familiar phenomenon. Every teacher has felt it, that ripple of unease too imperceptible at the first to quell but heavy with potential disaster.

Philippa set the older ones to copying their compositions on white paper, and called the lower grades up for their reading. The wind wailed through the belfry, but inside the fire burned redolent of well-seasoned birch. There was the scratching of pens, the shifting of feet, a mutter from Ralph Percy, and a subdued flurry of snickers.

Out of the corner of her eye Philippa saw Rob Salminen raise his hand to go out. She nodded at him. "Put on your jacket," she said. The boy grabbed it off the hook and went out with it half on. A gust blew in, rattling papers and causing exaggerated shudders among the girls.

A minute later Rob was blown in, gasping ostentatiously. Doors slammed behind him, the window shades flapped as if alive, and a handful of papers blew off Philippa's desk onto the floor. She leaned down to pick them up, and in that instant the thud, the cry, and the uproar came almost simultaneously.

When she straightened up, with the certain knowledge that the day's trouble had begun, most of the children were on their feet, gazing at Edwin and Peggy. An enthralled astonishment, not quite delight, seemed uppermost. Philippa had seen it before, on adult faces glimpsed in the light from a flaming house or circling a highway accident. Something had happened to break the monotony.

Edwin still knelt in his seat with the heavy geography book in his hands. Peggy pressed her cupped fingers over the top of her forehead. She looked white and sick. Rue stood by her own desk; she was as pale as Peggy.

"Everyone sit down," Philippa said to the rest. "What happened, Rue? Why did he do it?"

Edwin moved around and slid down into his seat, still gripping the book. Rue came forward and held out the paper to Philippa. It was Edwin's composition, half copied, entitled, "The Birds Around My House."

The white sheet had clearly been down on the muddy floor. The ink had run in places, the paper was smudged and wet, and marked squarely across it was the wet soleprint of a girl's shoe.

As Philippa looked at it, a hush of suspense fell over the schoolroom. They had seen what had happened, or part of it, and she had seen none of it. Yet she must judge, and they were waiting. She glanced at Edwin, who stared back with light, brilliant eyes. Peggy also watched Philippa. The involuntary tears had cleared away, but her fingers still moved tenderly over her forehead.

Rue said, "It blew off his desk and she stepped on it. It was delib-'rate."

"It wasn't." Peggy ignored Rue and smiled contemptuously at Philippa. "It was an accident."

How neatly and symmetrically the wet rubber sole had been printed, to make a dark diagonal pattern across white paper and blue lines and Edwin's meticulous writing—the writing he formed with a spellbound devotion as if it were his one art.

"What makes you think it was deliberate, Rue?" she asked.

"Sure it was delib'rate," Kathie said in a loud whisper.

"Be quiet, Kathie." Philippa turned back to Rue.

"It *was* on purpose," Rue stated flatly. "I saw. She stamped on it when he went to pick it up. She almost got his fingers."

142

"Rue, will you make Edwin understand that he mustn't take the law into his own hands? If he thinks someone is bothering him, he must let me know. I am the person to ask the questions and give out the punishments."

"He doesn't *think* someone's bothering him. He *knows* it," said Rue.

"Whichever way it is, I am still in charge. I know how Edwin feels. He's worked hard over his paper, and he was doing it beautifully. But next time he's to come to me."

Rue stood by her desk for a moment longer. Then she sat down, dipped her pen, and went on writing. Philippa went along the aisle and laid a clean piece of foolscap on Edwin's desk, along with the spoiled sheet. He sat forward as if to study the ugly mark. Philippa looked down at the rough whirl of pale hair at his crown and at the thin knobby neck. At least, she thought heavily, I didn't gush "Oh, I'm *sure* Peggy didn't mean to do it . . . !" I'm sure she did mean it.

There was a red place on Peggy's high forehead, half into the thick shiny hair. "How does your head feel, Peggy?" Philippa asked.

"Better," said Peggy indifferently.

Philippa went back to her seat and smiled at the awed fourth-graders. "Let's read some more," she said. She must not let the children know how angry she was.

Chapter 27

School had just begun in the afternoon when she saw Helen Campion emerge from the lane and pass the big boulder outside the windows. In spite of the dense fog and rough raw winds, she was dressed as for a formal call in her good fall coat of dark green tweed, and a green felt hat with a pheasant feather slanted recklessly. She passed by the window unaware of Philippa. Her face, fresh colored from the wet wind, was both troubled and determined.

Philippa glanced around at Peggy. But Peggy was studying the history quiz written out on the blackboard, as if all that concerned her in the world was the meaning of "Fifty-four forty or fight."

In a moment Mrs. Campion's firm step was heard on the doorstep, and the children looked up alertly. This morning there had been a crisis to enrich the monotonous passage of time. This afternoon, a visitor at school. When the knock came at the inner door, all heads but Edwin's turned, and Philippa, in spite of a slight dismay, remembered Charles Lamb's remarks on the drama of a knock on the door. The children and Charles Lamb understood one another. I must introduce him to them, she thought, and went to let Mrs. Campion in.

"How do you do, Mrs. Campion," she said, smiling. "What a nice surprise! You're our first visitor." Helen flushed. She gazed at Philippa with a strangely helpless expression.

Philippa said, "Come and sit by the fire." She led the way down the aisle.

Helen followed her massively, but when she reached the front of the room, she ignored the chair Philippa offered. She faced Philippa across the width of the desk; the effect of helplessness was gone.

"I don't need to sit down for what I've come to say," she said loudly. "It won't take long."

"I'm sorry you won't sit down," Philippa said. "We were all so pleased, thinking we had a visitor."

"There's no call for you to be sarcastic." Helen pressed her gloved fingertips hard against the desk. Her eyes, attractively crinkled and brilliant when she was laughing, now looked cold and small above her fleshy red cheeks. "You must know what I've come for, unless mebbe you figger to ignore it, seeing as you've some pets in the class."

"I have no pets, Mrs. Campion," Philippa said evenly.

"Then why did you let that Edwin Webster get away with practically knocking my girl out this morning?" She turned and stared glassily at Edwin.

There was a rustle through the classroom; the children, all but Peggy, were fascinated. Sky was in Philippa's line of vision. He was looking at his mother as if she were an interesting phenomenon of nature instead of a relative.

"Edwin thought Peggy stepped on his paper deliberately, Mrs. Campion," Philippa explained. "He shouldn't have struck her. He knows it now. He didn't get away with anything."

"Then why is he still sitting there, as if he was fit to mix with

144

the others?" Her voice trembled. "Why isn't he kept by himself where he won't be a danger? He could have killed her! She was scared to come back to school this noon. She kept saying she wanted her seat changed, but she knew you wouldn't do it!"

Philippa was skeptical about Peggy's fear but did not show it. She glanced around at the class. "Kathie, will you change places with Peggy, please?"

"Sure," said Kathie. "Edwin and I always get along." She began to take her books noisily from her desk. Peggy retired behind the lifted top of hers.

"I didn't know Peggy was afraid," Philippa said gently. "And she could have asked me to change her seat."

Somebody snickered. "Class," Philippa murmured. The two girls arose, their arms full, and passed each other at the back of the room. Kathie was grinning. Peggy's profile was haughty and immobile. As she took her new seat, her mother said emotionally, "To think I had to come out in this awful weather to see that justice is done for my poor child!"

Those at the front turned in their seats to study Peggy. She returned their look proudly, but the blush began in her throat and moved up over her face, and Philippa was sorry for her. "I'm sure you all have plenty of work to do," she said reprovingly, and then smiled at Mrs. Campion. "Now won't you sit down and visit with us awhile?"

"*No.* This isn't over yet, Mrs. Marshall. You keep trying to make light of it, but you'll find out that when we support a teacher, we're not paying her to keep critters in the classroom that should be taken off by the state! We're making it so you can have a living and keep your own little boy—but if you had *him* out here, you'd soon see to it that he wouldn't run afoul of the Websters!"

Philippa said coldly, "The incident is closed, Mrs. Campion. You've made your complaint, and that's your privilege as a parent. But your privilege doesn't include an attack on any of my pupils or on my personal affairs." She walked down the aisle in a profound silence and waited at the door.

Helen stood by the desk. The children were merciless in their avid curiosity. Her fine color became blotched, and she pressed her mouth into a small tight knot. Then with a defiant toss of her head, she went down the aisle. When she came to Peggy's desk she stopped, and touched the bruise with conspicuous tenderness. The girl pulled her head away and went on reading. Mrs. Campion's big face looked absurdly hurt, her eyes were swimming in tears as she came toward Philippa, but she managed to leave with dignity.

Philippa opened the door for her and said, "Good-by, Mrs. Campion."

There was no answer. After a moment the outer door slammed viciously. It might have been the wind, Philippa thought charitably, and went back to her desk. She saw the pheasant feather passing the windows again. Peggy saw it too. The child watched until it went out of sight past the boulder, and her expression was one of complete and unforgiving contempt.

She had dramatized herself at home in the noon hour, Philippa guessed, but she hadn't intended that her mother should visit school. She was humiliated now, and besides, she was probably sure that she could handle Philippa better than her mother could. She considered her mother stupid, and Peggy would never be able to excuse stupidity.

Philippa's own anger died quickly, and before the afternoon was over she had achieved a sort of pity for Helen Campion.

By the time school was out, the fog had lifted, and the island lay bleak and dark in the dreary light; the grasses looked dead, the woods sodden, the shingled roofs black with moisture. The tide was very low. The gulls picking around the refuse of old bait and fish entrails under the wharves looked chilly and desultory.

Philippa came out of the lane by the Foss Campion place and saw Perley lounging in the fishhouse doorway. He had his mother's coarse, vigorous, curly hair and big regular features, without her passionate vitality. In consequence, when there was nothing to animate him his dark face looked sleepy and stupid.

"Hello, Perley," Philippa called. "Wretched weather, isn't it? Is it going to storm?"

He was chewing on a match and now he took it out of his mouth, hawked loudly, and spat on the ground. He replaced the match and went on chewing.

Philippa walked on past the boarded-up house. She would have liked to knock the match out of his mouth and slap his face. Then

146

she was ashamed; her response was as childish as his action. And what else was she to expect from him? He suspected her, and therefore she was his enemy. She had seen his pursuit of the Webster children in the woods; she had coaxed those children into the safety of the school.

Nobody was home at Asanath's. Suze had left a piece of apple pie on the table, and Philippa made herself some coffee to drink with it. After she had tidied herself and put on fresh lipstick, she went to see the Webster parents.

No one had cleared the spruces away from the front of the Webster house for several years. They pressed close around the porch, and their branches scraped the roof. Philippa walked under them, turning up her coat collar against the drip. She went up the steps and knocked at the front door. The silence around the place made her uneasy. Surely the children didn't go to their brush camp after school in this bleak weather. She shivered; her raincoat seemed too clammy.

She knocked again, and suddenly Rue opened the door. "Oh!" she exclaimed. She put her hand up to her mouth.

Philippa smiled at her and said, "I've come to see your mother, Rue. Aren't you going to ask me in?"

"About Edwin?" Rue whispered, and Philippa shook her head. "It's just a call."

Rue's relief was like a light coming on. She stepped back and said huskily, "Come in. Be careful you don't fall over anything." Philippa went through a shadowy room oppressive with the raw, stale chill of a place kept shut up. Rue opened the door into the big kitchen, into lamplight and the scented warmth of a wood fire. The shades had been pulled down to shut out the dark day and the spruces. The big lamp on the table shed a kind light over the bare floor and cupboards scrubbed paintless. The children and the woman gathered around the paper-littered table and stared at Philippa as if she were an apparition. Then Faith shouted, drunk with excitement. "Hi, Mis' Marshall!"

Daniel grinned around his thumb. Edwin gazed at her defiantly. He had a pencil in his hand, and paper spread out before him.

"It's the teacher, Mamma," Rue said nervously.

Philippa had expected antagonism, or an obvious state of tension.

She had been unprepared for Lucy Webster as she appeared now, watching her from beyond the unshaded lamp. All her children looked like her, in the triangular face and wide-set light-colored eyes. But with her the eyes had a curious glow, unearthly in the lamplight; her hair fell in an untidy tawny mass to her shoulders. She had her arms folded on the table so that her shoulders were hunched, and in her whole pose and the unblinking stare there was a fantasy effect of youth. Rue looked older than her mother at this moment.

"How do you do, Mrs. Marshall?" said Mrs. Webster, smiling suddenly. She had a deep, hoarse voice. When she stood up she became tall, very thin and angular. The lamplight shining upward outlined the bony contour of her jaw and the strained slenderness of her long neck. She came around the table. "Won't you sit down?" she asked.

Rue pushed forward a small rocker. "You better take off your coat. It's hot in here."

"Lovely and warm," said Philippa. "You have a good fire going. It smells so nice."

Rue nodded primly and arranged the coat over the back of a chair. The children went back to their drawing and coloring. The square table was a litter of old coloring books, sheets of used wrapping paper, and cut-open paper bags. They seemed happy and busy, shut into their lamplit cave.

Mrs. Webster sat on a straight chair near Philippa and folded her hands in her lap. "I'm so glad that you came," she said with a meticulous respect for each word. "I've been wanting so much to meet you."

"I owe you an apology for not coming sooner," said Philippa.

Mrs. Webster's smile was constant, like a reflex. It followed a pattern; she squinted her eyes into bright slits, wrinkled her nose, and then curved her mouth widely without opening her lips. Philippa guessed that her teeth were bad, and also that her nose-wrinkling must have enchanted people when she was a child.

"I hope my children are a credit to me, Mrs. Marshall," she said.

"Oh, they are! I enjoy them very much!" Daniel was watching her soberly, and she gave him the ghost of a wink. He grinned and turned his head away.

148

"Well, I enjoy them too," said Mrs. Webster vivaciously. "You can see for yourself. Sometimes I play with them for hours, as if I was no older!" Again the smile. She arranged her dress over her knees. Like the children, she was extremely tidy though everything seemed faded and outgrown. "Probably you think it's silly," she said.

"I think it's splendid," said Philippa. "I wish more mothers felt that way. It's a tragedy not to enjoy your children."

"Oh, it *is!*" Lucy Webster refolded her hands in her lap, tightly. "We have a real snug little nest here. We don't care what goes on outside! We pull down the shades and forget the world!" The smile twitched around her mouth like a tic.

"It's a help to be able to do that, once in a while," said Philippa. "Not too often, of course, but it gives you a chance to rest when things seem too much for you."

There was a faint darkening like a cloud shadow over Mrs. Webster's face, and then she nodded her head and smiled fervently. But her eyes were different, a little distracted.

Daniel was watching Faith cutting paper dolls from an old catalogue. His mother looked around her in a distraught way, and all at once reached out her long arm and caught hold of him, sweeping him against her side. The boy gasped in fright at the sudden swoop, and Philippa felt Rue's uneasy stir behind her.

"Daniel loves school. It's so *sweet* of you to bother with him! He's lonely without the others, and of course when I'm not well—you wouldn't believe it but sometimes I have to stay in bed for days and days—I haven't the energy to *move,* but I have a *wonderful* hubby, the way he waits on me hand and foot, and such good darling children. . . . Sometimes I tell Rue she's the mother and I'm the little girl, she's so efficient and I can't do anything, really—" She stopped, panting, but the smile continued. Behind Philippa, Rue didn't move. Edwin went on drawing, Faith stolidly cut paper dolls, and Daniel tried stealthily to slide out from under her arm. But she was very strong. The bare arm was thin and sinewy.

"You're lucky to have Rue," Philippa said. "I love my boy, but I wish sometimes that I had a girl too." She wanted to leave, but she could not embarrass Rue.

"Even Edwin's a grand help to his silly mum," Mrs. Webster

burst out gaily. "Poor little Edwin! Folks think he's bad, but it's just that he doesn't *know*. His little brain stopped growing. I used to explain it to everybody and they were terribly sympathetic. Now I think they can just take him as he is, poor little addled chick! Of course it was an awful thing for my hubby—he just can't *bear* to mention it, but I believe a mature person should face those things, don't you?" She fixed Philippa with a brilliant gaze.

"I do indeed," said Philippa. She stood up. "I've enjoyed meeting you, Mrs. Webster, and I'd like to come again some time. Perhaps when Mr. Webster is home."

"Oh, do!" Lucy Webster cried. She released Daniel, who scuttled to the far side of the table beyond Edwin. The way she carried her lanky bony frame was a travesty of adolescence. "I'll go to the door with you."

"No, mamma," Rue said. "You stay where it's warm. You don't want another cold."

Her mother laughed and shrugged. She fluffed up her lank masses of fair hair with her hands. "You see? She's the mother!"

In the dark cold sitting room, Philippa said, "Hurry back to the fire, Rue."

"I'm glad you came," Rue whispered, "only . . . well, you see what I mean about Edwin."

Philippa put her hand on the bony shoulder and felt it stiffen. "Edwin's going to be fine, Rue," she whispered back. "Don't you worry. Between the two of us, we can help Edwin a lot." The shoulder relaxed.

Going down the steps, Philippa thought, Well, I've committed myself. And God help me. I don't know what I can do for Edwin or for any of them. Suddenly she remembered her resentment of them when they had first broken into her sight, that day in the orchard. She had resented them because she had known that once she had seen them like this, desolate yet brave in their fear, she would not be able to forget them.

Chapter 28

Philippa woke in the night and thought of Helen Campion and Mrs. Webster. She tried not to think of them; her consciousness slid to Steve and put her farther from sleep than before. She saw him against the darkness; there was a movement of his lips, as if he were saying her name.

When she was with him, it seemed to her that an entirely new personality had been set free in her, one with neither the wish nor the power to remain aloof. But apart from him she went on questioning her motives endlessly, even while her body was still warmed and invigorated by their moment of contact.

She hadn't known she could be so indecisive, and she tried to find reasons. I suppose at my age most women see all relationships with a view to permanency, she thought, lying in the chilly dark with the small wind crying past the window. That's why there has to be absolute assurance. He has it, and I trust it in him. It's entirely possible that he's an egotistical scamp trying to see how far he can get with an unattached woman. Yet I can believe with all my heart that he's honest and still doubt myself.

She slept finally, and when she awoke the wind had changed and brought a day with the texture of summer. The sea was an infinite and flowery blue. While she was dressing, Steve's boat went out of the harbor. She saw him turn and glance toward the house, and she stood very quietly behind the windowpanes, as if he could see her if she moved. The practical thing, she thought, the obvious solution to be seized upon by a sophisticated woman, was to have an affair with Steve. She would find out then just how deep her emotions went. But she was not sophisticated . . . or perhaps she was. Surely it was only a very naïve person who thought an affair solved anything.

It would set a dozen new questions for each one it answered and would be at best a shoddy compromise. One became neither fish nor fowl nor good red herring.

She walked dreamily to school through the light-dappled lane, her coat open to the morning warmth. The chickadees disputed her way in a noisy crowd; she laughed at them, wanting to stroke their black caps with her finger.

She was suddenly possessed with happiness, as if it had swept around her from the outside like the sun's warmth or the delicate springlike aroma from the ground. The moment had an almost unendurable sweetness; she knew it could not last.

The day was a peaceful one in the school. The children seemed to be soothed by the summery atmosphere. She tidied her desk after they had all gone, not hurrying about it; she had the doors open, and some of the windows, so that the scent of Schoolhouse Cove and the sun-dried sweet grass in the field could blow in on her. She could hear in the stillness the harbor sounds, boats coming in, a dog barking, a child shouting, the gulls' faint but everlasting crying.

Steve came so quietly through all this that he was in the schoolroom before she saw him. She looked up from her desk, and he was coming down the aisle. He smiled at her and didn't speak at once. His brown slacks and khaki shirt were freshly starched and ironed. Philippa felt at once mussy and smudged from her day in school.

"You look simply beautiful," she said.

"Behold, the bridegroom cometh," said Steve. "I could have come all scented up with bait instead of Red Maple. Maybe bait would be more virile."

"Dead Herring No. 5?" said Philippa. "Evening in Hogshead? No, I like Red Maple very much."

Steve sat on the edge of the desk. "I'll tell my niece. She gave it to me for my birthday, but she thought it would be wasted because I'd never get near enough to a woman to let her smell it." He gazed toward the open windows as if he had all time to spare. Philippa made a forcible effort to resume her tidying. "You'll notice too," Steve went on without hurry, "that I didn't take any chances. I put on a clean shirt. So if the Red Maple didn't work, the shirt ought to." He looked down at her; it was as if certain elements were focusing themselves into one powerful whole.

"I've come to ask you to marry me, Philippa."

She sat back in her chair, unable to speak.

"But before I can expect you to answer, there's something I have to tell you," he went on quietly.

She answered as quietly, "Why should you tell me anything? I know that you're sincere in this."

"Yes, and you know I'm thirty-eight, one of six children, and a good lobsterman." He was not smiling. There was an edge of white around his mouth. Suddenly she felt a pang of tenderness and remorse that shook her with its strength; she wanted to take him in her arms. Whatever forces were at work in him, this was a moment in his life that was at once terrible and exalted. She was humbled by it.

She said, "Listen, Steve, what do you know about me? I'm a widow, thirty-one, I teach school, I have an eight-year-old boy." She smiled up at him, wanting to take the intolerable edge off the moment. "You know, too, that I freckle in the Bennett's Island weather. But you know nothing whatever of *me*. I've lived a whole life before I came here. I know about love and birth and parting and death, the entire cycle of existence, but that part of me is as mysterious to you as—well, the universe. I've had all those very personal experiences with someone you don't know and can't imagine. So what you say about my knowing you works both ways; each of us knows only a tiny imperfect fragment of the other."

"We've got a lot of talking to do," he said.

"Let *me* begin." She sat forward, laying her arms along the desk and lacing her fingers loosely together. She determined to keep them loose. Steve did not move. She hadn't known that he could sit so still.

"Sometimes people have been amused or made uncomfortable to find my husband was a minister," she said. "They're the same way about clergymen as they are about undertakers. If a woman marries one, they think she has a queer, morbid streak in her; they set her apart from themselves."

"Did that faze you?" Steve interrupted. "I don't believe it."

She shook her head. "I could laugh at them, and Justin could understand them. They didn't matter anyway. We had our friends and we had each other. . . ." She put her chin in her hands and stared at him, wandering among her thoughts, seeing Justin and hearing his voice, yet fully conscious of Steve. "You would have liked him. You're something of the same sort. Wise about people, never shocked or surprised by anything that's within the bounds of human nature. It's the way a clergyman should be, and yet—have you ever noticed how some persons are so flustered and ill at ease in a clergyman's presence? They can't enjoy food, or talk, or joke. But if he weren't there, they still wouldn't be doing or saying anything out of the way. The biggest compliment they can pay is to say, 'You wouldn't think he was a minister at all.'"

Steve nodded. "Was he that kind?"

"I don't know. I never heard it said. But there was always a crowd around him. We were at a little church outside Boston, and he was able to draw the young people to him without neglecting the older ones. The small children used to run to catch up with him and take his hand." Her eyes went distant again. It was a blurred, yet bright scene; the drifts of yellow leaves on the lawn, the moving tree shadows blue across the white face of the church, the Sunday morning crowd, and Justin not quite distinct to her, a tall figure on the church steps in a black robe blowing in the October wind, the children running up the steps, laughing, and reaching for his hands. She had seen it so many times in sleeping and waking dreams, and always Justin's face was blurred, but the black robe, the yellow leaves, the moving shadows, and the laughter of children had been the same.

Suddenly, in this schoolhouse with this stranger waiting and listening, she remembered the first time she had seen him like this after they were married; she had stood across the street, waiting for him, and someone spoke to her, an old lady of the church. "You must be proud of him, my dear."

"I am," said Philippa. She was too consciously radiant, as if she were making a picture to touch an old lady's heart. But the truth was she had just received the frightening knowledge that Justin was not hers to keep. She had had, she supposed, what the older people of the church called an "experience." But hers was the wrong kind, and she stood there trembling inwardly and fighting against the powerful, bitter sense of her own selfishness. The morning had been like the awakening into sense from a long and delightful dream.

"Come back," said Steve. He touched her cheek with his forefinger. "What are you thinking?" He leaned down to her, his breath brushed her forehead. "He never held his own child's hand. Is that it?"

"Partly."

154

"What happened to him?"

"He went as a Navy chaplain," she said. "It happened on Iwo Jima. He was waiting with a wounded man for the corpsmen to come. It was a hand grenade that did it. But the wounded man lived. He wrote to me. Justin had protected him with his own body."

"I used to wonder when I was out there," said Steve slowly, "why it was. Why the man beside me, who had three children, and not me? Why did some rats come through a dozen messes without a scratch when some men who could have made the world a little better didn't have a chance?"

"I wondered," said Philippa. "I wondered for years. I used to try to think what I would tell Eric. I could say simply that his father was a hero, but what if he ever asked me if it was right to be that sort of hero? Suppose he thought his father could have done much more in the world if he'd saved his own life, so his heroism counts only as a senseless, foolhardy gesture?"

Steve's mouth curved wryly. "You could tell him it's a matter of reflexes. Look at the people who jump off bridges to rescue someone. Some of 'em don't even stop to remember they can't swim. It's a noble reflex, anyway. Better than pushing someone off the bridge in the first place."

Philippa laughed. "Well, so far Eric has taken it for granted. And by the time he does question it, if he does, maybe he'll realize that the same questions have been asked for a couple of thousand years. I suppose that ever since the beginning of Christianity people have been saying, 'Why, if there *is* a God—'" She shrugged and spread her hands out on the desk and looked at them. "There's never been a guaranteed, ready-mixed reply to that. You have to leave it to time to answer you."

"When you're a kid," said Steve, "time gets in your way. It's too long to Christmas, too long to summer. But the older you grow, the more you count on time." He stared out the windows at the wheat-yellow meadow stretching toward a white house mellow and assured in the sun. Without thinking she put her hand over his and held it firmly. "When you're grown," he went on in the same low voice, "you can say to yourself when you're going through hell, 'Five years from now, I'll be over this. At least I'll be able to live with it.'"

She said, "What happened after you were grown, Steve?"

For the first time he seemed conscious of her hand. He held it between both of his for a moment, then laid it gently back on the desk. He stood up. "That's what I came to tell you today," he said. "I'm married, Philippa. I haven't seen her for ten years, and I don't know whether she's alive or dead."

She was oddly shaken. She supposed she should have been relieved that he'd had a legitimate relationship with a woman, yet she was realizing that there had been a profundity to this experience that could still move him. But she would listen as objectively as he had listened to her, with no banal comments.

"Ten years ago," she said. "That would make it during the war. Were you away from home?"

"San Diego." He lit a cigarette, not nervously but with a deliberation as if he were gaining time. "I met Vinnie in San Francisco. The details aren't important. Except that she wasn't a pickup." He gave her a somewhat diffident grin. "I was too bashful to pick up a girl. I'd never had a girl, in fact. I suppose that's one reason why this went so deep."

"What did she look like, Steve?"

He didn't answer at once, but looked into the smoke.

She saw him adrift in San Francisco, skinny and straight as a bean pole in his blue uniform. The women in the railroad stations and bars must have fed their eyes hungrily on his island bloom; in the contrast between the strong, bony sweep of nose and jaw and the shy alertness of dark eyes, they would have seen a devastating mixture of maturity and innocence.

"She wasn't very tall," he said at last, "and she had light brown hair, a little wavy. She wore it short when everybody else wore it long. She had brown eyes. Light brown and clear, like brook water. She had a kind of thin little face, like a kid, and yet too old for a kid, as if she knew and laughed at things, inside, that no kid should know. She wore the same old raincoat all the time and flat-heeled shoes. But it was funny, she'd never go out without her lipstick. She could pull a comb through her hair and put on her lipstick all in a minute and look dressed up, even with the raincoat." He laughed, and he was not laughing at memories, Philippa thought, but at Vinnie; he had evoked her so that she was no wraith. Dead or alive, she was very much alive in the schoolroom at this instant. Philippa imagined the young Steve standing shadowy in a place where all the light was concentrated in a mirror. He watched the tawny image of his girl luminous against the darkness. The comb through the curly crop, the lipstick across the mouth, and the eyes smiling at him from the glass, brook water catching the sun and reflecting it back at him so he could only have a blind instinct as to what lay below.

He was speaking again. "She liked to walk at night in the blackout and the fog. She was crazy about the fog. She said she wanted to be lost in a Maine fog. She liked to cook spaghetti and drink wine with it, and have candles." He smiled sideway, at Philippa. "I didn't blame her. The place looked pretty tough in a bright light. She had a lot of cultch around."

"I like candles too," Philippa said. "Perhaps I should warn you. And I'm not what my mother used to call 'nasty neat.' What sort of work did Vinnie do, Steve?"

"It was in an office, but that's all I know. She didn't want to talk about it, even after we were married. She was an odd stick. It was always as if she didn't have anything but *now*, this minute, and the far future. She never had a day just passed, or a week or a year. I remembered afterward that she never once said anything about being little or having a family. There wasn't a thing to prove she wasn't born twenty-four years old into that rackety little flat on a hill in San Francisco. But she couldn't hear enough about *my* family and the island. I used to tell her she married me for what I came from, not for myself, and she'd grin and say, 'Tell me again the names of all the boats.' She always started out by saying, 'When we go home to Maine.' "

He stopped and went over to the stove. After he had tossed his cigarette into it, he stood there looking absently at the woodbin. Is this the woman in his bones? Philippa thought. Her hands were cold, but there was no way to get rid of the chill. She was tired, too. The night of the dance, the interlude in the dory, passed before her mind's eye in a swift and wearying brilliance. She remembered the red apples shining like jewels on the engine box and the quiet intimacy that had been theirs. Now Vinnie was a sharp and moving essence between them.

"What happened finally, Steve?"

"I was shipped out after a month. I'd made her an allotment and changed the beneficiary of my insurance. I hadn't told the family about her. We were going home together after I got back." He turned and gave Philippa a direct look. "Sometimes you want to keep a thing to yourself for a while."

"Too many fingerprints, too many people breathing on it—you think it will lose its brightness."

He nodded. "Afterward I used to think if I'd told them about her, maybe if I'd started her off for Maine before I left, it might have anchored her. And then I'd have the weirdest feeling that she would have gone into thin air halfway across the country." He was not a man feeding on memories after all; he seemed honestly puzzled. "She wrote three or four times a week for about six months. Then it stopped altogether. Things were tough where I was. I felt most of the time as if I was in hell with no claws. And I thought there was a mess with the mail. I kept writing whenever*I had a chance, and I thought she was writing too, even if I didn't get the letters. I could see her in that flat, ruining her eyes by candlelight. She had these ungodly big old candlesticks she'd picked up somewhere, and she'd have them on each side of her while she wrote. Said they made her feel medieval, as if she was in an old castle in Italy or somewhere, with walls five feet thick, and ghosts moving around behind her back."

He smiled at Philippa as if Vinnie were an endearing child they could both enjoy. "She sounds like a darling," Philippa said. "Your month must have been a very happy one."

"Well, it was. And it lasted as long as the letters kept coming, and afterward, when I thought they were piling up somewhere and I'd get them all at once. . . . Funny, I was out there two years, and I never doubted once that she was still there."

Philippa braced herself figuratively and literally. She put her elbows on the desk, her chin in her hands. "But she wasn't."

"She'd been gone so long," he said ironically, "that nobody else in the house remembered her. They were all new, even the superintendent. I remember standing in that hall with them all looking at me as if I had battle fatigue and they should call the shore patrol. 'Sure you got the right house, Bub? Try next door, huh, son?' Trying to ease me out. I kept telling them I was right, I kept hoping someone would remember. Then the man who had the flat now, a thin little weasel with yellow teeth, said, 'She's probably collected ten guys' allotments and now she's living in style in L.A.' "

"Did you—hit him?" asked Philippa.

He shook his head. "He was a little fellow, wore glasses. Besides, what he said didn't mean anything to me. Less than a gull hollering over a rotten fish head."

He came back and sat on the desk again. "I've never told this to anyone. They think I've lived like a monk, I guess. But you have to know. It's like what you said about being married to Justin. Someone else has had a hand in making you what you are, and so in a way I can't explain—I haven't the words—he's a part of you and I have to take you both. It's the same with Vinnie."

"Yes," said Philippa.

"I didn't know where she'd worked, so there was no one to ask. It was the strangest feeling, worse than being lost in the bay in a fog. I was surrounded by people, but there wasn't one who knew her. She was gone. I had a crazy idea there might be a gravestone somewhere with her name on it, but I never found it. For a long time I had dreams about it, not just when I was asleep. After I came home, I'd be out hauling sometimes when it would come over me, just as if she'd suddenly appeared in the boat, and I'd sweat and wonder if it had all been a dream—the flat, the marriage, the letters and all. . . . If maybe it *was* battle fatigue that sent me up to that tenement to make a fool of myself. . . . I'd heard of these fantasies people invent to get them through a spot they don't think they can lick. I got to thinking maybe that was my trouble."

"You know it was no fantasy," Philippa said. "You'd like to think it was, probably, but you know it wasn't. You know, too, that there was a good reason why she didn't mention her past. She might have had a wretched childhood. She might have been an orphan. Perhaps she hated her work because it went against her grain—she was an artist in her heart and soul, I imagine. But circumstances had locked her into herself." Her eyes were clear on his. "I don't think she ran away from you, Steve. I think something happened beyond her control. It might have been one of several things, death among them. But you would have set her free. On this island she would have found everything she lacked."

159

"I kept the book open for ten years," said Steve. He put out his hand and began to stroke her head with a gentle caressing motion; he touched her widow's peak, her temples, traced her eyebrows and the line of her nose. "I closed it because of you, standing in my sister's doorway and watching the Webster kids." Then he lifted her face and kissed her. "I'm not a haunted house, if that's what you think, Philippa."

"I don't think that," she said. But she wasn't sure.

First I doubt myself, and then I doubt him, she thought with a bitter amusement. But the feel of his mouth on hers and the pressure of his fingers along her jaw resolved everything for now. She shut her eyes, wanting to sink into the moment as if into sleep.

Chapter 29

She was working in her room that night when Foss and Helen Campion came to call. With her register shut and her radio on, their conversation was a blur, but sometimes Helen's voice pierced through.

Philippa had not met Helen or Foss face to face since the incident in the schoolroom. She had been disturbed by it, but there was no reason to suppose Mrs. Campion, once she had had her say, held a grudge. When her schoolwork was done, Philippa brushed her hair and put on fresh lipstick, and went downstairs.

The silence began in the kitchen as she started down the stairs. When she reached the doorway, Suze Campion was already manifesting the wan confusion Philippa had seen so often; she was hovering aimlessly around the stove, whisking off nonexistent crumbs with the turkey wing and trying to make the teakettle handle stand up straight. Helen Campion sat erect in her chair. She stared before her; her face had become very red. The men, in the captain's chairs drawn up to the stove, glanced around at Philippa. Asanath nodded.

"Shut up shop for the night, have ye?"

"Yes, and I thought I was just in time for a mug-up, but I guessed wrong." Asanath did her the favor of smiling. But Foss, who had never spoken to her without the caress in his voice that showed his affectionate toleration of all women, looked right past her. The intention was as tangible as a slap, and she felt a physical reaction she had not felt when Helen came to the schoolroom.

Foss pushed back his chair and stood up. "Time we were pushing off."

"Don't be in such a pucker to get under the kelp, boy," said Asanath. "It'll be no day to haul tomorrow. Full moon, flood tide, and easterly. That's what it'll be."

"Just the same, Asanath," Helen said portentously, "we shouldn't have come out tonight. Peggy's so nervous lately. I'm thinking we'll have to take her to the doctor."

"If she starts developing headaches," Foss said grimly, "there'll be some actions around here, I can tell you that."

"Oh, dear," Suze murmured. The teakettle handle fell down with a small crash. Asanath, sighing, pushed himself up out of his chair and went to the door behind them. Suze gave Philippa a distracted glance and followed.

It was time that she talked with Asanath, Philippa thought. She sat down in the chair Foss had left, trying to ignore the murmur out in the entry. Once Helen's voice rose shrilly, "I *haven't* forgotten it, Asa Campion, and I won't! If your Terence was school age—and Vi said—" The squeal dropped all at once, as if Foss had prodded her. What had Vi to say, Philippa thought cynically. No one had bothered Ellie.

When Suze and Asanath came back, she said to him, "I didn't tell you what happened in school the other day, did I?"

He propped his foot on the stove hearth and sucked on a cold pipe. "No, you didn't," he drawled. "No more'n you told me you'd fetched the Webster young ones into the fold. I heard right off, naturally. But I thought it was a queer kind of actions, you not telling me yourself."

She said pleasantly, "Well, I didn't feel that there was anything to tell."

"That ain't the way of it, according to my female relatives. They've been yammering around here for a week or more, and they don't show any sign of wearing out their lungs. They got more opinions than Congress conducting one of those investigations that cost us so much money. And it'll be only a matter of time before they get the rest of the women into it. For or against, it don't matter, it'll be a devil's broth however you look at it." He leaned forward and pointed his pipe at her. "Tell me something, my girl. What in the name of Jupiter possessed you to stir up a mare's nest?"

"*I* stirred up a mare's nest?" She stood up. "Do you mean that?"

"Ayeh." He watched her, she thought, with the stare of a marsh hawk on a high branch. She laughed disbelievingly.

"It doesn't seem possible that my interest in three harmless children should be the center of a storm. They should be in school, they're coming to school, and as far as I'm concerned, that's the end of it."

"You're either awful innocent," said Asanath, "or as crafty as some say you are." He shook his head. "Why you couldn't let those kids alone, I'll never understand. But no, you had to go out of your way to seine 'em in, and I ain't had a minute's peace since."

"Mr. Campion," said Philippa courteously, "do you really think those children aren't fit to be with the others? Or are you objecting because you're being disturbed by the talk?"

"Waal. . . . Six of one and half dozen of the other, I guess. The kids are queer, and I don't hold with the view that all kids are pure and harmless just because they're under twenty-one. Neither should you, being a teacher. And for the other, well, in a place like this, small and cut off from the cont'nent, so to speak, if you haven't got peace in the community, you got nothing."

"That's a very convincing argument, Mr. Campion. And nobody knows any better than I do that a child can be dangerous. I could tell some stories that would startle even you." Come down off your high horse, she told herself. He's not your enemy, this should be a genuine exchange of ideas. She smiled at him. "I agree about peace. But what I can't understand—and maybe you can explain it to me— is why there should be any storm and strife at all. These youngsters are odd, yes, but they've never done any harm, have they?"

Suze burst out in a trembling voice, "What about that Edwin almost splitting Peggy's head open?"

"I don't suppose it's the first time somebody's been hit with a geography book in that schoolroom," said Philippa, "or the last. It was wrong, I admit. But if Sky or Rob had done it, would it have been a criminal act?"

"I don't believe either of those boys has got criminal tendencies," Asanath said ponderously. "With them it wouldn't lead to anything worse, most likely."

"Edwin's wrong in his head, he can't even talk like a human being!" said Suze.

"Seems to me he's a matter for the state and not for you, my girl," said Asanath.

She looked from one to the other of them. Suze returned her look, her light eyes swimming without expression behind her glasses, her mouth tucked into silence. Asanath filled his pipe, his expression mild enough. Between them, with less conscience and imagination than if Edwin had been a sick cat, they had disposed of a child. She wondered what difference it would make to them if they knew that Edwin was deaf. She couldn't tell them, ridiculous as the vow of secrecy was. Besides, to explain would mean to go into the whole pathetic history, and still they would not understand; they would only look at her and say, *You see, they are all crazy in that house.*

Asanath tamped tobacco with a long forefinger and said on a yawn, "Ayeh, you'd have done a lot better by yourself and the rest of us if you'd left 'em running wild in the woods."

"*Wild* is right," said Suze. "What kind of actions went on down there in that brush camp? That Rue's got a queer look. I wouldn't let her get near any child of mine."

Perley's name was in Philippa's mouth; for a weird instant she thought she'd said it, but they had not changed, they were waiting complacently to see her submission. It took all her will power to speak in a suitable tone. "Of course I realize now just what I've done," she said softly. "I can see that either I've lost my sense of values or I've never had a true one."

Suze didn't grasp the irony. She wore a look of greedy satisfaction, as if she were already framing the words with which she would describe the scene; for once she would have something to tell Vi. Asanath put away his tobacco pouch and glanced across the stove at Philippa.

"It's not many folks who'd own up to being a fool and a meddler," he said. He had not missed her irony but had met it with his own.

"Good night," she said cheerfully, and went up to her room.

She was a long time getting to sleep that night. Nothing had been said, actually, that hadn't been said to her before. But this time Asanath Campion had said it. She had liked him from the first, she had liked him completely, and this made her sense of loss complete.

Chapter 30

The next day was Halloween, and Philippa planned an afternoon of games and ghost stories. But the southeasterly storm had begun at daylight, and all morning the gusts of wind broke against the schoolhouse like heavy seas. The peak of the high tide wouldn't be until noon, but by half-past ten the water had passed the limits of a usual high tide. Ralph Percy had to go out back; when he returned he was jubilant.

"Hey, it's coming in from the Cove and over the marsh from the harbor!" he shouted.

"Gently, Ralph," Philippa began, but no one heard her. They were all at the windows except for Daniel Webster, who looked around from his table with his long upper lip drawn down as if he didn't know whether to be amused or frightened.

"Come on, Dan'l," Philippa said. They went to the windows and she lifted him up to see over the heads of the others. A sheet of water reflecting the sky's lusterless gray was spreading over the marsh from the harbor; the harbor was sheltered, and this shallow flood moved slowly over the grasses with no racing crests. Gusts of rain scudded across from Schoolhouse Cove. On the brow of the harbor beach, men splashed around in rubber boots and oilskins, starting dories out over the marsh.

"The way Ralph came in and yelled," Kathie said languidly, "I thought it was a tidal wave. This isn't *anything*."

"Go look in the schoolyard, Miss—" He rolled his eyes at Philippa and cleared his throat elaborately. "Mebbe you'll see a little water there, enough to suit your Royal Majesty. Those old combers are coming right at the sea wall. Probably sweep us off any time now."

"Sweep us to where?" Kathie asked coldly. The smallest Percy began to cry. Philippa, still holding Daniel in one arm, reached down to the child's tense bony shoulder. "Look, Frances, they're coming for us in dories. I didn't expect a boat ride this morning, did you?" The younger children moved eagerly; only Frances Percy was frightened. Philippa said, "No school this afternoon, I guess. We'll have our party Monday, even if Halloween's gone by. Come on, everybody, let's get our things on." She handed Daniel to Rue and tapped Ralph's back. He came reluctantly from the window.

"You started the stampede, Ralph," she said briskly. "Now you can tell your little sister there's nothing to be afraid of."

Ralph glared at Frances. "Gorry, if you ain't the *biggest* bawl baby I ever see!" Frances butted him in his solid middle without a word.

The fright was over. They became busy with boots and jackets. A pleasant air of emergency pervaded the schoolroom. Almost everyone knew there was no real danger, but they could happily imagine that it was a thoroughly perilous situation.

"Jeeley, we don't get out tonight," Ralph mourned. "What a Halloween!"

"I been saving a swell trick on Gregg," Rob Salminen said. "Wish I'd done it before instead of saving it for tonight."

Clare Percy burst out, "I hate this island! I wish we'd stayed in Limerock! My father does too! *He* don't think it's so wonderful to be a fisherman!"

"Aw, shut up," said Ralph.

There was a dory coming fast over the rippling silver water. "Cheer up, Clare," Philippa said. "After all, this is a real adventure." Everyone crowded out onto the platform in spite of lashing rain and strong gusts; there was no use in trying to keep them inside to await their turn. In the schoolyard the water swirled around the flagpole and lapped at the steps. Out in the marsh, where dead grass should have been, a sheet of water spread a blurring mirror to the sky. Nils Sorensen's white lapstreak dory slid by a cluster of spruces and half-drowned wild rosebushes.

Behind Philippa there was a cry and a splash. She turned, still holding Daniel by the hand, and saw Kathie and Ralph down on their knees at the end of the platform hauling Faith up from the water. She was not crying, but she was drenched and shuddering violently. Her eyes seemed abnormally wide and black. Her old beret had gone and her pale hair was plastered, dripping, to her narrow skull.

Rue was already taking off her own skimpy coat, but Philippa stopped her. She wrapped her raincoat around Faith, and Kathie, not speaking, contributed her wool kerchief for the wet head. Philippa tied it under Faith's chin and looked fixedly into the child's face.

"What happened, Faith?"

Faith's teeth chattered in a new crescendo of chill; she didn't answer. Philippa looked around at the rest of them through the whip and bluster of rain. Their blankness infuriated her.

"What happened?"—she asked it of them all. After a moment Kathie said, "I guess she wasn't looking and stepped off the edge."

In the circle of Philippa's arm, Faith was shaken by fierce tremors. She had been tripped or pushed; it was as obvious as if she had cried it out. But no one would tell Philippa anything; she belonged in another world, an adult world, a mainland world. If Peggy had done it, Kathie might catch her later and twist her arm, as Perley had once done to Kathie, but Philippa would not know of it. If Peggy hadn't done it, who had? She looked once more at the ring of entranced wet faces and was relieved to see the dory slide alongside the steps. Nothing was solved; it was merely postponed.

"Faith will go in the first dory," she said. She handed the children down the steps to Nils, who lifted them in; most of them were sea-bred, they sat without moving where he placed them. "We had an accident," she said to him when it was Faith's turn.

He smiled at the child and said in his slow, even voice, "So you went for a swim, did you, Faith?"

Her lips moved nervously, but her eyes didn't change. She sat hunched in the stern like a small, bedraggled, and terrified bird.

Jude Webster's dory was already nudging the platform and came along to the steps as Nils left. The children got in while Ralph held the dory steady. Jude stood amidships, balancing awkwardly with his rain-streaked glasses in one hand while he fumbled with the other inside his jacket for a handkerchief. His oilskins were dirty, worn to the nap in some places and torn in others. The strap of his sou'wester hung loose, whipping in the wind. His eyes were narrowed as if they ached. Suddenly Philippa couldn't bear his futile motions; she was chilled to the bone, and Faith's accident had disturbed her unpleasantly. She took a clean handkerchief from her blouse pocket and gave it to him.

166

"Oh—thank you," he said awkwardly, looking at her blindly from slitted eyes. He began to clean his glasses. His thin features had a classic cut; they should have been scholarly and ascetic, but instead the whole effect was that of nervous indecision.

When he put on his glasses again, his high forehead smoothed out. He spoke to the children mildly, rearranging them so he could take one more. Rue took the handkerchief from him.

"I'll bring it back washed and ironed, Mis' Marshall," she said. As her father took up the oars and pushed away from the steps, he raised his voice with some effort above a gust of wind; it was not a voice for shouting down the gale.

"I'm sorry I wasn't home the other day, Mrs. Marshall. I'd like a talk with you."

"We'll have one," she called heartily. She wondered if all persons who seemed too heavily enthusiastic were driven to it by similar circumstances.

Kathie and Ralph were left with her, but they didn't have long to wait before the third dory came to the steps. Young Charles shipped his oars and swept off his sou'wester in front of Philippa. "The gondola awaits. Do we have to take all those old retainers too?"

"I never go anywhere without my train," said Philippa.

"Climb aboard, then, and get situated. They can stow themselves around ye." He took her hand firmly to balance her. His eyes, meeting hers, were smiling and friendly. She had not seen him at close hand since the night of the dance, and the thought of his grievance had sometimes bothered her.

He held out his hand to Kathie too, but she ignored it.

"O.K., Aphrodite," he said. "Well, if it isn't Pistol Pete with the tissue-paper drawers!" He slapped Ralph on his plump seat.

"That's fine, chummy," Ralph said calmly, "but you don't want to trust me to bag up for you next time you're looking for free help. I can fix them herring so they'll scare the lobsters ten miles away from your pots."

Charles grinned, and crowed like a rooster. "That's a bantam," he explained to Philippa. "We got an awful lot of 'em around here." Ralph scrambled aboard, swinging himself into the stern.

Charles first beached the dory in front of the long fishhouse, where there was a slight rise in the ground. Ralph and Kathie climbed out.

"By Gorry, we made it," Ralph said, panting. "Once back there I thought we was going to swamp, but we had a good man at the helm."

"What's he good for?" asked Kathie, and they burst into raucous adolescent laughter.

Young Charles rowed Philippa back across the marsh toward the flooded camps. They were blackened by the rain; their steep roofs seemed to huddle like bent and shivering shoulders. There was no living thing in sight, only the rush of the wind, the slop of the high tide around the lower shingles and the bottom traps in the stacks, and always the low roar of the sea on the windward side of the island. Young Charles rowed the dory past the traps and went aground by the boardwalk on the other side of the camps.

"Thanks for the ride, Charles," Philippa said.

"I'm available with my dory any time, ma'am. Bad weather or fine. He held her eyes with an easy, sardonic defiance. "Special rates on dark nights when the water's firing."

She ignored the reference. "Good-by," she said, and set off around the curve of the harbor. Rain ran down her neck and pelted through the back of her suit, making her slip and blouse cling unpleasantly to her flesh. Her stockings were tight and cold. The wood smoke from Foss Campion's parlor stove blew down on the wind, catching her in a sweet-scented eddy. The harbor waters surged around the rocks close to her feet, speckled with scraps of rockweed and dancing chips. She felt as if she were one of the chips, swept loose in a world of wind and flood.

Because of the wind she didn't hear Charles running behind her until he was close enough to touch her. She swung around to him, startled and angry. His expression was at once resentful and strained under the narrow yellow brim of the sou'wester.

"When are you going for a walk with me?" he asked accusingly.

"When you ask me." She was thoroughly annoyed; she had never been so cold in her life. "You've never asked me. You've never come to the house."

"And have Deacon Asa breathing down my neck, making home-spun remarks? But I'll come. There ought to be a pretty day after this."

"All right, then," she agreed, a little wildly. "On a pretty day after the storm." She added in a sudden burst of laughter, "Oh, go home, Charles! We'll both have pneumonia!"

He laughed too, excitedly, as if her half-promise had intoxicated him, and ran back along the boardwalk.

Chapter 31

When the tide turned, the wind came off northwesterly. The rain stopped, but gale-force winds kept up. Sometime in the dark hours Gregg's boat sank at her mooring; she was a round-bottomed little craft with an exhaust pipe pointing straight upward. Her mooring was to the leeward of Randall Percy's and Mark Bennett's. Their mooring had dragged, allowing Percy's boat to come down on Gregg's, and a night of pounding had finally driven a hole in the small boat's elderly planking. At least that was how the island construed it in the raw, wretched dawn of Sunday.

Philippa walked around the shore and watched from Nils's wharf with Joanna Sorensen while two dories, each with three men, went off to bring in Mark's and Randall's boats. The harbor was a heaving, bouncing mass of waves, tossed in by the strong northwester. To Philippa, it was an exciting battle of flashing oars and strong arms against the lifting white-capped waves. She caught her breath as Randall Percy watched his chance to leap into his boat from the small, prancing dory. When he was safe inside the cockpit, Philippa turned to Joanna, "Wouldn't it have been terrible if he had slipped and gone overboard!"

Joanna agreed seriously. "They're really very sure-footed," she said. "And it looks worse from shore than it does out there. It's when something like this happens in the winter that I hold my breath. When a northwester rips in here and everything's covered with ice and they have to go out like this, it turns my stomach. That's when I curse whatever it was that turned me into a lobsterman's wife."

Philippa nodded but did not speak. This was an ordeal of which she knew nothing. Joanna—at first merely an attractive and vigorous woman—seemed to take on greater depth and stature every time Philippa saw her.

"But it's like having a baby," Joanna was saying in an easier tone. She was holding Linnea on an overturned barrel and looked around her at Philippa, laughing. "While it's going on you swear it'll be the last time, but when it's over you forget the agony." She gave Linnea a squeeze. "Look at Gregg over there on Mark's wharf. He's one of the casuals of the storm. There's always someone."

Gregg was a fidgeting potbellied figure stumping from one group to another, talking and gesticulating.

"What will he do till he gets a boat again?" Philippa asked.

"He can go with Sigurd or Nils. For that matter, almost anyone would take him around to his pots. He's lucky, he still has traps to haul. Jude hasn't. He's about the only man who hasn't moved his traps offshore into deep water."

"What does that mean?"

"It means there isn't much left of them. In the last few days they've been dragged on bottom and smashed to pulp against the rocks. The undertow does it. Nils said this morning they might as well be called a total loss. And I don't suppose Jude has a cent put away."

Philippa felt sick. She was not seeing Jude, but Rue's face pinched with understanding, and the mother's voice going on and on in that frightening, febrile gaiety. "I don't know whether to be sorry for Jude or not," Joanna was saying. "He's been in love with the island since Cap'n Charles brought him out here, but it's like some hopelessly inadequate man being enslaved by a horrible and beautiful woman. Jude just can't take it, that's all. Not forever. But he'll keep trying. He's got more stubbornness than brains."

"Maybe this is his deliverance, then," said Philippa.

"I don't know. Nils says you have to let some people go on until their backs are broken as well as their hearts. He and Steve were saying this morning that Jude's likely to break up over this like one of his traps. He adores this island. If only there was enough carpenter work to keep him busy."

In a little while Philippa walked home. She was depressed; suddenly she wished that there was some place on the island where she and Steve could spend this long bleak windy afternoon alone, thinking only of each other, talking and dreaming; she found herself aching for it.

At dinnertime Asanath and Terence talked about Gregg's boat. She barely heard them for thinking about Steve. How can we carry on with this, she thought angrily, if we have no chance to be alone . . . ? She heard Jude Webster's name then and came back to the kitchen, the darkly varnished cupboards, the smell of the boiled dinner, the pattern of the oilcloth on the table.

"He's a sick pigeon," Terence said with neither satisfaction nor pity. "He looks like he's been dragged through a knothole."

"He should've stuck to his carpent'ring," said Asanath, taking a wedge of cabbage. "Perley's more of a lobsterman than Jude could ever be."

"He'll get off here now, won't he?" Suze didn't look at Philippa, but there was a barbed vivacity in her. "He'll have to."

"It's an act of God, looks like," said Asanath. "Better to have it this way, no violence except from old Mother Nature. She knows how to take care of the ones that ain't fit."

Terence grunted. His father went on. "I was hoping for something like this. There's uglier ways of getting rid of a nuisance, but I don't subscribe to 'em, myself. Though there's some that don't think much of the law."

"Who would bother a poor stick like Jude?" Philippa asked. "And why? He doesn't take up much room. There seems to be plenty of ocean around here for everybody to fish in."

Terence didn't look up from his plate. Asanath laid down his fork deliberately. "Well, my girl, it's like this," he began. "The Bennetts walk down the road like they owned the earth, not just this island. And they don't want any lame ducks flopping around and spoiling the looks of their paradise. Speaking of lame ducks, you know what a flock of healthy ones does to a lame one . . . ? The Bennetts might've brought Jude out here to shingle some roofs and build somebody a new fishhouse, but they didn't figger on him staying around and being a liability and a disgrace. They don't cherish him or his kids any more than the rest of us, but they'll smile in his face and do the dirty work at night." He picked up his fork and loaded it with food before he spoke again, gentle and smiling. "If an easterly didn't ruin his gear and run him off the island, something else would. Ever heard of Paddy's hurricane? And the next day the ones who did it would be as innocent as a nestful of newborn robins. And smug, too. They'd preserved the peace and the fitness of things."

Philippa's stomach contracted against the rest of her dinner. Bennett faces moved across her mind, vigorous, laughing, angry, contemplative. She could not believe there was a devious one among them; Steve was the only one who showed a trace of subtlety. And yet Asanath could be right. He was an intelligent man, and he had lived here several years; she had been here less than a month and had fallen in love with a Bennett. She had no moral right to judge. She said, deceptively agreeable, "It seems impossible that there could be people like that in this day and age."

"Oh, I know they've made a good impression on you," he said encouragingly. "That's fitting, I suppose, since they're all comely enough, and they're the kind who'll agree with everything. It's yes here, and ain't it a shame there, and they make you feel real fine and noble when you're talking with them. They don't keep a yammer going about things that don't suit 'em. But they're the ones, my girl, who think they made the law—or that it don't include them. They've been brought up to feel like little kings that don't have to complain like common folks; they just go out and do what comes into their heads to do, and the devil with the consequences."

Yes, it could be the truth he was telling; but there was something else revealed too. Apart from her oppressive doubts, she was painfully disappointed in Asanath. She could not have believed, a month ago, that he was capable of such hatred. She had seen him as a survival of a leisurely and tolerant age, a mellow man. But it had been borne in upon her during that month that the island, remote as it was, was not free after all but contaminated by rivalries and resentments. She would cling stubbornly to one belief out of all the rest, that Steve was different, that he was set apart.

She spent the afternoon walking around the western end of the island. If she could not be with Steve, it was best to be alone. It was satisfyingly wild and isolated at the far end, it claimed one's whole attention. She felt as if she were standing in the center of a world of water and primal mists. As far as she could see, there were green waves tumbling ceaselessly after one another, like explosions of water thrown up from the ocean bottom. The long white crests of foam rode, broke, re-formed. There was a dull booming each time a sea hit a long dark reef nearby. The sun was bright between gray masses of rushing clouds.

Gulls flew low over the waves and some small sea ducks rode on the surge close to the breakers. She watched them, wishing she didn't have to go back to the Campions'. The argument with Asanath a few nights ago had been one thing; this noon was something different. She did not want to sit across the table from him. But by all the laws of common sense she was bound to consider the significance of his words. Because of Steve, because she understood Mark's angry concern about Kathie, because she was drawn to Joanna and Nils—because of all this, had she any basis for believing Asanath was wrong about them?

She walked more slowly, and as she approached the village, she wondered how long it would be before the Websters, ruined by the storm, left the island. Then the rest could all settle back, as smugly sure as Asanath that the problem had been solved by an act of God. No one would really be the victor, though of course Helen Campion wouldn't be able to forbear acting like one. I'm getting to be horrid, Philippa thought. I should be relieved that my crusade is fizzling out so I can relax and go on pleasantly with my job.

Finally she left the shore and went up through the brambly field to Mark Bennett's yard, still sheltered and green within its surrounding spruces. She knocked on the back door and Kathie opened it; a warm scent of wood fire and cooking flowed out past her. She said in honest excited pleasure, "Hi, Mrs. Marshall! Come in."

"I was looking for permission to trespass," Philippa said. Helmi Bennett's quiet voice called from beyond, "Just in time for a cup of coffee."

"You'll have to come in, please," Kathie reached out and caught her by the arm, tugging hard. Her face was brimming with something that had been there when she opened the door, even before she recognized Philippa. "It's a celebration. You'll be glad of it."

Philippa went in, stirred without knowing why. Helmi was setting out cups on the big table by the windows that overlooked the island. There was no one else in the square bright room but her and Kathie and Philippa. She said, "The men wouldn't stay for coffee; they had other things to do. You'll have to help us drink it."

"Has anything happened?" asked Philippa.

Kathie tucked her thumbs in her belt as if she were confronting rustlers on her dream ranch. "Foss sent Perley over this morning to try to buy Jude's boat. They couldn't even wait for the funeral, could they? And Syd Goward had his eye on that dory that Mark let Jude have cheap!" She laughed in pure unabashed exultation.

"All it amounts to," said Helmi, smiling, "is that Mark's advancing Jude enough trap stuff for a good string, and the others will go good for it and help Jude get his traps built and set. Steve's going up to tell him that if he wants to try again they'll back him up."

"I'm so glad," Philippa said. She sat down gratefully. "I can't say how glad I am." She felt almost rapturously happy. The warmth from the stove and the smell of coffee were sublime. Her troubles had not ended with the storm; there was a prospect of more strife before there was less. After this pleasant interlude she must go back to sit at supper with Asanath. If he calls me "my girl," she thought, I shall tell him to watch his language. But for now she was happy.

Chapter 32

The wind stopped blowing so hard and life swung into its normal tempo. The men went out to haul in the mornings, and the women did their long overdue washings and hung out the winter clothes to air. It was early November weather; a pale warm sunshine lay in a thin wash over the fields, the wind was cold when it caught one unawares, and if it dropped at sundown, by morning everything was thickly coated with a glittering hoarfrost. If the northern lights bloomed ghostly in the sky over Brigport, it meant a southerly spell. If a day warmed to an exquisite windless hush and the Rock appeared to float weightless between sea and sky, there would be an easterly spell.

The days moved quietly in the school. Then, as she was picking up her papers one afternoon, directly after dismissal time, Sky Campion came in again. His round face was flushed, and he kept putting his hand up nervously to the back of his black head.

"Back to school already, Sky?" Philippa asked him. "Short night, wasn't it?"

He took off his thick glasses suddenly, and she saw his eyes without them for the first time; they were beautiful eyes, wide-set and of the brown that seems almost purple and heavily lashed. They stared at her wildly. She felt the imminence of panic as if it were in herself.

"What is it, Sky?" she asked sharply.

"Perley's up there." He pointed toward the Bennett meadow. "In the woods near the cemetery. He—" He stopped, breathing in short shallow puffs with his mouth open, then wet his lips and began again. "He got it all fixed up with Peg, to ask Rue and Edwin to take a walk with her after school, and Peggy did. She was sweet as honey, she said she was going to be friends." He was pale, and sweat showed on his forehead and upper lip.

Philippa picked up her coat. She wanted to run out of the schoolhouse. Instead she said quietly, "Tell me as we walk along. Where are the other children, Dan'l and Faith?"

"Rue told Faith to take Dan'l home through the village because she and Edwin were going to take the long way home, with Peggy. She was pleased because Peg was nice to her. She didn't know which way to look, hardly, she was so pleased."

They went across the shaded schoolyard and into the late sun with its faint, deceptive warmth. Far beyond them, Rue and Peggy and Edwin were halfway across the Bennett meadow. Peggy's red jacket blazed like rowan berries against the tall faded grasses around her.

If I could lay hands on Peggy now, I would want to kill her, Philippa thought. She went on speaking, calmly, keeping her hand on Sky's shoulder. "How do you know Perley's waiting?" she asked.

"I heard them planning it at dinnertime, down in the fishhouse. Perley gave Peg a dollar. But I didn't think she'd do it. Lots of times she gets money off him and doesn't keep her promises. I thought all afternoon she wouldn't do it. Then, after school, she started talking to Rue." He shuddered violently, as if with a chill.

Down at the harbor, men walked back and forth across the beach; the faint wind carried fragments of voices, of hammers pounding.

Philippa shook Sky's shoulder. "It'll be all right. Run down and get your father."

He hurried down the road. Up in the meadow the children had disappeared past a knoll of gray ledge and bay thicket. Philippa began to run. No stranger, she thought grimly, could imagine what infamy lay in this hush of bronze grass stirred gently by the wind and ringed with peaceful trees; who could imagine Perley waiting in the thick growth beyond the cemetery? *This* time, he must be thinking, *this* time maybe even Rue will cry out. He knew what strange terrified noises he could draw from Edwin, but to crack Rue's composure—that would be the challenge.

The thought of Perley waiting in the woods was monstrous enough to put the taste of nausea in Philippa's mouth as she ran. But at the same time she knew Peggy to be even more monstrous, for Peggy was intelligent where Perley was not. *My Peggy is a sweet-innocent little girl,* her mother was always saying fondly.

Beyond the knoll there was a lake of shadow cast by the woods. The three had just reached it, and for an instant the last edge of sun slanted across their heads. Peggy's motions were leisurely and good-tempered. Rue pointed to a crow in a dead spruce. Edwin, a skinny slight boy in overalls, leaned down to look at something in the grass. Then they strolled on into the shadow.

Philippa shouted Rue's name and the girl turned quickly. In the blue glaze of shadow, her face shone white. Peggy caught at Rue's arm, she strained toward the woods, but Rue hung back, looking over her shoulder.

"Wait for me, Rue!" Philippa called. "*Wait!*"

Peggy was trying to run, dragging Rue and Edwin with her. She was a strong girl, and they were frail. But they had spirit, and Peggy's sudden change of mood seemed to frighten them into revolt. If only Perley didn't come out of the woods to help. . . . The sweat burned in Philippa's eyes. She knew she was covering ground, but it was like running in a bad dream where one stays eternally on the same spot.

Someone pounded past her like a pony. It was Kathie. "Terence is coming!" she flung back at Philippa, and ran on. She reached the shadow and went forward in a series of long leaps. Edwin had already pulled free and was pounding at Peggy with his fists. When she saw Kathie she flung Rue savagely from her, and ran into the woods. Kathie passed Rue and Edwin and followed the other girl out of sight.

Terence and Philippa reached the children simultaneously. Terence knelt down where Rue crouched in the grass and took her by the shoulders. His hands were gentle, but there was no gentleness in his face. Philippa put her arm around Edwin's rigid shoulders; he ignored her, and kept staring toward the woods.

"Perley's waiting, isn't he?" Rue said in a bemused voice.

"I don't know," Philippa said. She sat down beside Rue, pretending to be merely companionable. Her legs ached and she felt weak. "I came after you because I wanted to talk to you about your work."

"You don't have to make up a story," said Rue. "I knew he was there when she started to pull at us." She rubbed her forearm gently.

Terence sat back on his heels and got out his cigarettes. "It would be easy to shoot him," he remarked.

"Then you'd have to pay," Philippa said. "There's a way to handle these things, and we've got to find it. Today is the end." She spoke in a reasonable way, as if it were a quite ordinary problem. "Where's Foss? He should have come. I wanted him to see for himself."

"See what?" asked Terence cynically. He blew smoke through his nostrils. "The only thing *he'd* believe would be seeing Perley in the act of slicing off their ears, and even then he'd tell you it was a mirage. . . . He's coppering his boat back there. Sky came falling down the beach, crying, and said the teacher wanted him to come quick, it was about Peggy and Perley." He watched Philippa over Edwin's head. Rue sat in a little dream, rubbing her arm and gazing at the woods as if she didn't see them. "Foss laughed," Terence said. "He said anybody worth her salary could handle most kids' foolishness. Randall Percy was hanging around, and he said where Sky was all hawsed up about something, mebbe Foss had better go."

He stopped. "Well?" said Philippa.

"Foss looked around with that rotten grin of his and said, 'Trouble with *her* is she's been livin' alone too long.'"

She felt the color rising in her neck, spreading heat to her face. She ignored it. "So you came," she said.

Kathie came up to them, breathing hard. "Not a hide nor hair of 'em," she said grimly. "But I've been thinking up a way to take care of that Peggy. Rob and I catch her on her way to Gowards' after dark some night, and we haul her off in the woods way behind Mark's, see, so nobody can hear her holler—"

Philippa had to laugh. It put strength into her and got her up onto her feet. "And Terence wants to shoot Perley. But let's be practical. We don't want Terence carted off to Thomaston, and you put into a school for delinquent girls."

Kathie shrugged. "That's where a lot of people think I should be. What was I doing today, instead of going straight home from school and doing chores for my auntie? I was hanging around the beach where that Terence Campion was working on his engine, shameless hussy that I am. . . . Come on, Rue." She hauled the smaller girl to her feet. Rue smiled in her odd, self-contained way. Edwin moved close beside her.

They walked back across the meadow. The day had become very still. For a little while the world had resounded with cries and violence, and now the damp shadow had crept imperceptibly across the meadow, smothering the echoes to silence. The strange thing was that the whole drama had been enacted as if on a desert island.

When they reached the shore, no one was left on the beach. They stood there a moment without talking, as if waiting in silent agreement to make a decision. The smell of fresh copper paint blew pungently from Foss Campion's boat. Nils Sorensen was rowing in from his mooring, and his son Jamie sat in the stern of the skiff.

"Well," Terence said, "what next?" He stood with his hands in his pockets as always, but there was a change in him. Perhaps it was not a change after all, Philippa thought; away from home, functioning as an individual rather than Asanath Campion's son, perhaps he often lost some of his vagueness and became this sharply limned personality.

"If you won't let me shoot the skunk, what then?"

"I think Rue and Edwin had better go home," Philippa said. "Will you walk home with them, Kathie?"

"Sure thing." Kathie put her arm through Rue's. "Think up something real elegant now, like pouring gasoline over 'em and lighting 'em up."

Rue said gravely, "I forgot to thank you."

"You're welcome," said Terence, unsmiling.

"Are you going to tell your father about this, Rue?" Philippa asked. She frowned. "I don't think so. It would worry him awful. He's got enough to fuss about now."

"If you want to tell him, we'll back you up."

Rue shook her head. In a queer way it was she who seemed to be most in command of the situation. "I don't want to tell him. He just wouldn't know what to do, Mis' Marshall. He'd be about crazy. I can manage all right."

"I'll help her manage," said Kathie. "I'll go back and forth from school with them. There'll be no ambushes without a few broken heads."

Terence grinned, and Philippa said, "I believe you."

The girls and Edwin went off past the long fishhouse, and Terence and Philippa turned toward the boardwalk. There was a faint rustle and a rattle of beach rocks from behind the traps stacked between the two camps, and Sky came out around them. At the sight of him, Philippa felt a jolt of desperation, almost as if she were ready to burst into helpless tears herself. At first he peered at the adults blindly through streaked glasses, until he took them off. His eyelids were thickly swollen, and the full childish lower lip had been bitten.

"Is it all right?" he asked thickly.

"Yes, because of you," Philippa said. She wanted to put her arms around him, but instead she took his glasses and blew on them and cleaned them with her handkerchief. The boy was sodden with his tears, and looked as if he had found no escape from misery in his crying.

"You're a quick thinker, you know that?" Terence ran his hand roughly over Sky's crew cut. It was too much. The tears sprang into Sky's eyes again and flowed over as if he had passed the point where he could control them.

"My father didn't think it was anything bad," he blurted. "That's why he didn't come, honest. He doesn't know about the way Perley is. He thinks it's just teasing. That's why he didn't come."

"I know that, Sky," Philippa said. "If he'd had any idea of what was going on, he would have come."

"I don't want to go home." Sky mopped his eye with his sleeve, but the tears ran without stopping. Terence gave him his handkerchief.

"Battery acid got onto it once, but a few holes don't matter," he

179

said. "You want to run away, Sky? That's what I always wanted to do."

Sky nodded vehemently. "I don't want to look at Peg and Perley ever again. She wouldn't *do* anything, but she's just as bad. First I only wanted—" his voice flooded again—"just to get even with Perley. He's always pushing rotten herring down my neck and pinching me on the inside of my legs where it hurts." He swabbed his face with the worn handkerchief. "All I wanted to do was get even with him. But the whole afternoon I've been thinking about how little and skinny the Websters are, and the things Perley can do to *hurt*, and Peggy making believe she was going to be friendly when all the time she knew—" The word climbed and cracked. "And I don't want to go home!"

Philippa handed back his glasses. "I'm licked at this point. I can't think of an answer. Can you, Terence?"

He stood looking at the boy, his face thinned and old. "I could give you an answer, but it wouldn't do Sky any good. I'm nobody to talk to a kid. Trouble with Sky is, he's in the wrong family."

Sky looked from one to the other from under his red lids. Philippa reached for him instinctively, and then put her hands behind her back. "Terence, he'd rather have *you* help him," she said.

"Oh, lord," Terence said between his teeth, but he put his arm around Sky.

Philippa went on past them; when she had walked by Jude Webster's camp, she was in full view of the Campion houses, and she wished at this moment more than anything else on earth to turn and walk the other way, to find Steve. But she could not in all honor do it. She had brought this upon herself; if she had left the Websters in the woods in the beginning it would be no concern of hers what Perley did and that Sky was at this moment wretched and trembling.

She must go to Foss about it, she knew; she knew also what the answer would be. Helen would show the honest, understandable fury of the mother animal, shrieking to protect her young. But Foss would be different. Couldn't she go beyond the stories of hysterical kids? he would ask her silkily. He would be generous in naming Sky a liar. Sky was a dreamer, Sky was inclined to be underhanded. He would tell her all this.

She had no logical reason for believing Foss would protect the others, including his stepson, rather than his own son, Sky; it was simply that she *knew*. It would be less harmful, Foss and Helen would reason, to name Sky a liar than to admit that Perley might be a dangerous sadist.

She couldn't face talking to Foss now. She could not guarantee herself the proper behavior.

Chapter 33

Steve came in after supper. At the sight of him in the kitchen doorway, she felt as weak and lost as Sky must have felt, coming out from behind the traps. She was tired from the afternoon, and meals with Asa and Suze were becoming a strain.

"Want to walk?" he asked her from the doorway. "There's one constellation I haven't shown you yet. Shows up real pretty tonight."

"Just what I need before I settle down to arithmetic papers," she said briskly, and went for her coat.

"By gorry, son," Asanath said, "there's one thing ain't changed over a thousand years and that's the way of courtin' a girl. Walk her out and show her the stars, that's the brave boy."

"Maybe he isn't courtin'," said Suze, quite pertly.

"No comment," said Steve. "That's what all the politicians say when they don't want to start a rumor." Philippa smiled in the darkness of the hall. She stayed there an instant longer than necessary, to keep the image of him in her mind as he had appeared in the doorway, wearing his big leather windbreaker and the dark blue ski cap.

"Enjoy yourselves," Asanath called after them.

When they reached the bottom step, Philippa slid her arm through Steve's, and without speaking, he pressed it against his side as if he felt her need without words. Almost at the same time she felt rather than heard an approach, and a light flashed in their faces. Young Charles said, "All nice and cosy."

"Almost like having an open fire," Steve said. His arm tightened on Philippa's hand. "Take that bug light out of our eyes, will you?"

The light went out. Charles's words moved toward them sullenly through the night. "So long. I'll be going. Sorry I rampsed in."

"No, wait." Philippa reached out and found the heavy wool of a sleeve. The arm braced against her touch. "Come for a walk with us, why don't you?"

"Look, I'm not Jamie. I don't have to be pacified with a nickel for a bottle of pop. Forget I was here. It won't happen again."

"But you must have come for *something!*" said Philippa. She wished she could cuff him out of his tough, hurt patience.

"Look," Steve said suddenly, "I'll go down to the shore and see a man about a punt." He left them with a faint scrape of moccasins on dry grass.

"What a guy," Charles muttered. "Always the perfect gentleman. It's enough to make me sick."

"I thought you and he were friends."

"We were. Well, now that everybody's made such a song and dance out of it, I'll tell you what I came for. I've got to go to Brigport for salt tomorrow morning—Mark's run short of it—and I'm taking my father's boat. You want to go?"

"I'd love it."

He couldn't keep the jubilance out of his voice now. "See you around eight, then. 'Night, Phil." When he got a little way off, he sang out in a clear ringing tone that pierced the island silence, "Watch that Steve now! He ain't been the same since he came back from the Navy!" He went away, whistling loudly.

Steve came up behind her and slid his arms around her. It was as natural as breathing for her to lean back against him; she shut her eyes and rubbed her cheek gently against his jaw. His arms tightened and she grew weightless within them. She felt that she could have stayed like this forever, cherished and hidden. But her natural pride canceled the weakness. It's because I'm tired, she thought, and straightened up. Steve released her and yet she was not released; it was a facet of him that he seemed to relinquish gracefully and hold fast at the same time. His hand slid gently from her waist and caught her fingers.

"Is Charles a problem to you?" he asked.

"Not in himself. But I don't like him to feel the way he does. All that energy and charm wasted, these bursts of anger, these grievances—"

"He'll live through it, you know, and be the better for it." As they walked along, they heard his whistle, sweet and shrill from around the harbor. "That charm you mentioned has been a trial to his mother. Too many women go for it like drunks for a bottle. It's been a tossup whether he'd break a good girl's heart or be ruined by a bad one. So you, my love, give him a true mark to steer by."

"Thank you, Steve," she said. They came to the Foss Campion house, whose lights shone out across the boardwalk and cast gleams on the restless water. The radio was on; they could hear indistinctly a man's voice talking fast and crackling bursts of laughter. She wondered what Sky was doing; there had been no chance to speak to Terence later. She refused to think of Perley and Peggy, or even of Rue. Tonight was for herself.

"Let's go to the clubhouse," Steve said. "It's too cold to stay out and look at stars."

"What's at the clubhouse?" she asked idly, contentedly.

"A place to sit in the dark and be warm. Come winter we'll have to marry up to get in out of the cold." He laughed and put his arm around her waist. They walked through the village like this, out of range of lamplit windows. Gregg was playing a simple tender song like a woman singing in the night. They stopped and listened to it, not speaking, and then they walked on again into the lane.

Steve had a key to the clubhouse. "One of the privileges of being on the Board of Governors," he explained. "I can entertain my girl in here. Of course there are plenty who aren't on the Board of Governors who can still entertain their girls in the clubhouse, but they don't come in by the door."

"One of the prerogatives of public office," said Philippa solemnly. "You come in by the door." He swung it open and she walked in. He came behind her, turned her toward him, and took her into his arms. She put her arms around him and said softly, "Steve, oh, Steve."

They put records on the old gramophone and danced, kneeling on the floor to read the labels by match light. And once as they looked at each other in the light of the tiny flame, they leaned toward

183

each other and kissed, and the match burned Steve's fingers. He dropped it and it went out. But in the sudden blackness he caught at her shoulders and kissed her with passion.

"Have you told your boy about me?" he asked.

"Not as a special person. But I've mentioned you."

"Tell him then." He was like a stranger in the dark, speaking in sharp laconic phrases. "Tell whatever you want, and however you want, but he should know."

"Yes, Steve."

"You're devilishly meek all of a sudden."

"It's the way I feel," she said. He pulled her against him then, holding her tightly. He was so still she thought he was holding his breath. She could feel the heavy beating of his heart. Suddenly he set her away from him and lit another match. "Let's dance again," he said. The match flame leaped in tiny reflections in his eyes. He picked over the records and held one out.

"'Do I love you, do I?'" she read aloud, and looked across at him. "Dancing won't help any, Steve."

He didn't answer but took her arm and lifted her to her feet. He put the record on and they began to dance, moving like one person in the dark.

Chapter 34

In the morning she was ready to go to Brigport long before eight o'clock. Wearing slacks, a warm sweater, and a topcoat, she walked out on the point beyond the Campions. The yellow tom went with her, conversing in little wooing dulcet sounds as he jumped from rock to rock. It would be another fine day; the sun was already warm though the frost was thick and slippery in the shade of the trees. The white houses on Brigport shone in the morning sun, and the fields sloping to the shore were warm bronze. She was thinking of Steve as she went down the twisting track among the spruces. She had been thinking of him more or less steadily since he had left her at the door last night. He was always in her consciousness now, sometimes directly, and even when she was disturbed by something else, her knowledge of him was subtly reassuring.

She had awakened early this morning remembering her promise to speak to Eric, and she didn't know how to begin. She had lain in bed watching the pearly light fill her room and rehearsed all sorts of openings in her mind. They all seemed too trite. Of course the situation is trite, if you want to niggle, she thought irritably. Why couldn't I say simply, *Steve has become a great friend of mine, and I'm hoping you and he will become friends too?*

She could imagine Eric's clear gaze moving slowly between her and Steve. The relationship between her and the boy was about to be changed; there was no question of admitting Steve into it. It would go, and the going would be like severing a second umbilical cord.

"Rubbish!" she said aloud. She had no right to conjecture about Eric and metaphysical cords when it was entirely possible that he would take Steve for granted and probably like him very much. Possible . . . but again she felt that faint inward quiver. How could you *know* a child? How could you guess, beyond a shadow of a doubt, what they really were inside the fragile structure of bones and flesh?

As she approached the harbor, she saw Charles coming fast from the far end of the boardwalk. She thought she saw a twitch of curtains in one of Foss Campion's front windows, but otherwise there was no sign of anyone. Foss and Perley had gone to haul. The three-colored money cat sunned herself on the high rib of granite behind the house. The fishhouse was open and empty.

She met Charles by the camps. "Coming to get me?" she asked. "Am I late?"

His brief grin was like a muscular reflex. He stood with his hands in his pockets and his legs braced in aggressive fashion, as if he wished to bar her way.

"What's the matter?" she insisted. "Is it too rough?"

"Yep. Too rough."

She didn't believe him. He looked at her too steadily; his lips were pressed into an unnaturally stiff line.

"What ails you, Charles?" she asked curiously. "If you've changed your mind about taking me, say so. I won't throw myself down and pound my head on the beach rocks or turn blue or anything of the sort."

His chest rose on a breath of exasperation that didn't get by his tight mouth. A dark blush flowed upward under his skin, and his eyes glistened suddenly as if with water.

She put her hands in her pockets and watched him, perplexed and compassionate. "Shall I go back home? No, on second thought, I'll take a walk around the harbor. I see Steve hasn't gone to haul, maybe he'll be more sociable." She moved forward and he made a motion to stand in her way; then he stepped off the boardwalk, but he fell into step beside her as she started on toward the long fish-house.

As they came to the giant fluke of the great anchor that had been imbedded in the earth above the beach so many, many years ago, she stopped and took hold of his arm and gave it a little shake.

"Something is the matter, Charles. What *is* it?"

He turned and looked out at the harbor. In the cold stream of wind all bows pointed northwest, and the dark blue water seemed to rush past the wet, rounded white or green sides of the boats. The big lobster boats rolled gently; the little skiffs jounced up and down on the water, and a gull perched on the bow of one suddenly launched himself into space with an effortless outward thrust of his wings.

"Look at Steve's boat," Charles said. *"That's* the matter, if you want to know."

Once she looked, she wondered why she had not seen it before, for now she could see nothing else but what had been painted on the white side of Steve's boat. Crude and gigantic, the words and the drawings were nevertheless plain. "Teacher and her pet" captioned caricatures of Philippa and Steve.

She laughed suddenly; the sound surprised her. "What a thing to call Steve, of all people!"

Charles stared at her, shocked and disbelieving. "Is that all you've got to say?"

"What else can I say? It's so—so foolish, somehow."

"You're a cool one," he said grudgingly, as if he felt his delicacy on her behalf had been wasted. "You cool enough to start off to

Brigport with me, in the face and eyes of all this?"

She didn't answer. An effect like delayed shock was creeping into her. She looked at the boat across the water, her face growing stiff and cold. The words were mocking but innocent; the caricatures were recognizable but not essentially more cruel than caricatures usually are. It was a silly, childish prank. At least it should have been. But as she looked across the bright dancing harbor, the great black lines sprawled against all the day's clean brilliance had an inevitable ugliness. And worse than the ugliness was the size of the hatred behind it. It was frightening but not in a physical sense that one could fight.

The rocks shifted under Charles's boots. He said gratingly, "I'd like to get a-hold of the critters who went out to haul early this morning and let it stand. Somebody should've gone and got Steve to tend to it. I suppose they thought it was funny." He brought out a crumpled pack of cigarettes and lit one as if it were the first after a long and exhausting mission. In the heavy silence between them he blew out smoke and stared at the harbor.

Then he said, with a restless motion of his head, "I hope you don't think just anybody did that, Philippa. Although I did it once." His expression was a mixture of bravado and embarrassment. "The woman was a fool, though. I was drunk and I thought it was a wonderful big joke. But when I saw it in daylight, I was ashamed and sorry. And the poor guy had to bring his boat in and clean her up, with everybody throwing wisecracks around like—" He took another deep pull on his cigarette. "Made me sick, all right. I knew most of 'em had gone around with her—he just happened to be the one of the moment."

"I don't think the wisecracks will bother Steve," Philippa said. "And I don't have to hear them." She sounded quieter than she felt; there was a stiffness to her lips and a churning in her stomach. Suddenly she wondered if anyone were looking from Foss Campion's, if they could see Steve's boat from there, and what they were saying to see her like this on the beach, staring out into the cold wind. The thought of eyes avidly watching was more terrible than the words and pictures.

"I lay it to either Terence or Perley," Charles said.

"Not Terence," she said quickly, turning away to rest her aching eyes with the sight of the russet marsh grasses bending toward the east.

"Why not?" Charles said belligerently. "He's too blasted quiet to be natural, if you ask me. There's something wrong with a guy like that."

"I'm not asking you, I'm telling you. It may be Perley, but it's certainly not Terence."

He shrugged. "Have it your own way. Are we going to Brigport?"

"We should, shouldn't we?" She smiled at him stiffly. "But I think not. I don't feel as excited about it as I did, somehow."

He could understand this; she was acting now as he expected her to act, and his voice gentled. He touched her lightly on the shoulder. "Sure. Take a rain check on it. There'll be other good days. I'll go up and get Steve." He looked out at the boat again. "If he was a fool or a coward, that'd be one thing." He shook his head and walked away.

Philippa went across the marsh to the schoolhouse. She would sit on the worn steps and collect herself, if such a thing could be done. She came into the schoolhouse yard and stopped involuntarily as she stared at the white, wide-paneled door. The violence of the black strokes stood out even at this distance. So they had done the same thing here, too.

"Teacher and her pet." And the drawings.

The lines seemed to breathe a palpable malevolence, bathing the schoolhouse in an aura of evil. She thought if she went inside, its familiar chalky and firewood scents would reassure her, but she could not bring herself to touch the door. Her squeamishness in turn dismayed her the more. She turned her back on the door and sat down on the steps to watch the gulls circle over the cove.

It must have been a half hour later when Steve came. He set down the can of white paint and looked at the defaced door. "Well," he said, "seems as if they thought it bore repetition. Good thing I brought my paint can along. I'll give it a coat after I have a cigarette." He sat down beside her and lit one before she spoke to him. Then she said in a tone of wonder, "Why did they do it, Steve?"

"Might have been because we were up at the clubhouse last night, dancing in the dark."

188

"Do you think someone was following us, to see what we—" She broke off, horrified. The island night had had such a primeval purity with only the sea sounds, the stars, and sometimes the shifting specters of the northern lights. As if he guessed at her horror, he took her hand and laid it on his knee and covered it firmly with his.

"Things like this have been done before. Kids looking for deviltry or full to the gills with stories they've read. Or women with nothing better to do, and bored. If you can get something on somebody, it can liven up things for a month."

"I'm afraid whoever looked in the clubhouse windows last night must have felt severely cheated," said Philippa, "to put such scorn in his paintbrush." She smiled at Steve and he gripped her fingers hard. The determined ease went out of his face. There was a frightening quality in his silence.

He got up and took the paintbrush from the can. "I've already done the boat," he said. "Now the door." She stood watching him, her hands in her pockets, her collar turned up against the wind, feeling no warmth in the sun on her back. She thought of the moments they had had together, the bits and pieces of time they could call their own; last night in the instant when the match had gone out, she had gone past all doubt and wondering. Afterward as they danced in the dark, she had realized that what she felt for Steve was not an echo of anything she had experienced with Justin; it was unique, it belonged to the Philippa she had become since his death. She had known instinctively it would have been impossible for her to feel it before. This is second love, she thought. It could never take the place of the first; it could never exist without the first, and yet it is an absolute and perfect thing in itself.

That was last night. But this was morning. Each of the other meetings had been an instant set apart from time, like a pebble of rose quartz separated from the others on the beach to be cut and polished into a gem. This morning the glint was gone. The attack had been made on her and Steve together, and whatever action they took would be given an undeniable significance. To ignore it or protest it, it didn't matter; all the cans of paint in the world wouldn't wipe out the hostility.

Steve painted without looking around, and she felt cut off from him. He cherished the way of living that had made him almost an invisible man, and now she had brought this upon him. The attention of the island was on him now, not casually, but with a sneer. Whether he was her lover or not didn't matter. The joke was on him. She wondered how long the chuckles and comments would last along the beach, and her anger sprang up strong and savage, in a desire to do physical violence to any who would dare hector him with their mockery.

But she knew even as she felt it that it was futile. Instinctively she straightened her shoulders and smoothed her features into aloofness, to meet the change that must inevitably come to his.

He said suddenly, still without looking around, "You told Charles you thought it was Perley. Any particular reason?"

Taken by surprise, she almost stammered her answer. "Yes." Then she told him in as few words as possible, undramatically, what had happened, beginning with her discovery of Perley in the orchard and ending with yesterday's affair. He didn't interrupt. When she had finished, he laid the paintbrush across the top of the can and turned to her.

"What made you figure on keeping this all to yourself?" he asked brusquely. "Where was I supposed to come in?"

"You've come in now. You're the innocent victim because I'm the real object of the attack." She managed to keep from sounding apologetic.

"There's such a thing as keeping too quiet. It could have been something worse than this. You're too blasted independent."

"As a hog on ice, my family always maintained." She realized weakly the source of his anger; it was not with the smear at all but with her secrecy. It was rather a domestic issue, as if between man and wife. She said eagerly, "Steve, listen. Without proof, I couldn't talk to the parents, so I felt in all honor I couldn't mention it to anyone else, even you. Don't think I wasn't tempted. I ached to drop it all in your lap. But that wouldn't solve anything. All I could hope was that when I had these children safe, in school, the trouble would have a chance to fade decently out of existence."

"But after what happened yesterday—"

"It was hideous. I wanted to walk into that house and hurl the truth at them like a pail of ice water. But how could I? Had I *seen* Perley hiding in the woods? How could I prove Peggy wasn't being sweet and generous to some little ragamuffins, who are vicious liars if they say Perley ever tormented them? The children themselves knew better than to start a row. The Websters were hounded out of school last winter, and not one child in that school told anyone about it. They just wanted to avoid trouble."

The skin was drawn taut over Steve's cheekbones. His eyes had a curious glitter she had never seen before. She went on, "Have you ever tried to talk to the parents of a boy like Perley or a girl like Peggy? If you had thirty pages of proof in black and white, they'd throw it in your face and revile you! Foss wouldn't come when I sent for him, and he didn't see Sky the way Terence and I found him behind a pile of traps. They'd tell me Sky was lying or even worse—they'd bully Sky into saying it never happened."

She leaned against the building, out of breath. Her throat was dry. He stood looking at her from under his lids as if he had never really seen her before. "I can understand why you didn't want to throw a match into the brush pile," he said slowly. "And that's what this place is. But good Lord, woman, the mess stinks to high heaven! I'm not going to wait until Perley hurts the kid to do something about it. How much proof do you have to have? Kids marked up with cigarette burns? Broken bones, or an eye put out?"

There was an undramatic violence in him that amazed her; she had not thought him capable of it. "What *do* you want to do?" he asked. "If you could handle this the way you wanted to, what would you do?"

She shrugged. "Rue doesn't want her father to know; she says it would drive him crazy, and I think she's right. Kathie walks back and forth with the Websters, and there'll be no long trips around through the orchard. And as for this—" she glanced at the door— "I suppose I'll ignore it. At least nobody will get any satisfaction out of seeing me squirm. What about you?"

"I put on some paint and act as if it hadn't happened." He pulled off his work gloves. Suddenly Philippa felt unsteady and her eyes burned.

"Steve, I feel responsible—I brought this on myself, I know, but I didn't think what I would do to you!" The words burst out. She had no control over them. "I came to this island, I loved it at first sight, I met you—"

"And loved me at first sight?" His mouth curved.

"Why should *I* have been the one to uncover the disturbances?" she protested. "Look what's happened to you because of me."

He put his hands on her shoulders and gave her a little shake.

"Listen to me. You didn't start anything. There never was peace here. Leaving the kids out of it, there still wouldn't have been peace. Oh, sure, all the talk's been involved with the kids, I know. The Campion women brought along some of their mainland ideas, and according to *them,* any youngster who doesn't seem right should be shut off from the rest. The way we've always done out here, a kid who was downright feeble-minded could go to school, if he was harmless. There might be something he could learn. And as far as plaguing them in the schoolyard, that's been done to other kids, and if the teacher didn't bother, it was just too bad for the victims, unless they went home and told their parents."

"But the men," she objected. "The way Foss reacted yesterday. The things Asanath says about my stirring up a mare's nest—"

"They probably mean just what they say, as far as the Websters are concerned. They hate to hear the women yammering, and you've started them up in good style. So the men don't bless you for it. They probably don't think anything's really *hurting* the Webster kids . . . nawthin' to get riled up about. . . ." He drawled it out like Asa, and grinned at her.

"But as for the other business—which didn't have anything to do with the kids in the first place—that springs from the fact that the Campions moved on here thinking it was El Dorado and found themselves pretty well surrounded by Bennetts. They'd like nothing better than to take over. Asa said in the store one day the island had had the Bennett religion long enough; time they showed us what the Campion religion was like."

"And how do the Bennetts feel about the Campions?"

He shrugged. "They don't bother us any. They bought their places here, and they don't look as if they'll become public charges. We've seen 'em come and seen 'em go. Why should they matter to us, as long as they don't haul our traps or become public nuisances? We were here before they came; we'll be here long after they go. If Young Charles's father was here, he might needle the Campions a little, just for the fun of it. But the rest of us are pretty peaceable."

She said thoughtfully, "Still, I can see why you make Asa's hackles rise. That air of careless power can infuriate."

"You wouldn't think Asa would be that easy to infuriate, would you? But he's been head of the Campions for so long, I guess he figured on being the Big Man out here. Probably thought this handful of Bennetts had gone to seed, intermarried till they were all soft in the head." He took out his cigarettes. "But this business with the kids may give them a good chance to prod us up. Jude's a Bennett man; we brought him out here and set him up, just as Foss brought Randall Percy. It's only a matter of chance that Young Charles isn't trying to fuss up Randall, by the way—just to raise hell and to annoy the Campions a little bit. Randall's easy to fuss up, he's scared to death of lobstering. But he's also Fort's father. So Young Charles won't plague him."

"What about the Campions and Jude?" she insisted. "You don't mean they'd condone anything that happened to Rue?"

"Oh, not that. I told you, they don't think there's anything to it. They told you the kids were feeble-minded. If you had believed them and ignored the kids, that might have driven Jude off sooner or later. He's no fighter. He's not much of a lobsterman either, and the space he takes up with his pots doesn't amount to Hannah Cook when the island territory is practically unlimited. So they don't worry about competition from Jude, but it would be one for their side if they drove him off. I don't know if you see what I mean."

"I do," she said quickly. "It wouldn't be much of a victory in a material sense, but it would be symbolic of something."

"That's it. You've fallen head first into island politics, Philippa."

She glanced at the newly painted door. "Is that island politics too?"

"If that's proved to be Perley's, the Campions will be properly horrified, but underneath they'll see it as an extra prod at the Bennetts. They won't be too shocked."

She said slowly, "I can understand the strain between the two families. That's more or less natural in small places, where the least thing can mushroom overnight into a big issue. But I can't stand thinking the children are going to be drawn into it." She felt cold and very tired. "I can understand how both things started. Maybe Helen and Vi would have realized after awhile that Rue and Edwin were all right, and the business with the Websters would have died a natural death. But now—" She kept looking at the door; it seemed to her she could see the letters through the paint. "Now they've come together; and each supplements the other and makes it far worse. It's not pleasant to think about, Steve."

"You don't have to think about it. After all, you said yourself a war of nerves is a natural state of affairs in most small places. It doesn't make the Campions any worse, or the Bennetts any better. We can all take care of ourselves, and nobody really wants a feud breaking out. It's just island politics." Unexpectedly he took her into his arms. "The devil with privacy," he said. He kissed her forehead and her eyelids with the faintest gentle brushing of his lips. She held her face up to him silently; she was quivering inwardly, as if at the end of a long race.

Chapter 35

Rob was doing well with his fractions, Philippa thought. She put the last of the arithmetic papers away and stood up to stretch, walking lightly across the room with an instinctive desire to make no sound. Whenever she caught herself like this, putting her feet down as the cat Tom did, she was amused; it was something that had come to her in the Campion household, where they were all so silent in their movements. It was not the cat's natural stillness but caution, as if they were treading on explosives. She wondered how it had been before Elmo died, if he had been a loud, happy, vigorous force in the house, making them all so conscious of him that they had forgotten themselves. Now that he was gone, perhaps they had all been thrust back into some dreary terrain of acrimony and resentment, and they could find no frontier by which to escape.

Terence was knitting trap heads down in the kitchen. Asanath and Suze were in the sitting room; the fatalistic tones of Asa's favorite commentator droned up through the ceiling. She wondered what Terence did when he was out. There were not too many evenings in the week when Gregg was sober enough for a nondrinker to want to sit in his kitchen. Kathie's aunt and uncle were strict about her studies and bedtime. What did it leave for Terence, except to stand in the lee of a fishhouse, to smoke and stare into the darkness pricked by mainland lighthouses?

The shocks of the morning had retreated safely into the distance allowed for dreams. She had gone through her day as if unconscious of the blatant black letters standing between her and the rest of the island, as if no one were staring at her back, snickering or shaking a head in sympathy. She had gone to the store in the morning and had waited with the rest for the mail boat to come. Joanna Sorensen had invited her to come in for coffee in the afternoon. Helmi had come too, and as the talk reached back into the past, Philippa sensed the solidarity that held these people, their unconscious assurance, inherent as the circulation of their blood or their ability to breathe, that this place was theirs. There was a timeless quality in the way they spoke; their memories began in the island, years before the Campions came. No matter where they went, they would always be islanders.

This was what the Campions hated. This was the source of the frustration behind their calm smiling eyes. They'd been able to buy property on the island besides their own houses; they owned the boarded-up house intended for Terence and the Percy place. But land and shore front weren't enough, Philippa knew, and she had a curious sympathy for them. A person could live out his life and go to his grave with his bankbook showing prosperity, and yet be sere and bitter from wanting an intangible. . . .

Now back in her room at the Campions', she thought that she heard voices outside. Sometimes the wind made queer sounds around the windows, and she went on with her writing. But there was no mistaking the heavy tramping on the back steps and the agitated opening of the back door; voices were raised, Terence pushed back his chair, and Asanath turned off the radio and went out into the kitchen with measured steps. Philippa stopped typing. Helen's voice rose by shrill stages to a passionate crescendo, and Viola's cut vibrantly across it. The men's tones mingled deep and unintelligible. Someone came out into the hall; she recognized Asanath's step again. He called to her.

She opened her door and went out to the head of the steep straight flight, and looked down at him. He was half in light from the kitchen, half in darkness. The melee went on beyond, and Helen was crying hysterically.

Her first thought was that someone had drowned, one of Foss' children, perhaps. She felt slightly ill.

"Has there been an accident?" she called down to Asanath.

"Nobody's dead. But you better come down, my girl." He cleared his throat. "They seem to think it's some of your affair."

Philippa started down. Her hands felt clammy and her heart was beating rapidly. She wished she could go back to her room and close the door, but that would have shut out nothing. It would be waiting for her tomorrow, whatever it was. *Tomorrow and tomorrow and tomorrow. . . .* She was astonished to find herself silently quoting the phrase in time with her feet on the stairs.

Terence came out from the kitchen. "Don't drag her into this," he said angrily. He stepped in front of Asanath.

Philippa stopped with her hand on the newel post and looked from one face to the other. Asanath smiled. "She's got a right to defend herself," he said.

"What's going on, Terence?" Philippa asked.

"Somebody just put the wood to Perley. Gave him a hiding over on the beach." He blew smoke from his nostrils. "The fools think you put a gang up to it."

"I think I'd better see about this." She stepped down, but Terence stood in her way.

"Don't *you* be a fool. Go on back upstairs and let 'em stew in their own juice." His face had the hatchet look she had seen before.

"I can't put it off, don't you see?" she said to him. "It'll come up again and again." They stood facing each other in an interval of silence laid against the confusion in the kitchen. Asanath stood behind them, defied and ignored. Past Terence's shoulder, Philippa looked into the brightly-lighted kitchen and saw Suze, the teakettle in her hand, staring down the hall. She realized then the appearance of intimacy between herself and Terence. She walked by him into the kitchen.

Foss was leaning over Helen, holding a glass of water. He straightened up when Philippa came in, and looked at her stonily. Vi was leaning against the dresser with her arms folded across her chest; her strong thin lips curled back from her teeth in a smile of anticipation.

"Well!" she said. "Here's the lady herself."

Helen whipped the wet cloth from her eyes. "You!" she cried in a thick, choked voice.

"What's the matter?" Philippa asked.

"*Matter!*" Helen exclaimed. "Matter! How can you stand there staring at us all so innocent?" Foss stroked her quivering shoulders, murmuring soothingly, but she shook him off and got to her feet.

"What about the gang you and Steve Bennett put onto my boy? Lying in ambush like a bunch of heathen savages, and him coming home with the blood streaming out of him like a stuck pig, and so sick to his stomach where they punched and kicked him—" She caught her breath sharply; her eyes flooded with tears as her throat and face turned a dark and frightening red.

"Oh, he was a handsome sight coming in the door," said Vi enthusiastically. "Like to scared Ellie into fits! All I can say is, it's going some when a gang of hoodlums have to lay into a seventeen-year-old boy out doing a chore for his father."

Philippa looked only at Helen. "Mrs. Campion, I know how upset you are. I'd feel the same way. But no adult in his right mind is going to be responsible for such a thing. Believe me, you're making a great mistake in blaming Steve Bennett and me for this." Helen opened her mouth, and Philippa hurried on. "Did Perley see any of the people who attacked him?"

Foss said implacably, "It was Young Charles spoke to him first. He started it. Must have given a signal to the others."

Perhaps Terence was right; perhaps she should have gone into her room and escaped this for a night at least. She put her hands behind her back, lacing her fingers to keep them still.

Viola's smile deepened. "Don't tell us you're at a loss for words, Mrs. Marshall. I didn't think that could ever happen!"

Terence said suddenly, "Why don't you tell them the truth, Philippa? They're asking for it. Sock it right to them."

"Terence!" his mother cried faintly. She put her hand up and twitched at her collar. "Terence, what ails you? Are you drunk?"

"I wish I was. Maybe you'd all look better to me. Go on, Philippa."

She glanced around at him quickly, and he grinned at her. "Want *me* to?"

She shook her head and looked back at Helen. "Perhaps I *am*

to blame after all," she said gravely. "In an indirect way. I didn't intend for anything like this to happen, I didn't dream it would. I
know for a fact that Steve Bennett isn't involved." She paused, and
the attentive silence in the room would have been flattering under
different circumstances. "This morning when we discovered the—
paint work on the boat and on the schoolhouse door, Young Charles
named someone I knew hadn't done it. I told him I thought Perley
did it. That was the extent of the conversation. I didn't ask him to
avenge me, I didn't act distressed. Later Steve and I agreed to ignore
the incident. If Young Charles took matters into his own hands, it
was without any encouragement from me."

"You *named* my Perley?" Helen's mouth worked. She flung out
her hands, desperately. "You *dared* to blame him!"

Asanath cleared his throat from the hall doorway, and they all
looked at him. "Waal, the girl was a dite foolish to go naming names
to that young devil, but like she says, no adult with the sense God
gave a codfish is planning to take any chances by instigating to
riot." Helen stared at him soddenly. "If I was you, Helen, I'd have
Foss get after the Bennett boy and give the Bennett family a sharp
prod where it'll do the most good, in its importance." He chuckled
softly, "But in the meantime I'd accept the girl's apology and let her
off, this time."

"It's not as simple as that, Asa," Foss said grimly. "There's been
an injustice done, and—"

"I said to tell the *truth*!" Terence turned on Philippa. "Why didn't
you?"

Suze's eyes swam between him and Philippa. "Is this any particular
business of yours, son?" Asanath said.

"Yes, it is," said Terence arrogantly. "All the Campions are wad-
ing around in it clear to their gizzards, so I guess I got a right to be
heard."

"Go ahead and talk, Terence," Vi invited. She laughed. "It ought
to be interesting."

"Terence," Philippa warned him, "you might as well drop a match
into a bundle of oily rags."

"They need a good rousing blaze," said Terence. He put his hands
in his pockets and smiled at them, rocking a little on his toes; he was
his father to the life, suave and leisurely. "You know what **drove**

the Webster kids out of the woods and to school, finally? It wasn't Philippa, here. They were scared out, just as they were scared away from school in the first place. Our Perley did it. Seems he's a great feller for tormenting the little kids half out of their minds."

Helen made an inarticulate sound and tried to rise, but Foss put his hands on her shoulders and held her down. He watched Terence with a contemptuous smile.

Vi said heartily, "What boy worth his salt never pestered small fry? It's part of growing up. So if the Websters run every time somebody makes a loud noise, well, that's no sign of a duck's nest."

"What's it a sign of," Terence asked softly, "when Perley gets somebody to help him ambush a couple of kids no bigger than Ellie? What makes those kids turn white as wax when he comes upon 'em sudden, and they think there's nobody around to save 'em? Pestering, do you call it, Vi?" He laughed. "Why don't you ask Ellie about some of the antics in the schoolyard before Foss took Perley out of the eighth grade, Vi? She'd probably tell you, if she wasn't scared he'd get even with her. He and Peg, that is."

There was a sudden harsh flush across Vi's cheekbones. Helen burst free of Foss' hands and rushed at Terence. "I know what you're getting at!" she cried. "They told me tonight just what was going on." Her fists pounded the air in a frenzy. "They didn't want to! I had to drag it out of them, and it just shows how *decent* those two young ones are compared to *her.* How any woman could *think* up such horrible things! And how'd she get such a holt on you, Terence Campion, let alone the way she's muckled onto those Bennetts?"

"Nobody's got a holt on me," said Terence. "Just happens that yesterday when something came up and Foss wouldn't go, I went. Did they tell you about what happened then, Helen?"

"They told me, all right! Told me the whole miserable story. Perley sat there with the blood running down his face, and said, 'Mama, I only painted that on the boat and the schoolhouse because they were saying those nasty things about me. I was driven to it.' And I could see what he meant, and I didn't blame him, so there!" She confronted Philippa with such a frantic hatred that it was like a physical blow. "Oh, yes, he told me, and Peggy said it was the truth, how you were stirring up a stink about him torturing those sneaky little Webster brats! Even Sky was upset, but he couldn't say why. He's like that. Perley was *driven* to what he did. He was trapped into it, and then they set on him like they were all so virtuous!"

She took a long moaning breath, and Foss said sorrowfully, "You see how it is. It's a rotten mess. The boy did wrong, painting up the boat and all, but the way I see it, he didn't know what else to do. It was self-defense. He was desperate."

"Sure he was!" said Terence. "Desperate because somebody's caught up with him!"

The lamplight that had always seemed so clear and bright had an oppressive glare. Each face was ruthlessly distinct. There was no answering them, she would not debase herself by protesting.

"Of course *I* didn't think Perley did the paint job," Vi said. Of them all, she seemed to be enjoying the situation to the limit. "I thought it was Young Charles, getting even with his uncle for having the schoolma'am up in the clubhouse with no lights on. But I certainly don't blame Perley a bit. We all know Perley doesn't realize his own strength sometimes, but he's no *monster!*" She grinned at Philippa. "Seems like the pot called the kettle black just once too often."

"Waal," Asanath began, "the boy shouldn't a done what he did with that paintbrush. But I can see what happened. Just natural resentment, that's all." He looked benignly at Philippa. "See what you've done, my girl, all by picking up with those young ones and letting them poison your mind against Perley?"

"I see a great deal," said Philippa. Her lips felt unnaturally stiff. It was not a Webster who told me, she thought, it was Sky Campion who came to warn me. . . . But she couldn't implicate him. She knew beyond a doubt that Helen would always sacrifice the healthy child for the sick one, without realizing that her unreasoning, passionate defense of Perley was only setting him more deeply in his ugly ways. Her blind protection would grow more blind, more intense, as his offenses grew more dangerous, and in the end she would weep, and blame everyone else as she was blaming Philippa now.

"No one poisoned my mind against Perley," Philippa said. "I've seen enough, and heard enough, to realize what the picture is. Every child on this island could tell you something about Perley—that is, if they weren't afraid of retaliation in one form or another. Mrs. Campion—" she gazed directly into the frantic, red-rimmed eyes.

"Believe me, I'm not blaming Perley alone for this. I think that in many ways he's unhappy. Maybe he feels slow and inadequate compared to Peggy and Sky. Maybe people have been too impatient with him, have called him stupid too often. He senses his own limitations, and feels trapped by them."

Now her eyes took in Foss, challenging him to face the truth for this once, instead of sliding away from it with a smile and shrug. "It may be that he's heard so much at home about Jude Webster and his wife and children being queer and slow-witted that he thinks he's at last found somebody inferior to him—and that whatever he does to them is perfectly fair, the triumph of the strong over the weak."

Foss's face was blank. She appealed to Asanath. "*You* must understand! Can't anyone be honest here but Terence? Do you realize that by calling me and everyone else a liar, you're condemning that unhappy boy to Heaven knows what?" Her voice got away from her in its desperation. "It doesn't stop at twisting arms and bending fingers and punching children in the stomach! It goes on and on, don't you realize? It could go from killing kittens to—to *killing*."

There was a short silence, and then Helen's voice rose in a wail. "You've just taken a dislike to my Perley, like all the other teachers!"

Philippa felt engulfed in a wave of despair, and the impulse to sickness was so strong that she turned involuntarily toward the door. Terence stopped her. He spoke to her alone, but behind them the others listened. "They're all tarred with the same brush," he said. "There's only one thing I wish. I wish my mother'd had the guts to step out on my father, so I could think I might be somebody else besides a Campion!"

He walked across the silent kitchen and went out. Philippa did not look at the other faces, but went directly to her room.

She turned on her radio; there was a demoniac outburst of old-fashioned jazz, and it shut out any sounds from downstairs. She picked up her hairbrush and began to brush her hair, hard. Sound came squealing and writhing from the radio; it seemed to bounce from wall to wall, and Philippa was caught in the center. But it was better than listening to what was said downstairs. As she brushed her hair, she looked at the room in the lamplight, at the small-flowered paper, the old-fashioned furniture, the bleak engravings and the sentimental prints, the drawn shades, the locked door. She had shut herself into her cave; she would snarl if anyone threatened her privacy.

When her wrist ached from the brushing, she went over to her worktable. She found that she was trembling, and thinking of Steve. Now there was no question of not telling him the things that had happened to her, only of how to tell him. What befell one of them was the concern of both; it was the beginning of their experiences together. I wish it could be a pleasanter beginning, she thought. He must feel that he's taken hold of a thistle. Then the rage she had suppressed downstairs engulfed her. She held to the edge of the table, watching her fingernails go from pink to white, and let the storm sweep past. If she had allowed it to possess her in the kitchen, she could have silenced Helen's hysteria and Vi's malicious gaiety without raising her voice; she would have shown them what a ruthless passion anger could be. But afterward she would have felt weak, chilled, and degraded. She had learned young the penalties of her tempers. Her opposition might be awed or even frightened by her icy intensity, but she was the one who, afterward, suffered as from any excess.

She could sit still no longer. She got up and began to take her clothes out of bureau drawers, with no definite idea except perhaps to rearrange them. She wanted to be out of the house, she wanted to see Steve with such a longing that her throat ached as if she were going to cry. But there was no way to manage it, until tomorrow. If only she could have gone for a walk to tire herself, but there were Asanath and Suze to pass in the kitchen, even if the others had gone.

She had laid all her clothes out on the Lone Star quilt and had begun refolding them meticulously when someone knocked at the door. The jazz program had ended and someone was playing Chopin. She snapped off the silvery flow of the nocturne and went to the door.

Suze stood in the hall. Her hands, swollen-knuckled and always pale as if their continuous immersion in strong suds had soaked away their color, were folded on her stomach. She looked at Philippa with bleached eyes and said, "I want you to leave."

"Tonight?" Philippa asked.

"Tomorrow will do. You can go to your friends. I don't want you here any longer."

She had never before spoken to Philippa with such clarity of intent. "I suppose Mr. Campion wants me to go too?" Philippa said.

"He's gone over to Foss's. But this time it don't matter what Asa wants. I want you to go." There was a faint but authentic emphasis on the *I*. "You're a bad woman."

Philippa said gently, "Because of the things they said tonight? Did you believe them all, Mrs. Campion?"

Suze shrugged. "How Foss runs his house don't concern me. Mebbe you're right about Perley. I shouldn't be surprised. I'm positive 'twas him strangled my nice little cat I had before Tom." She moved her head backward slightly, but she didn't look away from Philippa's face. "No, it's nothing to do with Perley. You're bad because of what you've done to Terence. He never talked in his life the way he did tonight, in front of people. I saw you talking to him in the fishhouse once. What did you say to him?" She didn't wait for an answer. "And I saw you coming down the road with him and that Finnish girl yesterday, like it was all right for them to be together."

"But Mrs. Campion," Philippa began. Suze peered up at her.

"You've changed him. He was bad enough, but since you came into this house, he's worse. Swearing and shouting, and tonight saying he wished he wasn't a Campion."

"That was a cruel thing," Philippa said. "But he was upset."

"It's your fault. It would be better if you got off the island altogether."

Philippa stepped back so Suze could see into the room. "Look, Mrs. Campion. I've started to pack already. I can move out of your house, at least."

Suze nodded, and turned away. At the head of the stairs she said in her usual vague manner, "Good night."

Chapter 36

Philippa stayed on at the Campions' for almost a week more. Asanath insisted, and Suze accepted the terms. Terence had nothing to say, and came in only at mealtime. They lived in the strained good nature of an armed truce. The eventful night was not mentioned.

Neither Foss nor Helen came to the house in that time, but one night Viola and Syd came to play cards. Syd gave Philippa his shy smile and duck of the head, and Viola was hearty in the overpowering way of one who savors her superiority.

There was no talk of a meeting to discuss the charges against her, though she had fully expected it. By the end of the week, the two rooms on the second floor of the Binnacle were ready. She had told only Steve about the affair in the kitchen; his face became drawn and austere as he listened, but when she said it was over and done with, he made no comment, except to say she could move into the Binnacle.

For the others she had simply said that she made too much work for Suze. She knew some other versions of the story would come out with the signs of Perley's beating so obvious, with Vi running up to the Percy house, and the men talking as they baited up. But she planned to say nothing, no matter what hints were dropped or what questions were candidly asked. She refused also Joanna's invitation to come and board with them, saying she wanted to keep a certain impartiality.

"I suppose that's best," Joanna said. "But we'd love to have you, just the same. Nils likes you. He says that you don't talk too much. A remark like that always knocks me into an unnatural silence for at least an hour, and then he asks me if I feel sick." They laughed, and then she added enthusiastically, "Anyway, I've found a *good* stove for you; it's up in the home barn, and the boys will get it down for you."

There was no way, after all, of being strictly impartial. The Binnacle belonged to the Bennett family, and it was Steve's idea that the rooms could be made habitable for her. Joanna and Helmi did most of the cleaning and painting; the children ran errands; the men got the heavy things up the narrow stairs and set up the stove. Sooner or later the entire family was involved.

One afternoon when Philippa walked around to the Binnacle after school, there was a blossoming geranium in a gaudily painted lard can.

"Guess who came scooting down here like a ghost and delivered it," Joanna said. "Lucy Webster. She looked scared to death to be caught out in broad daylight."

Philippa went to the window and touched the sturdy red blossom with her finger. Now that I am so nearby, she thought, I shall go to see her often. The neighborliness of the rest gave her a sense of riches, but the sight of the plant on the window, in vital up-springing silhouette against the eastward view, was like a cry in the room.

When the last of the painting was done and the stove newly blacked, Steve came across the harbor at high tide one morning in his boat, and loaded her luggage aboard from Asanath's wharf. Asanath carried it down from the house; he was as affable as if nothing had happened, and Philippa found it easy to behave in the same way. They were parting, apparently, as the best of friends. Suze stood like a shadow in the doorway; she had stood like that on the day when Philippa arrived for the first time.

The day was gray and northeasterly. It felt cold enough to spit snow, and the foam-streaked seas rolled down between the islands with monotonous regularity. It was an ugly day, a day to remind the islanders too vividly of winter. But when Steve had kissed Philippa and gone, and she stood alone in her rooms, she experienced an exquisite lightening of spirit. This was home. She tried the word experimentally. *Home.* However the days went now, she would come home at night to this precious solitude, and wake in it each morning. Joanna had been there already today and built a fire, leaving a saucepan of lobster chowder on the back of the stove and half a squash pie on the dresser. The red geranium blazed against the bleak prospect in the east. The pale yellow paint on the walls and cupboards gave an impression of faint sunshine. Through the open doorway into the small room tucked under the eaves, there was the mosaic of the Log Cabin quilt on her bed.

When she came back after Thanksgiving, she would bring some of the small personal things that she had always kept with her as her lares and penates; wherever she and Eric were, these things were as much their home as the shell is home to the snail. But for the first time, she felt almost as if she didn't need them. This was her home already. It lacked only Eric.

Steve and Joanna had reminded her of the drawbacks to the place. She would get up in the cold mornings and build her own fire; she would have to get her water from the well and take it upstairs. It didn't matter, she told them, when weighed against the fact that this was her own place.

After she had eaten her dinner that first day, in a sort of solemn rejoicing, she went to the store and bought staples for her cupboards. Mark Bennett, who was usually laconic, said, "Welcome to this side of the harbor." Kathie walked home with her and helped carry the groceries.

"Boy, am I glad you've moved over here," she said fervently. "I'll get out a lot more in the evenings now. I can say I'm coming to see you."

"Then you'd better show up," said Philippa. "I'm not going to uphold you in anything that's against your people's wishes."

Kathie laughed her great wholehearted laugh. "You think I'm stupid enough to try to put anything over on *you*? What do you think I do when I'm out running around, anyway? It's nothing *bad*. I just keep my eyes and ears open and find out things like—" she rolled her eyes around in elaborate unconcern—"like who beat Perley up, for instance. Perley says it was a gang, and everybody believes him, but I know better."

"You're a completely abandoned character, Kathie," said Philippa. She couldn't help laughing; she was happy today, the raw wind whipping across the harbor and stinging her face was part and parcel of her pleasure. Kathie was another portion of it.

"I suppose you think it's immoral or something," said Kathie. "Well, I wasn't sneaking around. I just happened to be there. It was some fight. Charles kept asking Perley what he saw in the clubhouse, and Perley said finally he couldn't see anything, it was dark. Now maybe he'll think twice before tormenting kids or marking people's boats."

Nobody else had mentioned the boat, but Kathie with her usual brash innocence saw no harm in it. Philippa said, "Maybe he will. Anyway, it's all water under the bridge now, Kathie. It's over and done with."

"No," said Kathie. They had reached the Binnacle, and Gregg was coming from the well. Kathie said under her breath, "It's not over and done with. Wait and see." She shouted at Gregg. "Ahoy, Skipper! How's life on the poop deck?"

Gregg gave her a sour look. "You got an awful loud voice for a female child. Shatters a man's eardrums." He set his pails down on his doorstep and hitched up his pants, which as usual were sagging down and under the round of his belly. "Jest keep in mind what the poet says, 'Her voice was ever gentle, low, and sweet, an excellent thing in woman.' "

"If you don't holler," said Kathie, "you get downtrodden. Who can afford to be gentle, low, and sweet these days?"

"You ask your teacher about *that*." Suddenly Gregg remembered his greasy and misshapen felt hat. He took it off and held it against his chest. Philippa smiled and said, "How do you do, Mr. Gregg. I hope you don't find it too unpleasant, having someone upstairs."

"Nothing I can do about it. Place belongs to the Bennetts. They could rent it to Hottentots if they had a mind to."

"I'll try not to make any noise, anyway."

"*You'll* try!" said Kathie with relish, as they went up the stairs. "Wait till he gets his next bottle, and he starts that clarinet a-going!"

Philippa hushed her. Kathie stayed long enough to look at everything, and then, while she was standing by the window, she saw Terence on his way to pick up the mail, and went downstairs with a coltish clatter. Philippa shuddered for Gregg, and wondered how much some cheap rag carpeting would cost.

The afternoon settled into a solitude that was rich and soul-satisfying. Rain began in hard showers against the window, but the fire threw out a live and crackling warmth. She lit her lamp early for the pleasure of its soft yellow light.

She wrote to Eric and told him she had moved in. She prepared schoolwork for the next week. She read a book with her supper, and while she was washing her few dishes, someone came up the stairs; she knew it was Steve and stood there listening, thinking that she had never heard him come up over stairs before. Suddenly the rightness of the scene possessed her, as if all that had gone before were unreality—the meetings in the Campions' kitchen, the escaping into nights that had become so cold. But this seemed as it should be; herself moving in the lamplight, putting dishes away in the cupboard; the sheen of the teakettle on the stove and its singing above the sounds of the fire; the night outside, shut away with its wind and rain beyond the black pane where the red geranium stood doubled by its reflection.

She went over and pulled down the shade just as Steve knocked softly at the door.

Chapter 37

Sunday Philippa awoke with the first of the engines in the harbor, but she did not resent the earliness. She built her fire and got back into bed, and lay listening to the engines, the gulls, the crows. She had no view directly on the harbor, but she didn't care; she could see if Steve went by, she could look eastward, and the sun poured in on her as she ate her breakfast.

When she had finished her breakfast, she took one of her pails and went to the well. From up behind Nils Sorensen's house came the sound of children's voices. Philippa hooked her pail on the pole and lowered it into the well. She had a great sense of leisure and lifted the pail up slowly, leaning over the edge and looking down into the wet darkness. She felt the pole grasped by someone else, and looked around to see Terence.

"Let go," he said. "I'll draw it up."

"Look here, I've got to get used to this," she protested, but she le: go, and he brought the pail up and set it dripping on the well curb "Thank you very much. I didn't know there was a man on the island this morning."

"My boat sprung a leak yesterday. I've got to ground her out and go all over her." He picked up the pail and started toward the Binnacle. "I'd like to see how you're fixed up, if it's all right with you." His tone was brusque and cool, as if he had just become aware of his voice as a means of expression.

"Of course it's all right with me. I can even give you a cup of coffee."

"Thanks." He gave her a slight sideways smile.

While she got out a fresh cup, she considered the incongruity of it. At first Terence had been as insubstantial as a spirit, then she had actively disliked him, and now he sat at her table and she was pouring coffee for him. She poured a cup for herself and sat down opposite him.

208

"I haven't had a chance to tell you," she said, "but I appreciated your coming in on my side that night. It meant a great deal to me. The only thing is, I've regretted getting you in trouble with your parents."

"I've always been in trouble with them," he said indifferently. The morning sun cast a harsh illumination on his lean features. "Ever since I was born, I guess."

"Were you in the service, Terence?"

"I tried to be. I started when I was seventeen, kept going the rounds, Navy, Army, Marines, Coast Guard. They wouldn't have me." He took out his cigarettes. "I was 4-F." He looked at her quickly, showing a ghost of defiance.

Philippa waited, hiding her sympathy. He wouldn't want it.

"One lousy kidney." He scratched a kitchen match with his thumbnail and lit a cigarette.

"I suppose Elmo was a perfect physical specimen."

The lighted match flamed in mid-air; his stare was cold and angry. "What do you know about Elmo?"

"Only that you had a brother, and he died a hero." She wondered if she had gone too far, but she hid her uncertainty. "No one's been gossiping, if that's what you think. Steve mentioned your brother when we were talking about the war. My husband was killed, you knew that."

He nodded, still staring at her defensively. "But why did you say that about Elmo—just then?"

"I was guessing." She drank some coffee. "I have an older sister who was very pretty and was always perfectly charming to everyone. But I never came into a room without knocking something down, and I used to blurt out everything I thought, no matter what. I hated Jenny for years."

"I don't know if I hated Elmo." He looked out of the window again. "He was a pretty nice guy. But I guess I hated them for being so foolish about him. He didn't ask for it. He didn't eat it up. Everybody liked Elmo. I would have, if he hadn't been my brother. He tried to—well, I guess you'd call it take me under his wing, but I wouldn't have anything to do with him. Hurt his feelings."

"I was the same way," said Philippa. "I'd lurk around the outside, scowling, and whenever Jenny tried to drag me in, I'd snarl."

"It was something like that with us. After he was killed, I used to think a lot of things. Sometimes I'd get sore as a boil at him and call him names, as if he'd gone out and got killed on purpose to make my father call him a hero. He should've come back and sooner or later got married, or done something else they wouldn't like, and then maybe I'd have a chance."

"I was lucky," Philippa said. "Nothing happened to Jenny."

He prodded the soil around the geranium with the match. "When I wasn't mad with Elmo, I'd get to remembering the way he looked at me sometimes when I'd tell him to go chase himself. Then I'd think what a crime it was, for him, to go off thinking I hated him. I can't remember acting as if I liked him even halfway."

Philippa put fresh coffee in his cup. "I'll have to bake some coffee cake," she said. "I'm quite a cook." She wished she could think of something to say to Terence, but nothing came to her except the time she had flung Cousin Robert against the door and his sawdust spilled out.

He was watching her warily, and she said, "Regret is the worst thing of all to live with. Rage and grief you can stand, you can get over them, but you can't ever get away from regret."

"I don't know why they didn't have another one, after me. Maybe they decided it wasn't safe to try again." He grinned derisively. "Anyway, I wished for a long time back there, when Elmo was dead and I couldn't get into the service, that there was a kid brother. I had all kinds of queer ideas. I thought I could be as decent to him as Elmo tried to be to me, and of course he'd be different from me, he'd be decent too, and in some crazy way we'd make up for the way it was between me and Elmo. See what I mean?"

"I see." She drank her coffee and looked out at the dark blue water beyond Long Cove, the long wavering ruffles of surf.

"Kathie's like a kid brother, isn't she?" she said finally.

"I guess you'd call it that." He flushed slightly. "You heard things about us around the house. Heard 'em elsewhere too, most likely. Some people have their minds in the gutter."

"I've heard both sides," she said. "There are some who don't believe any harm of you and Kathie, Terence."

"Good Lord," he burst out, "I'm twenty-seven and the kid's fourteen. What the devil do they take me for? Sure, *I'm* a half-wit, but Perley's all right, he's just a boy. Any boy worth his salt—" He mimicked his aunt, and for an instant he looked so comically like her that Philippa laughed aloud.

"I'm sorry, Terence," she said quickly.

"That's all right, I hate the woman." He pushed back his chair. "Thanks for the coffee. I guess I've been doing a lot of gassing around here this morning. Thanks for putting up with it."

"It was good for me." She was lying again, looking at him with the eyes of innocence. "It's the first time in my life I've admitted to anyone how I felt about Jenny."

He leaned down and carefully dropped his dead cigarette butt in the cuff of his rubber boot. "I've never talked about Elmo either."

"Then it's been good for both of us." She walked to the door with him and stood at the head of the stairs while he went down. "Come in again, Terence," she called after him. "Thank you for carrying my water pail."

As he went out, she heard Kathie's surprised shout of greeting, ringing from a distant point like the call of the Valkyries. In a little while she saw them from her window, walking toward the beach. She wondered why the innocent must be forever damned by their sense of guilt, while the truly guilty were always so vain about their virtues. Terence walked lazily, his hands in his pockets, and Kathie strode beside him like the young boy she was meant to be.

Joanna had invited her to Sunday dinner, and afterward she and Steve were going to walk around the Eastern End, where she had never been. She was putting her topcoat on when, inexplicably, she remembered Vinnie. She had thought of the girl often since Steve had told her the story, but never with such a cruel brilliance as now. If whatever had happened to Vinnie hadn't happened, she, Philippa, would not be standing here now with Steve's image as tangible a part of her as her own hands and feet. If Justin had not died at Iwo Jima, Steve would not now be waiting with a strong intimate consciousness of her. Each of them had lived through the long agony of disbelief and then the forced brutal realization of the truth. Each of them loved the lost one still, with a particular tenderness burnished by the years. The first love, the lost love, and yet not lost, she thought; for from the first there remained a portion for this slow sweet second flowering.

Chapter 38

Young Charles had not been near since she had moved in, though he had been busy enough helping to collect her heavier furnishings. She had met him several times then and wondered if his curtness was due to the fact that other people were in the rooms at the time.

After she moved in, she saw him sometimes from her window, and whether he was alone or with Fort, he seemed morose, walking with his head down and his hands in his pockets. She hoped it was not because of her; by all the laws of high-spirited male youth, he should have come to her in the full panoply of his manhood to claim credit for punishing Perley. He was not one of the silent Bennetts, and the sight of the slow-fading bruises on Perley's face should have made him crow.

She met Charles and Fort by the beach one day when she was going home from school. Charles became busy rolling a cigarette, but Fort's broad merry face broke into a grin.

"Well, how is it, perched up there? Gregg been up yet?"

"No, and neither have you." She looked from one to the other. "You'll have to see how it looks. It's a real home now. Everybody's been dropping in."

"Well, sure," Fort began, his light brown eyes crinkling happily. Charles looked up from his cigarette.

"I see you've been entertaining Terence," he said in mock elegance. "Among others."

She lifted her eyebrows, and Fort laughed. "Don't mind him. He's melancholic. You ought to hear the way they cart it to him down at the shore."

"Cart what to him?"

Fort shrugged his shoulders up to his ears and spread out his freckled hands. "Oh, you know the way they do when they find a new way to twit a feller. Talk about that fancy reparty! They got some real flashing wit going around. Sparkles to beat all get-out."

Charles swung his head around and said viciously, "Oh, go fry—"

He threw down his cigarette and went down the beach. Philippa looked after him regretfully.

"I'll fetch him up some night," Fort said. "Mebbe you can cheer him up." His voice grew sober. "He'll get over it sometime, but I know why the girls over at Brigport don't look like anything to him any more. They're kind of raw, kind of like green apples, if you know what I mean. Well, so is he, but he can't see it."

"What makes you so wise, Fort?" she asked.

His grin seemed to shatter his face into twinkling fragments. "Oh, I learned young the girls warn't ever going to look at me, so I better not waste my heart looking at them."

" 'Waste my heart,' " Philippa laughed. "Fort, you're a philosopher and a poet."

"You say that real pretty, ma'am," said Fort. "Thank you kindly." They both looked down at Charles, a solitary dark figure at the edge of the water, kicking beach rocks overboard. "I'll bring Gloomy Gus up real soon."

"Do that," said Philippa. "We'll make a party out of it." She called good-by to Charles, but he didn't look around.

But Charles came alone, and earlier than she had expected, just as she got home from school one blustery afternoon. He walked into the kitchen and stood against the door.

"Sit down, Charles," she said. "It's nice to see you."

"Haven't got time." He stared at her broodingly, then blurted out, "What in Old Harry did you have to stop off in the clubhouse for, that night?"

She was measuring coffee, and she put the spoon down and looked at him. "What business is it of yours, Charles?" she asked quietly. "It was nothing in the first place, and it's gone by long since."

"You think so?" His laugh was exaggeratedly sinister. It would have been funny if she hadn't been so angry with him. She went back to measuring coffee. Suddenly Charles came forward and knocked the spoon out of her hand.

He shouted at her, "Don't you care what they're saying? And now you're living up here alone, that just makes it worse! How can you stand there and not turn a hair? Vi and Helen are out for your

213

scalp, and they're dirty. They won't stop at anything till they get everybody wondering if there isn't some fire under all that smoke. And Asa won't call 'em off. He could, but he won't till he gets tired of listening to 'em."

"I know all that, Charles," she said. "And it's not a pleasant prospect, but I don't think they can hurt me very much. I'm thinking about you at the moment."

"*Me?*" He flushed.

"I'm not in the habit of discussing my conduct with anyone. But because you were one of my first friends here, I'll make an exception and ask you a question: Do *you* believe Perley had any good reason to paint what he did on the boat and the door?" He stared at her almost in horror, and then his blush deepened. He opened his hand and studied his palm. When he looked up again, his eyes were shiny, as if they were wet.

"I was mad," he said harshly. "You giving that moron a chance to get something on you."

"But he didn't get something on me," she argued. "You've done me an injustice, Charles. You could at least have given me the benefit of the doubt."

"I never really thought anything! I just—"

"You just thought *maybe*. And the *maybe* was enough. I think Perley got a little extra on the beating because you were so mad at me."

"I'm not sorry I mohaggled him," he said defiantly. "He had it coming to him." Then he smiled at her, tentative and appealing. " 'Course it made you a lot of trouble. I guess I've been a fool. Think there's any hope for me?"

"Well, you're still a growing boy. I'd say you had quite a future ahead of you."

"Go ahead, cart it to me." But his smile became a grin, charmingly vain once more.

Charles and Fort came up the next evening, just after Steve had arrived. Fort had his fiddle case under his arm. "Thought we might have some music, if you're agreeable," he said.

Charles was aloof again, as if he hadn't forgiven her and Steve. He sat forward, his elbows on his knees, and stared at the floor as Fort tuned his fiddle. Philippa watched him covertly while she knitted on Eric's sweater.

Fort began to play, and "The White Cockade" was brave in the room. If Gregg had his fifth, the time-keeping foot couldn't bother him. Steve was trotting his foot too, lightly, and one of Charles's began to move, jerkily, as if it were entirely separate from his mood. Fort went from "The White Cockade" to "My Love Is But a Lassie Yet." He loved to play; it was in his face and the way he pressed his cheek to the smooth tawny wood and curved his hand about the neck. The fiddle was cheap and old, but the tones were true.

Fort clowning on the beach as he scrubbed out hogsheads that had held rotten bait was one person; Fort with his cheek to the fiddle and the scroll turning back from his big hand, the bow dancing staccato in the other, was someone else.

There were tunes that Philippa didn't know, and still he went on, as if he were caught in a mesh of his own weaving. Sometimes Philippa and Steve smiled at each other faintly across the room. Then she caught herself glancing quickly at Charles to see if he had noticed, but she couldn't tell.

Fort stopped at the end of a reel to adjust a string. Steve held out his cigarettes to him, but Fort shook his head and went on playing. Now it was something quiet, as simple as Brahms' "Lullaby" and with much the same quality. His eyes were half shut, and his freckled face took on a peaceful maturity. By middle age, Philippa thought, Fort would be a rare person. Now he veiled his sensitivity with unsubtle humor, but it showed in spite of himself when he played.

Suddenly he took the fiddle from under his chin and blinked around at the others like someone waking good-humoredly from sleep. "I'll have that cigarette now," he said.

Steve handed it to him silently. Charles sat back in his chair, sprawling his legs before him; somewhere during the playing he had relinquished his antagonism for the time being. "You and Cynthy make a real purty pair, Fort," he said. "Of course, if you were a singer, you'd be drier than a cork leg by now."

"I am, bub," Fort wheezed in suitably parched tones.

"Oh, I can take a hint," said Philippa. "He deserves champagne, but coffee will have to do." She pushed the teakettle forward on the stove. At the same time there was a clatter in the entry downstairs, thumpings and incoherent mutterings.

"Sounds like somebody was trying to herd an elephant upstairs," said Fort. "Where would anybody get an elephant, this time of night?"

"It's probably one of Gregg's," said Steve. He went across to the door and put his ear to the crack. "Or one of Syd's, gone astray," suggested Charles.

Gregg's voice came in squealing outrage through the door. "I'm a-comin' up there! Anybody makes music in this house, a-poundin' them big hummels of feet right over my bed so the plaster's comin' down like snow, I got a right to make music too!"

"Open the door, Steve," Philippa said. "Tell him to come up."

"He isn't waiting, he's on his way," said Steve wryly. He opened the door and shone his flashlight down the stairs. "Come on up, Gregg."

There were frantic scrambling sounds, and Gregg's panting. The boys leaned past Steve and urged Gregg on. "I bet you can hear this all over the island," Fort said enthusiastically. "They'll think we're having one of those Roman debacles."

In the beam of the flashlight, Philippa saw Gregg's red, sweat-shining face and the whites of his eyes rolled wildly toward her. He had his clarinet in his hand. Finally he reached the top step. "Now don't tell me I'm drunk!" he commanded. "I got no more rum in me than—than—"

"Than an old sponge dropped in a barrel of rum," said Charles. "Hurray for Gregg!"

Gregg, wiping his wet face on his arm, grinned. He staggered only slightly before he reached a chair. He lifted the clarinet to his mouth at once, and his blue eyes turned toward Fort.

Fort nodded. Gregg began to play something that sounded like Mozart to Philippa, and Fort joined in. She could hardly believe it was Mozart, played in this island kitchen by a quarrelsome little man in clothes that smelled of liquor and bait, and followed with such fidelity by a boy with no education, who could not read music; but the indefinable stamp was there, a nagging familiarity, and if she shut her eyes, she could almost catch it. . . . Shouldn't the violin have been a flute . . . ? Gregg had taught Fort this part, obviously. It was exciting and incredible. It ended too soon; Gregg put down his clarinet in a gust of foolish laughter, and said, "Where's 'at coffee?"

"I'll have it ready in just a moment," she said quickly. "Keep on playing." She thought suddenly, If only Justin were here! She looked around quickly, as if she had said it aloud. Charles was fascinated, as lost in the moment as a child. Steve's face was calm and distant. She wondered if he had listened to such music with Vinnie.

They had no more music after the coffee. As Gregg sobered slightly, he lost his good nature and became sad. The others had been talking around the table, but Gregg's depression cast a silence on them. Fort laughed less and kept looking nervously at Gregg. Charles stared into his coffee cup. Gregg muttered to himself at intervals; all at once he reared back in his chair and stared across the kitchen into the shadows of Philippa's room.

"Is my boy in there?" he asked loudly.

"You got no boy, Gregg," Charles said uneasily. Gregg ignored him.

"Tell him to come out," he said, lurching to his feet and still staring at the door.

"There's no one in there," Philippa told him kindly. "Really there isn't. Show him, Steve."

Steve helped him to the door of the little room and flashed the light around. Gregg grabbed it from him and flashed it around again. Turning back to the others, he looked incredulous and sad.

"Where is he?" he asked faintly. "I just saw him. Standing there in the doorway, all a-grin." He wiped his hand across his eyes and then pulled away from Steve toward the door. "I better git down below," he muttered. "No place for me here."

"Wait up, man," Steve said. "I'll help you. If you fetch up with a bang at the foot of the stairs, how's the schoolma'am going to lug her wood and water over you?" He put his long arm firmly around Gregg's pudgy middle, and started down the stairs with him. Philippa held the light and watched their descent. She felt chilled and tired; Gregg's change had shattered their happy mood. She rested her head against the door frame, and stood there even after Gregg and Steve had gone out. The cold night air scented with rockweed blew up the stairs toward her.

"I thought Gregg always saw cats when he was polluted," Fort said in a subdued tone.

"I never knew he had a boy," Charles answered.

When Steve came upstairs, she thought he seemed tired too. He refused more coffee and stood leaning against the dresser, smoking. He too had no answer for Gregg's strange behavior except, "He's an old man, a drunk. Maybe he had a boy once, I don't know." Philippa wished urgently that the boys would go. As if he sensed it, Fort put his fiddle away, but Charles got up and went over to the stove. He propped one foot on the stove hearth and rested his folded arms across his knee.

"I guess this is kind of an anticlimax, after Gregg," he began rather diffidently. "But somebody's fooling around my traps who has no business to. Some have been hauled and dumped with the doors left open; some are gone clip and clean, I can't find them at all."

"Well." Steve watched him through smoke. "That looks like a fine way to spend a Saturday, messing up another man's gear. Why didn't you say something before? You mean you and Nils kept that under your bonnets all day?"

"I wanted to think about it awhile. Try to figure out what to do. But I can't figure anything." Charles scowled. "Must be why Foss and his ocean pearl went out at the crack of dawn today. We met 'em coming home when we were on the way out."

Philippa poured fresh coffee for herself and held the cup in both cold hands.

"I had a hundred traps set out," Charles went on. "Half of 'em are gone. That's three hundred and fifty dollars just disappeared, and nothing but crabs and sea urchins in the rest. And Foss waved at us real cordial when he went past."

"What does Nils say?" Steve asked.

"We were hauling together so he couldn't tell me it was all in my head. I've had him tell me my traps got drowned in deep water because I had short warps on 'em. Well, he didn't tell me anything like that today. And he had to admit it was most likely Perley, because Foss cornered him at the shore the other day and claimed I had roughed up Perley. He also had to admit Foss knew what Perley was doing, because Perley goes with him this time of year, same as I do with you or Nils, and Fort with his old man. After he admitted all that, he chewed his lip and did some plain and fancy thinking."

"Then I suppose he said, 'Let's go and cut off every last trap of theirs,'" said Steve.

Charles grinned. "Yeah. I had my sheath knife all ready and he

218

said, 'Put that away, boy. The family will set you up with some new gear if you've got nothing saved. We're not starting any lobster war.'" Charles shrugged. "I told him it was already started, but you know how he is. I suppose you think he's right." He pulled his brows together aggressively.

"I know he's right," said Steve. "Listen, I remember when your father had *his* knife ready, and called your grandfather soft as warm wax for not wanting a lobster war. Now we've got some sense on us along with our gray hairs. A lobster war could clean out everybody on this place as fast as a shooting war could do. No man in his right mind wants trouble in these waters."

"Foss must be out of his, then," said Charles.

"I admit I never thought Foss would get mixed up in anything like this. I thought he was too cautious. Well, he's safe enough. You and Nils didn't *see* anything." Steve glanced over at Philippa. "Got some more coffee there?" As she refilled his cup, he went on talking to Charles. Fort sat by the table, his red hair coppery bright in the lamplight, staring down seriously at the pattern of the tablecloth.

"Maybe he figured it would be a good lesson for you. Teach you to mind your own business. Foss knows your family won't let you get back at him, so he feels safe with his revenge. I doubt if you lose any more traps. So just figure you had your whack at Perley and he had his whack at you and forget it."

"Fine speech." Charles was sarcastic. "You ought to run for Congress. Look, if I ever get out to haul without you or Nils, I'm going to get even with those two."

"Nobody ever gets even in a lobster war," Steve said somberly. "It might turn out that a warden will close the grounds and then none of us will tend any pots. The Campions don't want that any more than we do; they've made money since they came here, and they want to make some more. So if you just stop breathing so hard and calm down, this will fade out and be forgotten and no real harm done."

Charles slapped his own chest. "Look, *I'm* out three hundred and fifty bucks in trap stuff and all the lobsters I lost besides! I've got something coming to *me!*"

"Sure." Steve nodded imperturbably. "A job on the mainland. Or you can go into the Navy. You go out and touch their traps and you'll wind up pushed right out of lobstering and off the island. Your father won't fit you out with new traps forever."

He carried his cup to the table and put cream and sugar into it. Charles said angrily, "No use talking to these Bennetts, they think they know so much. They're so scared of something happening to their island paradise anybody could spit in their faces and they wouldn't fight back! It might cost money, it might bring the warden down!"

"Charles, have some fresh coffee," Philippa said. Her words sounded inane to her. She didn't blame him for the curt sideways look.

"No, thanks. I guess I'll go home. Been a nice evening." He took his cap and jacket from the hook by the door. Fort got up.

"Thanks for the coffee and cake, Mis' Marshall. I hope you didn't mind Cynthy's squawks and squeaks too much."

"Cynthy sang like a bird. I've never had a private concert in my life. I'm greatly honored."

"By gorry, you say that nice, now." Charles was going down the stairs and Fort called, "Hey, wait up!"

Chapter 39

After the sound of them had died away, Steve still stood by the table, stirring his coffee. He looked meditative and aloof. Philippa felt loneliness like a physical chill. Now she was out of his sphere; certainly in this affair she was an outsider, yet an outsider who had become irretrievably enmeshed in their troubles. She took a step toward him and said sharply, "Don't tell me I'm not responsible for all *this*."

He gave her a severe, incisive glance. "Don't be a chowderhead. You're not half as important as you think you are."

"Oh, I see," she said distantly. She turned back to the stove and put an unnecessary piece of wood on the fire.

"I wondered when you were going to start acting like a woman in love," Steve said.

"How is a woman in love supposed to act?" she asked without expression, gazing at the stove lifter in her hand.

"Touchy," said Steve. He came up behind her and put his arms around her. She stood there stiffly. She thought almost with longing of the sheltered uneventful life she had led with Eric before they came to Maine. There might have been no moments of sweet and unexpected passion, but neither had there been anything like this; she felt angry, confused, and tired all at once. I should never have come here, she thought.

"I'm sorry I bit you," Steve murmured. "But you deserved it. If you're going to be an island woman, you'll have to stop thinking everything that happens is personal."

"I don't know if I want to be an island woman."

Steve said evenly, "That's right. You've never told me you'd marry me." He didn't take his arms away, his breath was warm against her ear. "Tell me now," he said. "Let's be engaged." His arms tightened around her waist, and gently he touched the side of her ear with his teeth.

Why can't he be bad-tempered this once? she asked herself helplessly. She knew she was going to be petty and waspish. She was dismayed, but not enough to put a stop on her tongue. The mood had been common enough with her when she was young, and she had taken a perverse satisfaction in it. She knew now it was a hunger to provoke violence, as a sort of catharsis for the stress of the moment. If Steve refused to admit there was stress, after what they had listened to tonight, he deserved to see the worst of her.

"What about the island?" she asked in a constricted voice. "What about all these troublesome things?"

"The island will take care of itself," Steve answered. "It always has. Never mind that, now. Think of us. Look, we could have one of the Eastern End houses for the best seasons and move back to the harbor in the winters."

"What about Vinnie?" The name crackled in the room like the sudden blaze of a match. She turned in his arms to look squarely at him. "You told me once you didn't know if she was alive or dead. How can you talk about marriage when you're not sure about her?"

He said equably, "I don't know in black and white whether she's dead or alive. But I've had a feeling for a long time that she's—

well—" He took his hands from Philippa's waist and put them in his pockets. "She's been blown out like a lamp or like one of those candles she was so crazy about. She just *isn't.*"

"But suppose you're wrong—suppose that occurred to you just because I came along. It's always easier to focus on something tangible. Even *I* know that dreams can die for lack of nourishment. Then suppose that after we're married a letter comes one day. Or Vinnie herself steps off the mail boat. It's happened to other people. Why not to you?"

She was rewarded by the almost inimical contraction of his pupils. "What's possessed you, Philippa? You've never trotted Vinnie out before. Leave the poor kid in peace, and tell me what's really on your mind."

"I've just told you," she said airily. She moved away from him, loathing herself and wishing he would go.

"Is that all you intend to say?" he asked.

"There's nothing else." She leaned over the lamp and adjusted the wick. She felt the force of his bewilderment and his losing struggle against anger filling the room.

"I guess you're right. There isn't anything more." He reached for his windbreaker and put it on, and picked up his cap. He came toward her and stood waiting. She didn't look at him. There was a peculiar sensation in her lips. They wanted to tremble. "If you don't want to marry me," he said, "why can't you say so? You don't have to tell me the reasons for it. You don't have to make up a story for yourself around Vinnie."

"It's not a story. I haven't made it up." Her voice rose a little. Suddenly she thought in the wild relief of self-pity, It's the truth; I've never really been sure that it's over between him and Vinnie, whether she's dead or alive. "If she should all at once appear—"

"I'm going to get a divorce, Phil, just in case," he said patiently.

She shrugged. "What's a divorce? Would it end what you feel in your heart for her? No, if she should come and we were married, everything you felt for her back there in San Francisco would come alive again—because it's never really been dead. I can't take a chance on that, Steve."

His skin had an odd pallor in the lamplight. "What about Justin?" he asked in a low voice. "I'm taking a chance on *him.*"

"We know Justin won't be back," she said, looking at him steadily. It was like a nightmare, but there was no awakening from it. She had to go on talking. "I fought this at the first, Steve, and then I gave in because I thought it might be something real and wonderful. But I'm seeing the facts now. I've been an unqualified failure all around on this island, and tonight I know that I can't compete with Vinnie, whether she's alive or a memory."

She thought in surprise, He looks actually ill. There was a fine film of sweat on his forehead. He was staring at her as if he, too, realized the nightmare and their helpless participation in it.

"Philippa—" He half whispered it.

She wanted to say to him, Steve, please go. I have to be alone to see things clear and rest my bruises. She knew that if she did say it, it would be all he needed; but this was part of the familiar mood, that she could be weeping and desolate inside and still show an arrogant indifference.

"Good night," he said finally. The words dropped into the quiet with a cold separateness. He waited for a moment more and then went to the door. A passionate wish to stop him sprang up wildly in her; when he paused at the door, it might very well seize control and spin her toward him. She stared past the lamp at the window and waited in a lightheaded expectancy to be overpowered.

He didn't pause at the door. It closed gently behind him and he went down the stairs. She turned and gazed at the door with a burning sensation in her face and eyes; she could hardly believe he had gone.

She lay awake for hours, dry-eyed and feverish; she tried to cry, but she could not. She heard the wash of water on the harbor shore, and the far-off rote, and saw the first gray light come around the edges of the shade. There was no quick, slick solution for the consequences of her behavior. A mature woman has no excuses. She could hear Justin saying it, in a level, impersonal voice. Human weakness he could condone, but not human pettiness. Even Justin had never understood what caused these moods in her. It was not the sort of thing one explains easily. She knew there had to be a certain emotional climate, and a particular conjunction of events like the meeting of tide and wind that made the violent rip tide outside the harbor mouth.

She slept finally, all through the early morning departure of the boats, and awoke just in time to get ready for school. As she walked through the village, for the first time she saw the winter look of the island; the houses seemed to huddle in dun-colored loneliness at the edge of the harbor, and the wind sliced through her clothing and into her flesh. She thought with longing of the snug shell of her rooms; she would have liked to remain there immobile all day, neither stirring nor thinking. Everything was finished between her and Steve, she was sure of it. It was her doing. The thing was preposterous, but it had happened. In time the ache would fade to dullness and perhaps disappear altogether, unless, she thought wryly, she felt it in certain weather, like an old scar: whenever she saw a sparkle like diamonds overlaying a blue sea, or tried to pick out Andromeda with a night wind blowing around her, or whenever she smelled a freshly ironed shirt.

The next few days went by as if nothing had happened, except that she saw Steve only at distances. From her kitchen window she might see him in the road; as she walked from school, she might see him at his mooring. Once when she went out to the well, she saw him going home with two pails of water. Linnea bobbed behind him like a puppy. She saw Philippa and called "Hi!" in her clear round voice, and Philippa answered, but Steve didn't turn.

In school there was peace. Sky was absorbed with his work, as if Philippa had never seen him sick and weeping behind a pile of traps, and Peggy went through her classes with a haughty indifference. Outside, everything looked the same. But it seemed to Philippa that there was a queer, invisible distortion, as if under their surface all things had changed their shapes. She had experienced the phenomenon before, in a much stronger degree, when Justin died.

She made some calls on parents, first Mrs. Percy and then Helmi Bennett. She tried the Webster door, but no one answered. People called on her; Joanna came upstairs for coffee and a chat. Ralph and Rob visited her early one evening. The young Percys and Ellie Goward came up and looked at everything with the frank, scientific interest of clerks making inventories. Helmi Bennett sent her a loaf of Finnish coffee bread. Philippa wondered when they would all realize that Steve was no longer coming to see her; perhaps they knew already, but they wouldn't mention it to her, of course. No doubt it had taken precedence over the Websters and Young Charles's traps and Perley's beating.

One afternoon as she came home from school, she saw Foss Campion's boat tied up at the head of the long wharf. It had been only a few weeks since he'd overhauled and repainted her. Now he stood on the wharf with Asanath and Randall Percy. Syd Goward sat on a lobster crate a little distance from them, his back against a pile of traps. He smiled vacantly into the pale warmth of the sun. There was no one else on the beach except Jude Webster, who was piling the last of his new traps onto his dory to take out and load on his boat. There had been no really bad weather since he'd started fishing his new string, and the children were coming to school with new shoes and more substantial clothing.

At least she could feel a twinge of satisfaction about that, she thought, but felt nothing. As she passed the men on the wharf, she said pleasantly, "Good afternoon."

Asanath nodded. "Afternoon, Philippa." Randall's round face, lacking the comic ease of his sons', puckered in his habitual grin. Foss looked down at the ground.

After she had gone by, Foss spoke up distinctly. "I lay it all to her. Neither father nor mother can hold a hand over their kids when there's one like her loose in the neighborhood."

The words stopped her as effectively as a hand pulling her around. For a second she considered going on; here was something surely on which she could close a door. But for the first time in three days, she felt a violent response. She walked back to the men. Randall Percy was blushing and kicking at the stones, and Asanath watched her speculatively, but she kept her eyes on Foss.

"Was that remark intended for me, by any chance?" she asked pleasantly.

"If the shoe fits, wear it." Foss spat on the stones.

"Hey, listen, Foss," Randall said urgently. He pulled out a bandanna and mopped his freckled forehead.

"What is it that you lay to me?" Philippa asked.

Foss nodded his head toward his boat. "You know as well as I do. Warn't it planned up in your place to begin with?" His light eyes glinted in the shade of his duck-billed cap.

She looked at Asanath. "Will you please explain, Mr. Campion?"

"Why, certainly," Asanath said. "Seems that when Foss here just got out of the harbor a little ways this morning, his engine died and he had to h'ist a distress signal. Nils Sorensen come by and towed him in." He smiled amiably at Philippa. "Well, when Foss here got to looking at his engine real close, it turns out that somebody'd gone and dropped a hunk of lead down his exhaust pipe last night."

"What does that do?" Philippa asked.

Foss spat again, and Randall fussed with his pipe.

"*Do?*" said Asanath. "Waal, my girl, when the engine gits to running, the lead melts, and it gets around in the engine and raises partic'lar hell. In some cases, it costs a lot of money to fix an engine up afterward. It *always* costs a man more time than he'd ought to take from his pots this time of year." He smiled again. "So you see, it's a real unkind prank."

"And I'm supposed to be responsible for that." Philippa smiled too.

Randall, obviously embarrassed by the talk, started to move away, toward Syd, and Foss called after him, "I got ten new pots needing to be headed, Randall. Why don't you go over in my shop and make a start on 'em?"

Randall looked around, blinking. "Why, sure, Foss," he said eagerly. "Sure!'" He hurried across the beach at an awkward trot. Foss turned back to Philippa, hostile again.

"You've made a serious accusation," she said quietly. "Are you able to back it up?"

"As able as you are to back up the yarns you told about the kids."

"You're very sure of your facts, aren't you? Even without proof, you're sure I put foul ideas in people's heads, and stir them up so they'll go out and drop lead in other people's exhaust pipes."

"I'm damn' sure of it. There was never any such actions before you came here. My wife's boy getting beat up in a dirty fight, and then this."

She looked at him incredulously. He knew even as he challenged her that Perley had damaged Young Charles's gear, but perhaps he felt that was justified by the beating.

"Look, Mr. Campion," she said gently, "I had nothing to do with the beating, and I had nothing to do with this. I admit I've been disturbed by Perley's behavior, because it affects all the other chil-

226

dren on the island. And I've been angry—and still am—because you and Perley's mother choose to ignore the fact that the boy's heading in the wrong direction and might some day be in terrible trouble. Believe it or not, I have as much concern for Perley's problems as for any of the other children's."

Foss' mouth twisted. "I've heard fine words before."

"And you're not convinced, but at least I've had my say."

"It's a free country," said Foss. He jerked his head backward in an effort to cut himself free of her, and jumped down into the cockpit of his boat.

"Foss is all haired up about this," Asanath explained kindly. "Can't blame him none. It was a dirty thing to do to a man. I couldn't do it to my worst enemy." He shook his head. "It may have ruined his engine for good."

"I suppose that *is* more of a tragedy than ruining a boy for good," Philippa said. She walked past Syd Goward, whose small pinched face was as peaceful as a sleeping child's. He stirred and looked up at her, squinting because she stood between him and the sun.

"Yonder's a hard crew," he murmured. "You get 'em stirred up, it's worse'n running afoul of a hornet's nest."

"I'll manage," Philippa said. He shut his eyes again, and she smiled and went on. From start to finish, the whole encounter had exhilarated rather than upset her. After the stagnation of a week she felt at least alive again. The accusation was ridiculous, she had no reason to brood. She resisted scrupulously the premise that whatever happened to Foss he deserved, although there was no possibility of there being anyone else but Young Charles to blame. Perhaps this was the end of the episode, if he felt he'd paid them back for the traps.

But to think *I* put it into his head! she thought, ready to laugh at the incongruity of it. Wait until I tell Steve!

Then she remembered, and her smile grew set on her face.

She went up the stairs to her own kitchen, and the darkness of the passage enclosed her like nightfall. If only it *were* nightfall, she thought tiredly. She came into the kitchen, aching in the final collapse of her defenses and yet grateful for the chance to let them collapse in secrecy. In the morning she would build them back again.

Kathie sprang up from a chair by the table, laughing. She had

Philippa's field glasses in her hand. "What made Foss look so ugly?" she cried. "You said something that gave him an awful sour stomach!"

Philippa looked at the glasses. For once she could think of nothing to say. She put her books on the dresser and looked around the room in a camouflage of absent-mindedness, as if Kathie had interrupted some important mental process. Then she saw Rue sitting on the couch, her arms wrapped tightly around her knees, staring at her with a timid intensity.

"Hello, Rue," Philippa said. "I wondered when you were coming to call."

"We stopped on our way home from school. Is it all right?"

"Of course it is." Now she could deal with Kathie, but the moment of blankness had left an alarming memory. "Kathie, watching with glasses is as bad as eavesdropping. It's a wonder you don't learn lip reading. Then you'd be all set."

Kathie grinned. "Gosh, why don't I?" She put the glasses back on the shelf beside the radio. "I wasn't gawking on purpose. We were just waiting for you, and then I saw you coming and I wanted to see how you looked in the glasses. You looked just like a movie star. You have an awful good walk, did you know it?"

"Flattery will get you nowhere," said Philippa. "I'll make some cocoa."

Rue said nervously, "I can't stay."

"You can stay fifteen minutes," Kathie told her with an exasperating assurance that precluded all argument. Rue sat down again. There was a faint softening of added weight around her face, and she wore a skirt and blouse that made her look closer to her age. Her straight fair hair was tied back with a ribbon instead of bait-bag twine. She had not lost, and would not lose, the awareness that gave all her movements the subtle high-strung grace of something wild; and if she became as lost as her mother was, this particular quality would turn febrile and destructive.

Kathie was talking. "So I said," she went on, " 'You can't tell me anybody's bothered Young Charles's gear because he would've gone out and cut off every one of *theirs* by this time. He's a real heller. He doesn't give a damn.' "

"Kathie," Philippa said mechanically. Kathie grinned.

"I love the geranium your mother brought down," Philippa said to Rue. "I went up to thank her the other day, but she wasn't home."

There was a shadowy line between Rue's brows. "Maybe she was asleep. She doesn't go out anywhere."

"She *must* have been asleep," Philippa agreed. She wished she hadn't mentioned Mrs. Webster. Her sense of oppression deepened. Just how much had she done for Rue after all? Perhaps Rue was doomed by her own sensitivity; in five years she could be burned out, a gaunt fey eccentric tending her mother in the frightened seclusion the woman had already built around them.

Kathie rattled on while they drank their cocoa, her bright brash voice clattering against Philippa's ears. Rue watched with noncommittal amber eyes over the rim of her cup; she followed Kathie's every move as if she couldn't look away. If Rue could catch some of Kathie's egotism, now. . . . But Philippa was too tired to go further with the thought. The week had been one enormous exertion, half as long as eternity. She wished the girls would go and leave her alone; or that she herself could go. If the mail boat were at the wharf this instant, she thought, I would go aboard it. It was a brave and stimulating idea, even though she knew that if the boat *were* there, actually, she would not go aboard; there was only a half week left of school before the Thanksgiving vacation.

Rue was ready to leave, and she stood by the door. "Thank you very much, Mrs. Marshall. I have to go home now."

"Well, I do too." Kathie stood up and stretched. Her cowboy belt slipped down an inch from her lean middle. She hitched it up again. "I'm supposed to keep store this afternoon. Mark's going to throw me out, come the first snowstorm, if I don't tend to my chores better." She chuckled, and thumped down the stairs. Rue waited for an instant. Then, with a darting, furtive gesture, she reached into her coat pocket and brought out a wad of papers.

"Here's some things I wrote," she whispered huskily. "I thought maybe you'd see if they were all right." She pushed the papers into Philippa's hand and then ran down the stairs.

Philippa opened the package and looked at the first paper. It was a poem, called "The Gray Wind." The first line read, "There is a wind that comes over the sea."

Tears came into Philippa's eyes. She could not have explained them; she was not a sentimentalist. But it was really more than she deserved for her frailties, to have a handful of poems thrust at her at the end of the day.

She sat down at the table and began to read them.

Chapter 40

The last day of school before Thanksgiving was mild and still, with a smoky haze along the horizon. The sun came through the filmy overcast with a pale warmth. School closed at noon, and Philippa left on the *Ella Vye*. She expected to be the only passenger, and she was surprised to see Nils Sorensen swing aboard with a small canvas zipper bag in his hand.

Joanna, kneeling on the edge of the wharf to talk to Philippa, at the *Ella's* stern, seemed to be trying not to laugh. She moved her head cautiously toward Perley, who lounged against a hogshead a little apart from the others on the wharf. "He's been watching Nils," she whispered. "Nils is going in to see about an infected finger, and he'll be out tomorrow morning on the lobster smack, but before night somebody will be saying he's gone to get the rest of the Bennetts to come home and start fighting. As soon as Perley's sure that Nils really went off on the boat today, he'll be around the harbor in a flash . . . if you can imagine Perley moving like a flash."

Philippa smiled with her face, and wondered if Steve was staying out of the harbor purposely until she should be gone. Some of the other men had already come in from hauling. Young Charles gave her a dozen lobsters in a cardboard carton; he held her hand, regardless of the others watching, and said huskily, "Don't forget to come back."

"I shan't." She worked her hand gently free. Her whole body strained backward without moving outwardly, listening and watching for Steve. There was still a chance for him to come around the point. She tried to concentrate on the others, on Kathie wigwagging from up on the wharf, on Mark Bennett pegging lobsters on the big floatlike car, on what Joanna was saying. The Webster children stood in a little cluster apart from the rest. She must say a special good-by to them, even though it was only for a few days.

When it was all said, Steve still hadn't come. The Diesel engines were starting up. Philippa turned her back on the wharf and pretended to see if her suitcase was securely fastened. The voices, the gulls, the engine sounds, all blurred into a steady din in her ears, and when she looked once more at the harbor mouth, the sun burned in her eyes. She was despairing and afraid, not so much because Steve hadn't come, but because of the depth of her disappointment.

Then she settled herself on the bench across the stern, looking as if she expected to enjoy her trip, and waved to the people on the wharf across the widening and bubbling strip of water.

She didn't see Steve's boat between Bennett's and Brigport. Two men came aboard at the bigger island, one obviously a salesman and the other a fisherman dressed in his shore clothes. They went up into the pilothouse where Nils and the captain were. There were no other women to share the sunny solitude of the stern, and so Philippa came without interruption to what seemed a necessary and logical premise; if she had not been so miserable, she would have congratulated herself on her clear thinking.

He never really loved me, she thought. He was lonely, and he thought I was lonely too. He tried to make something out of nothing, but he must know by now that it would never do for him. She looked back across the pale satiny sea to the mauve haze that veiled the island from her, and the facts moved on irrevocably. . . . Vinnie is the one, she thought. I never had a chance.

They were within clear view of the mainland, and the hills were changing color against the sky, when Nils came astern and sat down beside her on the bench. He gave her his slow warm smile and said, "I thought I'd better show up before we reach the breakwater. Jo told me to be sure to talk to you on the trip."

"That's not fair," she protested. "Why should you have to bother with me instead of staying with the men?" Joanna was sorry for her, she thought; Joanna had guessed at the break between her and Steve.

"It's no bother," Nils was saying. He held out his cigarettes to her and lit one for himself. Watching him, she thought how much she liked his square-cut ruddy face and thoughtful dark blue eyes. In his fairness he all but shone among the dark Bennetts. "I wish I'd come astern sooner," he said. "It was pretty tough in the pilothouse, hemmed in between Link's cigar and that rope salesman who got on at Brigport. He had a lot of jokes—real hot stuff, he kept telling us—and he had to tell each one twice, because Theron Pierce is deaf as a haddock."

"Were they funny jokes?" Philippa asked.

He gazed at the match solemnly before he threw it overboard. "No," he said. Then he looked directly at her. "Is Steve coming in for you Sunday?"

She answered too quickly, "No, I'll be on the *Ella*, Saturday." She felt the heat rising in her neck and face. He would see it and read his own interpretation into it. He must know there was something wrong between her and Steve, if Joanna knew it.

"Then you *are* coming back," he said gently.

"Of course." She smiled. "Unless you all get together while I'm gone and decide to discharge me on grounds of moral turpitude. I incite riots and tell people to drop lead into other people's engines."

"Good Lord! What have you got to do with that?" He was staring at her in genuine astonishment; then he burst into laughter. "Foss has been on our necks about Charles, but I didn't know you were in on it. You're what Syd calls a femmy fatallie, aren't you? Leading poor weak males astray!" He was still laughing. Then he turned serious and said, "Charles won't admit anything, but he's the one who tampered with Foss's engine, all right. We've read him the riot act about any more such nonsense, so maybe now he thinks he's got even for his traps and can leave well enough alone. None of us wants to get into a tangle down there and lose our summer's work."

They were almost into the big harbor, and he began pointing out landmarks along the shore and naming off the hills behind the city. His orderly presence was subtly calming; it had driven away the anguish that had begun to wrench at her a little while ago, and now she wore a shell of cheerful composure over her sadness.

Chapter 41

The children rushed around the house to meet the taxi, and Jenny came out on the steps. They were all far more effusive than Eric, who stood a little to one side while his cousins hugged her; then he gravely

232

received her kiss, and at once started upstairs with her bags. Her first thought on seeing him was, How he has changed. He seemed to have grown both taller and heavier, his slightness was becoming a lithe, springy slenderness accentuated by the dungarees and cowboy shirt. Even the back of his neck was changing; it had always seemed such a slim babyish neck, with the brown drake's tail curling on it, and now it had a sturdiness like the set of his shoulders. I suppose it's from riding a bicycle so much, she thought irrelevantly, trying to curb the first instinctive dismay. He was getting to be like other boys; he spoke in curt monosyllables. He smiled at her with a conventional motion of his lips and didn't look at her for very long. It was the right way for him to be. He had passed into a different world, as he had changed from one to another with his first day in kindergarten.

Just before supper she escaped Jenny, saying she would tell more about the island at the table, and went up to her room. She sat by her window looking out across the bare elms and the street lights glimmering in the dusk at the great mysterious dark of the harbor. The light on the breakwater sliced through it at intervals. Eric was down in the cellar with the other children. Philippa sat alone in the dark, ordering her thoughts. Steve and Eric were inextricably entwined. She remembered with what happy innocence she had contemplated her new job at Bennett's Island, how she had looked from this window without knowing how the island looked on the sea, without knowing how the people lived, worked, thought. Now she was no longer innocent or happy, and the change in Eric suddenly seemed abnormal; in this oppressive mood she saw it as one with Steve's aloofness. She thought, in fright, Suppose that Eric has turned on me too, that he's had some psychic warning about Steve. There was a more logical reason; Roger and Jenny might have made joking remarks. *There seems to be a lot about this Steve in your mother's letters, Eric.*

But she could hardly believe they would do it, and the psychic idea was idiocy. Eric was simply becoming all boy, he was becoming independent of her in an ordinary way. She leaned her forehead against the cold windowpane and shut her eyes, and thought, In a little while no one will need me. Steve's face came before her, smiling intimately and tenderly, the way Justin's face used to come to her in her dreams after he was killed.

Someone tapped at her door and then turned the knob gently.

"Are you asleep, Mother?" Eric whispered hoarsely.

She sat up. "No, just resting. Come in, dear. Is supper ready?"

"No, I just came up." He shut the door and came toward her, like a small ghost in the dusky room.

"I'm glad you did. I was just thinking about you. Bring the hassock over."

He dragged it across the floor and sat down near her. The faint light reflecting up from a street light just below the window glimmered in his eyes. The particular scent of boy, overlaid with the odor of soap and dampened hair, came to her. Her fingers realized in anticipation the way his hair would feel, and the heated tightness of his bone and flesh under the fringed shirt. He was near enough to touch, but she would not touch him yet.

"Mother," he said tensely. "You never wrote me how long the boat was you went hauling in."

"Thirty-eight feet, I think." Exhilarated, she rushed into facts. "It's painted white with a buff deck. It has a nice cabin."

"They say cuddy," said Eric.

"That's right. I forgot."

"What kind of an engine does she have?"

"I don't know." She felt a damning sense of failure. "I didn't get a chance to ask," she explained hurriedly.

"But you've been there since September," Eric said with patient reproof.

"Well, it's a big engine," she said tentatively. "Almost all of them have big engines. But there's one with a little old one-cylinder engine, and I don't believe she could go as fast as you can on your bike."

Eric chuckled. In an instant he had been restored to her. The shadowy room had taken on a dim, comfortable safety. She said, "You know the boat that sank at her mooring. Well, they've got her up, and Mr. Gregg is fixing her bit by bit. She had a big hole in her planking, up near the bow."

"Mm," he said absently. "Gee, I'd like to ride in one of those big ones. Sometimes Tad and I ride our bikes down to the public landing, and we see the boats coming in. Gee, those big draggers at Universal Seafoods. . . . But I like the lobster boats best. Some of 'em are neat, boy. Hey, Mother, after you live in Maine three years, you

234

can have a lobster license. There's a kid in school—well, he's in the seventh grade—and he had pots right in the harbor last summer. Right down here, with all those yachts and draggers and Coast Guard boats whizzing around. Golly!" He blew loudly. There was no need for her to make even a pretense of answering. He was off on one of his speaking reveries, his voice dreamed, and all that was required of her was to sit still and listen.

She turned her back on the window and the blank dark of the harbor; she shut her mind to the image of her island kitchen and the sound of feet on the stairs. This, in this room, was the reality. Here was the core of her existence.

On the afternoon after Thanksgiving she had an appointment with Jenny's dentist. It was not as bad as she had expected, and she came home feeling the mild exhilaration that is the peculiar aftermath of dental appointments. It was a cloudy day of quiet cold, and when she had gone out, the children had been trying noisily to decide between the cowboy picture at the Lux and the vaguely Arabian fantasy at the Metro; both had horses galloping for dear life across desert sands. Marjorie had been holding out with great fortitude for life among the beautiful veiled women and the gallant French Foreign Legionnaires, while the boys had abjured such trappings.

When Philippa reached home, they were gone. Jenny was drinking coffee before the living-room fire and reading. "Come in and collapse," she invited. "Did he take your jaw off? Can you drink coffee, or do you have a brand new filling?"

"I think I can channel the coffee around it," said Philippa. "Who won out on the movies?"

"Ha!" Jenny's eyes gleamed. "Wait till I tell you!" She sat forward to pour the coffee. She was not as tall as Philippa, and her features had a softer mold. Her fair hair curled around her face. She had lost the deceptively delicate appearance that had wrung boys' hearts, but now looked very pretty and domestic, like a poet's version of a good wife. She tucked in the corner of her mouth in a way Philippa knew well, and said, "A tall dark stranger won. When they laid eyes on him, they forgot all about movies. And he's abducted them like the Pied Piper." She pointed her finger at Philippa. "You've been holding out on us, haven't you?"

"I don't know what you're talking about." Philippa sipped coffee carefully, bracing herself against an illogical excitement. "Who was it?"

"A man named Bennett," said Jenny. She leaned back and gave Philippa a long meditative stare. "Phil, you've always been careful when you wrote not to mention this Steve any more than anyone else, but sometimes it struck me that you were a little too careful. I mean—well, sometimes sisters do have a sort of telepathy system between them, you know. And I've wondered about him. I didn't tell Roger, because you know how men are. He'd say I was seeing a beau for you behind every bush." She laughed a little, but her eyes were as tender as they had ever been for Philippa. "But when I opened the door today and saw him standing there, I had a queer feeling even before he told me his name. I knew he'd come to see *you,* and that it was something more than casual."

"Darling, you used to tell *me* I had a terrific imagination!" Philippa couldn't taste her coffee; she knew only that it was wet and she needed it for a drying and tightening throat.

"It isn't imagination in this case, Phil. Do you know, he knew right off which one was Eric? And the way he looked at him, such a long, *sweet,* serious look—" Her voice sounded odd. Philippa glanced up quickly and saw that Jenny's eyes were full of tears.

"Why, you old sentimentalist! Jenny, you amaze me!" But her laughter sounded false and breathy.

"I can't help it," said Jenny belligerently. "He was so nice with the kids, and he took them all down to the harbor to see his boat. He was going to take them out as far as the breakwater in it. And I got to thinking how Eric hadn't ever known his father. And Phil!" She sat up, shedding one mood for another; it was Jenny's own, sometimes incomprehensible, trait. "Those island lobstermen make a good living. I don't have to tell you that, you've been out there. Why, when they come to the mainland, they spend hundreds of dollars, and then earn it back again in a week of good fishing. You could go farther and fare a lot worse than marrying a lobster fisherman."

"Jenny Hathaway," said Philippa. "You are shameless. You deserve everything that Roger would say to you if he could hear you." She put down her coffee cup and stood up. "I don't know what Steve Bennett came here for, but I don't think he came to ask me to marry him. I'm going upstairs and lie down awhile. Dr. Elliot didn't drill very deep, but the very sound of that thing is shattering."

Upstairs she washed her face in cold water and brushed her hair. She sometimes wondered how many million strokes her hair had had in her moments of stress; she remembered the hours after Justin's death when she sat brushing her hair and staring at nothing. The awakenings at dawn, when she sat up in bed in a cold room and brushed her hair because she did not smoke, and if one sat motionless, the grip of one's arms around one's knees gradually became a crushing vise and sent arrows of pain through the whole body. If she brushed her hair until first one arm and then the other was aching, her passion of grief was spent.

She looked in her mirror now and saw her brilliant eyes, her flushed cheeks. A number of fine pulses beat hard through her body. She tried consciously not to think Steve's name, but it clanged on and on, like the strokes of a clock gone wild. He had come; he and Eric were together. The other children didn't count.

She reasoned that he had come over from the island on an errand of his own, and through common politeness he would ask her if she wanted to go back with him. But the clamor still went on, and in the course of her reasoning she came to the window and looked down toward the harbor, straining unconsciously for a sight of his boat.

She was still in her room, going aimlessly from one thing to another, hating her indecision and yet wryly amused by the state she was in, when she heard the children come in downstairs. They were wildly excited, shouting like gulls. She put her ear against the door, listening for Steve's voice. At first she didn't hear it and was sickeningly disappointed. Then she heard Jenny's high, sweet, social tone.

"Children, cease and desist! We can't hear ourselves think. Do come in and sit down, Mr. Bennett. I'll call Philippa." She trilled up the stairs in the blithely artificial fashion she had taken on at fourteen and never outgrown. Oh, for heaven's sake, Philippa thought in a sudden nervous spurt of irritation. She opened her door after a moment and went sedately down the stairs.

The lamps were lit and a new birch log was on the fire. Jenny smiled at her and put an arm tenderly around her waist. Steve stood by the mantel with Eric and Tad, looking at Roger's clipper model;

he turned and looked across the room at them with a formal pleasant-ness. Philippa felt a thrill of dread. The whole scene was a re-creation of scenes that had caused some of the worst crises between her and Jenny, the older sister presenting the graceless and recalcitrant jun-ior to the young man she had dredged up from her acquaintances. All that was missing was the chat in the bedroom beforehand, half wheedling and half menacing. *Now, Phil, darling, try to walk across the room like a lady, not like the captain of the girls' hockey team going up to bat or whatever it is they do . . . and for heaven's sake, be decent and show an interest in him. After all, you're darned lucky to get him for tonight.*

Philippa looked across the room at Steve, remembering the sim-plicity of their meetings on the island, and the whole situation be-came suddenly nonsensical. Jenny urging her by the pressure of her arm to be decent and show an interest, thinking she had a finger in the pie after all. It was all so idiotic. Her laughter was going to break loose in a moment, she knew it. She stepped skillfully away from Jenny's arm, reached out one hand to touch Eric's shoulder, and put the other one out to Steve.

"Hello, Steve," she said.

"Hello, Philippa," he answered. His fingers closed around her hand with an irrevocable tightness. "I've come to take you home."

"That will be nice." That will be nice. How simple it was in the last reckoning, in spite of Jenny beaming from the archway, and the children. She felt a splendid indifference to them all, not caring if they saw the knuckle-whitening clasp of Steve's hand and the sud-den convulsive movement as if he would have pulled her toward him.

"You'll stay for supper, won't you?" Jenny was with them again, judging it was safe to pounce. "I'm sure the children can't bear to part with you, and Roger will want to meet you." Steve let go of Philippa's hand, and Philippa turned smiling to Jenny. There was a calm exhilaration in the moment; in the old days she would have been seething by now.

"I'm sure he'll stay for supper, Jenny," she said.

"Yay, stay!" shouted Tad, and Marjorie said, "Please!" Her tone was an echo of her mother's; she hadn't taken her eyes from Steve's face. Eric said nothing, but he looked around at Philippa and grinned.

238

"I'd like to stay," said Steve.

"Oh, lovely!" cried Jenny. She crinkled her eyes at him, and then whirled like a ballerina toward the kitchen door. "Come, Marjorie, Tad! Eric, you can help too!"

"I'd like Eric for a moment," Philippa said. Jenny gave her a brief, wary frown as if to say, *Why* can't you be cooperative, it's for your own good! Philippa looked at her blandly and held Eric back. The door shut behind Jenny and her children with a suggestive finality.

"What did you think of Steve's boat?" Philippa asked Eric. She remembered not to push his hair back or fuss with his collar. He held his thin, childish mouth still with an obvious effort; he could do nothing about his eyes.

"She's swell," he said huskily. "Just swell." He gazed at Steve with a lustrous, unbelieving awe, as if he had found himself suddenly in the same room with Robin Hood or Kit Carson.

"Some day Eric's going out to the island with me," Steve explained to Philippa.

"That will be wonderful," she said. She gave Eric a little push toward the door. "You'd better see what Aunt Jenny wants." He went, looking back over his shoulder. His gaze moved seriously from one to the other. He seemed still to be moving in a dream. When he had gone, Steve took a step forward, reaching for her.

She went into his arms, shutting her eyes against their sudden burning. Her face felt unsteady. She put her hands on his shoulders, kneading with her fingers through layers of pull-over and shirt. "How did anyone with your disposition have such a nice kid?" he murmured.

"*My* disposition!" She felt slightly drunken. She had not forgotten what it was like to be this near to him, to move her temple back and forth against his jaw in urgency and wordless longing, but she had forgotten how intolerably sharp the edge of the instant could be. "My disposition," she repeated dreamily, not remembering why she said it.

"The last time I saw you, it wasn't very good." He barely spoke aloud.

"You called me a chowderhead."

"You were one. You are one." He folded his arms behind her and rocked her in them. His lips brushed her forehead and cheekbones. "Marry me, Philippa."

"Yes, Steve." It wasn't the way she'd wanted it; in Jenny's living room with the city outside, no sound of the rote seeping in past the windows. But the time and the place had no significance in the last analysis. She had said it finally, she had said it meaning it and wanting it, knowing they must not be separated again. All other issues must fall into place, and Eric was included among them.

As if he knew what she was thinking, Steve said, "We'll give Eric time to get used to the idea. Kids can't be rushed."

"No." She thought she heard Roger's car in the driveway. She loosened his arms, with the languid reluctance of awakening. "I love you, Steve."

"And I love *you*."

They were apart, Steve with his elbow on the mantel throwing a match into the fireplace and Philippa sitting in a chair, when Roger came in.

Chapter 42

When they went back to the island the next morning, the day was overcast but not windy. Behind them the mainland hills were purple-brown in their November coloring, and sharply lined against a pearly sky. The city dwindled to nothing; the lighthouses of the breakwater and then of Gannet Head were left behind, the closer islands fell away, and the bay opened before them. The gray sea glistened like pale silk.

Out here a gull rode solitary on a marker for the course which the destroyers followed on their trial runs. A big dragger passed near, heading home after a successful trip that put her low in the water. Now and then there was a lobster boat rolling in the sleek swells as the lobsterman hauled a trap. But nothing destroyed for Philippa the total effect of solitude with Steve. She had never been alone like this with him before, standing beside him at the wheel with her arm through his while the boat headed out toward the horizon.

They hardly spoke until they were halfway, when they opened

up the thermos bottle of hot coffee and the dozen fresh doughnuts Jenny had given them. Philippa sat eating and drinking in what seemed a state of nirvana. The boat slipped forward over a sea that might have been timeless and endless.

"I saw a lawyer yesterday," Steve said suddenly.

At first she could not connect his words with herself and looked at him blankly. Then her mind cleared of its detachment, and she waited for him to go on.

"I've filed suit for divorce. Desertion." He reached out and moved the wheel a degree, sighting a mark invisible to Philippa. "It will come up in the February term of court."

"It's not a very pleasant thing to have to do." She put her half-eaten doughnut down on a paper napkin, no longer hungry.

"It's just a formality." He was sitting on the engine box. Philippa sat near him on the washboards, and he touched her cheek with his finger. "Do you want to get married on Washington's Birthday?"

They reached the island just before noon. Everyone else was out to haul, and gulls had possession of the skiffs at the moorings. They were finishing dinner with Joanna and the two children when Nils and Charles came home from hauling. Nils greeted them pleasantly, washed up, and sat down at the table. But Charles was flushed and blazing-eyed, as if with fever. He paced nervously around the table, the children watching him curiously, until Joanna said, "For heaven's sake, Charles, sit down and eat!"

"Eat!" His voice was too loud, his motions violent. He stared hotly at Nils. "Let *him* eat! Good Lord, nobody'd ever think he'd just found at least half his traps cut off!"

Joanna put her fork down and looked at her husband. The children were suddenly silent. Steve, too, turned toward Nils. Philippa's throat closed against food. She felt a little sick.

Nils spoke softly. "Sit down, Charles. Don't make a fool of yourself. It's not the first time I've lost traps, and it's probably not the last."

Finally the meal was resumed, and the conversation, somewhat awkwardly carried on by Steve and Joanna and Nils, didn't touch at all on island affairs.

Joanna refused help with the dishes, and Philippa was glad to leave. The others would want to talk about Nils' traps without an outsider listening; what concerned them now was not to be discussed lightly. And she wanted to get away, to stifle the stir of dread, and try, if she could, to remember the trip this morning, the perfection of those two hours alone with Steve when they had belonged neither to the island nor to the mainland, but solely to each other.

On the island nothing had changed. The evils still went on. The important thing was not to let her dismay become as strong a poison as it had been before Thanksgiving. It should be easy to be courageous now, she thought, to fight off the damning sense of failure; there was her new and incorruptible agreement with Steve that they could not be parted again.

When he came in the evening, she asked him what would happen now, and he shrugged. "I don't know. Nils is one of these slow-to-anger guys. But when he does get mad, he's pretty deadly, and he likes to do his fighting in the open."

"Maybe that's what we need," said Philippa. "Something to bring it all out in the open where everybody can see it."

They had no more chance to discuss it then. Kathie and Terence came in, and they talked about other things. Young Charles showed up briefly; Philippa told him how everyone had enjoyed the lobsters, and he nodded and left. "Guess he was surprised to see you had company," Kathie said maliciously.

"That's enough for you," said Terence. "Time you went home, anyway. Come on." He herded her out. Steve went over to where Philippa sat on the couch, and sat down beside her. He put one arm around her tightly, and took her chin in his fingers, pulling down gently with his thumb until her lips were parted. Then he kissed her. "Let's not talk any more about the neighbors," he murmured.

On Sunday there was no escaping the fact that a really serious situation was upon them all. It had been another good hauling day, and by nightfall everyone knew that Asanath Campion's traps had been bothered.

"Do you think Nils did it?" Philippa asked Steve.

"It doesn't sound like him." His frown made him look tired. "But maybe he's changed his tactics. Anybody could have done it. Foss could have, to get Asanath to join in on the mess. Maybe they think

I'm the one. The only one who knows is the one who did it."

That night Philippa dreamed of faceless figures reaching out from boats to slash off buoys; everything was shadowed by a strange twilight except the knives, which flashed with a burning brightness.

Chapter 43

The whole island was uneasy. There was only one topic of conversation wherever Philippa went. Conflicting theories came from every side; the stir spread to the school, and there were loud arguments and threats at recess, with the boys telling what they would do if they caught anyone messing around *their* traps. Philippa felt a twist of dismay when she saw Sky and Rob going home separately. Sky was such a lonely boy, he couldn't afford to lose his friend.

Kathie, staying after school to help tidy up, wanted only to talk about the trouble. "Imagine being caught in a lobster war!" she exclaimed. "That's what it is. Mark says it's no use beating around the bush, it's a lobster war, all right. Did you know the Campions stopped selling to him? They take their lobsters over to Brigport and sell to Freeman. All but Terence. He says he'll do as he pleases. I asked him who he thought cut off his father's gear, and he just gave me a look, without saying a word."

"Let's talk about something else," said Philippa.

Kathie looked at her in honest astonishment. "You mean when something like *this* is happening on Bennett's Island you don't want to *talk* about it? But golly, nothing ever happens here very much, and when it does, you have to make the most of it!"

"Not me," said Philippa. "And I don't think we should have so much talk about it in the schoolyard. It's split up Rob and Sky already."

Kathie sighed. "I told Rob he shouldn't have called Foss a hypocritical louse in front of Sky. He heard Mark say it. Rob didn't mean anything by it. Nothing against Sky, I mean. He's sorry for Sky."

"Sky is loyal to his father," Philippa said. "He loves him. He wants to think his father is the most wonderful man on earth, any son does. It's cruel to tell him anything else."

"But Sky *knows!*" Kathie spread out her hands. "That mess with Perley and Rue and Edwin, when Foss wouldn't come!" She thought Philippa was becoming stupid and conventional; her angry disappointment was plain.

"Don't you think that hurt Sky enough? Now he's lost Rob." Philippa went to the windows; the island was russet with coming winter, but in the afternoon sun the sea had a gemlike blue. The meadow grasses bent in the cold wind like rockweed in the tide. "I don't suppose there's any chance of stopping the children's guesses and suppositions and rumors. It's all that they hear at home these days, and it's exciting, I know. But it's not exciting to the grownups, Kathie. It's a terribly involved thing that pulls at your nerves and makes you suspicious and always angry. It's like any kind of war."

"I know," said Kathie with one of her sudden switches from a garrulous childhood to maturity. "I listen around. It's already cost Mark plenty, with the Campions and Percys and Syd selling at Brigport. And Mark's got some big bills to meet, so he's worrying. Terence won't talk about it at all. We always used to have an awful lot to talk about, but now we can't think of anything. If his father wins out and gets him to sell at Brigport, Mark'll clamp down on me faster than you can spit through a knothole, and I won't be allowed out of the house, even to come and see you." She stared down at the window sill where someone in the past had carved initials. Years of paint work hadn't quite filled in the rough letters. Her face had a look of sadness Philippa had never seen on it before. "I don't know what Terence will do without me. I'm his only friend."

"I believe you are, Kathie," Philippa said softly.

When she was leaving, Kathie said, "I'll try and get Rob to tell Sky he didn't mean it."

Philippa gave Kathie a chance to get well ahead of her before she left the schoolhouse. December was beginning, but there had not been too much wind yet, and the men had had an almost uninterrupted spell of good hauling weather. As she walked across the marsh, the sounds of homecoming boats were borne to her loudly on the northwest breeze. It was a time she loved, the time when the boats came home, gliding in past the harbor points on a pearly stillness of sea or plunging spiritedly across the tide rip. Sometimes she had been at the store and walked down on the wharf to watch the tubs of lobsters being weighed out and dumped into the car, where they lived in a dark-green tangle, moving with slow, deliberate motions. She liked to look down at the boats; into the cockpits wet from dripping warps and littered with the clean sea-soaked litter of the business; the bait tubs covered with old canvas; the bucket of used bait bags that had been emptied of their old herring on the way home, bringing the gulls in a crowd of wings over the wake; the gaff lying handy along the washboard; the oil clothes hung up inside the cuddy. She had watched Mark put the brass measure to a lobster which had caught his eye and might be an eighth of an inch too small; she had watched him punch the tail of a seed lobster, which could not be sold but must be returned to the water.

Sometimes she had felt herself to be a real island woman when she watched for Steve's boat to come in. Now she dreaded it, and wondered if the other women felt the same way, anticipating with this quick cramp of dread what their men would have to say. A trap cost five dollars at its cheapest, if a man made the bows and funny-eyes himself, from supple spruce limbs which he cut in the woods on the gale-swept winter days, and if he knit his own trap heads. He could reduce the cost even more, perhaps, if he owned spruces he could cut and saw into laths. But most of the men had to buy their laths through Mark. Some had their heads knit for them, and a few used nylon instead of marlin. Only a few, however, for out in the exposed waters around the island a trap's life was short enough by due process of nature without the interference of a human agency. A bad storm could wipe a man out overnight, but that was part of life out here. It was either feast or famine, and most of them were ready to endure the spells of famine for the days of feast.

But what a devastating experience, Philippa thought, to go out to haul and find nothing, when there's been no storm to do it but just someone who got out ahead of you. To come back to the beach and look around at the other men, trying to read behind the calm, pleasant faces, thinking you knew whom to suspect but having no way to make sure. If you were one man, you fought down your suspicions; if you were another, your knife was sharp when you went to haul again. And so the vicious line of battle was spun and pulled taut to make a hard cord that wouldn't fray. That was a warp nobody knew how to slash once it had been drawn tight around the island.

As Philippa came to the beach, the harbor moved and glittered in the late sun. The days were cold now, and there was hardly any loitering at the shore for the sake of talk. But there were men baiting up in the long fishhouse. Someone was whistling, and she guessed it was Charles. Smoke came up from Jude Webster's shop. Gregg's boat was high up on the beach alongside the wharf. He had replanked the place that was damaged when she sank and now was caulking the new seams. Seeing Philippa on the path, he waved a handful of caulking cotton at her.

"Kind of late gittin' out, ain't ye? Teacher keep you after?"

"Yes, and she made me clap *all* the erasers," said Philippa virtuously. Gregg cackled. There was a skiff coming in through the shady lee of the wharf, and she stopped to see if it was Steve. It was Randall Percy and Fort. Fort was rowing, and his father sat hunched in the stern of the shallow boat. The plaid hunting cap looked incongruous above his round, puckered face; he was red from a day in the wind, and so were Fort's ears.

"Wondered what kept 'em so long," Charles said from behind her. He was standing in the doorway of his part of the long fishhouse, wiping his hands. "Thought maybe they'd had a breakdown somewhere and I'd have to go out after 'em." He held up his hands. "Don't you think I need some real expensive perfume to get the stink off?"

"I think anchovies smell worse, and they're a delicacy, supposedly," said Philippa. "I wouldn't say this bait smelled bad at all."

"That's because it isn't rotten. Good corned herring, that's what tolls the lobsters in. If you've got any traps left to catch 'em in." Charles watched Fort beaching the skiff. "Randall looks real worn and miserable now, doesn't he? Never saw a man hate lobstering the way he does. He's so scared in a boat he won't even look aft to see the following waves when the wind is behind him." His whistle pierced Philippa's ear. "Hey, Fort! You got flatirons in your boots to make you drag your feet like that?"

Fort didn't even look up. His father seemed a little unsteady getting out of the skiff with his dinner box under his arm. He glanced toward Philippa and Charles with a sickly smile and stood uncertainly by the bow of the skiff while Fort walked up the beach with the painter. Fort's head was down, as if he were counting beach stones.

"He must be thinking up something real good," said Charles audibly. "Something that'll really cut the legs out from under me."

246

Fort tied the painter to a bolt in a rock. His father came up the beach, moving heavily. "Fort," he said in a winded voice. "Listen to me, son."

Fort straightened up; he looked neither at his father nor at the others. His chubby face was smoothed to a stolid indifference. Randall reached out his hand in a tentative gesture; the fingers fell just short of Fort's sleeve. "You don't want to go off without giving me a fair chance to explain, son," he said pleadingly.

He might not have existed. Fort walked away from him, out of reach of those groping fingers. He passed Philippa and Charles with no apparent consciousness of them.

His father stood numbly watching him, his mouth pursed and his cheeks crumpled. His eyes grew watery; he looked distracted with weak, tearful anger. The false jauntiness of the plaid cap and the heavy shoulders of his jacket, the distraught way he rubbed his nose with his hand in the thick white cotton glove, made him as ludicrous as a clown.

Fort's boots crunched on the stones. He was walking fast toward home. Gregg glanced up from his work as Fort passed him. Philippa looked around at Charles; his eyes were half shut and he was chewing absently on the inside of his lower lip.

"Well?" she said softly.

"I don't know what the devil all that meant," he muttered. She saw that he was disturbed beyond mere annoyance. For Fort to ignore her was one thing, but to ignore Charles was another thing entirely. Whatever had happened to set Fort in this desperate mood bothered Charles deeply; Philippa could see it plainly in his face.

"I must be getting home," she said. She gave one backward glance along the beach and saw Randall trotting over the boardwalk toward Foss Campion's.

Chapter 44

The next mail day was a Saturday, with a wet southerly wind piling great graybacks against the island. No one went to haul, but the mail boat, the *Ella Vye,* would come as usual. At Mark's store

there was a fire in the potbellied stove and a warm scent of damp
heavy clothing and cigarette smoke. A few women's voices leavened
the soft rumble of men's conversation. Helen Campion turned her
back ostentatiously at Philippa's entrance and drew Peggy toward
her with an elaborately protective gesture. Peggy resisted with no
change of expression. She gave Philippa a calm blue look. Philippa
said, "Hello, Peggy." Taking her time about it, to give the full
flavor of the snub, Peggy moved her eyes and stared at a point behind Philippa's head.

Philippa smiled. She made her way around the groups of men
toward the post-office window, speaking in a general friendliness to
anyone who glanced at her. Foss Campion gazed through her, as
usual, but Asanath said in his amiable drawl, "Well, now, young
woman; wet out, ain't it?" Syd Goward was with him; he said,
quite distinctly, "Mornin', Mis' Marshall."

Mark said from inside the post office, "Anybody'd know Syd's
wife wasn't here, he's speaking out so loud and clear to a good-look-
ing woman." There was a ripple of laughter, and Syd blushed.

"Well, I may be a gray-haired old wretch, but I ain't completely
dried up yet!"

"That's the boy, Syd!" said Asanath.

"Old fool," Helen hissed.

Syd said bravely, "Just because Foss never says ah, yes, or no
when you're around, Helen, you don't want to figure he's not cutting up when you're stuck in the kitchen."

Helen flushed. Her hand closed spasmodically on Peggy's shoulder.
"Foss," she said.

"Now, Helen," Asanath soothed her, "a fine-looking woman like
you hadn't ought to worry about what her other half's doing when
her back is turned."

Helen ignored him. "Foss," she commanded, "you get the mail.
Come, Peggy." She went out, leaving a wake of heavy silence behind
her.

"Gorry, Foss," Syd said, looking up meekly at his brother-in-law,
"I guess I ruffled her up a bit."

"You sure did," Foss agreed. "But I don't reckon as she'll leave on
the next boat on account of it." He turned back to his conversation
with Asanath.

248

Behind the post-office window Mark fastened mailbags. Jude Webster leaned against the shelves, staring abstractedly across the store and out through one of the small-paned windows that gave on the harbor. He seemed totally divorced from the others in the room.

And so am I, Philippa thought. She stood with Joanna, but the tide of talk eddied around her and past as if she were a rock in a stream. What a pleasant scene this would be, she thought—the old store smelling of a good fire, the water sloshing and slapping under the floor, the easy voices—if I didn't know what lay behind it all. The rest can take it for granted, but I can't. I don't think I ever could. Perhaps you have to be an islander born and bred to live under such conditions in any sort of tranquillity.

She hadn't seen Fort and Charles together since the day Fort had walked by the bait house, away from his father. Steve hadn't been concerned. "It's only natural for a boy to have a chew with his father once in a while. Fort's probably sore at the whole world right now, but he'll get over . You should've seen the fireworks when Young Charles used to lock horns with his old man."

If he could dismiss it so casually, she supposed it was no affair of hers, but she thought of Charles and Fort often.

Randall Percy came into the store. He looked around apprehensively, slid by the Campions, and reached his wife. In a little while there was a heavier trampling on the wharf outside, and Steve, Nils, and Young Charles came in. Steve saw Philippa near the post-office window and smiled. Here was her tie with a reality that was strong, warm, and sweet, and just as much of a reality as the slashing of traps.

Nils took a position in front of the stove, his feet apart and his hands in his pockets. He was not a big man, and he was certainly a quiet one. But almost instantly he was the focal point. Talk ebbed into silence, and those who did not look at Nils stared nervously at the floor. Randall Percy was one of the latter.

"Somebody's been at my gear," he said in a cool, moderate voice. "Everybody knows it. And now that we're all here, most of us anyway, it seems like a good time to mention it."

Asanath Campion leaned back against the candy case, smiling. "Well, now, Cap'n, you're in the same boat with the rest of us."

"There's a difference, Asa," Nils said quietly. "The knife that started this dirty business didn't belong to me or mine. But however it started, I know how it's going to end. It'll end with the wardens down here, and we'll be shut out of our own waters. Well, I say if we're going to have a warden down here, let's have him now and save a lot of woe. Because I'm going out to haul my traps—and find my traps in good condition—if I have to take a warden with me every day."

"Who needs a warden?" Charles blurted out scornfully. "I'm taking a rifle with me. It's faster."

"Seems to me you're talking pretty wild," said Asanath. "Of course, what the boy says don't surprise me none, but I never knew you was such a hothead, Nils."

Foss watched bleakly. Syd Goward looked unhappy; he began to fill his pipe.

"Pretty wild," Asanath repeated. "Carrying on about wardens and rifles. It don't sound very seemly, Nils. No matter what you say, you still better look to home. I ain't one to condemn youth—I guess I was jest about as hot-blooded as a young one could be." He laughed gently. "But I figger a father—or uncle—has to know enough to haul back on the reins when a boy gets all fouled up and carried away with evil influences."

Young Charles straightened up; his hands came out of his pockets, clenched. "Why don't you talk like a man and name names instead of sniffing around like a contriving mealymouth? What do you mean, evil influence? You got Terence reined in so close he's strangling to death right under your nose, and you stand here talking about other people's boys—"

"Shut up," said Nils without raising his voice.

"I've got a right to be in on this," Young Charles said passionately. "Who's an evil influence, Cap'n Mealymouth?"

"I said shut up," repeated Nils, "or get out of here. The thing's over. I've given notice of my intentions. Anything else that's said is just so much spray on the wind."

"That's a matter of opinion, ain't it?" asked Asanath. Nils walked over to the post-office window. "Give me ten three's, Helmi," he said.

"There's a lot of queer stuff going on around here," said Young Charles. He was springy with tension. His eyes moved shining over the others, slid by the Campions, and rested again on Randall

Percy. Randall gazed at the canned tomatoes. His face glistened with wet; he kept wiping at his forehead with the back of his hand.

Philippa turned and looked out at the harbor. She wanted to leave, but it would have been too conspicuous for her to reach the door from where she stood. They all know Asanath meant me, she thought. I'm the evil influence. It's getting to be the accepted thing. How long before the others, outside the Campions, begin to wonder if I'm the trigger that set off all these explosions?

Someone moved close to her, shutting off the rest of the store and creating an illusion of privacy about her. She knew it was Steve; she would have known if the place had been pitch dark. He didn't speak, and she remained motionless, watching the gray surge in the harbor and the pelting drive of rain over the wet wharves. Suddenly Joanna said, as if she had just remembered something she had meant to say earlier, "Philippa, Jamie told me to invite you to dinner today. It's lobster chowder. How about it?"

It was in Philippa's mind to refuse, but she recognized the intent behind Joanna's gesture. It was to show Asanath Campion beyond a doubt where the Bennett family stood. If he could make his assertions, veiled and yet definite, in public, so could they. Philippa had no right to withdraw.

Chapter 45

The island's tension could be felt everywhere. Kathie, Rob, and Ralph had a serious fight in the schoolyard Monday morning, and Philippa kept them all after school that afternoon. The boys seemed to have forgotten their differences by noon, but Kathie remained unnaturally sullen all day.

She had lost her shimmering mobility of expression and now appeared merely stolid. Her mouth drooped and her eyes were without depth, like a doll's. Philippa tried several times to establish contact; it was hardly possible that they could look at each other for any length of time without the dissolution of this new barrier. But the girl sat lumpishly at her desk and ignored Philippa.

That afternoon she dismissed Ralph and Rob after a short discussion of proper conduct in the schoolyard. Kathie sat in her own seat, reading her next day's assignment of *Julius Caesar*. Philippa reached into her handbag for some new snapshots of Eric, taken on Thanksgiving Day, and laid them out on her desk. "Come here a minute, Kathie," she said.

Kathie came and stood by the desk, her hands hanging heavily at her sides.

"I have some new pictures of Eric," Philippa said. "Aren't they nice?"

Kathie had always been interested in Eric. Now she didn't lean forward, didn't even incline her head. Her eyes moved across the pictures without a pretense of looking.

Philippa motioned to the chair beside the desk. "Sit down and be comfortable, Kathie."

Kathie obeyed, staring patiently at Philippa. It was incredible that she should have been capable of such moronic stillness. It was a defense, and as such Philippa respected it. But a defense against what?

"You don't remember what started the trouble this morning?" she asked. Kathie shook her head.

"I have a hunch that Ralph said something to plague you," said Philippa. "I know something about boys. And Rob helped you fight, didn't he? If I'm right—well, next time, Kathie, ignore Ralph's remarks. I'm not advising you to be like Peggy, but it's a pretty sure thing that anyone who gets under Peggy's skin isn't going to have the satisfaction of knowing it." She gathered up Eric's pictures and looked at the top one seriously. "I like this one where he has his bicycle. No cowboy was ever more devoted to his horse." She put them back in her bag. "Aside from everything else, Kathie, we can't have these tangles in the schoolyard. I've always counted on you to help keep things on an even keel."

She smiled, her eyes holding Kathie's and willing them to respond, to begin to crinkle at the tilted outer corners. "That's all, Kathie. Or are you going to wait and walk home with me?"

"I guess I'll go home now," Kathie said. Nothing had changed, but for a moment Philippa wondered if there was a tremor in her, as if Kathie were reaching the end of her endurance. The girl got up and went quickly down the aisle to the door, and left without looking back.

All at once the emptiness of the schoolhouse became more than

252

the ordinary emptiness at the end of the day; it seemed especially significant, as if this were a schoolroom that had been emptied years before by some great catastrophe.

Steve came in soon after supper, and she went to him with an ardor that surprised them both. He held her away from him, laughing, "When we're married you can have everything I've got, but right now I keep my sore throat to myself."

"How sore is it? Have you got a temperature?" She laid her hands on his cheeks. "I can't tell, your face is cold from the wind."

"I'm going to bed," he said. "It'll be gone in the morning. How are *you*?" He held her by the shoulders and looked at her narrowly.

"Fine," she said. "Except for taking my pupils a little too seriously. There's something bothering Kathie." Now that she said it aloud, it was miraculously minimized. "A case of ordinary adolescent megrims, I suppose. It's not fatal, but it can be so darned uncomfortable."

She reached up and held his wrists. "Have you heard anything more about anyone's traps?"

"Nobody's made any more complaints, as far as I know. Maybe the thing has reached its peak, and now the mess will begin to slack off."

"I hope so," she said fervently. "The contagion's getting into the children. And what with Asanath's comments about evil influences, I feel like something out of the *Scarlet Letter*."

"There's some women would be set up by that."

"Not me," she said. "I'm easily intimidated. I can feel guilty even when I know I'm not."

He canted an eyebrow. "I know how to cure that. What you need is a man."

"*Steve!*"

"What are you blushing for?"

"I'm not blushing!" But she could feel it; the heat rushed over her and she was released from the day's tensions by an emotion as pure and single as rain. "How long ago was it you said good night? Now I'll say it. Good night, darling."

"Good night, darling." He almost whispered it; he had changed in an instant to a somber tenderness.

He had been gone only a few minutes, and she was settling down to work, when someone slammed the door at the foot of the stairs, and she heard Gregg yell, "What you doin' out there, you omidon?" There was no answer; the visitor came noisily up the stairs, hammered at the door, and came in without waiting to be told. It was Young Charles. He didn't take his cap off but pushed it back, and sprawled familiarly into a chair.

"Well," said Philippa in mild disapproval. He took out his cigarettes and put one in his mouth without looking away from her; his face was flushed to a warm red-brown. With his dark curly forelock and black brows, he was almost theatrically handsome tonight.

"Well what?" he asked. There was a sickish scent of gin around him.

"That's for you to answer," she said, going back to Jamie Sorensen's composition on *Heidi*.

"Do you think I'm drunk?" he demanded. She didn't look up from the paper.

"I didn't say that."

"But you think it, don't you? Well, I am. I've been drunk before, too."

"I'm sure you have," she said politely. "Where's Fort tonight?"

"The sneaky louse!" He tucked his match with delicate caution into the cuff of his boot. "I don't mean Fort's a louse. But his father is."

"He seems like just a nervous little man to me," said Philippa mildly.

"*I* know what he's up to." He stabbed a finger at her, and his eyes grew glistening. "Fort hasn't been to haul since that day on the beach. I don't know what he's doing, but he doesn't go to haul. And *I* know why."

"Why?" she asked. It seemed to be demanded of her, but Charles shook his head, smiling shrewdly.

"I don't tell everything I know. It don't run out of me like gruel out of a goose."

"You're wise."

"I never tell anything," said Charles, "till it suits my purpose. Then I let fly with facts. You got to have facts. I've got enough facts in my noggin to patch hell a mile. . . . What did Rob have to stay after school for? He was s'posed to bait up for me."

Philippa put down her red pencil and sat back in her chair. "It

254

wasn't anything bad, Charles. They were plaguing Kathie."

"Oh." He frowned, rubbed his hand over the deep furrows in his forehead, and yawned with convulsive suddenness. "Ayeh. Guess it was about Terence. Mark put the wood to her about him. If she gets caught talking with him, she gets sent back to the main so fast she'll never know she was ever on the island."

So that was it! *I'm Terence's only friend,* Kathie had said. Philippa kept down her anger at the way children must be swept helplessly along in the wake of their parents' stupid involvements. "Is that because the Campions don't sell to Mark any more?" she asked.

"Not exactly. Terence still sells to him. It's turning old Asanath sick to have a Campion boat go up alongside a Bennett car, but Terence still holds on." Charles yawned again. "No, Mark's just sore at all the Campions, and Terence is one of 'em. So he clamps down on Kathie, and she stays away from Terence." Charles teetered back and forth. The heat from the stove was making him sleepy, and his words grew more blurred as his lids grew heavier. "God, I got to get out of here! But I can't go home like this. Jo will wring my neck. Guess I'll have to go up in the hayloft." He gave her a drowsy, sweet-tempered grin. "Be something, now, if I passed out in here and you had to keep me all night."

"I don't imagine you've had enough to pass out," said Philippa. "But you'd better go anyway. I have a lot to do this evening."

"If *Steve* came up here three sheets to the wind, you'd let *him* stay, wouldn't ye?" he asked craftily.

"I wouldn't let anyone stay." She got up and went to stand by the door, taking her flashlight from the shelf. "I'll light you down the stairs, Charles."

" 'Course *I'm* not good enough, being just a young squirt. I'm not all used up and wore out with life, I never had another woman to—" He yawned tremendously, and then stared at her as vacantly as a sleepy baby. "What was I saying?"

"Good night," said Philippa.

"Oh." He came to the door, eddying out toward the table like a skiff swung by the wind. She held the light on the steps, and he began a cautious descent. Halfway down he made an attempt to snap his fingers, but failed. He turned and gazed up with blind, luminous eyes into the light.

"I know what I was saying. You're not so smart. I know what I was saying. And I'll tell you the rest of it."

Philippa lowered the flashlight. It was useless to warn him about Gregg. She sighed and said, "Yes, Charles."

"You can have Steve. That's it. I don't care, because I don't even *want* you. I did, till I found out the facts. You know what I said about facts." He pressed his hands flat against the wall behind him and spoke with quiet drama. "A man's friend means more to him than his woman. A man's *friend*. And that's a fact."

"It certainly is," said Philippa. He should have been funny, balancing on the stairs like a tight-wire walker while he pontificated. But he wasn't. She watched him with tenderness. "You've hit upon a great truth, Charles."

"Of course it's a great truth!" His passionate nod almost threw him down the stairs. "So that's why I don't want you." He went down the rest of the way in a headlong rush, and opened the door. The night cold came blowing in as he raised his arm toward her in a sweeping salute. "Farewell!"

He stepped out and pulled the door shut behind him with a shuddering crash. "Thunderation!" Gregg shouted.

Chapter 46

The next day, just before the afternoon session was to begin, a rock came through an upper pane of the middle window on the side of the schoolhouse away from the marsh. Up till the moment when the crash and the shower of glass occurred, there had been a healthy uproar around the schoolhouse. The day was free enough of wind for the children to play outside, the sun was warm in the lee, and the earth had thawed overnight to a deceptive, springlike juiciness. Philippa had seen Kathie perched immobile on the big boulder outside the windows facing the marsh, and the boys were nowhere near her. Peggy Campion had come along the lane in her new bright-red topper and tartan skirt, and would now be waiting aloofly at the corner of the building for the bell to ring. Rue crouched at the foot of Kathie's boulder, sitting on her heels with her back against the warm slant of rock and holding Daniel between her knees. As far as Philippa could see in her carefully nonchalant errands near the windows, the three girls were not in contact with each other or with the rowdy sounds at the front of the building.

Then the rock came through the window on the other side, and the shouting stopped with an appalling finality. It was like the end of all sound. Philippa went slowly to pick up the rock. It had landed on Rue Webster's desk, scarring it, and bounced into the aisle. It was a rough oval of quartz, about the size of a goose egg. She weighed it in her hand. Then she went out onto the doorstep.

She looked into all the faces, from Daniel's to Kathie's. Edwin stood out by the flagpole, with one arm around it. His wild fearfulness showed in the meager pale face framed by the overlarge cap and the unnecessary earflaps.

Philippa held up the rock. "Who threw this?" she asked.

Faith kept buttoning and unbuttoning her coat. Frances Percy moved her feet in a soggy place, making a rhythmic squelching sound. No one spoke. Rue, holding Daniel by the hand, edged toward Edwin at the flagpole.

"I think it's only fair that you should speak up," Philippa said reasonably, "whoever you are. I know you didn't intend to break the window, but there'll have to be a new pane put in. And we don't want rocks thrown anyway. If that had hit a person instead of a window, someone could have been hurt very badly, even killed."

They gazed at her solemnly, the older ones because it was the proper mood for the occasion, the younger ones awed. Rue stood by Edwin; she had a look of ancient resignation.

It was Edwin who had thrown the rock. Philippa knew she must have realized it all along. Last year, when Edwin was disturbed, he threw rocks. She beckoned to him and went back inside. In a few moments he came in with Rue. He stood before her, his lower lip under his teeth. He showed a rigid avoidance of the broken pane and the glass strewn on the floor.

"He doesn't know why he threw the rock," Rue said. "He hasn't thrown any for a long time, Mis' Marshall."

"What was going on outside just before it happened?"

"I don't know. I was out by the big rock with Dan'l." She held the little boy in front of her by the shoulders. "I could hear them racing around and shouting. I don't think that had anything to do with it." Her amber eyes worried patiently. "I guess it was something else."

"Rue," Philippa began tentatively. "Is anything wrong at home that could upset him?" She smiled at Edwin and motioned him to sit down. "Is your mother sick?" she asked Rue. "I stopped by there yesterday, and no one answered."

"No, she's not sick." Rue's voice dropped to an almost inaudible tone. "But my father almost is. Yesterday somebody hauled all his traps. He says it's a warning. He says next time they'll cut them all off. Mrs. Marshall, he can't lose them. They're all he's got."

She felt rage like nausea. It was hard not to show it. "I know, Rue. It's a terrible situation. And something will have to be done. But can you make it clear to Edwin that he mustn't throw rocks here? He could go down on the beach and throw them into the water."

"He won't do it any more. He's about scared out of his head because he broke the window. I'll tell my father, and he'll put some new glass in." She pressed Daniel close against her legs. "I guess it was because Edwin saw them all shouting and acting crazy, and the way he felt inside—well, I *know* how he feels, but I can't explain it."

"You do very well, Rue." She heard Rob stamping in the entry, and then the bell began to ring for the afternoon session. Rue started to take off Daniel's new snowsuit, the precious outfit that had been a sign of the Websters' new grip on life. Edwin, seeing her, kicked off his boots. The other children came in.

As soon as school was out and she was walking home, her mind swung to Jude Webster. As she came across the marsh, she saw him through the open door of his workshop, a patient harassed man at a workbench. She wondered if he had told anyone about his traps and decided not; last night Steve had said with casual optimism that perhaps the tangle was beginning to loosen and slacken off.

She wanted to go and speak to him, but she didn't know what to say. It was like Edwin's deafness; she couldn't violate Rue's confidence. Besides, theoretically, what happened to his traps or anyone's was none of her business. But she would go up to the Webster house after supper when there would be someone to open the door for her; Lucy Webster was to be thanked for her geranium in spite of herself.

The beach was deserted today, except for Jude in his shop. The other men were making a long day of it out to haul. But Jude was afraid to go. She walked on quickly.

The weathered gray bulk of the Binnacle lay before her like a refuge. There seemd to be no one about this afternoon; nothing moved but a few leisurely gulls. Children were playing somewhere out of sight; she could hear them. She was unprepared for Viola Goward, who came along the path by the well at a smart pace.

Before she reached the corner of the house, Viola hailed her. Her voice rang through the moist, mild stillness. Philippa stood still and watched Viola come toward her. Her tweed coat was open and she wore no hat; her hair had rusty glints in the sun. Her dry skin showed its pale freckles and fine tissue of creases more distinctly than usual.

"It's as hot as love in summertime," she exclaimed. "Good pneumonia weather!"

"It's nice," Philippa said. "It's a bonus, to shorten the winter."

"Well, there's all ways of looking at things." There was faint contempt in the swing of her head. "Like all the ways different people could look at a young man coming drunk out of a woman's house."

Philippa felt a prickling along her backbone. She continued to gaze at Viola with a polite, quizzical expression.

Viola said, "There's some who'd say, 'Too bad he's been up there bothering her, I hope she didn't try to be polite to him.' And there's others who know he wouldn't take himself where he wasn't wanted."

Charles declaiming all the way down the stairs in a voice that would have carried through the door for anyone who cared to stop and listen; Charles standing on the doorstep and shouting, "Farewell." Viola couldn't have made out all the words, Philippa thought, or else she'd have known he was renouncing me. She smiled, made weightless and exhilarated by anger. It was a splendid sensation; she chose her words with a lofty disregard for the consequences, cherishing each syllable.

"I take it you were passing by last night, and you stopped to listen. You know, there are some people who would hesitate to give such a picture of themselves. And there are some who are so anxious to spatter filth they don't care how much blows back into their own

259

faces. They can reek with it, but they don't care, or they don't know. Which is it with you, Mrs. Goward?"

The deep-seated lids slipped over Viola's eyes. She looked at Philippa from under them; her mouth was bloodless. *"Your time has come.* Do you realize what that means? The Bennetts know now what you are and what you've done, with all this cutting and vandalism, and that boy starting to drink."

"Perhaps," said Philippa. "But tell me something, Mrs. Goward. Did I really start anything? Wasn't it always here? Didn't it start when the Campions moved out here and found that if they owned deeds to half the houses on the island, it would still be *Bennett's* Island? Didn't it start because some persons have a hate born in them for the ones who have a little more, who always have had it and always will have it?"

"You're talking like somebody escaped from the state hospital." Viola was trying to keep her voice down, but it had a wild stridency. Her gaunt cheekbones were blotched with color. "Nobody sane could understand a word of it. The trouble started when you brought those dirty little wretches in from out of the woods! We were supposed to *pay* to let our children sit next to them and have their heads bashed in!"

"Did anyone ever hurt Ellie?" Philippa asked.

"Not yet, but it's coming. What about that rock Edwin threw today? Big as a pot buoy. He's getting wild again. He's going to kill somebody, and it'll be all your fault. I suppose you'll say he was driven to it." Her chin jerked upward and the cords of her neck were taut.

"Mrs. Goward," Philippa said with a patience calculated to madden, "are you sure the Webster children are so important? Aren't they just a symbol, something you and your brothers and your sister-in-law can wave around like a flag and cover up the things you won't admit even to yourselves?"

"The Websters will be cleaned out of here yet," said Viola. "And as for you, if you get off with being fired, you'll be lucky. You've sowed the wind, Philippa Marshall, and you'll surely reap the whirlwind." She held up her strong bony hand and ticked the charges off on her fingers. "You've been carrying on ever since you got here, not content with a man somewhere near your own age, but you had to get boys under your influence. Nobody in this world ever heard Terence Campion swear at his mother and father the way he did that night on *your* account! You started this trap war by persecuting Perley. You can't keep order in the school. And let me tell you one thing more, Mrs. Marshall!" Her long forefinger lunged forward like a rapier. "We're not paying—neither Campions nor Bennetts—to have a teacher entertaining her men friends in the schoolhouse after hours and sending the kids high-tailing it for home so she can have privacy!"

Philippa said out of her weightless calm, "I suppose it will all be brought out into the open when your brother Asanath gives the word. Thank you for advance notice, Mrs. Goward." She looked at her watch. "Now, if you'll excuse me, I have work to do."

She nodded at Viola and left her. As she unlocked her door, she thought something wavered at the side of her vision beyond the corner of the entry. She glanced past the side of the building, out by Gregg's workshop, toward the Gowards'. Nothing moved in the thin, subtle sunshine. When she looked back, Viola was walking fast toward the beach.

Going around to tell brother Asa, Philippa thought. It didn't matter. She had spoken her mind to Viola, and whether it had been wise or not, she was past caring. She was carried on by a wave of heady satisfaction.

Chapter 47

Steve stopped in after he had come back from hauling to tell her in a windy, ludicrous whisper that he had laryngitis. She said aggressively, "Why did you go out today?"

"It was lonesome in bed." He laughed at her.

"You'd better go back to it and continue to be lonesome," she said. "Honestly, Steve, men are all alike. They think it's noble to go staggering on. If you get pneumonia so Viola Goward can look smug, I shan't marry you."

He leaned against the door. "What has Viola Goward got to do with it?" he whispered.

"Nothing, except that she said this was pneumonia weather." Suddenly she felt burdened with exhaustion, not so much of the body as of the spirit. "Steve," she said quickly, and put out her hands. He caught them, lacing his fingers through hers and pressing palm against palm.

"Don't come any closer, sweetheart. If we were married now, the germs wouldn't matter, would they?" He squeezed her hands until he made them ache, and then let go. But she held on, twining her fingers insistently around his.

"Steve, stay in bed tomorrow or at least in the house, and get over this, please. I don't want another evening without you." She was too depressed to put the story about Jude's traps into words. He'd know about it sooner or later. "Darling," she said.

He whispered it back at her. "Darling. All right. It's hell to miss somebody, but it's close to heaven to be missed. Good night." He kissed the backs of her hands and went out.

The early winter dusk came down quickly in a soft blurring dark that still kept the deceptive Marchlike scents of damp earth and spruce. As she ate her supper, she thought of Kathie, then of the Websters, then of Fort, whom she had not seen since the day he left his father on the beach. From him she returned to Kathie, and the ugly cycle began again: the light blown out in Kathie, Edwin's disturbed condition, Fort's new anger. She wondered sadly if he missed Charles as much as Charles missed him. The night when he and Gregg played their music here in the kitchen seemed very far away.

She washed her day's dishes and put them away, then got ready to go out, not sure where she would go. As she stood before the mirror of the old-fashioned bureau, she thought, I don't look a bit like a bad woman. I wish Justin could know what a reputation I've got. He'd laugh and tell me it was my just deserts for wanting to look like a siren at eighteen. He said I could never look anything but what I am. . . . The child that is born on Sabbath Day is blithe and bonny and good and gay.

She laughed aloud. She didn't look as if she were morbidly preoccupied with good and evil, but like an agreeable young woman setting out to call.

The knock on the door was a timid one, and there had been no

262

warning sound of footsteps on the stairs. She thought it was a child. It was Jude Webster, his cap in his hand; he smiled at her anxiously.

"Are you just going out? Or expecting company, maybe?"

"Neither," she lied. "Just fortifying myself for an evening of spelling and arithmetic papers. Come in, Mr. Webster. Do you know how many ways there are of spelling the word 'weather,' as in climate?"

He managed a hushed, uncertain laugh. "I imagine the kids put down all sorts of things." He looked around the room, his thin face flushing. She took his cap and hung it up.

"Sit down, won't you? Would you like to see what your youngsters have been doing?" She shuffled through the papers, taking longer than necessary, hoping he would soon collect himself. His hands laced and unlaced over his knee; he moved continuously.

"Mrs. Marshall," he said abruptly. "What I came to see you about —well, it's not the children's work—or maybe it is in a manner of speaking—" He was red again; his eyes were feverish and distressed behind his glasses. She looked squarely at him and realized that there was a quite primitive panic in his face.

His hand plunged swiftly into his mackinaw pocket and came out with a folded paper. He gave it to her with no explanation. She opened it. It was a piece of plain white letter paper of poor quality. There was a message on it, pieced together of words and individual letters cut from newspapers and magazines. It read:

"Jude Webster: If you're any kind of a man, you'll take your kids out of the school and get yourself off this island bag and baggage. You've got no right to keep them in school with bright decent children. They aren't fit. Take them and get out of here."

There was no signature, of course. Philippa sat down by the table, spreading the note out under the lamp. She felt the same way she had felt when she saw the defacing of the schoolhouse door. But Jude could not know that any more than he could know how her legs felt at this moment. "When did this come?" she asked.

"About fifteen minutes ago. Rue found it, pushed under the back door." He put his hand up to cover his mouth. "I—I couldn't hide it from my wife. Rue opened it up before we knew. She was all excited." His fingers kneaded his lips apologetically. "She thought it was a party invitation—one of the Percy girls was talking about a birthday party."

"How did your wife take it?" As long as I keep asking questions, Philippa thought, I shall keep calm.

"Well, she—" He took off his glasses. "You see, we've always sort of sheltered her, and the way she lives, it's like nothing comes through from the outside. She—" He cleared his throat and put his glasses on again, blinking exhaustedly. "It was an awful shock. She —she can't understand. And neither can I, for that matter. Mrs. Marshall—" He sat forward. "I'm going to leave this place, I have to. I've had another warning before this. All my traps were hauled a few days ago. But this. This about my kids—" His voice seemed to gather the strength of desperation.

"I had to see you about it and ask you before we go. What's wrong with 'em? I'm their father, maybe I'm too close. You read about kids committing terrible crimes, and their parents never knew what they were really like. Mrs. Marshall, what's wrong with my kids? I know Edwin's deaf, but that's no crime. So what else is wrong?"

"Nothing," said Philippa. She turned the note over, to hide its obscenity from them both. "They're what you think they are, Mr. Webster. Good children, sensitive children. Edwin's deaf, but he keeps up in school. Rue is what I'd call a gifted child." She looked steadily into his beseeching face. "Do you believe me?"

"I have to. You wouldn't lie. But *that*—" He pointed to the note.

"It doesn't amount to a hill of beans. It's a blow struck by the losing side, just for the sake of striking a blow. They don't care where it hits. I might have got a note, or one of the Bennetts, or Nils Sorensen. It's a cruel thing but completely idiotic." She wondered who could have concocted the note. Viola and Helen would shout their accusations for the whole village to hear. Was it Peggy, working secretly? Or Suze, who never dared raise her voice? She looked at Jude again and said, "It doesn't matter. It's just words."

He was slumped back in his chair, wiping furtively at the corners of his eyes. She did not like to think what he had gone through in the short time since the note had come. "I'm grateful to you," he mumbled. "I kept remembering the things I read. They say there's always a warning if a child's not right. And I kept wondering if I'd missed a warning. I didn't know how I could. Rue's such an old-fashioned young one. But kids live a secret life, I know that. I *could've* missed something."

"You haven't missed anything, but some others have," she said.

264

"They'd better look to their own children. But will you talk to Steve or Nils or any of the others before you decide definitely to go? They have a right to know about your traps, and they may not want you to go."

"Why not? I'm just a liability to them." His face gathered a worn determination. "I've just come to, I guess."

"*Please,*" she said.

"I'll do anything you say. I'm grateful to you." He got up with caution, like a man who has been sick for a long time and can't gauge his strength. He reached out tentatively for the note, and she put her hand over it.

"You don't need it now, do you? I'd like to keep it for a while." She smiled at him. "And tell your wife everything's all right, at least as far as the children are concerned."

"That's all she knows about, anyway. I didn't tell her about the traps. The kids know, but not Lucy." He fingered the edge of his jacket while his mouth worked painfully at shaping words. "She wouldn't understand. She—well, you see, it's like she lived in a world of her own. Sometimes I have a feeling she never wanted to grow up, and she's tried awful hard not to."

Oh, Jude, Jude, Philippa thought, keeping her look of calm omniscience while she could have wept for him. Had Justin ever felt like this when they came into his study, all their anguish explicit in their fingers while they tried hard not to make a show of themselves, telling their tragedies in bare apologetic words? Perhaps they didn't have to try too hard; how numbed and inarticulate they could be, patiently accepting, mutely trying to understand. *Blessed are the meek,* Justin had said with a particular emphasis. And had he ever hated their meekness because it made him feel so furiously helpless? Perhaps *for they shall inherit the earth* meant the terrible burden the meek put on the strong. So in the end, the meek were the strongest after all.

Jude misinterpreted her silence and her downcast eyes. "Maybe you think she could do better," he said humbly. She looked up at him and shook her head.

"No, I know she can't help the way she is. None of us can. Even the person who sent this note must have something hateful driving her."

"Well—" Jude went toward the door. He smiled in a shy illumined way that reminded her of Daniel. "You've been more than kind, Mrs. Marshall. You kind of steadied me. A man can take most anything except what touches his kids. I'll go round now and talk to Nils, I guess." He nodded at her. "Good night, now."

He had just gone when Gregg's clarinet began. It was too much; she could not mesh its pure note of grieving with the letter lying across the table under the lamp. She wondered tiredly where she would go to be cheered. Certainly not to Mark Bennett's, to see Kathie as lusterless as a dandelion gone to seed. Besides, there were her papers to correct. Downstairs the clarinet went on and on, as if it had a life of its own. She had a fantastic picture of it dancing around the kitchen in the smoky glow of the hand lamp, slim and black with its silver fittings glowing like the frogs on a hussar's tunic. A drunken hussar.

She started to put the letter away and then decided against it. Let it lie there on the table and lose its power. She was through with hiding; she had made a brave start this afternoon with Viola. She went back to work. Downstairs the clarinet went on, reeling one moment and waltzing the next.

Because of the clarinet, she didn't hear a definite set of footsteps on the stairs, but a wary creaking came to her ears during an interlude when Gregg presumably stopped to wet his throat. She sat gazing at the door, listening.

The creaking came again; she sensed the held breath, the painfully exact placing of the feet. Then the clarinet began. She was doomed by sound; she felt deaf and defenseless. She got up quickly and took her flashlight from the dresser, opened the door, and turned the light down the stairs.

At first she didn't recognize the two faces that stared blinking into the glare, two white ovals that seemed to bear no connection with living bodies. Then Syd Goward said timidly, "It's Ellie and me, Mis' Marshall."

She laughed aloud in her amazement and lowered the light to the stairs ahead of them. "Come up, come up! I think I was expecting ghosts."

They came up very carefully, Syd holding Ellie by the hand. He had a small cardboard carton under the other arm. He kept smiling

266

a bashful, delighted smile at finding himself here. Ellie's narrow pinched face was immobile framed in the red hood of her parka, but her eyes moved everywhere.

"Well, this is *nice,*" Philippa said warmly.

Syd pushed the carton at her. "Brought you a few lobsters." He chuckled and ducked his head. "They're all cooked. We got a small washtub full of 'em in the shed. Tomorrow's Helen's and Foss' anniversary, and we got a gatherin' of the clan comin' up."

Philippa wanted to laugh. It was an incredible situation. Surely Viola hadn't sent the lobsters. She looked into the box and saw three.

"But can you spare them?" she asked earnestly.

"They'll never be missed." Syd chuckled again. He looked down at Ellie. "Will they, Missy?"

Ellie shook her head. "Mamma never counted them," she said primly. "She's over to Uncle Asa's."

"It's a wonderful surprise," said Philippa. "Sit down, both of you. It's nice to have company, with or without lobsters. This is my night, I guess. Jude was just here."

Syd said, "Oh, we didn't come to stay. Jest to bring the lobsters. Hope you like 'em." He turned to the door, still holding Ellie's hand tightly in his. She remembered, then, how, as she had come to her door that afternoon, she had seen a wispy flash of something. She would never know, and she could never ask, if it had been Syd who had stood there listening to her and Vi and then had ducked out of sight into Grègg's shop.

She said quickly, "At least stop long enough to see some of Ellie's papers. She does beautiful work, Mr. Goward." She went across to the table and they followed her, holding hands like the two babes in the woods. She shuffled through the papers and found Ellie's spelling and arithmetic tests.

"Ellie's one of the best spellers," she explained. "These are seventh-grade lists. She takes spelling with the older children."

"Her mother was always good that way." Syd studied the papers, bemused and shaking his head. "Now me, I can't even spell *cat* straight." He looked lovingly into Ellie's face. "These are real beautiful, Missy. Real beautiful."

Suddenly Philippa felt anxious to please him further; he was such a pleasant little man, his eyes so humbly bright and friendly under his brindle forelock. She said, "I've been saving some of the best papers to make up a notebook. It will be like a record of the year. I'll get it."

She went into her bedroom, and when she came out, they were still standing by the table, hand in hand as if Syd were no older than Ellie. She thought, Tonight Ellie has changed for me. She keeps her hand in his with perfect confidence. His "migraine" means nothing to her.

Syd looked at Ellie's papers in the notebook, and Ellie waited, her small face content and quiet. Whenever he ducked his head down to smile at her, she gazed at him seriously. In a little while they left, Syd thanking Philippa profusely.

"Thank *you*, Mr. Goward," she said in return, and she was not thanking him for just the lobsters.

Chapter 48

Philippa settled down with difficulty that night. By a pure effort of will power, she could refuse to go over the day's snarl of events. She put Jude's note in the bottom drawer of her bureau, under her clothes. She found some dance music on the radio and turned it to an intimate tone. She took a sponge bath; then, in pajamas and robe, with her feet on the oven hearth, she ate a lobster sandwich and read *Boswell's London Journal* until she felt sleepy.

She slept heavily. Toward morning she dreamed of turbulent, distressing events, none of them very clear to her. At first she thought the knocking on her door was in her dream, but it went on and on until she thought it had lasted all her life. She fought against it at first. Then, with a sick reluctance, she came awake. It was nearly eight o'clock. She called in a faint, drunken voice, "All right, I'm coming."

It was Kathie. "What's the matter you aren't up?" she exclaimed. She was no longer apathetic. She came into the kitchen smelling of the cold morning. "Look," she cried, holding out her mitten. "It's snowing! Oh darn, they've melted already. Well, it is snowing a little, but they all say it's not cold enough to amount to much." She went over to the table and leaned across it to look out the window. Philippa began to make the fire. Kathie said, "There's nobody in sight. Rob must've got Foss and Asanath started all right. Golly, do you suppose they'll find her?"

"Who?" said Philippa. The kindling caught fire and began a fierce blaze.

"Lucy Webster," said Kathie. "She's run away in her nightgown and bare feet. All the men are out looking for her. I wonder what set her off?" She came away from the window, entranced with speculation.

It was the note, Philippa thought, the vile note. I should take it down and put it up outside the post office and write under it, This is what made Lucy Webster run away in her nightgown and bare feet.

She said aloud, "It's hard to tell what makes people do things. Where are the children?"

"Down to Jo's. Steve came over and told us." Philippa caught at his name.

"Steve? Was he out? How's his laryngitis?"

"Oh, he's croaking some. He's gone with Mark down the west side. They started right beyond the breakwater. Max is with them. That dog's awful good at finding things."

"Steve shouldn't be out," Philippa said. "There are enough men to look without his going." She set the teakettle over the fire and went into her room to dress. Fool, she thought bitterly. Chivalrous, softheaded fool. What's Lucy Webster worth to me, compared to you? What if they never found her, how much of a loss would it be even to Jude and the children? And you have to go tramping over the rocks in this air, wheezing and croaking. . . . Shocked at her venom, she put her hands over her face. Poor Lucy, plunging out into a world that terrified her because suddenly the place of safety had been made even more terrifying. Poor Jude. The meek shall inherit the earth, Jude. Remember that, if you can take any comfort from it.

She went out into the kitchen again. Kathie had taken off her things and had set the table for her. The water was beginning to boil. It was curious what an atavistic sense of security came to one from the sound of a fire, the growing warmth, the positive sound of water boiling.

"Have coffee with me, Kathie," she said. "It won't hurt you for once."

Kathie grinned. "You know Finns and coffee. I keep telling Helmi she's sold her birthright because she makes me drink cocoa in the morning." Suddenly she became sober. "I shouldn't be laughing about anything, with Lucy . . . you know. But I can't help being excited, because it *is* exciting. Everything that happens, I think, 'This is Life. I'm living Life.' I go along for days thinking I'm half dead, and then something comes along to make me know I'm alive. Then everything changes for me. I'm sorry for Lucy and Jude and the kids. I'm not glad this is happening, but I'm glad I'm not feeling stupid any more."

Ralph and Rob were in the search party, and they returned to school before noon, flushed with windburn and an exalted sense of their own importance. They reported the news antiphonally.

"Syd found her," Ralph began, "under a big spruce down near Sou'west Point—"

Rob objected. "Max found her. Syd was just following, because he knows that dog's smart."

Ralph shrugged. "Well, anyway, she was sitting under the tree, and she wouldn't speak to Syd. She was scared of him. She was scared of everybody."

"Not Max," said Rob. "She patted *him*." He looked proud.

"How is Mrs. Webster now?" Philippa asked.

"She's all right, I guess," said Ralph, with a rapid descent from exhilaration to boredom. "Scratched up, kind of, with her nightgown tore, and she was about blue with cold. But I guess she's learned not to go hypering off like that. She was some quiet when they took her home in Nils' boat."

"You ought to have seen Jude shake," Rob said in awe.

"He's had a terrible experience," Philippa said. "You boys will have time to get your arithmetic done before you go home to dinner."

"Oh, Golly," Ralph blew out in a loud stage whisper. "Back to the old grind."

As she was leaving school that afternoon, she saw Joanna Sorensen coming down through the meadow from the Homestead, and waited for her. Joanna always carried with her a special sense of sanity and humor. Philippa envied her; she had grown up on this island and could meet it on its own terms. What Steve called "island politics" could never defeat his sister.

"I've been up prowling around the old house," she said. "Thinking of the past and trying to convince myself that the human race hasn't gone so far downhill after all."

"Did you succeed?" Philippa asked. Joanna made a wry face. They laughed and started across the marsh toward the gray harbor.

"Have you seen Lucy Webster today?" Philippa asked.

"Yes, I went up when they brought her home. I had all the hot-water bottles I could collect. We tucked her in, as snug as an incubator baby." She looked down at the path, frowning. "It's all the same to Lucy. She might as well still be down on Sou'west Point under that spruce tree."

"What do you mean?"

"I'm not exactly sure what I mean. Jude keeps saying over and over that it's nothing strange, she just walked in her sleep. He says it so much you're darned sure there's a lot more to it than sleep-walking. He's so wrung out it's heartbreaking. And in the meanwhile Lucy lies there staring with those yellow eyes, not saying a word, and Rue waits like a devoted little dog."

"That's a tragic family," Philippa said.

"I'd almost think Lucy was having a tantrum, like a young one holding his breath. Maybe she's getting even with Jude for something."

Philippa didn't look at her. "It might be that," she said vaguely. "Maybe she hates the island and thinks Jude's indulging his own wishes at her expense." She thought of the note, lying buried at the bottom of the bureau.

They had reached Philippa's doorstep. "Well, I'm going to the store," Joanna said, "to see if Mark got any fresh vegetables on the boat this morning. Come up to supper, will you? Steve slept all day after they came back from the search and woke up with his voice."

"I'd love to come," Philippa said. Steve is my talisman, she thought as she went upstairs. Some people touch wood or cold iron to protect them from evil; I touch Steve. She looked at her watch. In two hours she would be seeing him; if she worked in the meantime, the hours would pass with blessed speed.

When she had replenished the fire, she took one of her water pails and went downstairs. She stood for a moment on the doorstep, listening to the silence and looking out at the harbor, where a pale cold glint of sunlight had suddenly appeared on the water from a break in the clouds. Gregg was coming home from the beach at his rolling, limping gait. When he saw Philippa, he gave her a watery smile and said gruffly, "Well, I can't say as I object too awful much to seein' a good-lookin' woman standin' outside my door."

"Why, thank you, Mr. Gregg," she said.

"I s'pose I'd ought to follow that up by luggin' your water for you, but I ain't that gallant." He squinted past the corner of the house. "I gorry, here comes one larrupin' along like the devil in a gale of wind."

It was Joanna running back, laughing and excited. "I'm a sinner," she said to them. "A downright sinner. I shouldn't laugh, but I can't help it. I heard all this racket from the Goward house, so I took a short cut up around there and went by as slowly as I could and still be decent." She let out a long breath and looked dramatically from one to the other. "You won't believe this. But Syd's beating his wife!"

"You mean he's landin' blows on the harridan?" Gregg asked.

"Well, he hadn't made contact while I was there, but maybe he has by now. The Salminen children are out in the yard watching; Randall Percy is shaking like a leaf in the entry; his wife is shrieking, 'Do something!' Ellie isn't in sight. And Syd is chasing his wife with a kitchen chair."

"I gorry," Gregg whispered reverently. "I gorry. That'd be a sight to see."

Joanna put her hand on Philippa's arm. "You aren't saying a word, as much as Vi's been on your neck. Is it sordid to you?"

Philippa shook her head. "I've been trying to imagine it, that's all. Since there aren't any of my pupils around, I can safely say I think it's wonderful and I'd like to be over there watching, but being an adult *and* a teacher has its disadvantages." She was mildly exhilarated

272

at the thought of Syd's wrath; but another current ran below the surface, the strong and sinister current that she was never able to forget. "Was Syd saying anything that you could hear?" she asked Joanna.

"When Ella Percy tried to push Randall into the fray, Syd flourished the chair at him and said he'd break Randall's thick head in for interfering. And he said Randall was such a yellow belly anyway that he'd hang himself to a spruce tree if the Campions told him to."

"That's no lie," Gregg said.

"Then Ella told Clare to go get Foss and Asa. Of course Viola was screaming all the time that Syd had gone crazy, so he told her she was the crazy one to think she could start *that* again. I didn't find out what *that* was, because just about then Kathie lit on me and said, 'Isn't this a swell fight?' So I thought I'd better move on."

"Here comes Foss now," said Gregg. Foss came by Sigurd's house, walking rapidly, with Perley a little distance behind him. Neither looked at the three on the doorstep. Asanath came by in a few minutes, walking at his usual gait. He nodded at them.

"He don't seem to be in no pucker," Gregg observed. "Mebbe he thinks it will do the old witch good to be trimmed up a little."

They stood on the doorstep, all caught up in a meditative silence. Philippa was not seeing the harbor but her table under the lamp last night. Syd had had a chance to see the note Jude had brought; she'd forgotten it was in full sight when she handed him Ellie's papers to read. Syd was not dull. He was a very acute little man who could listen around corners and be invisible afterward. It was Syd, too, who had reached Lucy Webster first this morning, and she had not known him; it must have struck him like a blow, that light unrecognizing stare. . . .

It was strange that she had never connected Viola with the note, for now it fitted; it was just the sort of thing such a woman would do to provide herself with something to watch. The note had been concocted of the purest essence of mischief. Having no luck with the schoolteacher, who refused to be intimidated, Viola had looked around for a more vulnerable set of victims. Jude Webster would surely squirm like an insect on a pin.

"Come on, Philippa," Joanna was saying. "Let's walk slowly up past the well. Maybe we'll hear Vi whinnying."

"Lord, what a day," said Gregg blissfully. "Wish I'd seen it, that's all. Wish I'd seen old Syd a-cornerin' her with that chair."

Chapter 49

There was a week of winter weather when the wind blew day and night, first from the northeast, alternating with rain and wet snow; then the wind backed around to the west, and the cold became a dry and chilling certainty. Where once it had crept, now it seared through the flesh and into the bones. The radio said that all of New England was having a premature cold snap, but to Philippa it seemed that no other place could so vividly express the cold in color and sound and sensation. The wind howled past the Binnacle's eaves by night and around the schoolhouse all day. The surf piled on the harbor point in glittering masses. In the early mornings when the sun came up in a glazed unclouded sky, the water appeared to steam as far as one could see. It was her first experience with vapor, and she realized after the first day that if she saw it from her window while she ate her breakfast, her face would be aching with cold before she reached the schoolhouse. She was cautioned by Gregg and Steve both not to load her stove too heavily; in turn she cautioned Rob about the schoolhouse stove, and he gave her the patient, bored politeness of all males when given advice by women.

The men didn't get out to haul, but every morning they rowed out to the moorings in bouncing dories to pound off the ice that had formed over their boats during the previous night.

"This is what it'll be all winter," Steve warned her. "You'll get pretty sick of having a man underfoot before it comes March."

"I don't think so," she said. "It depends upon the man. And it's been a long time since I've had a man around the house."

They were walking down the field one evening, hurrying against the unbroken sweep of wind across the flatlands. He turned her to him and kissed her; their cold mouths warmed in the instant of contact and, as they separated, grew even colder than they had been before.

Then they hurried on, arm in arm. They were taking it for granted now that they would be married in February. Sometimes when she was alone and thought of it, she tried to imagine how it would be to live in the intimacy of sleeping and waking, dressing, calling back and forth between the rooms. She wondered if he would put his arm over her in his sleep as Justin had done, if he would dream of Vinnie and she of Justin. In the past their bodies had learned certain responses; had time merely sent those reflexes burrowing deep into the subconscious, or were they really over and done with, with new responses to learn from new persons?

In this cold week she dwelt on their marriage more and more, and was grateful that other issues seemed to have fallen back. Fort was hardly ever seen these days. It was quiet in school. Rue and Edwin had come back. Vi was not seen striding around the harbor or hurrying up the back path to the Percy place, but then not many of the women came out into the wind that week. The story of the attack with the chair had gone the rounds, but to see Syd scurrying meekly before the wind to his fishhouse, like a gull feather blown over the water, was almost enough to make anyone believe it had never happened. The preponderant reaction was a delighted incredulity. Philippa wondered if this was to be the finish of the long siege, this ridiculous pursuit with a kitchen chair, captioned by Gregg's hoarse whisper, "He must've thought she was one of them Ben-gal tigers." If he had killed her, it would have been tragic; but he had not killed her, so one could overlook the intent or the intensity of passion to which he had been driven. The end was ridiculous, and Vi's yammer was hushed for a week, though no one expected it to be hushed for long. But was this to be the end, after all? Philippa hoped so with the devoutness of prayer.

Steve went ashore on the *Ella Vye* in the middle of the week to have a lost filling replaced. From the schoolhouse windows she watched the stubby-nosed boat plunge along outside Long Cove. In two or three days he would be back; until then she would move in a sort of pleasant vacuum, marked off in patches of light and dark.

On her way home she stopped at Jude Webster's shop and knocked.

When he opened the door for her, she saw a half-finished trap on the bench. He was nervously cordial.

"Come in, come in! Sit down!" He brushed off the top of a nail keg. His eyes were shadowed behind the glasses, and his face seemed sunken around the mouth.

She said, "I only wondered if you were going away after all."

"No. No, I'm not." He gestured toward the trap. "You see. Well, Nils and I are going to work together from his boat, for the winter at least."

"Oh, I'm glad," she said sincerely. "Nobody would dare bother you then. At least I don't think they would." She laughed at her own extravagance. "Nils doesn't say much, but people seem to stay away from him."

"Yes." He laughed too, jerkily. He scuffed shavings with his foot and looked out, squinting, at the dazzling surge of the harbor outside the small window. The fire snapped in the oil-barrel stove.

"How's Lucy?" she asked him.

He still watched the harbor; she saw his Adam's apple slide as he swallowed. "She's all right, Mrs. Marshall. She didn't even get a cold out of—out of that sleepwalking. I can't understand it."

"Perhaps she's stronger than she looks." Philippa got up. She knew when the key turned in the lock. Jude had his pride, after all; he might be poor in everything else but that. He had come to her humbly in his distress, but she needn't expect him to come again. She put her hand on the thumb latch, and at its click Jude looked hopefully around.

"I must get home and do my housework," she said. "Would Lucy like some company, do you think? Or something to read?"

"I don't think so," he said with his painfully courteous smile. "She never gets bored."

"Then she's very lucky," Philippa said.

Quite suddenly during the night the wind ceased, and when it began again, it blew gently from the south, the sea paled, and the sound of surf decreased so sharply it seemed almost quiet for a little while, till one became again aware of the rote.

The men went to haul that day. Hardly anyone had come in by the time school let out. They went farther from the island in their winter fishing, and traps shifting during storms had to be found and returned to their original places.

Philippa had been at home for nearly an hour when Kathie knocked on the door with the usual fanfaron.

"Come on to the shore!" she cried. "Hurry up, or you'll miss it!"

Philippa had been writing to Eric, but Kathie's excitement was contagious. "What is it?" she asked, rising from the table.

"You'll see when you get there!" She had Philippa's coat off its hanger and was holding it out.

"Tell me what it is," Philippa demanded while she put on her things. "It must be a whale at least, the way you're acting."

Kathie laughed. Philippa remembered the first time she had heard that laugh outside the windows of the schoolhouse, and she had wondered whether the unique and vivid possessor of it would be her friend or her enemy. Still remembering, she allowed herself to be swept down the stairs as if by a strong wind and along the road to the beach.

In the late afternoon light, the beach at first glance looked as it always looked at the end of a working day. Most of the men were there. Foss and Perley were dragging a skiff up to high-water mark, Young Charles was hauling bait boxes behind him over the wet stones with a clatter. Nils stood alone outside the long fishhouse, smoking and gazing meditatively at the scene.

Philippa looked the length of the beach and then at Kathie. "Well, where's the whale?"

"I never said it was a whale!" Kathie's laughter spilled out of her, loud and delighted. Nils Sorensen looked around, taking his pipe out of his mouth.

"*Allmägstige Gud,*" he said solemnly, "I just heard a loon."

Kathie, holding Philippa's arm, hurried her on for a little distance and stopped at the far corner of the long fishhouse.

"You've brought me out on false pretenses," Philippa said. "I thought I was going to see a sixty-five-foot whale at least, with a mermaid sitting on his head. I'm going home."

"No, wait," Kathie said under her breath. She took Philippa's arm in a tight grip. "Look, Randall Percy's rowing ashore."

"I've seen Randall Percy rowing ashore many times. And there's

Fort, over there by the anchor, talking with Jude Webster. What's so strange? What ails you today, Kathie?"

"Come back a little," Kathie said hoarsely. She glanced quickly at Nils. They turned and walked a short distance from the head of the wharf. "Nils is waiting for Randall," she said. "I don't know what he's going to do. And Randall, he's been fussing around in the harbor for a long time, because he's scared to come ashore. Rob heard Nils talking to Mark about it, and he came flying to tell me; then I came to tell *you*." She said it with extravagant pride.

"But I don't understand," Philippa said.

Kathie explained patiently, "Nils caught Randall cutting off Steve's traps." She gave each word an equal value, as if explaining to a young child. "Don't you see? He came into Sou'West Cove all throttled down because he was looking to see if any of his traps had drifted in from outside, and there was Randall. Nils saw him cut off a buoy, and when he came up alongside, Randall like to've fainted dead away. The buoy was still on the washboards; he hadn't had a chance to throw it overboard. Nils took it and went off and left him, without saying a word." She nudged Philippa's side. "Look, there's the buoy on top of those traps on the wharf, the black and red one. I'll bet Randall was some sick all the way home. I'll bet he'd have gone straight to Spain if he'd had gas enough."

Philippa thought despairingly, How can there be anything more? Aloud she said in an aloof, cold voice, "Is that why you wanted me to come out here, Kathie?"

Kathie's blue-green eyes had the glitter of the sun on the sea. "I knew you wouldn't come if I told you why," she said, "and you'd tell me I shouldn't come back either. When something happens around here, you have to take advantage of it, good or bad." Her excited glance swung back to Randall, then to Nils standing on the beach.

"But Kathie, this is terrible, can't you see?" She longed to turn and run back to the Binnacle; she felt as if she could not endure any longer the dreadful inconclusiveness of the war of nerves. Yet some pride held her there, with the girl and yet opposing her. Kathie looked at this with the eyes of fourteen, avid for experience. Anybody's experience would do; she would rejoice in its drama even if, as in the case of Lucy, she felt the tragedy. But Philippa looked at it with the eyes of thirty, eyes that told her someone was going to get hurt.

"Look," Kathie said, clutching her elbow.

Randall appeared at the head of the beach. He walked slowly, as if he could hardly lift his boots. He had been walking slowly whenever Philippa had seen him since Fort had stopped going to haul with him, but today he showed a meek and dreadful resignation, as if he were ascending the steps to the headsman's block. It was not easy to watch. Philippa moved, but Kathie, spellbound, tightened her grip, and there was no way to remove it short of slapping the tense hand.

"How's he ever going to get by Nils?" Kathie whispered. "I bet his stomach's twisting."

Randall kept on coming. He took a diagonal way across the beach so that he would reach the road at a point beyond Nils, nearer home and safety. He kept his eyes rigidly forward, as if to catch Nils' eye would be to spring the trap. Philippa sensed the aching effort it cost him not to wipe his forehead, not to hurry. At last he was on the path toward home. And then Nils spoke to his stiff back.

"Wait a minute, Randall," he said without raising his voice.

Randall whirled. "*Sure!* What is it?" He bared his teeth in a smile.

"I guess you know what," Nils said. He tilted his head a little as he looked down at Randall and seemed friendly, almost affectionate. "You aren't going to try to put anything over on me, are you, Randall? You been thinking up a good story about how that buoy got to be in your boat?"

"I don't have to think up no story," Randall burst out. "I got Steve's warp caught in my wheel, that's all. You went high-tailing off before I got a chance to tell ye." He sounded near tears. "I figger that's why you're suspicionin' me. S'pose *you* never got a warp in *your* wheel and had to cut it free, 'n' tell the man afterward, 'n' pay him if you spoilt the warp and lost the trap."

"I've had to cut warps out of my wheel, yes," admitted Nils. "But I never could figure a way to get the trap up and take the lobsters out of it before I cut it off. Kind of a hard chore to do." He took his pipe out and pointed it toward the black and red buoy. Randall's watering eyes followed the pipestem. But Nils, while he pointed at the buoy, was watching Foss' bent head as he tied his punt painter. He raised his voice slightly.

"That buoy, there," he said, "will convince just about any warden and any court that the man who cut it wasn't up to his neighbor's best interests. It will probably convince them the man ought to lose his license for six months while he meditates on his sins."

Randall made an incoherent noise; he clawed at the neck of his jacket and finally got it open. "They're your brother-in-law's pots! He'd never make a complaint with no more evidence than that!" He looked around wildly, but Foss had moved away.

"Wouldn't he? Listen, Randall. Isn't this—" he pointed to the buoy again— "just what all of us have been waiting for, your crowd as well as mine? Just one thing to get the grappling into somebody's hide and put an end to this foolishness. Well, it was a tossup for a while whose hide it was going to be.".

Charles appeared in the door of his bait shed in the long fishhouse. "Looks like it's sunk real deep into that fat butt of yours, Randall," he shouted. "You're the one to be hung up like a dead gull in a blueberry patch."

"Shut up," said Nils without looking at him. He watched Randall quietly.

Randall's head swiveled; he stared all around the beach. "You wait," he muttered. "You just wait. You can't ruin me. My house, my kids—" He shook his head and hurried toward the other end of the beach. Foss was there, lighting a cigarette and talking with Asanath.

"Come on," said Kathie, "let's take a walk up the road to the Homestead."

"I'm going back to the Binnacle," said Philippa.

"We can be taking a walk along the beach as well as anybody, can't we? Golly, if we just happened along, we can't help it!"

Philippa would have laughed at another time. She said coldly, "I've seen and heard all I want. More than I want." She pulled her arm free of Kathie and turned back.

"*Look*," said Kathie. "He's talking to Foss."

Randall's voice came to them indistinctly, and they couldn't hear Foss at all, but they could see Randall's arms flung out in imploring desperation and the way Foss kept looking down at his cigarette. Then Philippa saw Fort take a few steps toward them from the big anchor and stop uncertainly.

Suddenly Foss dropped his cigarette, rubbed it out with a twist of his boot heel, and walked away from Randall.

"He's turned his back on him," Kathie breathed. "Supposed to be his friend, and he's turned his back on him."

Randall took a few blundering steps after Foss. Philippa felt a tremor of disgust with everyone concerned, with herself for being there, with Randall for his stupidity and his shameful terror, with Nils for his quiet cruelty, with the others for their indifferent stares.

Foss didn't turn. He walked faster as if in a few yards he would be forever out of reach of those frantic fingers. Fort ran down from the anchor and caught at his father's arm. Randall fought him off, and their voices rose in the quiet air.

"Don't speak to him!" Fort cried. "Don't even look at him! If I catch you doing it again I'll beat you to a pulp, even if you are my father!"

"Leggo!" Randall struck at Fort's hands. "You git! Git home with your mother where you belong!"

"This time I *am* going," Philippa said. She went home without looking back to the beach.

Her fire was almost out and she rebuilt it, wondering if a cup of strong tea would take away the faintness in her stomach. Kathie came in a few minutes. "I know you think I'm awful," she said cheerfully, "but you might's well hear the end of it. Randall kept fighting Fort off, and finally Fort said, 'Well, you can go fry in hell for all I care,' and he stomped off up toward the woods. Young Charles went right behind him. Maybe they'll make up now; it's out in the open and Fort doesn't have to keep it locked in any more."

"Keep what locked in?"

"He had such an awful fight with his father about bothering gear that he wouldn't go to haul with him any more." She said it as a simple, unassailable fact, as obvious as the weather.

"Of course everybody knows Randall didn't do *all* the damage, and what he did he *had* to do because Foss told him to. Foss owns him lock, stock, and barrel. But Randall's that stupid, he'd cut off a trap in the face of everybody and get made an example of."

I'll never ask this child another question as long as I live, Philippa thought, but almost at once she asked it, out of her astonishment. "How do you know all that for the truth?"

Kathie's eyes narrowed; she lifted her head with that indefinable air of assurance. "Oh, I told you once," she answered casually, "I know almost everything that goes on. I keep my ears open."

Chapter 50

Steve came on the mail boat on Saturday morning. It was not too cold for December, and most of the women who had stayed under cover all week appeared at the store. Viola came out at last, with a fading bruise on one angular cheekbone and a small cut almost healed along her jaw. The story of the quarrel's end was somewhat blurred, since Foss and Asanath had arrived and driven away the spectators just when it appeared that Syd was to corner her in the pantry. Syd had dropped back to his usual obscurity since the occasion, but Viola's laughter rose again above the other voices by the door. Joanna edged closer to Philippa and murmured, "She's in fine fettle today. Maybe he just succeeded in tuning her up."

When the boat whistled outside the point, there was a general stirring, but only a few went down the wharf. As Joanna and Philippa came out of the shed, the northwest wind struck them across their faces. The *Ella Vye* was rolling through the whitecaps in the tide rip. "There's Steve standing outside the pilothouse," said Joanna. "He hates a fuss. I can't see him making an example of Randall alone when the rest have all been mixed up in it. But something will have to stop them, somehow."

They stepped over to one side where a stack of traps gave a little shelter from the wind. Terence Campion appeared from the shed. He nodded at the women and went out to the end of the wharf, where he stood braced against the wind with his hands in his pockets. There was an air of energy and determination about him. He kept his eyes fastened on the *Ella Vye*.

Asanath Campion came out onto the wharf. He glanced around at the women and grinned. "Ain't a very summery mornin', is it?" Foss came a little behind him but said nothing. Joanna went across the wharf toward the boat, but Philippa hung back. She wished she had not come; it was hard, after even this few days' separation, to greet him before people as if there were nothing between them.

Without apparently hurrying, Terence reached the head of the ladder before Joanna did. He leaned down and took Steve's bag; Philippa saw Steve's surprised smile as he looked up at Terence. He came over the top of the wharf, his dark eyes narrowed and good-natured going past Terence, Joanna, and the boys guiding the loads of freight to the wharf. He is looking for me, Philippa thought. In a moment he will find me. Her face felt frozen in a conventional smile.

Terence spoke, and Steve looked back at him. Philippa couldn't wait after all. She went slowly out by the traps, passing Asanath and coming up to Joanna. Then she heard what Terence was saying. He spoke in a flat voice, ignoring everyone but Steve.

"I'm getting my licks in first," he said. "They'll all be at you by the time you reach the store." He nodded across the water at the road going by the Binnacle.

"Well, what is it?" Steve asked patiently.

"Randall's been at your traps," Terence said. "I don't know what the damage is, but I'll make it good, every cent of it, if you'll leave him alone."

"Randall?" Steve stared at him. "Good Lord! What's *he* in it for?"

Asanath drawled from behind Philippa, "Ask my boy what *he's* in it for. It's none of his business; he ain't got the money to throw away. Randall made his bed, now let him lie in it."

"Wait a minute," said Steve. He put his hand on Terence's shoulder. "I guess you hadn't finished what you were saying."

Terence looked at his father and at Foss behind him; the one brother wore a patronizing smile that did little to soften his bony face, the other stared coldly. Like two figures set barrenly in a modern painting, Philippa thought. And Terence was like them, physically shaped in their image. He was an uncanny mirror of them both, first in the cold stare and then in the corrosive smile.

"I wasn't figgering on saying anything more," he said. "But now I guess I will. The reason I'm going good for Randall is because he's no more a crook than anybody else. He's been at your traps, sure, but he was drove into it. The Campions kept him in their ranks when they thought they could use him. But he hasn't been much good. Kind of stupid. So now they see fit to turn their backs on him."

"Son," said Asanath. "You're talking too much." He scratched his head and looked sadly perplexed. "There's times lately when I don't think the boy's well."

"I've never been so healthy," said Terence. He kept his eyes on Foss now, whose expression never changed. "Randall's crime—according to some—wasn't cutting off somebody's traps. It was getting caught at it. Foss twisted him into it; he clubbed him over the head with his kids and his house and his boat, and now Randall can go to hell on wheels. My old man could have stopped it. They all listen to Asa like he was the Almighty himself. But he sat back and gave Foss his blessing." He laughed suddenly, but his eyes didn't change. "Know what? Foss and Vi don't even breathe unless Asa tells 'em to."

Foss turned abruptly and walked away. Asanath said, "That's an awful hard statement to make about your family, son. In a war, even the enemy don't think much of a traitor."

"I'm glad you admit it's a war," said Terence.

"I was just generalizing." Asanath's gaze moved over Terence, down to his feet and up again to his face. He smiled distantly. "I wonder what your brother Elmo would think of you now."

There was a flicker across Terence's lashes as if he had been slapped, and Philippa's hands clenched in her coat pockets. She implored Terence silently not to lose his temper and give his father a weapon. Steve stood with his head bent forward a little, staring at a crack in the wharf as he listened.

Suddenly Terence let out his breath hard through his nostrils. "That's a good question, now," he said. "What would he think of all of us? He'd think we were a passel of fools, wouldn't he? Getting a footholt on a place like this where you can set traps in your dooryard and catch lobsters in 'em, and then proceeding to foul our own nest!"

Asanath stood there listening with a stiff, distant dignity. "I suppose," his son said in a brutal parody of his father's drawl, "that Elmo would say, 'Go to it, fellers, this is what I was fighting for.'"

Asanath was pale. "You were never like the rest of us. I ain't surprised at the way you're acting now. And you always hated Elmo." He walked away.

"*Hated* him!" The words jolted out of Terence. "Sure, I always

284

did! That's the big joke!" His father didn't hear. Philippa put her hand on Terence's arm.

"I don't know what it's all about, Terence." Steve spoke quietly, "but I won't get after Randall. You keep your money. We've all got to carry part of the cost of this mess."

"I meant it," Terence protested. "As soon as you figure out the damages, you come to me."

"All right, all right," said Steve. "I will, I promise you." He put his hand on Terence's shoulder. "Now promise me something. Go and straighten things out with the old man. It's an awful fix, to have trouble between father and son."

"Straighten what out?" said Terence. "It'll never be straightened out. When they can't think of any other way to knock me flat, they bring it up about Elmo. They tell me I hated him, they'll always believe it, and they'll always hate me for being the one that's alive." He put his hands into his pockets and watched a load of laths come up the wharf. Without looking at the others, he said, "I'm sorry I hauled you all into the mess."

"We were in it anyway," said Joanna.

"Clear to our necks," Steve added.

"Thanks," Terence said, and left them.

Chapter 51

A few mornings later Philippa awoke with an unpleasant start to the raw red light of sunrise in her room. She could not remember ever seeing such a crude and ugly glare. She tried to shut her eyes against it, but the impression persisted; her small room seemed filled with the fierce glow. She got up finally, shivering, and looked out. The east flamed, but the rest of the sky was gray, and the sea was a flat dark gun-metal.

No one went to haul that day, and Philippa knew why by morning recess. The feeling of snow was imminent; its smell was in the sunless, heavy air. The children's voices rang piercingly, but there were few gulls to cry from the harbor ledges.

The snow began at noon. Philippa walked back to school in it after lunch. It was a soft, theatrical snow, falling gently with no wind behind it yet. Brigport and the farther places of the island itself were obscured. There was a peaceful silence everywhere. As the roofs and chimneys of the village became outlined in the clinging wet snow and the spruces were frosted on one side with white, the place took on the quality of a black and white drawing. The wharves above the quiet water and the old workshops along the shore became irresistibly picturesque.

The children had collected early for school and were playing wildly in the snow, wrestling like puppies. Some tried to scrape up enough for snowballs, and others were trying to make angels. Kathie had Rob by the neck and was trying to wash his face with snow. He called her horrible names, which Philippa ignored as she passed them, and Kathie was laughing tremendously. Of all the children, only Peggy Campion hadn't come yet.

How attractive they all are today, Philippa thought. Even the sharp little faces of the Percy girls were softened and gay. Sky Campion stood by the steps, wiping the snow off his glasses, and he smiled at her. Sky had not smiled directly at her since that terrible day Perley hid in the woods waiting for Rue. It was the snow, of course. Even Sky was not immune to the spell of the first snow.

In this mood she was unprepared for trouble. The bitter feelings between Bennetts and Campions, the miserable plight of Randall Percy, Nils' anger—all this seemed far away. When the screams went up from the lane behind the schoolhouse, she thought it was a game. When she realized a certain quality in the shrieks, she got up, thinking tiredly, At least it's not Edwin this time. She could see him standing by the boulder, staring intently toward the lane.

She ran down the steps and around the corner. There was an indistinct tangle in the narrow wet space between the spruces. Kathie stood looking on with enthusiastic interest. Rue and Faith stood behind her. Rob circled the tangle warily. Sky was not there at all.

The tangle became Peggy Campion and the Percys. Clare and Frances hung on Peggy with a clawing tenacity. Ralph had her by the hair. His voice sang out in exultant incantation over the screams of his sisters. The pain from her scalp and the little girls' nails, the shrieking so close to her ears, must have added up to an agonizing result. But Peggy fought them off with a dispassionate patience. It was as if her pride were inviolable even when she was outnumbered. She would go down despising them, her contempt for them was absolute, and they knew it.

It was an infinitely more dreadful scene than if Peggy had been screaming back at them. Philippa rushed at the tangle and caught Ralph by the shoulders. Her strength surprised him; he stared at her, gaping, and let go a handful of fawn-colored hair.

"Ralph, I'm ashamed of you!" she said angrily. "Go inside at once."

He backed off from her, shouting, "If my old man's a crook, hers is a worse one!"

"*Go inside,* Ralph!"

He ran around the corner, swearing; she heard the door bang. She reached out to Frances and Clare, but they dodged back, too transported with excitement to be afraid. She looked around at the others. "Kathie and Rob," she said coldly, "I'm ashamed of you both. Do you think it was a pretty sight, Ralph attacking a girl? Don't you have any conception of fair play?"

Rob pulled his cap doltishly over his eyes. "*She* never worried much about a fair fight, did she?" asked Kathie.

"We'll talk about this later," Philippa said. "We'll all go in now." She beckoned to Frances and Clare, took Daniel by the hand, and said in a pleasant, ordinary voice, "We start our Christmas cutouts today. Be thinking what you want to make first, a Santa Claus or a snow man or maybe a house for Bethlehem on the sand table."

"Is it going to have a stable and a little Lord Jesus?" Faith asked excitedly.

"It will have everything," Philippa promised. The children looked at each other expectantly; the balance of the day was restored. The teacher's promise belonged with the promise of the snow and superseded completely the brawl in the lane. When they had gone in, outtalking each other in the excitement of anticipation, she turned to Peggy. They were alone in the lane. The snow fell thickly around them. The sound of the foghorn at the Rock came blundering out of the thickening storm. Peggy's face was white, streaked with thin red scratches. But her mouth was perfectly steady.

"Come in, Peggy," Philippa said, "and let me do something about those scratches."

"I'm not coming in," Peggy said. "I'm never going to that school again. I hate it and you. That's final."

She turned around and walked down the lane toward her home. There was no use in calling her back; she would not have answered. She had made her decision in some climax of emotion, icy and hidden. She walked proudly with her head up. When her red coat faded in the snowfall, Philippa went into the school. She would, of course, be called to account by Helen Campion, but the prospect was not even mildly alarming. She had a curious sympathy for Helen, who would have to bow to Peggy as she had always done. What Peggy wanted, and perhaps had wanted for a long time, was a school on the mainland where there was room for her talents; she despised the little island schoolhouse as a piece of the existence her parents had forced on her. Everything about Peggy pointed to her inherent conviction that she had been thrust by the unfairness of birth into the wrong station in life, an inferior station. Some day she would free herself of it with a vengeance. Her mother was part of it. Helen adored Peggy and in turn was only tolerated, but probably not for long. Today, Philippa thought, perhaps Peggy had taken her first positive step toward freedom. One had to keep reminding oneself that Peggy was still a child. There was such unchildish strength of purpose behind those cool eyes.

As Philippa came into the entry, the clamor inside died down abruptly, leaving Ralph Percy's voice nakedly proclaiming, "I don't give a hoot what she says to me!"

Sky had mysteriously reappeared, although he had apparently been absent during his sister's beating. Helen did not come that afternoon. The Christmas decorations were begun, and the session passed quietly except for Ralph's tendency to be on the defensive. She kept him, his sisters, Rob, and Kathie after school. The smaller girls were dismissed after a brief discussion. Had Peggy harmed them, personally? If there was trouble between Peggy's father and theirs, was that Peggy's fault? They said *yes* and *no* in the right places, which did not deceive her; she knew they had taken a passionate pleasure in the attack. She let them go and turned to the older ones. There was a different sort of discussion with Ralph and again the same conviction of failure. From Ralph's viewpoint, he had been entirely in the right. Peggy deserved a comeuppance for a number of reasons,

288

and he was as certain as he was of his own name that she was in the wrong. He, too, said *yes* and *no* in the proper places, fixing Philippa with a glazed stare, and she said the conventional things and tried not to be too stuffily virtuous.

"The thing is, Ralph," she explained to him, "that while you may get a certain amount of satisfaction from lighting into Peggy, you and she aren't the only persons concerned. It makes trouble for me; I'll be blamed for what happened today. It might make more trouble for your father, and he has enough on his mind, don't you think?"

At mention of his father Ralph looked at the floor. A quick fierce blush flowed up under his freckles. She looked past him at Rob and Kathie. "Almost the same thing goes for you two. You're old enough to have a sense of responsibility about what goes on here. Regardless of the things you've seen Peggy do, if you use her tactics, you're sinking to the same level."

"It's the only thing she can understand," said Kathie. "Some people despise you for being decent. They think you're soft."

"I know," said Philippa. "But the only way to keep the last shreds of goodness from passing out of the world is to practice it. I'm not preaching. This is just common sense. I don't even expect you to see it my way until you're my age. When you have children coming into the world, you'll want to feel they have some security, that you haven't turned them out to the wolves."

"Well—" Kathie was wavering. Suddenly she smiled at Philippa. "O.K. But I'm going to teach mine to fight for their rights. Fair, of course."

"Of course," said Philippa. The boys had nothing to say. The session had been a dismal failure.

Chapter 52

The wind was rising when she came home from school, and the temperature was dropping. As she passed the deserted beach, the dry snow blew in stinging, powdery clouds across the rocks. From the harbor points came the dull rhythmic roar that meant storm.

It was dark enough in her rooms for her to light the lamps. The snow hissed dryly against the windows, and the gale made the familiar bagpipe sounds that meant it came from the northeast. She felt safely immured in solitude at the top of the Binnacle, and she took a purely sensuous delight in the storm.

Steve came earlier than she expected him, his clothes sugared with snow, his cheekbones red from the stinging wind. He carried a bowl of lobster meat and a covered pasteboard box containing hot biscuits. "I've come to supper," he said. "I've brought it with me."

She could only smile at him without words for a moment; she felt something she had not felt for years, a happiness that was almost too extreme for a frail human body to contain. After he had set the food on the dresser and taken off his jacket and boots, she said, "Steve, do you think we've reached a turning point? That things are straightening out at last? This is the first time for a long while that I haven't felt burdened down with all sorts of problems."

"You mean you've decided you're not personally responsible for all the wild goings on around here?"

She laughed and moved into his arms. "I don't know whether I'll feel like that tomorrow or not, but right now I feel very calm and hopeful. A storm always affects me like this when it's time to light the lamps, and all the boats are safe in the harbor, and the island's all battened down for the night."

"Not all the boats are here," said Steve. He brushed his lips across her cheekbone and she shut her eyes, the better to savor the caress. "Gregg went over to Brigport before the snow began. Fort and Charles went with him."

"I thought it was awfully quiet downstairs." She tilted her head back to look at him in some alarm. "They won't try to come back tonight, will they?"

"Good Lord, no. They'll have themselves a good time visiting around. Lots of girls over there for Fort and Charles and liquor for Gregg. That's what started him off today." He grinned reminiscently. "He was moaning around the shore all morning, saying he was dryer than a cork leg and couldn't stand it, and finally he said he'd go to Brigport and see if there were any Good Samaritans over there. None on Bennett's, he says, and gives me a hard look from those bleary eyes. The kids had been up in the woods cutting pot limbs, and they showed up in the fishhouse about that time and heard him talking and decided to go along. Just for the ride, I guess."

"I'm glad they've straightened things out between them," Philippa said. "You know, those two were my first friends on Bennett's Island. I hated to see them separated. Who would have thought Fort had so much pride, to let his father's behavior cut him off from everything like that?"

"Everybody's a mystery to everybody else," said Steve. "You, for instance. You'll probably surprise me every day of our life. Let's sit down on the couch and make love in comfort."

"You sit down." She unclasped his hands from behind her back and moved free of him. "I'll set the table."

While she worked, he lay on the couch smoking and gazing at the pattern made on the ceiling by the old-fashioned lamp shade. The wind rushed over Campions' point and past the Binnacle with a roar, the hard snow hissed on the windows, but neither could penetrate her shell of wood and glass. She didn't talk to Steve; their silence was restful and as full of communication as words could be.

When she had supper ready, she looked over at Steve. She was used to the solemn dark absorption with which he followed her every motion. At first she had been self-conscious, feeling big and gangly and thinking too often of Vinnie, who had probably moved like grass in the wind. But now she hardly ever thought of Vinnie, except with a curious stab of pity, as if the girl had never been Steve's wife and known his body but had been instead a child who had died.

Now Steve's eyes were closed. His face was so peacefully clear of all expression that she thought suddenly of death, and this time it was a personal terror. She remembered the times she had watched Justin sleeping and had never been afraid. But because Justin had died, she would never again know that serenity. She felt heavy with too much knowledge. It was only the ignorant who began their new lives so gaily.

She knelt beside the couch and lifted his hand, watching his face. She held the hand to her mouth; then she caught the glistening line between his lashes. He opened his eyes and looked into hers.

"What are you thinking about?" he murmured.

"Death," she answered honestly. "I watched you sleep and thought

I should wake you and tell you all the things I want you to know. That's the horror of death, I think. There's always so much left unsaid."

"Start telling me now, then," he said. He reached out and pulled her onto the couch beside him and into his arms. She put her hands on his face, the fingers curving and their tips moving along the contours of his cheekbones and into the faintly hollowed temples. She felt her eyes smart as if she held back tears.

"I don't know where to begin," she said. "Yet it all comes crowding when I see you sleeping, and I wonder how I can endure lying beside you every night if I feel like this now."

He smiled. "It'll be different then. Don't you know?"

His body was warm against hers; they were locked together in drowsy sweetness. She did not answer.

"It's a long time till February," he said. "That's half of it. I go home at night when the two of us are beside ourselves with wanting to stay together." His eyebrow moved questioningly. "There's one way around it, Philippa."

"There's no way around it," she said. She put her hands on his shoulders and gripped tight. "We've waited all this time for each other. Can't we wait two months more?"

"I don't know," Steve said. She was not strong enough after all to hold him back; her braced wrists gave way, her arms went around his neck. He kissed her mouth, easily at first and then hard; he thrust at her chin with his, to turn and tilt her head, and kissed her throat. Close by her ear, he said in a low voice, "I'm not going to die between now and February either in my bed or in my boat. So stop working up nightmares for yourself." He laughed, and whispered the last word. "Chowderhead."

She said defiantly, "What I was thinking about didn't have anything to do with waiting until February. But I suppose you think there's only one cure for a woman's megrims." The fear was gone; there'd been no room for it in the brief but vigorous struggle between them. Perhaps he was right after all. She pushed a lock of black hair off his forehead, and he kissed her again, looking marvelously young; there was a fine flush across his cheekbones.

"I think I'd better get up," she said.

"Why?" He didn't move his shoulders; they walled her from the rest of the room. She laughed but she was uneasy; she felt as if they were reaching a point of no return. Then she heard feet stamping downstairs, and she cried, "Listen! Company coming."

He kept her pinned down, but he turned his head, listening. The door at the foot of the stairs was flung violently open. Steve was up like a cat, pulling her after him. She stood somewhat unsteadily, running her fingers through her hair because there was no time to reach for a comb. Steve propped one foot on the stove hearth and took out his cigarettes.

There were heavy steps on the stairs. When they reached the top, Philippa opened the door. Mark Bennett stood there, his clothing whitened with snow, snow melting on his thick eyebrows. He stared by her at Steve, and his face was unexpectedly gaunt.

"Randall Percy just came down to the store," he said in a flat voice. "They found a note in Fort's room. He left to join the Navy. I called Brigport. They never touched there. They must've talked Gregg into taking them to the mainland." Steve had a match halfway to his cigarette. It burned forgotten in mid-air while he gazed at his brother. Terror began in Philippa while she watched his eyes and waited for his lips to move. When he spoke, the words came with an effort, as if he too were borne down by the sheer weight of fear.

"There isn't any chance they could have reached the mainland before it started to snow? They could have fetched up somewhere in the Mussel Ridges."

Philippa knew the words had no conviction behind them; more than her personal thoughts of death had violated the warm shell. What the men believed was as clear to her as a shout.

"They left about an hour before it started to snow," Mark said. "You know what Gregg's boat can do. They couldn't have been any more than out of sight by the southern end of Brigport before the weather shut down thick."

"Called the Coast Guard?"

Mark nodded. "I'm on my way up to see Jo now."

"Wait a minute." Steve reached for his boots. His face had become worn and aged in a matter of moments. Philippa clasped her hands tightly behind her back to keep from touching him.

"Come inside and wait," she said to Mark.

He said unsmilingly, "This is all right. I don't want to mess up your floor."

As if that matters, she cried at him silently, when you think Charles is dead . . .! and then the meaning of the words burst on her like a monstrous light, and she could have cried aloud, Oh, No! I can't believe anything's happened to them! It can't! They're too much *alive*.

But she had cried the same thing about Justin, and all the time the telegram was telling her the truth. Steve turned back after Mark had started, and kissed her cheek. She found herself stroking his arm in a futile gesture of reassurance—for him or for herself, she didn't know which. He did not seem to feel it but turned and followed Mark down the stairs.

Chapter 53

Alone, she felt as if someone had slapped her repeatedly until her head was ringing. Then she went through the terrible process of imagining; she saw Gregg and Fort and Charles in the little boat, peering out by the spray hood and seeing not the faintest spark of light through the dark and the snow. The gusts of wind blowing past her window were intensified to a roar until she wanted to clap her hands over her ears, and she was very cold, as if the brutal chill of the night out there on the water were creeping into her room. Huddling over the stove, she gazed around the room that had seemed so warmly radiant and saw Steve's face, changing in an instant from the face of love to that of anguish. Then she saw the Percy family; Randall standing by while Mark called Brigport and the Coast Guard, perhaps with Fort's note in his hand, his face shriveling; young Ralph gone stolid and pasty white with his efforts to be a man when he wanted so much to cry. And what of Joanna? Just about now her two brothers were coming into the kitchen.

Whichever way her thoughts turned, there was a reason to escape them. She snatched at Steve's remark that they might have reached the Mussel Ridges. She tried to see them making a brush shelter on a scrap of wooded island. She heard Gregg swearing, and Fort and Charles laughing at him, jibing cruelly to keep him angry and active. . . . And then she felt guilty that she hadn't thought of Gregg before, as if he didn't matter because he was not a boy like the others but simply a drunken derelict. Yes, he would be swearing and snarling, wanting a drink to warm his sagging old body. Then the sound of Fort's laughter was so clear in her ears that it rocked her with sickness. He had sat by her table, his cheek laid to his fiddle and his eyes closed as he played. Charles had stopped halfway down the stairs, shouting, *A man's friend means more to him than a woman.*

So he had gone with his friend. She looked wildly around the room. She would not believe they were dead. If only the picture of them in the woods would come clear and bright, she could seize it as an omen and shut her mind to its deceit.

Steve did not come again that night. When she went to bed, she looked out of her window and saw no lights; the snow was too thick. It swirled out of the dark toward her lamp. The sense of the bay lost in storm and night was like a sense of the edge of the world.

She awoke at daylight. Without stopping to revive her fire, she went downstairs, just as she was, in heavy robe and thick slippers. She opened the outside door to the cold and smothered silence, like the death stillness over a deserted city. She went back upstairs and lit her lamp; she drank coffee and did schoolwork with a painful concentration until the east began to brighten with color.

Then she saw Nils, Steve, and Mark tramping a path through the deep snow from the Sorensen house to the fishhouse and wharf. Across the harbor the Campions were moving around. When the first sound of engines broke the unnatural stillness, she dressed to go out and followed somebody's tracks around the shore to Mark Bennett's wharf. The sun was rising fair and clear; the windless air had a dry bite in the throat and nostrils. Between the long blue shadows of the buildings, the powdery snow glittered; trees and terrain had changed their shape under the unique sculpture of the drifts.

All the boats that were fit to go would join the search, fanning over the bay while the Coast Guard worked from the mainland. Their planes were out already, Kathie told Philippa. She had come out of the store when Philippa passed by, and joined her at the end of the wharf. Rob, awed into silence, lurked behind Kathie, never letting himself get very far from her.

Kathie herself was shadowy-eyed, as if she had cried a great deal in the night. "Fort and Charles came into the store yesterday morning," she said huskily. "Charles started plaguing me. You know the way he does—*did*." She bit her lip. "And I wouldn't laugh, I was awful snotty to him. I wish it was yesterday again. I'd do anything to make it yesterday again."

The sounds of the engines warming up were loud. "We're all wishing things, Kathie," Philippa said. "That's the way it always is. It's part of this." She moved her head toward the boats. Some were leaving. Steve stood on the bow of Nils' boat, casting off the mooring. He was a lean silhouette in the sun glare. She thought, If I hadn't come here, the trouble wouldn't have started. Randall Percy wouldn't have cut Steve's traps. Fort wouldn't have fought with his father, wouldn't have gone off to join the Navy and taken Charles with him. They'd still be alive. The words sprang up, bristling with unexpectedness: *They would still be alive.*

Nils' mooring buoy splashed into the water, and the boat cut free toward the harbor mouth. This is what it is to feel old, she thought, this is when you hate life, when you have to ask yourself questions. For instance, are the Webster children worth the lives of Fort and Charles?

Rue and Edwin were coming down through the shed, their wan faces framed in the peaked hoods of their new red parkas. For these children she had begun a chain of circumstances that had broken, horribly, somewhere in the bay during the night. For the moment she could not look at them objectively, and she stared out at the other boats as they circled the harbor and went out, dancing, across the tide rip.

Rue and Kathie talked in awed tones behind her. "Look, Randall's with Terence," Kathie said. "They're coming over for gas."

"Ralph was splitting kindling in the back yard this morning," said Rue. "He looks awful." Her voice was thin and hoarse.

Terence's boat came swiftly across the water toward the wharf, and Mark went down the ladder to the car with the gas hose. Randall stood beside Terence at the wheel, his chubby face almost unrecognizable in its strain. Philippa turned quickly toward the children. "Let's go up to the store," she said. "The Coast Guard might have called."

Their eyes became wide with hope; they turned and ran across the snowy planks. It was cruel to arouse them like this, but even more cruel for them to stare at Randall as if his grief were a wound visible to the eye. She was walking behind them up through the shed when Terence caught up with her.

"I need cigarettes," he said. "Funny how you can't do anything without cigarettes; they get so darn important even if you're walking to the electric chair. How's the Bennetts?"

"I suppose they're like everybody else. Pretending there's hope when they know there isn't. How's Randall?"

"Numb. His wife's wound up like a talking machine. I don't know which is worse. He's so stunned you could bawl for him, and she's keeping up a front for the kids and working so hard at it she makes you ache." His eyes had the pale, old look again, and there was a twitching in one lid. "Fort was getting out because he couldn't stand it. It came to me last night that I didn't have half his guts. Maybe I can say he was a fool, setting out with Gregg in that leaky little tub with a storm coming, but calling him a fool doesn't change anything. The fact is, he wasn't scared to start out. Neither was Charles. He wanted to stick with Fort. They had courage. They stopped at the end of the shed nearest the store. Terence kept on talking as if he couldn't stop. "Maybe if I'd done a little more before this, they'd still be here."

"What could you have done?"

He shrugged. "I dunno. I just got the feeling there was a lot everybody could've done." He looked down at the snow around his boots. "I'm getting off this island. If I don't get a chance to talk to you again—" He looked at her directly. "I guess I owe you some thanks for being a friend to me."

"I haven't done anything," she protested.

His mouth twitched. "You listened. I dunno as anybody ever listened so much to me in my whole life as you did at one stretch. So, thank you." He went into the store.

She stood for a few minutes by the bench, looking at the harbor. The climbing sun was a blessing on her face. Charles will not feel the sun on his face again, she thought incredulously and remembered when it first had struck her that Justin would never again see the Atlantic break against its coast.

Philippa walked back to the Binnacle slowly; she met no one else.

Chapter 54

When the fire and sun had warmed her rooms thoroughly, a compelling drowsiness crept through her. The shock, the disbelief, and now the beginning of acceptance left her stranded as if by a neap tide of emotion. She lay down on her bed and watched the sunlight move along the wall until she fell asleep.

Sleep was no cure; one escaped the truth in sleep but awoke to instant awareness of it. She arose lightheaded and slightly ill, so tired of disaster that she could not even weep. She put more coal on the fire and set the teakettle on a front cover. The rooms were dim, and she could tell by the long shadows that it was late afternoon. Her first thought was that the boats had all come back. She ran down the stairs and opened the outer door. The pure icy sweetness of the still air washed around her. No one moved as far as she could see, though smoke wavered thinly upward from several chimneys. The world was perfect in its stillness and brilliance; it was also empty. The harbor, dark blue in the shadow cast by Mark Bennett's point, held only the skiffs at the moorings and the few boats whose owners had gone with someone else."

No one had come back, but there was no hope implied by their lateness. She waited a moment longer, almost convincing herself that she heard the distant hum of an engine somewhere outside the harbor. But all she heard was a door closing somewhere; then Nils Sorensen's dog barked perfunctorily. Joanna was up there, alone with the children, but she was strong and had no need of Philippa.

It was a long way upstairs. The water was boiling; how long ago was it, she wondered, when she had thought that the sound of boiling water was a comfortable thing? All comfortable things lost their comfort, all beautiful things their beauty, when you remembered that someone would never feel or hear or see them again.

While she was drinking the coffee, not tasting it, she heard the first engines. She didn't move. She had no right to be out on her doorstep like the other women; she was not an island woman and never would be. Never would be. . . .

As she sat at the table, she could see along the path to the beach. Presently she saw two skiffs, almost abreast of each other, approaching the beach. Foss and Perley were in the first one to reach the shore. They hauled up their skiff. Perley made it fast and then lumbered off after Foss, his natural awkwardness intensified by the long cold hours spent aboard the boat. Terence, rowing his father, came in next. He had set out with Randall that morning, and Asanath had gone with Foss and Perley. They must have given up the search first, Philippa thought tiredly, and so Randall had transferred to another boat, a Bennett boat, for they would stay out to look as long as there was light on the sea.

All that had passed between her and the Campions was meaningless now. She had set herself against them, against all intolerance, and for what cause? For a handful of wizened children or for her own arrogance? And this was the end of it. She sat alone at her table, wrung so dry of emotion she could at last think of Charles and Fort without a surge of incredulous horror. And in this interval of dead calm, she knew what she must do.

Terence and Asanath were standing at the head of the beach, talking. As she watched idly, Terence turned quickly from his father and started home. He walked rapidly, like a man on an important errand. Asanath watched him for a moment, and then he looked up and down the empty path before he began to walk around the shore in the direction of the Binnacle. Philippa supposed he would be going up to tell Joanna when to expect the others. She took her coffee cup to the sink; it was while she was washing it that she heard the door open downstairs. She swung around, her heart beating hard. But it wouldn't be Steve, she remembered, and walked quietly to the door and opened it.

Asanath was coming up, slowly. She said in a steady voice, "Come in."

"Thanks." He was breathing hard when he reached the top, and his face was deeply lined. He stood before the stove, his cap pushed to the back of his head and his mackinaw unfastened, his hands in his pockets. He contemplated her under wind-burned lids. But she was beyond apprehension.

"Well?" she said calmly. "What's the news?"

For an instant she had a crazy suspicion that he might have come to say, "You satisfied now? You ready to get out before you kill off any more?"

"No news," he said. His voice rasped. "There'll be no news till somebody finds a spray hood or a piece of the engine box washed up somewhere."

She looked down at her hands, resting on a chair back, and willed them to relax. "Would you like some coffee?" she asked.

"I might, at that." No mellowness here, just dry, short words. She poured the coffee for him and put it on the table. He sat down to it stiffly, and she sat opposite, waiting.

When it did come, it startled her, though she had thought herself beyond amazement. He took a swallow of coffee and then looked hard into her eyes and said, "Terence is leaving here. He told me just now. He wouldn't say why, so I've come to ask you."

"Why should *I* know?"

"Somebody's got to know!" It was almost a cry, coming from Asanath. Quickly he took another mouthful of coffee. "Spent all night wondering what's going on out in the bay, and seeing those kids' faces till I had to get up and walk the floor. Spent all day looking till I'm half blind—seen more logs floating that we thought was one of 'em held up by a life belt. . . . Come home just able to crawl, and then my boy tells me he's getting off here for good. And he won't say *why*." Something flickered wrathfully in his tired eyes. "You see a lot of that kid Kathie—"

"Kathie's a loyal friend to Terence, Mr. Campion, nothing more," Philippa interrupted. She was too weary to talk, but she forced the words anyway. "Terence is a much better man than you think he is. I know it, and Kathie does, but—" Her voice trailed off. She couldn't think.

"That's it," he said. "That's it. You *do* know. He talks to ye, don't he? Look." He sat back in his chair. "Whatever you know about him—whatever mess he's in—I got a right to know." He gripped his long chin in his hand. "He's my son. I got a right to

300

straighten it out for him. It'll kill his mother if he goes. Specially right after this."

It'll kill you too, Philippa thought. You're scared, aren't you? But she felt neither anger nor satisfaction. She said, "The mess he's in doesn't have anything to do with girls, or gambling, or anything simple. The mess is—" she hesitated and was unexpectedly moved by the eagerness the man tried to hide. She was too tired to pick subtle words. "He thinks you wish he'd died instead of Elmo. He thinks you always liked Elmo better than him. That's at the bottom of it."

"That ain't so."

"You think I'm lying?"

"No, no. I mean, what he says isn't true. Of course we wanted Elmo back, but we didn't wish Terence dead in his place! It's just because he's always had this queer kind of hate for Elmo, even when he was a little tyke. We couldn't understand it."

"He loved Elmo," she said. "Whenever you think how you and Mrs. Campion grieved for him, you might wonder what Terence was feeling. He knew he'd never have a chance to let Elmo know he didn't hate him . . . and at the same time he knew nobody was ever going to call *him* a hero and weep over him the way you must have wept over Elmo." She sighed and tried to find the rest of the words, staring away from Asanath's face to the snow outside. "He lost a brother he'd never had much chance to enjoy, and he felt he didn't have any parents either."

Silence hung in the room for a long time. Asanath's face was bleak. "How do you know all that?"

"We talked about it."

He pulled at his lower lip and watched her for a moment, then said slowly, "So now he's getting out. After all this, we got no boy."

"If he goes with your blessing," said Philippa, "he'll still be yours. That's all he wants. Pretend you think he's bright enough to make his own way . . . even if you don't believe it."

"Lord, girl, I always said the young one was *smart* enough!" he said angrily.

"Did you ever say it to *him?*" She got up and went over to the stove, trying to warm her hands that had been cold all day with an inner chill. Asanath remained at the table, his head bent.

"Seems like anybody can make a yellow million mistakes without even trying," he muttered.

"Yes, anybody can," she said. "I don't know which is worse, to make a mistake that way, or to do the thing you think is absolutely right—and find out too late that it was absolutely wrong. Like my taking this job."

She hadn't expected to say it. It came out because she was too tired to exercise control. But perhaps it was just as well. The Campions, at any rate, would be glad of her decision. "I'm leaving just as soon as you can get a replacement," she said.

Asanath's sandy head came up. "What for? You and Steve had a falling out?"

"No. But you were right when you said the island was no place for me. I know it now."

He said with a touch of his old humor, "I don't figger you been too conspicuous a failure, as the feller says. I hear you got Rob Salminen doing fractions."

"Your brother and his wife don't like me," she continued doggedly. "Peggy's left school and swears she won't come back."

"Stuck-up little piece, that one. She'll be back, if Foss ain't altogether lost his manhood. If she doesn't, well, it's your gain." He picked up his coffee cup and drank. "Sky likes you fine. He's the brains of that family—if they don't ruin him."

"I don't know why you're defending me," she persisted. "You certainly haven't forgotten all the fuss about the Webster children, and the things you said to me about stirring up trouble."

"Since last night," said Asanath, "they don't look awful important. 'Course, that Edwin not being right in the head and throwing rocks—he could be dangerous, you know that."

"Edwin is deaf," said Philippa. "It's been criminally foolish to keep it a secret all this time, and allow that child to be victimized. How would you behave, Mr. Campion, if you lived in a world of absolute silence, and people treated you as if you were either insane or idiotic? Wouldn't you fight back?"

"*Deaf*, you say?" He scowled at her. "Stone deaf? What ailed his folks not to do something about it? I always knew Jude was an odd stick, but not *that* odd."

302

This was no time to defend Jude. Besides, there were other things to say.

"What ails Perley's folks?" she asked. "Do they think, like poor Lucy, that if they ignore the problem it will cease to exist?"

Asanath's tired eyes didn't blink. "Foss always was stubborn. But I've got after him about the boy, if that's any satisfaction to ye. He'll keep him from doing any more harm."

"That isn't enough," she protested, but she was too weary to find the sharp imperative words. "There must be someone, somewhere," she said vaguely, "who could puzzle Perley out, channel that destructive energy into something safe and useful—" She pushed her hair back from her aching temples.

"Foss isn't altogether numb," said Asanath. "If he can just break Helen down." He smiled wryly. "Talk about tigers!"

"But a mother tiger tries to teach her children." Her voice trailed off, and she roused herself. "Anyway, I'm glad the younger children will have some protection after I leave."

He got up, slowly, as if his aching joints had stiffened while he was sitting. "Steve going with ye?"

"I wouldn't ask that of him. This is his home."

"You're just about the most honest woman I ever knew." He stared fixedly at her face in the failing light. "But that don't signify I think you're right about this. Whatever bee you got in your bonnet, better give him a while longer to buzz around before you decide for sure about leaving us. . . . I'd ought to thank you for telling me about my boy, I s'pose. But it's cussed hard to thank somebody for pointing out my mistakes."

"I know what that's like," Philippa said dryly.

"But I figger it's better to have him go on a good day, all open and aboveboard, than to run off at night and end up in the bottom of the bay." He cleared his throat. "So I'm putting my pride in my pocket, young woman. You've helped out."

"You're welcome," she said. "Good-by."

He didn't answer but went on down the stairs, slowly. As he opened the outer door, she heard several boats coming into the harbor at once, the echo of the engines reverberating from the harbor points, and she knew that Steve had probably come home at last.

Chapter 55

She stood at the window and watched Joanna Sorensen with her children and the dog go by on the way to the wharf. Philippa knew that Steve was coming when she saw Joanna going home again. Nils walked ahead of her in the narrow path through the drifts, with Linnea on his shoulders and Jamie plodding behind him. They were unnaturally quiet; Joanna looked down at the broken trail thoughtfully, and it was strange to see her not walking with her head up.

Steve's feet were slow on the stairs. She sat listening, deliberately stilling the clamor that his footsteps had always stirred in her. She was a little shocked that it should start up now, when he was returning from such an errand.

As he came in, he didn't look at her but leaned against the wall to kick off his boots. His motions were heavy and tired. Standing in his thick white boot socks, he took off his mackinaw and stripped off the navy turtle-neck he wore under it. She did not stir until he padded over to the stove and lifted the coffee pot. Then she moved quickly, setting out a cup and saucer for him and putting yesterday's meat pie in the oven to warm.

He caught her by the arm as she passed him. His mouth was chapped; the usually clear whites of his eyes were bloodshot, the lids were reddened and dry, the lines were deeply accentuated from his nostrils to the corners of his mouth. She wanted to put her arms around him and lull him into sleep, but she said quietly, "You'd better sit down and eat, Steve. You look exhausted."

"What's the matter with *you?*" he asked hoarsely, holding her by both arms.

"Did you find anything out there?"

"No. Neither did the Coast Guard. We didn't expect to." He tightened his grip deliberately on the soft flesh inside her upper arms. "It's over. Randall's moving his family off. There's nobody to notify about Gregg." There was a tremor of his eyelids. "So tomorrow we start new."

"You say that as if it were all so simple!" she burst out. "Like wiping off a blackboard at the end of a lesson!"

"But it's the truth, isn't it?" He looked at her angrily. "We can't help the kids by mulling it over and over. We can't take the load off the Percys, any more than they could take ours. These things have happened before; they'll happen again. I should have taken you with me, then you'd know what I mean."

"I do know, Steve!" Her voice was sharper than she had intended. "You've been out doing something about it, you've worked something out of your system, and you've come to a logical conclusion." She moved restlessly, and then her self-control splintered.

"But it's so *unbelievable!*" she burst out wildly. "And at the same time so *final!* You know it's happened, but you can't—you can't—" her voice went high and broke. Through a blur of tears she saw his face contort as if in pain. He reached for her, but she held him off while she fought silently for composure.

"Steve, I can't live on this island," she said at last. "I'll never belong, and I don't think I want to belong. What the island has done to me, and what I've done to the island, make a pretty rotten story." She waited, but he made no offer to speak. His dark eyes watched her with neither pity nor anger.

"You told me there was always trouble, that I didn't start anything. But Steve, since I came here two months ago there's been nothing but the *worst* trouble. If that's the true state of affairs here, I don't think I can endure it even with you, either for myself or Eric." This time he opened his mouth, but she shook her head. "And if you tell me it's not usually *this* bad, then it comes back to me, that I started everything. Steve." She leaned toward him. "Can you say, and believe it, that these things would have happened anyway? Can you say in all honesty that it's not in everyone's mind that Fort was hounded into running away—and Charles went with him because Fort was his friend?"

"You didn't do it."

"If you want, you can trace it from the beginning. From the time I saw the Webster children in the orchard." She gestured helplessly, in despair of explaining. "And they led directly to yesterday."

305

He shook his head. "You're so very mistaken. And so conceited, taking it all on yourself. Listen to me, for a change." He kept one arm hard around her, the other hand holding her chin so she could not turn her face from him.

"Justin never stopped to figure out if that man was worth saving when he threw himself on the grenade," he said cruelly. "You'd have been some kind of monster if you'd turned your back on those kids. You've got to stop weighing them against Fort and Charles. You understand? As for Fort being hounded, what I told you in the first place still goes. The Campions felt like crowding; place wasn't big enough for 'em. So they used you for an excuse, and the mess began, and every man who took part in it, Campion *or* Bennett, was equally to blame."

She tried to free her chin from his grasp, but he wouldn't let go. "Let me tell you another thing, Philippa. Gregg and Fort and Charles caused their own deaths. They knew the condition of Gregg's boat. They knew there might be a storm. But Gregg was thirsty and the boys were mad, so they took a chance. And that's the story behind everything like this, Philippa. You're going to be a lobsterman's wife, so you might as well learn the thing first as last. They took a chance."

He released her abruptly and went to the window. He was a blurred dark figure against the dusk outside. "Here's something else. Maybe you can figure out how you're to blame for this, too. Jude broke down today and told Nils he's got to take Lucy back to the state hospital at Bangor. Seems she spent some time there after Rue was born. Now she's going back." His voice failed tiredly; he seemed to have run out of words.

"No!" The cry was torn from Philippa.

"Yes. The way Jude puts it, she never did think much of this world, so she's chosen up one of her own." He turned around. "Can't you figure out some tie-in with yourself?" he asked savagely.

"No, I can't. I knew when I first saw her that something was wrong. This was inevitable, I suppose."

"So was the other.... It would have been something, wouldn't it," Steve murmured, thinking aloud, "if Perley ever had got hold of Rue and Edwin? That would have set the whole family off for fair. And you stopped that.... Those kids are Jude's lifeblood. They'll make out, Philippa." His voice came clearer. "They've got you to thank for that."

"But the boys—"

"Listen, I loved Charles as if he was my own kid. I've loved him longer than you've known him. And I can't figure how we're going to get used to not having him around. But I'm telling you the truth when I say they should have known better." He came back across the room, walking softly in his stocking feet, and stood above her where she sat huddled on the couch. "Listen, my darling, we'll live somewhere else, where you won't have to look at the Campions and hear Vi's horselaugh, where you won't have to remember Lucy Webster or Charles or any of the mess at all. We'll go wherever you want. You pick the place on the coast where you want us to live and where you want Eric to grow up. I can live without this island, Philippa, but I can't live without *you*."

She tried to say his name but could not. She leaned forward and put her arms around his waist and laid her head against him. His belt buckle cut into her cheek, but the pain was a lifesaving reality and she cherished it. He reached down and pulled her up so that he could look into her face. Her eyes filled with tears.

"Oh, Steve, what do you take me for, a cosset lamb, a child bride? We won't go anywhere else to live! This is your place, and it can be mine. But thank you for offering. If you never gave me another gift as long as we both live, that one would be enough."

"What about Eric?"

"Eric will have us, and the family, and the island itself, the boats —he'll have so much that's wonderful that it will take all the sting out of the bad things." She moved into Steve's arms and put her cheek against his wind-burned one. "He'll probably learn his lesson much easier than I'm learning mine, Steve. He has so much common sense."

Steve kissed her. It was a gentle kiss that neither compelled nor demanded. There was no reason for any urgency to cut through their weariness. Their lifetime lay ahead of them. They sank into exhaustion with their arms around each other, as if into sleep, mutely grateful for each other with an emotion which for the moment had no concern with love or passion.

Philippa stirred, once; a threadlike lilt had come unexpectedly into her head, a thin gay ghost. "What was that one Fort played so much?" she murmured. "It had a strange title for a square-dance tune—'The Dawning of the Day.' That was it."

That's what we're waiting for, she thought. The end of the night, the dawning of the day. Only Fort and Charles aren't waiting. The day was over for them before it really began. Grief was sharply aroused in her again, but as if he sensed it Steve tightened his arms around her.

The island night deepened into its long, starlit winter solitude. The darkness flowed into the room, and they rested in it.

About the Author

If it can be said of any author that she *lives* the subjects and settings of her books, it certainly can be said of Elisabeth Ogilvie. Although she was born in Boston and at first only summered in Maine, Miss Ogilvie now resides most of the year on Gay's Island off the Maine coast, where she "writes, gardens, and tries not to suspect that a bear is at the door, a moose is lurking in the alders, or a bald eagle hovering overhead about to bear away my red-gold shag cat, Tristan." She keeps a big black sheep—who does his share by cropping the grass—and occasionally sees a fox saunter nonchalantly across her lawn.

Her novels, all of which have a Maine seacoast setting, have earned her a wide and faithful audience: STORM TIDE, HIGH TIDE AT NOON, EBBING TIDE, and ROWAN HEAD. She has written one book of nonfiction, MY WORLD IS AN ISLAND, in which she describes in humorous and delightful detail her unique life on Gay's Island. Even as a child, when she spent vacations in Maine, she was fascinated with the fishermen's life, its freedom and independence, the excitement of the sea, the remarkable lobstermen in their sturdy boats. The conviction grew—and has remained ever since—that this was the life about which she wanted to write.

The Tide Trilogy

The first three volumes in the continuing narrative of Joanna Bennett of Bennett's Island, Maine.

High Tide at Noon (I)
Storm Tide (II)
The Ebbing Tide (III)

The Lovers Trilogy

Down East Books is pleased to reissue the second series featuring Joanna Bennett Sorensen and her family.

Dawning of the Day (IV)
The Seasons Hereafter (V)
Strawberries in the Sea (VI)

An Answer in the Tide (VII)

Following the fortunes of the third generation of Bennett's Islanders, *An Answer in the Tide* focuses on Joanna's son Jamie.

The Day Before Winter (IX)*

This long-awaited latest volume in Elisabeth Ogilvie's series of Bennett's Island novels rejoins Joanna Bennett Sorensen's family during the Vietnam era.

The Jennie Trilogy

Spanning eighteen years and ranging from Scotland to the Maine coast, the Jennie Glenroy saga offers vivid historic settings and unforgettable characters.

Jennie About to Be (I)
The World of Jennie G. (II)
Jennie Glenroy (III)*

My World Is an Island

Miss Ogilvie's entertaining autobiography of early days on Gay's Island back in the 1950s, updated with new photo-graphs and an epilogue by the author.

All titles are paperback unless otherwise noted.
*Also available in hardcover.

CHECK YOUR LOCAL BOOKSTORE, OR ORDER
FROM DOWN EAST BOOKS AT 1-800-685-7962